THE WITCHES SABBATH

A STUDY OF WITCHCRAFT AND DEVIL WORSHIP IN EUROPE UP TO THE MODERN AGE

INCLUDING A SECTION OF SHORT STORIES ON WITCHCRAFT

British Library Cataloguing-in-Publication Data
A catalogue record for this book is available from
the British Library

Contents

Part II: Of English Witchcraft from the
Passing of the Statute of 1736 until the

Fictional Accounts of European Witchcraft

Selected Author Biographies

CHAPTER I

Of the Profession of Witchcraft; of the Contract, and of the Familiar

In order to the proof that there have been, and are, unlawful
Confederacies *with evil Spirits, by vertue of which the* hellish accom-
plices *perform things above their natural powers : I must premise that
this being* matter *of* fact, *is onely capable of the evidence of* authority
and sense ; *and by both these the being of* Witches *and* diabolical
Contracts *is most abundantly confirm'd.*
JOSEPH GLANVIL, *Saducismus Triumphatus.*

" A sorcerer is one who by commerce with the Devil
has a full intention of attaining his own ends, and I
give this definition because not only is it necessary for
the full understanding of my book, but also because it
explains and supplies the reason for the divers laws
which in all Christian countries have been directed
against sorcerers, and furthermore because no concise
definition has hitherto been supplied by the many
authorities who have written upon witchcraft, whilst
at the same time it is essential that we should be quite
clear and exact in regard to the use of our terms."
With this sentence the erudite lawyer and politician,
Jean Bodin, one of the most acute and liberal minds
of his age, opens his famous treatise *Demonomania, A
Scourge for Wizards and Witches,* which was first published
at Paris in 1580, and in the opinion of not a few scholars
is still distinguished as being the most copious and
most closely-argued manual of its kind.

It would be, I imagine, hardly possible to discover
a more explicit, precise, comprehensive, and intelligent

definition of a Witch. Bodin was thinking only of European witchcraft, but actually his words carry a complete and universal connotation, and we find, for example, that Father Joseph J. Williams, S.J., who is Professor of Cultural Anthropology at Boston College Graduate School, in his *Psychic Phenomena of Jamaica*, writes : " Certainly we have this definition [of Bodin's] fully verified in the case of the Jamaica obeah-man as the direct descendant in theory and practice from the Ashanti *obayifo*," a term which Captain R. Sutherland Rattray in his *Ashanti Proverbs* (Oxford, 1916), explains as follows : " Obayifo, deriv. bayi, sorcery (Synonymous term ayen), a wizard, or more generally a witch. A kind of human vampire, whose chief delight is to suck the blood of children whereby the latter pine and die. Men and women possessed of this black magic are credited with volitant powers, being able to quit their bodies and travel great distances in the night. Besides sucking the blood of victims, they are supposed to be able to extract the sap and juice of crops. (Cases of coco blight are ascribed to the work of the obayifo.) These witches are supposed to be very common, and a man never knows but that his friend or even his wife may be one."

Such characteristics can be closely paralleled in the history of European Witchcraft, Some are frequent, others are more rarely met, but all occur, and this in itself goes far to show how in spite of external differences and even climatic and regional variations, the horrid cult is essentially one and the same the wide world over, the witch near home or in the remotest and most savage quarters of the globe serves only one master, is the bondslave of one only lord, the fallen angel who is the Prince of Darkness, " that old serpent, which is the Devil, and Satan."

It must be borne in mind that the word " witch ", although in recent usage almost invariably applied to a woman, may with perfect correctness be employed of a man, and it seems a pity that the meaning should be narrowed and curtailed. The great *Oxford English Dictionary* defines " witch " (a word of Anglo-Saxon derivation) as " A man who practises witchcraft or magic, a magician, sorcerer, wizard ". Also, and to-day more generally, " A female magician, sorceress ; in later use a woman supposed to have dealings with the devil or evil spirits and to be able by their co-operation to perform supernatural acts." The word " sorcerer " is from the Old French, and is derived from a popular Latin term signifying a caster of lots, a diviner, a charmer.

" The father of the English law," Sir Edward Coke (commonly called Lord Coke), defines a witch as " a person that hath conference with the Devil to take counsel or do some act ".

Whilst he was Bishop of Luçon, and before he had received the red hat, Cardinal Richelieu, in 1618, with considerable pains and application, composed for his diocese a catechism which became famous under the name *A Wholesome Instruction in the Christian Faith*. The Cardinal thus distinguishes between Magic and Sorcery. " Magic is the art of producing extraordinary and supernatural effects by the power of the devil : Sorcery or Witchcraft is the art of injuring men in their persons or their possessions by the power of the devil. The difference between Magic and Sorcery strictly lies in this, that the former has for its chief aim and end the design to excite wonder and vain esteem; whilst the latter in its malevolence seeks to injure and harm."

Magic, says Swedenborg, is an abuse of the correspondences of the natural world with the spiritual.

Black magic, which is magic proper, produces effects which are beyond the reach of any forces of nature, and which could not be contrived by any skill of legerdemain. These effects, moreover, are produced by the power of the demon, with whom the witch has commerce and has entered into a contract.

In order clearly to understand and fully to realize the shuddering horror and heart-sick dismay any sort of communion between human beings and evil spirits, which is the very core and kernel of Witchcraft, excited throughout the whole of Christendom, to appreciate why tome after tome was written upon the subject by the most learned pens of Europe, why holiest pontiffs and wisest judges, grave philosopher and discreet scholar, king and peasant, careless noble and earnest divine, all alike were of one mind in the prosecution of sorcery; why in Catholic Spain and in Puritan Scotland, in cold Geneva and at genial Rome, unhesitatingly and perseveringly man sought to stamp out the plague with the most terrible of all penalties, the cautery of fire; in order that by the misreading of history we should not superficially and foolishly think monk and magistrate, layman and lawyer were mere tigers, mad fanatics—for as such have they, too, often been presented and traduced,—it will be not wholly impertinent briefly to recapitulate the orthodox doctrine of the Powers of Darkness, facts nowadays too often forgotten or ignored, but which to the acute mediæval mind were ever fearfully and prominently in view.

And here, as in so many other beliefs, we shall find a little dogma ; certain things that can hardly be denied without the note of temerity ; and much concerning which nothing definite can be known, upon which assuredly no pronouncement will be made.

In the first place, the name Devil is commonly given to the fallen angels, who are also called Demons. The precise technical distinction between the two terms may be seen in the phrase used in a decree of the Fourth Lateran Council, which was convened under Pope Innocent III in 1215. The assembled Fathers spoke of " The Devil and other demons ", i.e. all are demons, and the chief of the demons is called the Devil.

As Cotton Mather explains in his *The Devil Discovered* : " It is not *One Devil* alone, that has Cunning or Power enough to apply the Multitudes of *Temptations*, whereby Mankind is daily diverted from the Service of God ; No, the *High Places* of Our Air, are Swarming full of those *Wicked Spirits*, whose Temptations trouble us. . . . But because those Apostate Angels, are all *United*, under one Infernal Monarch, in the Designs of Mischief, 'tis in the Singular Number, that they are spoken of."

Mention is made of the Devil in many passages both of the Old and New Testaments. Thus, as he is multifold in evil, so is he known under a variety of names. Beelzebub is prince of the devils (St. Matthew, xii, 24) ; he is Satan (St. Luke, x, 18) ; he is Belial (2 Corinthians, vi, 15) ; he is the angel of the bottomless pit, " whose name in the Hebrew tongue is Abaddon, but in the Greek tongue Apollyon " (Revelation, ix, 11). He is proud (1 Timothy, iii, 6) ; powerful (Ephesians, vi, 12) ; wicked (1 John, ii, 13) ; subtle (2 Corinthians, xi, 3) ; deceitful (2 Corinthians, xi, 14) ; fierce and cruel (1 Peter, v, 8). He is the father of lies and a murderer from the beginning (St. John, viii, 44) ; one who loves to work lying wonders, that is to say the craft of magic (2 Thessalonians, ii, 9). He is the prince of the power of the air (Ephesians, ii, 2) and a sinner from the beginning (1 John, iii, 8) ; finally he was cast out into the blackness of darkness (St. Jude, 6 ; 13).

It is interesting to note that even so extremely advanced a writer of the modernist school as Dean Inge, when preaching at St. Mark's, North Audley Street, London, W., on Sunday, 6th March, 1932, remarked : "Liberal theologians may jeer and philosophers scoff, but there it is. We cannot get rid of the Devil. ' Deliver us from the Evil One,' is the right translation. I have not the slightest doubt that Christians are enjoined to believe in a positive, malignant spiritual power."

An obvious question which next arises and which has been amply discussed by the fathers and school-men is : What was the nature of the sin of the rebel angels ? This point presents some difficulty for theology has logically formed the highest estimate of the perfection of the angelic nature, the powers and possibilities of the angelic knowledge. Sins of the flesh are certainly impossible to angels, and from many sins which are purely spiritual and intellectual they would seem to be equally debarred. The great offence of Lucifer appears to have been the desire of inde-pendence of God and equality with God.

It is theologically certain that Lucifer held a very high place in the celestial hierarchy, and it is evident that he maintains some kind of sovereignty over those who followed him in his rebellion. There can be little doubt too that among their ranks are many mean and petty spirits—to speak comparatively—but even these can influence and betray foolish and arrogant men.

There are many historical examples, indeed, of men so besotted as to cause themselves to be saluted and even worshipped as God—Herod, Caligula, Heliogabalus, the Persian king Khusrau.

To come down to more modern days. About 1830 there appeared in one of the American States bordering upon Kentucky, an impostor who declared himself to be Christ. He threatened the world with immediate judgement, and a number of ill-balanced and hysterical subjects were much affected by his denunciations. One day, when he was addressing a large gathering in his usual strain, a German standing up humbly asked him if he would repeat his warnings in German for the benefit of those present who only knew that tongue. The speaker answered that he had never been able to learn that language, a reply which seemed so ludicrous in one claiming divinity that many of the auditors were convulsed with laughter, and so profane a charlatan soon lost all credit.

John Nichols Tom, the son of a Cornish publican and self-dubbed Knight of Malta, early in 1838 was shot near Blean Wood, Kent, during a riot which he had incited owing to his having persuaded a number of rustics that he was Christ returned to earth. He exhibited the five wounds in his hands, feet, and side, and gained no inconsiderable following. Upon the tree beneath which he fell some fanatic actually attached an engraved plate : " Our real true Messiah, King of the Jews." Henry James Prince, " the Beloved " founder of the Agapemone, openly claimed divinity, whilst his successor T. H. Smyth-Pigott in 1902 declared to the congregation of his church at Clapton : " I am that Lord Jesus come again in my own body to save those who come to me from death and hell." Smyth-Pigott died in 1927.

It is apparent then, that although rationally it should be inconceivable that any sentient creature could claim divinity, actually the contrary is the case. The sin of Satan would appear to have been an attempt to usurp the sovereignty of God. This is further borne out by the fact that during the Temptation of Our Lord the Devil, showing Him " all the kingdoms of the world and the glory of them ", said : " All these will I give Thee, if Thou wilt fall down and worship me." Here the Devil is demanding that divine honours should be paid him. And this claim is perpetuated throughout the witch trials. The witches believed that their master, Satan, Lucifer, the fiend, the principle of evil, was God, and as such they worshipped him with the supreme honour due to Almighty God alone, they adored him, they offered him homage, they addressed prayer to him, they sacrificed.

The Devil, Satan, was and is the god of the witches, and we may now inquire concerning their practice and profession, how a novice joins that horrid society, and what obligations so damnable a state entails.

The first business required of a candidate who desired to become a witch was to make a formal compact with Satan. This might be either expressed or tacit. The expressed pact consisted of a solemn vow of fidelity and homage paid before witnesses, to the devil visibly present in some bodily form, or else to some wizard or magician acting in the devil's stead. The tacit pact involves the offering of a written petition to the devil, and this is not unseldom done by proxy through the medium of a witch when the contracting party is afraid to summon or directly have speech with the fiend.

That a determined man will be able in some way or another to get most intimately into touch with the dark shadow world is not to be denied. The existence of evil discarnate intelligences it is impossible for any thinking man to doubt, whilst it is certainly established that this realm of rebellion and disorder owns one chief, and it is reasonable to suppose, many hierarchies, a kingdom that is at continual warfare with and opposed to all that is good, ever striving to do ill and to bring man into bondage. It is this connexion between man and the demon with its consequences, conditions, and attendant circumstances that is known as Witchcraft. Thus, even so ultra-cautious and indeed frankly sceptical a writer as Father Herbert Thurston, S.J., finds himself bound to acknowledge : " In the face of Holy Scripture and the teaching of the Fathers and theologians the abstract possibility of a pact with the Devil and of a diabolical interference in human affairs can hardly be denied." Plainly, a man who not only firmly believes in a Power of evil but also that this Power can and does meddle with and mar human affections and human destinies, may invoke and devote himself to this Power, may give up his will thereunto, may ask this Power to accomplish his wishes and ends, and so succeed in definitively and explicitly entering into a mysterious contract with evil whose slave and servant he is become.

St. Jerome explains that a contract with Satan is spoken of in plainest terms by the prophet Isaiah : " We have made a covenant with death, and with hell are we at agreement " (xxviii, 15). St. Augustine too discusses such compacts at length. There were few better known histories throughout the Middle Ages than the sixth century legend of Theophilus of Adana, who when bitterly disappointed and wellnigh disgraced, concluded a pact with the devil, to whom he delivered a document he had written and sealed with his own hand. Presently, repenting most heartily of the evil he had done, he besought with fervent prayer and fasting the Mother of all Mercies. Our Lady wrested the fatal parchment from the demon and returned it to the penitent, who cast it into the flames, shortly after passing away in peace.

Stevenote de Audebert, a witch of the Pyrenees, who was executed in 1619, actually showed the judge, Pierre De Lancre, " the contract and agreement she had made with the demon. It was scrawled in blood and feculent matter, enough to turn a man's stomach to see."

Elizabeth Style, a witch of Stoke Trister in Somerset, in 1664 confessed before a magistrate, that the devil who visited her " in the shape of a handsome Man " promised that she should " have the pleasure of the World for Twelve years if she would with her Blood sign his Paper, which was to give her Soul to him . . . and with a drop or two of her Blood she signed the Paper " with her mark. In 1672 a

Nottingham boy inscribed a formal agreement with the powers of evil.

The most famous and most infamous of these written pacts with Satan is probably that made by the arch-magician, Urbain Grandier, a holograph which is preserved in the Bibliothèque Nationale at Paris.

These formal contracts with the fiend are still made to-day, and indeed *Le Petit Dragon Rouge*, one of the vilest and happily one of the scarcest of the grimoires, sets out in explicit terms (although, I am bound to add, not without a note of caution), the precise formula to be most efficaciously employed.

Maître Maurice Garçon, one of the leading French barristers, in the course of an address delivered before the Institut Métaphysique at Paris, September, 1929, affirmed " The first step for novices in sorcery and witchcraft is to make a contract with the devil ". Among ancient French legal documents and records of the courts there are many examples of these pacts, and those which are being written and signed in blood to-day appear practically identical with the older screeds. The substance of all is that the neophyte pledges his soul to the Evil One in return for power, or wealth, or some other object he desires. " I have not only held some of these contracts in my hand," said Maître Garçon, " but I actually witnessed one of these strange businesses quite recently." He proceeded to relate how it had come to his knowledge that a candidate was going to invoke the devil in a wood near Fontainebleau. Maître Garçon and another witness concealed themselves whence they had a clear sight of the appointed spot. The sorcerer arrived at midnight, and proceeded with the dark ritual, tracing a circle on the ground, lighting two candles, and with hideous blasphemies calling upon Satan, from whom he demanded the fulfilment of his quest. At the climax the man raising himself on tiptoes threw out his hands at full stretch proffering the infernal charter scrawled in his own blood, and promising to win the devil a human soul for every wish that he was granted. That the fiend did not appear was doubtless owing to the fact that these ceremonies were being spied upon and overseen by those not of the wizard fraternity. But, as one of the greatest of theologians and profoundest of philosophers, Francisco Suarez, observes, even if no response be obtained from the demon, " either because God does not allow it, or for some other reason we may not know," the guilt of the experimenter in this dark art and his sin are in no wise lightened.. Maître Garçon further related that he knew of numerous cases of persons both of poor estate and in the highest social positions who had signed these protocols with Satan, and he instanced (without naming the individual) a leading French banker who openly attributed his worldly success and his immense riches to a diabolical compact.

It is true that the great moral theologians and doctors teach us that such abominations as a contract with the demon are in their essence null and void, a question discussed at length and thus decided with much learning by Jacques D'Autun. Arguing on different lines and from another point of view, the same conclusion was arrived at by so profound a student of occultism as the Marquis Marie-Victor-Stanislas de Guaita.

None the less it is certain that anyone who is cankered

and infect with evil to such a degree as actually to submit himself a bondslave of Satan, and who signs these charters of hell stands in the utmost peril. For, as Jules Bois says, the interior pact of which the written paper is in some sense an outward sign and symbol is not so easily broken. The infernal yoke, the serfdom of Satan, is not lightly cast off; the intellectual sin it is hard to atone.

In the fifteenth century when a novice joined the Waldensians, who are the Vaudois sorcerers, the demon insisted that he should swear implicit obedience to evil and sign a formal document yielding up his soul, without which no business could be done.

The formal contract in fine opens the door to every kind of witchcraft and black magic.

The second point in the profession of a witch follows upon and may be regarded as essentially a part of the impious compact which has been made. At the devil's instigation the neophyte with horrid imprecations and blasphemy abjures the Catholic Faith, explicitly and in set terms withdraws from and denies the obedience due to God, and is therefore, as the older authorities so justly observe, a rebel, guilty of high treason towards the Almighty King.

Mention of these infernal dedications and the ruthless renunciation of all good occurs in almost every witch-trial. Martin Delrio briefly sums up the matter by pointing out that certain articles are common to all these declarations. "The Christian Faith is rejected and denied with contumely; the worship of and the honour due to God are transferred to Satan; the Patronage of Our Lady is repudiated; the Sacraments are scorned and derided; every divine ordinance is profaned." The actual words may be a shortened formula, or they may be delivered at some length and garnished with revolting profanities, but the substance of the matter is in every instance the same.

The Waldensian disciple upon his full profession denied God and Christ, Our Lady and the Saints, in plain set terms. He blasphemed the Sacraments and vowed never to enter a Church, or if indeed he were obliged for safety sake to be present at Mass he muttered a foul curse at the Elevation of the Host, and if bound to take Holy Water he whispered to the demon : " Sire, ne te desplaise," " My Lord, thy pardon."

The witches are required to be active in their profession, for the devil is a hard taskmaster, although indeed it is true that but seldom do they need any spur to wickedness. It is, however, much to be suspected that any person who renders himself notorious by his contempt for and a certain abhorrence of all sacred things has dabbled (and it may be deeply) in black magic. Not very many months ago I was informed by a friend that one afternoon as he found himself by chance near a small church in a London suburb he went in to pay a visit to the Blessed Sacrament. The church was empty, save for one man who was standing at the sanctuary rails, facing the tabernacle. To my friend's surprise he noticed that the stranger was shaking his fist with wild threatening gestures towards the altar, and muttering to himself in tones of horrid menace. When he heard a footstep he turned and hurried from the place. His mouth was writhed in a bestial grimace of derision, his teeth snarled, his eyes were blazing with maniac fury and hate, and it seems plain that this wretch was a Satanist who had entered the church to curse and insult the Sanctissimum, and who perhaps had he not been interrupted would have proceeded to worse indignity and violence.

From time to time the daily papers tell us of some apparently senseless piece of mischief or damage that has been done in a church. In May, 1936, for example, an extraordinary sacrilege was committed at St. Cuthbert's Church, Stanley. The parish priest found that during the night the church had been entered, and the intruder seemed "to have concentrated upon the tabernacle of the high altar". A Ciborium was lying upon the altar table, and around it the consecrated Hosts were scattered pell-mell. The pix containing the lunette which had held the larger Benediction Host was found on the roof of the school. There can be no doubt that this desecration and many another similar outrage are the work of Satanists, whose vile society is only too rife and too industrious amongst us here in England to-day.

The ordinary man—the man in the street, as the phrase goes—was wont to regard Satanism as incredible, or at any rate a myth of the far-off Dark Ages, but to-day he has been forcibly brought face to face with a tale of horrors that will admit of no other explanation save the potency, the intensely active and purposeful potency of the powers of evil. Who can doubt that the revolution of Russia, the persecution in Mexico, the anarchy and atrocities of Spain, have been fomented, energized, and directed by Satanic agency? The wholesale carnage of priests and nuns; the torture of innocents ; so deliberate a destruction of most holy and most ancient shrines ; the burning to the ground of churches, convents, and every home of prayer ; all unmistakably betray their ultimate source and author, hell and the devil. It is reported that among the red raving mobs, the dregs of the populace unleashed to slaughter and the most inhuman savagery, there mingle demons under the form of men who urge on and encourage the bloodshed and the fires, nor have I for one any difficulty in believing that this is indeed the case.

As Archbishop Hinsley said in August, 1936 : " The Spanish terror would seem to aim at the wreck of Christianity and the ruin of civilization." *The Universe*, 7th August, 1936, spoke of " Demoniacal Fury in Spain", and described by an eye-witness fiendish attacks upon the Blessed Sacrament and on priests and nuns. " When the Reds set about the task of destroying practically every church in Barcelona, they went first to the altars. Pulling the vessels out of the Tabernacles, they scattered the sacred Hosts on the floor and in the street, and completed the sacrilege by trampling on the Hosts." The Barcelona Reds were " like maniacs possessed by the devil ", which pregnant phrase in its literal truth sums up the position. " To batter off the head of a dying priest, to outrage a girl little more than a child and then riddle her with machine-gun bullets—these are the pastimes of the beast that roams under the name of Communism "— or Satanism, call it what you will (*Daily Mail*, Monday, 10th August, 1936). Sir Edward Russell wrote : " For the true Communist there is no God . . . Russia sets up a completely atheist state " (*Hibbert Journal*, July, 1936). This may well seem to be the case, but the gist of the matter lies deeper. The Communist denies God, it is true, he is superficially atheist, but he certainly has a god, for he has set up Satan as his god, who is worshipped not with prayer and in churches or holy places, but by violence, by cruelty, and every atrocity, by anarchy and blood.

We need not in view of the events which have happened in our own day be at all surprised when we learn from Bodin that Trois-eschelles du Mayne, a notorious sorcerer, told King Charles IX that there were at that time more than three thousand Satanists in France. It was said that in the fifteenth century so vast was the army of witches that had a leader arisen and an international organization the whole of Europe would have been thrown into chaos, nihilism, and war. To-day leaders have arisen, an international organization has been formed, and Europe is honeycombed by the vast society of devil-worshippers whose members may be found everywhere, in crowded capital and remotest hamlet, ever busy at their evil work, ever recruiting, ever flaunting their doctrines now glossed under some specious name, now hardly disguised in their native licence and horror, and if unchecked the result must be universal confusion, discord, red revolution, and the ruin of humanity.

" To worship the Devil is Witchcraft," says Cotton Mather. Satanism and Witchcraft are one and the same thing.

From the pact struck by the witch or Satanist with the fiend and the formally expressed renunciation it logically follows, that the novices must cast away such holy things as the Rosary, or the girdle of St. Francis, the girdle of St. Thomas Aquinas, the leathern cincture of St. Augustine, the Scapular of the Carmelites, or any other Scapular. They will also trample under foot the Cross, the Medals, or other objects of devotion they possess or once carried on their persons.

The Medal of St. Benedict, who was endued with an especial influence over the dark power, is particularly dreaded by witches, and is extremely potent against all evil spells. During a trial for sorcery in 1647 at Nattenburg, near the Abbey of Metten in Bavaria, the necromancers acknowledged that the attempts against the monks were foiled by the holy Medal. The two possessed boys of Illfurt (Alsace), 1864-9, exhibited the utmost dread of St. Benedict's Medal. A wizard, then, would plainly get rid of so sacred an emblem, and cast it from him with hate and fear. The Carmelite Scapular, bestowed by Our Lady on St. Simon as a sure pledge of final grace and salvation, is equally abhorrent and detested by the servants of the devil.

Suspicion was first aroused in the case of Ernest von Ehrenberg, a cousin of the Prince-Bishop of Würzburg, when he was observed to show a strange contempt for holy things, and was one day seen to burn his scapulars and medals.

It was found that the Waldensians did not know the Lord's Prayer, the Ave Mary, or the Creed, but they would secretly make the Sign of the Cross in the dust and spit upon it.

Boguet notes that the demon forbade the witches of the old town of St. Oyan de Joux (now Saint-Claude) to say the creed.

On the 16th April, 1594, died Ferdinando Stanley, the young Earl of Derby, and although he suffered from a bladder complaint it was commonly believed that his sickness had been much aggravated and his end hastened by witchcraft. Rumour, and something more than mere rumour, accused a number of crones of the worst possible reputation, and these were promptly haled before a magistrate : " One of them being bidden to say the Lord's Prayer, said it well, but being conjured, in the Name of Jesus, that if she had bewitched his honour, she should not be able to say the same, she could never repeat that petition, *Forgive us our trespasses*, no not although it was repeated unto her."

Florence Newton, the Irish witch of Youghal, who was arraigned at the Cork Assizes in September, 1661, when put to the test could not say, " and forgive us our trespasses " in the Lord's Prayer, but boggled at the words, and " being oft pressed to utter the words as they were repeated to her, she did not," which left a very ill impression. Julian Cox, the Somerset witch, when asked by Serjeant John Archer to recite the Lord's Prayer, went over it very readily until she said " *And lead us into temptation*," which she repeated again and again, and could not otherwise.

Since the devil is the " ape of God ", whilst Holy Baptism is the " first Sacrament " and in the phrase of Eugenius IV " the door of the spiritual life ", Satan bathes in a new mock baptism, the witch, who is thus fully incorporated (as it were) into the infernal conventicle. Both Bodin and Boguet comment upon this scurril baptism, the latter giving it as his opinion that the fiend thereby seeks to persuade the witch that the first baptism is thus annulled, and that it can be of no more service to him. This accords with what Nicolas Remy states in his *Demonolatry*, for he was astonished to find that many of the Lorraine sorcerers who had fallen into the hands of justice asked to be purged by a second baptism, and it became necessary to explain to them the folly and the futility of such a request, since Holy Baptism impresses an ineffaceable character on the soul, a spiritual and indelible mark.

Jeannette d'Abadie, a witch of the Pyrenees, confessed that she had often witnessed at the sabbat the impious baptism of children, and among the Swedish witches of Mora on Lake Siljan in the years 1669–1670 the rite was regularly practised. They confessed that the devil " caused them to be Baptized too by such Priests as he had there, and made them confirm their Baptism with dreadful Oaths and Imprecations ". The Salem trials of the New England witches supply very ample accounts of baptism, but concerning these it will be sufficient to quote from Cotton Mather's *The Wonders of the Invisible World*, a passage from the trial of Elizabeth How on 30th June, 1692 : " there came in the Confessions of several other (penitent) Witches, which affirmed this *How* to be one of those, who with them had been baptized by the Devil in the River at *Newbury* Falls : before which he made them kneel down by the Brink of the River and worship him."

In some instances at this baptism the witches forswore their old names and were given new, as for example a sorcerer of Cuneo, della Rovere, who was renamed Barbicapra. The author of *A History of the Witches of Renfrewshire* lays particular stress on this, and writes : " Renouncing of baptism is by Delrio made an effect of paction, yet with us it is *per se* relevant, as was found in the former process of Margaret

Hutchinson [1661] . . . and our witches always confess the giving them new names, which are very
ridiculous, as Red-shanks, Sergeant, &c."

Another detail in the profession is that the witches
give the devil either a lock of their hair or some piece
of their clothing in token of their vassalage, for as
Guazzo explains the fiend is eager to make them his
own in every particular, and this gift establishes a
psychic sympathy or copula. Moreover these objects
are often utilized in confecting a charm.

The Waldensian upon his reception into this horrible
company of devil-worshippers was required to offer
the demon a lock of his hair, nail-parings, and a few
drops of his blood.

In January, 1929, intense excitement was caused
in the United States by the trial at York, Pennsylvania,
of John H. Blymyer, a voodoo-man and professed
witch-doctor, for the murder of Nelson Rehmeyer,
who was locally notorious as a practitioner of black
magic. Blymyer and two companions, Wilbert Hess
and John Curry, visited Rehmeyer, who lived at a
lonely farm, in order to secure a lock of his hair which
was required for removing a "hex" or spell he had
cast on the Hess family. The hair had to be buried
eight feet underground, and the charm would be
dissolved. Rehmeyer refused, and in the course of
the fight which followed he was struck on the head
with a billet of wood and killed. Milton Hess and his
wife Alice testified that Blymyer, who was a pow-wow
man, told them they had been "hexed", and they
firmly believed such was the case. Blymyer, when
examined, stated that for ten years he was under a
"hex" cast by "Old Man Rehmeyer", and that

Mrs. Noll, a sorceress, instructed him how to free himself by getting a lock of the wizard's hair. When asked by the judge, " What does hexing do to you ? " Blymyer replied : " You can't rest. It takes the appetite away."

Blymyer was sentenced to imprisonment for life. None the less, " The pow-wow doctors and the necromancer who told Blymyer that he was bewitched by Rehmeyer continue to do business in York County to-day, unmolested and unconcerned over Blymyer's fate . . . York's trust in ' medical ' treatment by charms and incantations, based on mysterious rites culled from mediæval books on witchcraft, seems unbreakable " (*Daily Express*, Friday, 11th January, 1929).

An essential part of the profession is that the witch should swear allegiance to the devil, and do homage. " They who swear fealty to the feudal Lord do so by falling on their knees before him, giving the required kiss and placing their joined hands between his hands, thus symbolizing a lowly and willing obedience of spirit, and the Demons must strictly exact a similar homage from their subjects whenever they hold their assemblies, although the ceremony is conducted in the strangest and most degraded manner, as is everything else they do." Thus Remy. A witch of Lorraine named Beatrix Bayona described how when this horrid society assembled " one of the Demons always sat on a high throne with a proud and haughty demeanour, and so each in turn approached him with awe and trembling and, in sign of submission, fell prone at his feet and reverently embraced them ". Marion Grant, an Aberdeen witch (1597), confessed that the devil " causit the Kis him in dyvers pairtis, and worship him on thy kneis as thy Lord ". Elizabeth Style and the Somerset witches (1664) were very particular in their mention of the ceremonious salutation when they met the devil. " Alice Duke, Anne Bishop and Mary Penny had their rendezvous about nine of the Clock in the Night, in the Common near Trister Gate [Stoke Trister is some two miles from Wincanton], where they met a Man in black Clothes with a little Band, to whom they did Courtesie and due observance, and the Examinant verily believes that this was the Devil."

The allegiance vowed by the witch to the devil at her profession was renewed at almost every Sabbat, and in fact became part of the ritual observed on these occasions, as is noted by many authors.

" They swear allegiance to the devil," says Guazzo, " within a circle traced upon the ground. Perhaps this is because a circle is the symbol of divinity, and the earth is God's footstool ; and so he wishes to persuade them that he is the God of heaven and earth." Mother Humphrey, an old witch of Maplestead in Essex, instructing Joan Cony in the craft bade her kneel within a circle on the ground and pray to Satan when the spirits would come to her (1569–1570). Jules Bois in his study *Satanism and Magic* speaks of homage rendered to Satan by those who stand within the circle.

A familiar, an attendant spirit or demon to obey the commands and serve the pleasure of the witch, is assigned to the newly-professed upon admission. In Holy Writ we are told that King Saul " had put away those that had familiar spirits, and the wizards, out of the land ", but when on the eve of Gilboa " the Lord answered him not, neither by dreams, nor by Urim, nor by the prophets ", he said to his servants, " Seek me a woman that hath a familiar spirit, that I may go to her and enquire of her. And his servants said to him, Behold there is a woman that hath a familiar spirit at En-dor " (1 Samuel xxviii, 3, 6, 7, *A. V.*). In Leviticus we have the divine injunction : " A man also or woman that hath a familiar spirit, or that is a wizard, shall surely be put to death" (xx, 27).

William Forbes in his *Institute of the Laws of Scotland* writes that " to some [the Devil] gives certain Spirits or Imps to correspond with, and serve them as their Familiars, known to them by some odd Names, to which they answer when called ". The familiar assumed various forms, sometimes human, sometimes animal, most conveniently to suit the business upon which he was employed. Bishop Binsfeld in his *A Complete Review of the Confessions of Warlocks and Witches* lays stress upon these particulars, and (in agreement with all other authorities) shows how the familiar can disguise himself in that form which is most apt for his requirement. Many writers, however, assert that the familiar can never assume a perfect form, whether human or animal, that is to say there will always be some ugly blemish, some deformity, although of course this may be cunningly hidden and disguised.

In his celebrated *A Treatise of Ghosts*, the Capuchin Father Noel Taillepied writes : " Solid historians tell us that the Pagans had their Lares, Penates, and inferior household deities, whom they honoured as the protectors of the family and the home, and who were none other than familiar spirits who manifested themselves and made it their business to interfere in mortal affairs in order that they might induce and entice men to worship them. Thus the account given by Froissart of the demon Orthon is deservedly famous."

Raymond, lord of Corasse, which is about seven leagues from Orthez, Béarn, having affronted a clerk curate of Catalonia, was by the command of this necromancer visited by a familiar, Orthon, who arrived amid a great gale and tempest. Raymond, however, struck a pact with the demon, who was wont daily to bring news from almost all quarters of the globe, but who stoutly refused to say how he travelled to and fro, whether or not he was winged. Being pressed to manifest himself under some visible form he bade Raymond look from his window early in the morning. There was nothing to be seen save two straws twisting and untwisting in a gust of wind. That night Orthon revealed he was one of those straws. He agreed to show himself again, but when Raymond saw a huge sow, very lean and ill-favoured, in the courtyard, he cried to loo the dogs at her, whereon the shape melted into air, and never again did Orthon return to the castle. Raymond died within the twelvemonth.

The witch's familiar or Astral Spirit is a demon, and as such the word will be used here. Other names signifying a familiar are bunn (generally a term of endearment), imp, likeness, spirit, devil, fiend, angel, maumet, puckrel, nigget.

In reference to this connotation of the term "familiar" it is interesting to note what Professor

T. Gwynn Jones tells us in his study *Welsh Folklore and Folk Custom*. Having discussed haunted houses, ghosts, and poltergeists, he continues, "There is in Welsh tradition some uncertainty as to the character of the Familiar Spirit and its relation to the person whom it serves. Codi cythreuliaid, 'to summon devils' is properly a matter of witchcraft, depending upon certain formulæ which even professed magicians sometimes failed to control. That the familiar spirits in Wales, like those employed by magicians elsewhere in the eighteenth and preceding centuries were mostly 'demons', there is no reason to doubt. Although they were generally invisible, at least to others, they were also frequently visible in various shapes—those of a fiery ball, a roaring flame, a round bowl, a goose or a gosling, a dog, especially a mastiff, a bull, and a lovely young woman are noted. . . . Persons who had seen such demons refused to describe the sight and often died soon after the occurrence. There seems to have been belief not only in a demon coming when called and doing what he was told to do, but also in a comparatively harmless type of familiar, attaching himself to certain persons without invocation and performing certain duties of their own choice."

Mr. Wirt Sikes, who was the United States Consul for Wales, writes in his *British Goblins* : "The sort of familiar spirit employed by magicians in the eighteenth and preceding centuries was distinctly a demon." Thus the familiar controlled by Sir Dafydd Llwyd is celebrated throughout all Wales. Sir Dafydd Llwyd, who lived in Cardiganshire in the reign of Charles II, had studied black magic at Oxford. He practised as a physician and was far famed for his skill and the wonderful cures he effected. Originally he had held a curacy but he was deprived on account of his abominable sorceries. The chief source of information concerning this old magician is a work very seldom to be met with, *A Relation of the Apparition of Spirits in the County of Monmouth and the Principality of Wales* by Edmund Jones, who in the first years of the nineteenth century was Pastor of the congregation of Protestant Dissenters at the Ebenezer Chapel near Pontypool. The Rev. Edmund Jones, commonly known as " Prophet Jones ", was himself a very extraordinary character. Not only his fervent piety and eloquence in the pulpit but, as evidenced by his nickname, his insight into the future made him remarkable. As he himself often averred, a belief in ghosts, witches, fairies, and the whole order of supernatural beings was part and parcel of the Christian faith, and the man who denied the goblin world was no better than a Sadducee and a rank infidel.

" It was Sir Dafydd Llywd's great wickedness to make use of a familiar spirit. . . . The bishop did well in turning him out of the sacred office, though he was no ill-tempered man, for how unfit was such a man to read the Sacred Scripture ! With what conscience could he ask the sponsors in baptism to undertake for the child to renounce the world, the flesh, and the devil, who was himself familiar with one of the spirits of darkness ? . . . Of this Sir Dafydd I have heard much but chiefly depend upon what was told to me by the Rev. Mr. Thomas Lewis, the curate of Landdw and Tolachdy, an excellent preacher of the gospel ; and not sufficiently esteemed by his people, (which likely will bring a judgement on them in time to come). Mr. Lewis knew the young woman who had been Sir Dafydd's maid servant, and the house where he lived." The story went that Sir Dafydd kept his familiar locked up in a book of spells. On one occasion he accidently left this book behind him, and at once sent his page home to fetch it, strictly charging him not to open it. The lad being, as boys use, of an inquisitive turn of mind, on his way back to his master began to turn over the leaves, and read although the words were quite unintelligible to him. Suddenly there issued forth a huge cacodemon who with a frowning face in a gruff grumbling voice asked to be set to work. The boy in spite of his terror had the wit to say : " Fetch me some stones out of the river Wye." In a few moments stones and pebbles began to fly through the air, when Sir Dafydd, who from the delay had a shrewd suspicion of what must have happened, came hurrying upon the scene, and conjured the spirit back into the book before any serious mischief had been done.

Whilst Cornelius Agrippa was lecturing at Louvain there happened to be lodging in the same house as this famous occult philosopher and his wife a young student, who had long been very anxious to pry into all the secrets of divination and goety. His chance he thought with glee was now surely come. But Agrippa when he went abroad invariably double-locked his study door and carried the keys in his purse. The youth who was handsome, rash, eloquent, and of a warm amorous complexion, as a preliminary began to woo the lady pretty hotly, nor was it long indeed before she granted him an ample share of her favours. This wanton was Agrippa's third wife, a

native of Mechlin, who had much beauty but so little
honesty that he was at last compelled to divorce her.
Nor would she have hesitated to filch her husband's
keys had opportunity offered, as her gallant often
wheedled and pressed her, but they were too safely
guarded for even her nimble fingers to reach, and
conscious of her adulteries she shrank from arousing
suspicion in any direction. At length urgent business,
a wealthy and exacting patient—for Agrippa was
practising and highly esteemed as a physician—
compelled him to be absent for some days, and meanwhile he entrusted his keys to his wife, most strictly
enjoining her that nobody should so much as venture to
set foot across the threshold of his study. She promised
that he should be obeyed in every particular, and no
sooner had he ridden off than she hastened to hand over
to her lover the bunch of keys, only begging him not
to move anything or displace a single caliper or sphere.
He protested that he would use every caution, indeed
he desired no more than a peep at the workshop of so
great and reverend a master, at the same time in his
own mind he had determined to purloin some manuscript or formula which might instruct him in the art
of turning metal into gold, perhaps he might even
secure a pinch of the powder of transmutation itself.
It was late and the house was wrapped in sleep when
the adventurous young man crept softly down the
stairs and unhasped the door of the mysterious sanctum.
As half-daring, half-afraid, he held the flickering lamp
high above his head he saw that upon the philosopher's
desk there lay open a huge book close written as it
seemed in scarlet characters which might be blood.
Gently drawing to the door, lest he should be interrupted

at his unhallowed task, he advanced, set down his light upon the table, and seating himself in the quaintly carven chair he bent to con that cabalistic page. What secrets did it hold, what runes of awful power? The cipher was strange, in no tongue he knew, but he made shift as he pored thereon to pronounce some few words. Suddenly he fancies he hears a sharp knock upon the door. He listened for a moment, but all was still. He turns to his task. Hardly has he uttered some half a dozen syllables more than the knock is repeated with awful force. Leaping to his feet he tries to speak, but his tongue is parched and dry and he cannot articulate a sound. His hair bristles, and his body is cold with the sweat of fear. The door, slowly turning on its hinges, discloses a stranger of majestic form upon whose face there sits eternally a grim black scowl and whose eyes glow with fury like red coals of fire. Advancing he sternly demands in threatening tones why he was summoned. "I did not call you," stammers the wretched youth. "You did!" cried the stranger, "and learn that demons are not invoked by fools in vain!" His crooked claws are at the young man's throat, and a moment later he cast aside his body as it were some empty husk upon the floor. Not many hours after dawn Agrippa in silence and with frowning brow comes swiftly back to his house. He enters the study, and with a glance he realizes what has happened, even as he guessed whilst many leagues away. With mighty gestures and impious charm he recalls the familiar whom he sharply upbraids for so rash a deed, commanding the murderous spirit to assume a human form, and then immediately to reanimate the poor dead body and to walk forth with it up and down in the market place and crowded streets. With horrid mutterings the demon obeys. He appears as a grave and sober burgher of middle years in rich attire. The student revives, and putting his arm through that of his unearthly companion, they go forth together very friendly in the sight of all the passers-by. They even enter the college courts and quadrangles and are hailed by the dead man's comrades with jest and merry greeting as they bustle to and fro to lecture-rooms and classes. It is noon ; from tall belfry and from lowlier convent gablet rings forth the Angelus. Cold and lifeless the youth falls to the ground ; his companion is nowhere to be seen. At first it is thought he has expired in some apoplexy or fatal fit. But when they examine his body marks of strangulation are found on the neck. The prints of the cruel claw of the demon are only too plain. It is whispered that his companion vanished in a flash of flame. Suspicion is aroused. The magistrates institute inquiries. They visit Agrippa's house, and question those dwelling there. That evening Agrippa and his wife fly from the town.

So the legend runs. Similar stories are related of many warlocks and there is no reason why they should not in effect be substantially true. The ignorant who meddle with magic out of the itch of an idle and wicked curiosity are courting dangers whereof they are wholly unaware.

It was a very ancient and widespread notion, possibly of oriental origin, that a witch might keep and confine his familiar in some one instrument or place. There was a common proverb, for example, in the fifteenth century, " Beware of the devil in Ossiach."

Now Ossiach was a Benedictine monastery in Austria, and the story went that the monks had imprisoned a demon in a crystal or glass vial. Paracelsus was believed to have confined his familiar in the pommel of his sword. There is nothing either theologically or philosophically impossible in the fact that a spiritual body, an angel (either good or evil) can be contained in even a point of space.

In the Canary Isles, before the natives embraced Christianity, familiar spirits who had assumed human forms could be seen walking about, not only at night but in broad day, conversing with and accompanying their wizard masters on various businesses.

A famous Spanish scholar and physician of the sixteenth century, Dr. Eugenio Torralba (who incidentally is mentioned by Cervantes in *Don Quixote*) was for many years ministered to and served by a familiar. Whilst Torralba was still a young man, a student of medicine, he formed, owing to their interest in the same pursuits, an intimacy with a certain Fra Pietro, a Dominican. One day the friar in close confidence imparted to his friend that he was attended by an angel or genius named Zequiel (Ezechiel). He was bound by no pact or vow, however, to this spirit upon whom he merely had to call for help to be relieved in any necessity and advised as to his future undertakings. Fra Pietro promised to present Torralba to Zequiel, and at a fitting opportunity the form of a young man with fair hair and a mild countenance stood before them. Addressing the doctor the spirit said : " I will hold myself at your service so long as you live, and I will follow you faithfully wherever you go." There was no suggestion of any other bond or agreement between the two. Henceforward Zequiel appeared to the doctor at the quarterly changes of the moon, and more often, whenever he was summoned, if there was need of him. Torralba expressly stated that the spirit had never uttered a word contrary to religion, never given him bad counsel, never inspired evil thoughts, and not infrequently even accompanied him to Holy Mass, so that he verily thought an angel was his monitor and guide.

On one important occasion Torralba was consulted by Cardinal Bernadino Lopez de Carvajal, a theologian of acknowledged eminence, concerning a dark and mysterious business. A lady of wealth and position had with great trepidation and alarm informed the Cardinal that she was nightly disturbed by the phantom of a man, completely unknown to her, who declared that he had been murdered and unavailingly sought rest. The Cardinal had directed his body-physician Morales to watch with the lady and report what occurred. Morales for several nights had remained in the chamber but could discern nothing, although at a certain hour he felt a chill as if of the grave, accompanied by a loathly smell of corruption which filled him with no ordinary horror and fear, whilst the lady cried out that the ghost had appeared. Cardinal Carvajal, knowing Torralba's deep studies in occultism, prayed him to join Morales at the next opportunity, and accordingly the two doctors took their station in the haunted room. About one o'clock they heard an anguished cry, the air grew deathly cold and was filled with the stench of human decay. Torralba saw by the bed the figure of a man covered with wounds, the countenance distorted and pale with pain. A little further there lurked an even more terrifying apparition, the half-formed shadow of an evil woman, her vile face leering horribly from the darkness. " What would you ? " demanded the scryer. " The treasure ! the treasure ! " moaned the vision. Upon being questioned, Zequiel informed Torralba that in a cellar long years before had been buried the body of a miser, assassinated, all unshriven and unhouseled, for the vast sums it was known he had concealed in the house. The woman, whose spectre had been seen, was his servant who had admitted the ruffians with whom she was in league, but after the murder they could not find the hiding-place of the money-bags, and so perforce remained unsatisfied. The crime had never been discovered. Zequiel revealed the sliding panel which gave access to the secret room where the wealth was stored, and which actually opened out of the lady's bedchamber. The money being thus recovered, a part was devoted to masses for the dead man's soul, the remainder to other pious and charitable uses, and so the unhappy and unquiet house found rest.

Eventually Torralba was denounced to the Inquisition as a sorcerer. When examined he frankly acknowledged his intercourse with Zequiel, who was, he maintained, a good spirit, perhaps an angel. After a long investigation the lightest of sentences was passed, mainly consisting of a formal and public abjuration of all heresies and magic. He was, however, bound by a solemn oath to hold no further communication with the familiar.

Zequiel, as we have remarked, appeared as a comely fair-haired young man. A Suffolk witch of the reign of Charles II confessed that the demon visited her. " in the form of a Pretty handsom Young Man first ". More often the familiar is evil-favoured and misshapen, so ugly indeed as to betray his diabolic origin. The late Mrs. Violet Tweedale saw a familiar of this kind at Nice. She noticed that a certain Prince Valori, who frequented the fashionable Riviera, seemed always to be attended and shadowed by a man in grotesque attire. This personage was gaunt and emaciated, " with very long thin legs, and he was dressed entirely in chocolate brown—a sort of close-fitting cowl was drawn over his head, and his curious long, impish face was made more weird by small, sharply pointed ears rising on each side of his head. He appeared to have ' got himself up ' to look like a satyr or some such mythical monstrosity." At a fancy-dress ball Mrs. Tweedale saw Prince Valori magnificently costumed as a French courtier of the eighteenth century, and by his side moved the man in brown. They came up to her, and she naturally concluded that he was about to present his friend. The Prince, however, seated himself by her and talked whilst the satyr stood behind them in perfect silence. Mrs. Tweedale says that she felt exceedingly uneasy all the while. Later she took the opportunity of quietly asking a Russian lady, a clairvoyante, who the brown satyr was. " Why don't you know ? " was the reply. " It is his familiar who constantly attends him. People say they became attached whilst he was assisting at a Sabbath in the Vosges, and he can't get rid of it. Sabbaths are still held at Lutzei, and each initiate receives a familiar. The familiars have names —Minette, Verdelet, and so forth. One of my ancestors de Laski, the Polish boyar who patronized Dr. Dee, owned a familiar called Sainte-Buisson." "Then the satyr attached to Prince Valori is not flesh and blood? Horrible!" exclaimed Mrs. Tweedale. "Is he always there?" "Oh yes. Any one who is clairvoyant sees him. I myself have seen him in Paris." A few mornings after, Mrs. Tweedale meeting Prince Valori on the Promenade des Anglais boldly asked him, "By the way who is that tall man so curiously dressed in brown I have seen with you lately?" The Prince's face changed: "You also," he muttered. "My remark was a thoughtless impertinence. I am sorry to have hurt you. Pray don't answer." He shook his head gloomily, and after a moment's silence, "I am not the only one in the world so afflicted," he said.

Mrs. Tweedale knew General Elliot, who commanded the forces in Scotland, and was a distinguished figure in society in the nineties. The General had a familiar "Wononi", to whom he actually used to speak aloud in the middle of a dinner party.

The animal familiar, imp or maumet—"puckrel" is the old English country name—was quite distinct from the familiar in human shape. In England, most frequently in Essex, Suffolk, and the Eastern Counties, and in Scotland there is abundance of evidence concerning the puckrel. "To some of the baser sorte of them [witches] he [the devil] oblishes him selfe to appear at their calling upon him, by such a proper name which he shewes unto them, either in likenes of a dog, a Catte, an Ape, or such-like other beast; or else to answere by a voyce onlie. The effects are to answere to such demands, as concernes curing of diseases, their own particular menagery : or such other base things as they require of him. But to the most curious sorte, in the formes he will oblish himself, to enter in a dead bodie, and there out of to give such answers, of the event of battels, of maters concerning the estate of commonwelths, and such like other great questions : yea, to some he will be a continuall attender, in forme of a Page : He will permit himselfe to be conjured, for the space of so many yeres, either in a tablet or a ring, or such like thing, which they may easily carrie about with them." Thus concisely King James VI of Scotland (not to be James I of England for another half a dozen years) in his famous *Dæmonologie* summed up the question of familiars.

At Windsor, in 1579, Mother Dutton, who lived at Clewer kept " a Spirite or Fiende in the likenesse of a Toade ". Mother Devell, whose cottage was " nigh the Ponde in Windesore " had a spirit in the shape of a black cat, called Jill. Mother Margaret, a cripple, who was in the Windsor almshouses, maintained a " Kitlyng or Feende by her named Ginnie ". One notorious witch of that knot " kept a Ratte, beeyng in very deede a wicked Spirite, naming it Philip ", and this rat she fed with blood " issuing from her right hand wrest, the markes whereof evidently remain ". The Lancashire witch Mother Demdike entertained a familiar who first appeared in the shape of a boy, but later in the likeness of a brown dog, and was called Tibb.

This was in the early seventeenth century, the reign of James I, but to come down to the present day, a resident of Horseheath, a village about fourteen miles from Cambridge, gave the following details regarding the sorceries of Mother Redcap, a notorious witch who died in 1926. " One day a black man called, produced a book, and asked her to sign her name in it. The woman signed the book, and the mysterious stranger then told her she would be the mistress of five imps who would carry out her orders. Shortly afterwards the woman was seen out accompanied by a rat, a cat, a toad, a ferret, and a mouse. Everybody believed she was a witch and many people visited her to obtain cures" (*The Sunday Chronicle*, 9th September, 1928).

Very frequently the witch did (and for the matter of that does) keep some small animal which is nourished on a diet of milk and bread, and often stimulated with drops of her own blood, in order that she may divine by its means. The details of this particular method of augury are by no means clear. Yet it seems certain that something unhallowed and even diabolical must enter in, and we are bound to regard the medium as magical or ensorcelled. Probably of old the witch observed the gait of the animals, and its actions ; the tones of its voice were easily interpreted to bear some fanciful or likely meaning, whilst no doubt a dog, or such a bird as a raven, a daw, a pie, could be taught tricks to impress the simplicity of inquirers. At the same time it is a very well known fact that most animals are not merely extraordinarily intelligent but also extraordinarily psychic. The dog and the cat and many birds are in close touch with the unknown. Both dogs and cats are aware of any coming misfortune in a house, especially if it be a death. Dogs, moreover, have the faculty of seeing ghosts and are afraid of the supernatural. This is common knowledge.

The witch's familiar might be obtained in various ways. The demon familiar who appears in human form can only be procured at the sabbat, or else by some very explicit covenant with the fiend following upon a direct invocation. Thus, as has been noted, Prince Valori obtained his infernal companion at a sabbat in the Vosges. Virginie, the maidservant of Madame Belloc, a pious lady living at Agen at the beginning of the last century, confessed to her mistress that she was a Satanist and at a Sabbat had been assigned a familiar, an unclean spirit, who appeared as a young man and frequently had commerce with her.

"The Laplanders bequeath their demons as part of their inheritance which is the reason that one family excels another in this magical art." So often the puckrel was presented by the older witch of a family to the younger witches. Alice Hunt and Margery Salmon, two witches of Saint Osyth, were given two familiars apiece by their mother, Mother Barnes. Sometimes too a witch would present a familiar to another member of the society. Mother Waterhouse, a Chelmsford witch, possessed a black cat sent to her by the grandmother of Elizabeth Francis, a fellow witch. The old woman added instructions that the cat must be carefully nourished with blood and bread and milk.

The demon familiar, even in animal form, could converse. The Devil appeared in the size and shape of a dunnish coloured ferret to Joan Prentice, who dwelt in the almshouse at Hinningham Sibble. She was preparing for bed when the ferret, whose eyes glowed red as fire, came out of a corner and cried : " Joan Prentice give me thy soul." " What art thou ? "

stammered the wretched old woman, sore afraid. "I am Satan," came the reply, "fear me not. I am here to obtain thy soul." At night a grey shadowy thing stood by the straw pallet of Elizabeth Clarke in her miserable hovel at Manningtree and talked with her, and anon brought her victuals. The imps of Elizabeth Hubbard, a poor widow of Stowmarket, were like three children who kept whispering that she must deny God, Christ, and all good works. By their aid she wrought fearful mischief throughout the neighbourhood.

The familiar might also be procured by certain impious rites or actions involving a profanation of Holy Communion. As early as the twelfth century Gerald de Barry, the distinguished Welsh writer, warns priests against letting the Host by any accident get into the hands of magicians. In the thirteenth century Jacques de Vitry has an account of a woman who kept the wafer in her mouth intending to convey it out of church for witchcraft. A little later we find Berthold of Ratisbon, one of the most famous preachers of the day, denouncing those, "who do witchcraft with God's Body, for that is the greatest of all sins that ever the world committed," whilst those who are guilty of such horrid impiety are "to the devil the dearest that he hath ever begotten".

On Spy Wednesday the Waldensians were wont to attend the confessional with a great outward show of penitence and devotion, and when they made their Easter Communion they would secretly let slip the Host out of their mouths and under cover of their sleeves hide it in a handkerchief or glove. Then they would carry it home and throw it to certain toads

THE SABBAT AT NORTH BERWICK CHURCH
Dr. Fian and his Coven

41

which they used to keep and nourish in earthen pots and other vessels. Sometimes when the toads had eaten the Host the reptiles were killed and their blood employed to confect a certain charm. Occasionally the wizards were commanded to bring the Host to the Sabbat in order that they might defile the Body of God with every possible circumstance of filth and profanity.

In 1582 the wife of Edward Jones was called upon to prove to the satisfaction of the Archdeacon of Lewes " that she did eat the Communion bread and put yt not in hir glove ".

James Device, one of the Lancashire coven, was bidden by his grandmother old Demdike on Sheare Thursday morning to go to church to receive the Communion (the next day after being Good Friday), but not to eat the Bread the Minister gave him, since he was to deliver it to such a thing as should meet him on his way home. Yet he did eat the Bread, and as he was returning home, not more than a couple of hundred yards away from the church door, there met him a thing in the shape of a hare, and this asked him if he brought the Bread as his grandmother had bidden him. When he replied he had not, the thing threatened to tear him in pieces. Shaking with fear, he made the sign of the Cross, whereupon the thing vanished from his sight.

At the beginning of the eighteenth century two old dames attended the morning service at Llanddewi Brefi Church, and partook of the Holy Communion ; but instead of eating the sacred bread like other com-, municants, they kept it in their mouths and went out. Then they walked round the church outside nine times, and at the ninth time the Evil One came out of the Church wall in the form of a frog, to whom they gave the bread from their mouths, and by doing this wicked thing they were supposed to be selling themselves to Satan and become witches.—There was an old man in North Pembrokeshire who used to say that he obtained the power of bewitching in the following manner : The bread of his first Communion he pocketed. He made pretence of eating it first of all, and then put it in his pocket. When he went out from the service there was a dog meeting him by the gate, to which he gave the bread, thus selling his soul to the Devil. Ever after he possessed the power to bewitch.

The same profane practice persisted both in Berkshire and in Lincolnshire. Not fifty years ago in the latter county an old woman tried to persuade a young girl to keep at least half the Bread in her mouth at her first Communion, promising her that thus she should become a witch.

In July, 1873, Mr. W. H. Gamlen, of Brampford Spoke, Exeter, read a paper at Sidmouth, which was afterwards printed in the *Transactions of the Devonshire Association*. He exhibited and discussed that curious talisman, the toad-stone. The specimen in question had belonged to a Mr. Blagdon, of Puddington, to whose house persons from all parts of the county constantly resorted to borrow it, since it was supposed to cure complaints that were presumed to be beyond the skill of regular medical men to aid, such complaints having been caused by some wicked person having obtained power from the devil to do mischief. The person to obtain the power must be a communicant of the Church of England or Rome. " The power was said to be obtained by keeping such a portion of the elements on receiving the Sacrament, and, after carrying them round the church and using certain incantations, giving them to a toad met with in the churchyard."

A Manx " Obbery " (superstitious sorcery) is " Bringing home some of the Sacramental Bread and making crumbs of it, when a huge black stag-beetle will come and eat it ".

Grotesque names were generally given to the familiar : In France, Lizabet, Verd-Joli, Maître Persil (parsley), Verdelet, Sainte-Buisson, Abrahel (a succubus) ; in Germany, Reicheher, Schwarzburg, Jammer, Helle-krug, Kuhfuss ; and in England, especially to animal familiars, Grissell, Greedigut, Blackman, Jezebel (a succubus), Ilemanzar, Jarmara, Pyewackett, Elva, Jeso, Arouta, Cramega, Panu, Vinegar Tom. Among the imps which Marion Hocket gave Sarah Barton of Harwich were two called Pretty-man and Dainty. So one of the Italian witches named his familiar, Fiorino.

Michael Dalton, the famous legal writer and author of *The Country Justice*, who died about the middle of the seventeenth century, summarizes the following articles from the Rev. Richard Bernard's *Guide to Grand Jurymen* as being (among others) of prime importance in trials for witchcraft.

1. These witches have ordinarily a familiar or spirit, which appeareth to them ; sometimes in one shape, sometimes in another, such as in the shape of a man, woman, boy, dog, cat, foal, fowl, hare, rat, toad, etc. And to these their spirits they give names, and they meet together to christen them (as they speak).

2. Their said familiar hath some big or little teat upon their body, and in some secret place, where he sucketh them. And besides their sucking, the Devil leaveth other marks upon their body, sometimes like a blue spot or red spot, like a flea-biting; sometimes the flesh sunk in and hollow (all which for a time may be covered, yea taken away, but will come again, to their old form). And these the Devil's marks be insensible, and being pricked will not bleed, and be often in their secretest parts, and therefore require diligent and careful search.

These first two are main points to discover and convict these witches; for they prove fully that those witches have a familiar, and made a league with the Devil.

The " big or little teat " or pap upon the witch's body, said to secrete milk which nourished the familiar, and which was one of the main points to discern and convict witches, must be carefully distinguished from the insensible devil-mark to be considered later.

In the case of the Witch of Edmonton, Elizabeth Sawyer, who was in spite of her resistance searched upon the express order of the Bench, it was found by Margaret Weaver, a widow of honest reputation, and two other grave matrons, who performed this duty, that there was upon her body " a thing like a Teate the bignesse of the little finger, and the length of half a finger, which was branched at the top like a teate, and seemed as though one had suckt it ". A boy, only nine years old, who lived at Rattesden, a small village in Suffolk, confessed that " he suckled an imp, and commanded it to do mischief". He came of a bad stock, being the son of a witch, who had been hanged

(1645). John Palmer, of St. Albans (1649), confessed that " upon his compact with the Divel, hee received a flesh brand or mark, upon his side, which gave suck to two familiars ". The Kentish witch, Mary Read, of Lenham (1652), " had a visible Teat, under her Tongue, and did show it to many." At St. Albans about 1660 there was a wizard who " had like a Breast on his side ". There is similar evidence adduced in the accounts of Rose Cullender and Amy Duny, two Suffolk witches, executed in 1665 ; Temperance Lloyd, a Bideford witch, hanged in 1682 ; Widow Coman, an Essex witch, who died in her bed (1699) ; and, indeed, innumerable other examples might be quoted affording a whole catena of pertinent illustrations. The phenomenon, it is observable, seems to be stressed only in the records of England and New England, where, however, it is of exceedingly frequent occurrence. No doubt many of such instances are explicable by the cases of polymastia (*mammæ erraticæ*) and polythelia (supernumerary nipples) of which there are continual records in recent medical works. It must be freely admitted that these anatomical divagations are commoner than is generally supposed ; frequently they are so slight that they may pass almost unnoticed ; admittedly there is exaggeration in many of the inexactly observed seventeenth century narratives. However, it has to be said that when every most generous allowance is made, the facts which remain (and the details are very ample) cannot be covered by physical peculiarities and malformations.

As we know, a number of devils were permitted to enter swine, and certain writers have held (and nothing is more probable) that demons entered into these animal familiars, and that bound by a blood contract with the witch and nourished with human blood by the reeks and vapours of which they are recreated for "her young ones also suck up blood", they obeyed the commands of the person they served, going forth to do mischief even to the destruction of life. When they thus assumed the form of or entered into an animal they are clearly "not perfectly *abstract* from all *body* and *matter*" wherefore the natural appetite of the animal would persist, and hence it must needs be fed in the ordinary way as well as rewarded with the sip of blood. This seems a simple and satisfactory explanation of various details in the mystery of the familiar which may appear puzzling. Glanvil suggests that further the sucking of blood "may be onely a *diabolical Sacrament* and *Ceremony* to confirm the *hellish Covenant*", whereby the witches become "*mischievously influential*".

What wonder then that in 1604 there was passed an Act, 1 Jas. I, c. 12, against Conjuration, Witchcraft, and dealing with evil and Wicked Spirits, whereby it was ordered that if "any person or persons . . . shall use practise or exercise any Invocation or Conjuration of any evil and wicked Spirit, or shall consult covenant with entertain employ feed or reward any evil and wicked Spirit to or for any intent or purpose . . . then every such offender or offenders, their Aiders, Abettors and Counsellors being of any the said Offences duly and lawfully convicted and attainted, shall suffer pains of death as a Felon or Felons, and shall lose the privelege and benefit of Clergy and Sanctuary".

CHAPTER II

OF THE PRACTICE OF WITCHCRAFT ; OF THE MALICE AND MISCHIEF OF WITCHES ; OF THE DEVIL'S MARK ; AND OF THE GRIMOIRE

Then flourish Hell, and mighty Mischief reign !
DRYDEN, The Duke of Guise.
Many of them also which used curious arts brought their books together, and burned them before all men : and they counted the price of them, and found it fifty thousand pieces of silver.
The Acts of the Apostles, xix, 19.

The most complete, as it is certainly the most authoritative, summary of the mischiefs wrought by witchcraft is that delivered in the famous Bull of Innocent VIII where the evil is set forth in words of burning eloquence and conviction : " Many persons of both sexes unmindful of their own salvation and straying from the Catholic Faith, have abandoned themselves to devils, incubi and succubi, and by their incantations, spells, conjurations, and other accursed charms and crafts, enormities and horrid offences, have slain infants yet in the mother's womb, as also the offspring of cattle, have blasted the produce of the earth, the grapes of the vine, the fruits of trees, nay, men and women, beasts of burthen, herd-beasts, as well as animals of other kinds, vineyards, orchards, meadows, pasture-land, corn, wheat, and all other cereals ; these wretches furthermore afflict and torment men and women, beasts of burthen, herd-beasts, as well as animals of other kinds, with terrible and piteous pains and sore diseases, both internal and external ;

they hinder men from performing the sexual act and women from conceiving, whence husbands cannot know their wives nor wives receive their husbands ; over and above this they blasphemously renounce that Faith which is theirs by the Sacrament of Baptism, and at the instigation of the Enemy of Mankind they do not shrink from committing and perpetrating the foulest abominations and filthiest excesses to the deadly peril of their souls whereby they outrage the Divine Majesty and are a cause of scandal and danger to very many."

This historical pronouncement carries no mere historical interest. The wisdom of Pope Innocent is speaking to us to-day, and his words are as awfully solemn and as eternally true in the twentieth century as they were four hundred and more years ago. We have in these noble sentences set forth the very essence of witchcraft, that is to say the implacable hate the witch bears all mankind, and the dark power these slaves of Satan have obtained to contrive damage and destruction, ay, even of life, to the glut of their murderous malice and malignity.

The witch is an evil thing, indeed ; a social pest and parasite ; the devotee of a loathly and obscene creed ; an adept at poisoning, blackmail, and other creeping crimes ; a bawd ; an abortionist ; a minister to vice and corruption, battening upon the foulest passions of the age. Witches

                                       raise jars,
Jealousies, strifes, and heart-burning disagreements,
Like a thick scurf o'er life.

Their baneful activities range from domestic annoyances and accidents, singly trivial enough maybe, but in sum horribly fretting and vexatious, to the most serious injuries, the ruin of property, sudden illness and wasting death, and ultimately to the embroiling of nations, to anarchy and red revolution, for the witch is and always has been a political factor. The witch is, in effect, a perpetual menace, a source of instant danger to any ordered society. In the humblest walks of life, in townlets and small villages, witches although almost isolated members of the infernal organization are yet potential murderers, even as the master whom they serve was a murderer from the beginning.

A correspondent in *The Times*, 19th September, 1930, writes : " In 1900 I was living in a small Sussex village between Groombridge and Eastbourne. An old villager one day began to talk about witches. ' The worst on 'em about here's not long dead,' she said. She told me a few of the common tales, injuring children, damaging poultry, &c. Then she warmed up. Pointing to the adjacent cross-roads, she said: ' I was standing just there, one day, and *she* was there. Along come one of Squire ———'s big farm carts, you know, him at the Park.' (Just then ' the Park ' was let to ' furriners '—i.e. non-Sussex people.) ' *She* looked at it, and down went the horses into the road over their knees, and the cart over the axles.' "

Another correspondent in the same paper, three days later, related that when he was living in a small town in Somerset about 1912–13 he used to visit an old woman who told him that she had had an ulcerated leg ever since she came to the town and that there was no hope of her getting any better, since her ailment was due to a bad woman next door who had come and overlooked her one midnight. She further remarked that Somerset was particularly full of " bad folk ", that is to say witches. I suggest that the secret tradition has been handed down from the days of Julian Cox, Ann Bishop, and Margaret Agar.

In February, 1923, at Gorefield, a small village in Cambridgeshire, Mr. Scrimshaw and his family were bewitched, and much distress ensued in the house. Mrs. Holmes, who lived about a mile away, claimed to be able to break the spell as she had been " born in Chime-hours ". I will do what I can to help neighbour Scrimshaw," she said, " if they are witching him I can stop them." She collected some apple pips ; some locks of hair and nail parings from each member of the family, and these with two black pins she put in a bottle which was thrown on the kitchen fire. As the bottle burst she declared the charm was broken. However, new disturbances took place at the farm, coincident with which Mrs. Holmes died (*The Evening Standard*, 19th March, 1923).

Four peasants were tried at Szeged (Hungary) in January, 1928, for having killed an old woman, alleged to be a witch. The defendants were near relations of Vincent Tokar, who had long been bedridden owing to the malice of this hag. She visited him at night, and by her cantrips drained him dry as hay so that he dwindled, peaked and pined, and was left in so pitiable a state that his cousins resolved even with violence to free him from the evil spell. That evening they waited in the bedchamber, and when the woman entered swiftly dispatched her. The court acquitted the accused since they had acted under irresistible compulsion being compelled to believe in the stated origin of Tokar's illness. Moreover in the circumstances the case indicated the existence of a witch.

Some two years later there was a similar occurrence in a Hungarian village. A well-to-do farmer was seized with a sudden fever. One evening the sick man, raving in delirium, shouted that a witch had seized him by the throat and cast a curse upon him. "Save me from the witch," he cried, "she will appear at midnight." For three nights the family kept vigil, and on the third night as the church clock was striking twelve the door was flung open and a fearful crone hobbled in, but the men of the house sprang on her and a blow laid her dead on the floor. At that very moment the farmer rose from his bed, completely cured. Those concerned were tried for homicide and sentenced to short terms of imprisonment, which were much reduced by the Supreme Court at Vienna.

In September, 1928, Camilla Illasi was convicted at Padua of witchcraft, cruelty to animals, and extortion. She had terrorized the village of Bassanello for years, trafficking in black magic. She kept numbers of birds, dogs, cats, and rabbits which she used for her foul charms and auguries. The peasantry feared and hated the witch, who long cunningly evaded the law, but at last she was caught and reaped the full reward of her iniquities.

Writing in *The Church Times*, 8th May, 1931, and describing the Essex village of Good Easter, Donald Maxwell remarks that the people are still firmly convinced of the power of witchcraft and the evil eye. "There was no doubt whatever that old Mother Blankley was a witch. There was proof of it. What about Farmer Attridge's heifers and the strange litter of pigs in Old Mead's barn ? She was a witch right enough."

A tourist in Cardiganshire writing in *The Daily Express*, 27th December, 1932, evinces surprise that in Wales to-day many people believe firmly in the power of witchcraft and the evil eye. " I was positive that my little pig was bewitched when one day he sat up on his haunches in the sty and laughed at me like a woman I know. I went to the wizard about it," one woman told him. Another woman said that when her two pigs refused to eat she consulted a wise man, who instructed her : " After sunset take a few hairs from the pigs' backs. Rub them into a ball of lard. Put the tongs over the fire and place the ball of lard on it. You must be alone. You will see a blue flame and in it the face of the person who bewitched your pigs. Feed the pigs next morning." This was done, the pigs were cured and the following day they ran to their food.

A few years ago a lady who was walking through the market square at Tavistock saw an old woman pilfering small articles from the stalls. She called the attention of one of the sellers to this, whereupon the hag swiftly turning round asked : " With which eye did you see all this ? " " With both my eyes," was the reply. The old woman muttered quickly to herself, and added aloud : " For meddling with what does not concern you, by this and that you shall see no more." So saying she waved her hand swiftly across the lady's face, not touching her, and hobbled away. Within an hour the lady lost her sight, and blind she remained until the day she died, which was in 1931.

A correspondent in *John O'London's Weekly*, November, 1936, observed that " even now belief in witchcraft in the upper parts of the Wye Valley is not quite extinct ". Mr. E. Thomas, writing in the following month, remarked, " when we lived in a small village in Montgomeryshire some years ago we found a widespread belief in witchcraft among the farmers of the district." If the cattle became sick the farmers visited the conjurer at LL—— to inquire who had bewitched their beasts. When two farmers had a serious quarrel, one of them went to the conjurer to procure a charm to injure his neighbour.

Other methods a witch might employ to plague her neighbours were by making the cows go dry, and so stealing the milk ; by enchanting the churn, whence butter would not come ; by burning the bread in the oven or souring it ; by spoiling the ale at brewing time. To us to-day generally these mishaps may not mean so much, for they can at least fairly easily be rectified, they may even appear a trifle ridiculous, not to say comical. But two centuries and less ago (and in some remoter districts now) when a household might depend for its comfort, nay, even for its sustenance, upon the success of these domestic operations things wear a very different face, and such malicious interference would have very disastrous results. Examples of all these mischiefs occur again and again throughout the witch trials. Alice Martin, a Devonshire witch, arraigned in 1565, used to enter houses begging for milk. If refused she would mutter " Give no milk : give no milk ", and from that day they could make no butter nor cheese nor have milk from their kine. About ten years ago there was a notorious witch living in

Caithness who wished to buy a young cow from a neighbouring farm. The owner refused to sell, saying he needed the milk. The witch replied that he would never again get milk from that cow, and her words came true. More recently a Welsh farmer was charged with assault. He had drawn blood from a reputed witch, and had compelled her to come to his house and unspeak the churn. He probably acted under great provocation and was justified in his somewhat rough and ready procedure.

Mother Waterhouse, one of the Chelmsford coven, who was hanged in 1566, confessed that she had sent her familiar to destroy the brewing. Mother Palmer, of Framlingham, came to Robert Waite's house and asked for a draught of beer. She was refused, and answered the goodwife, " You will want a cup o' beer yourself before long." After that they could make no beer which did not sour in a couple of weeks. The demon of Tedworth, who incited by the villainy and witchcrafts of the drummer, so plagued Mr. Mompesson's house, used to spoil the food by filling the porringers with ashes.

In Guernsey, not many years ago, a witch ruined the melons by the blight of a small black fly which the scientists found it impossible to recognize.

A particularly loathly annoyance whereby witches tormented their victims was through an uncouth spell to render them verminous. This filthy cantrip persists to-day. I have known the threat used and the dirty charm employed by sorcerers. In 1617 three Guernsey witches, Collette du Mont, her daughter Marie, and Isebel Becquet, were tried on multiplied charges. The household of James Gallienne, his wife and children had been cursed, and many other depositions of neighbours proved the accusation. Cattle died, mares miscarried, cows could give no milk, sheep sickened and fell, children and women were taken ill, men were lamed and palsied. There was no end to the mischief. Horrible black pimples broke out on the bodies of the afflicted persons ; insects swarmed in their houses, and lice in such abundance that they had to be swept away with brooms. The witches were found guilty by the Royal Court of Guernsey of having practised the damnable art of sorcery and of having thereby caused the deaths of many persons, of having destroyed and injured much cattle, and of many other abominable crimes. They confessed, and were very justly strangled and burned at the stake.

At Bedford, about 1637, old Gammer Rose amongst other charges was accused of making " a man to be alwayes lowsie ". The matter was proved beyond any question.

In 1645 a fearful witch, Elizabeth Fillet, of Witherenden, was put on her trial for various misdeeds. The wife of John Spink having made a slighting remark which was overheard by Mother Fillet, their child sickened and was suddenly covered with lice. In the same year Thomas Monticute refused old widow Thomazine Ratcliffe, of Shelley, some faggots. He became full of strange lice. A very respectable Norwich woman in 1843 made complaint before a magistrate that an old hag had bewitched her by sending her and her children a vast number of vermin. There dwelt as lately as 1874, in a lonely hut hard by the rugged promontory "La Roque du Guet", Caûbo Bay, Guernsey, a known witch of long continuance, who plagued the whole countryside by her spells. A woman scrupulously clean in her person and attire against whom the witch had a previous grudge chanced to make use of some not very complimentary expressions in speaking of the old hag, and instantaneously her clothes were covered with vermin of the most loathsome description.

A Guernsey lady, Miss E. Le Pelley, in 1896 related that two young fellows, still in their teens, one day happened to chaff an old woman, when suddenly she got furiously angry, and stooping down gathered a handful of dust which she flung in the air, at the same time gabbling a sentence very quickly. The boys went home, and found they were covered with vermin. One was so enraged that he took his gun, ran back to the witch's house, and levelling it at her cried : " Now rid me of the lice, or I will shoot you." The old wretch was really frightened. She took up some dust, scattered it on him, repeated some words, and the vermin disappeared. The other youth was worried for three days.

Mrs. Le Patourel, of St. Martin's, was told the following by the lady to whom it happened, her own mother-in-law, at the time of the incident Miss Mauger, of Saints. Miss Mauger and her sister, who came of a wealthy old family, went to school in England at a new fashionable academy, where they imbibed rather grand notions. On their return home, being very handsome girls and fond of gaiety, they used to go to all the country dances, and were much sought after as partners by the beaux of the Island. But as young ladies sometimes will they held their heads pretty high, and only cared to dance with the most select and most eligible gentlemen. One evening when they were present at a dance with a girl friend and all three happened to be particularly smartly dressed in new frocks, some man whom they did not know came up without any introduction and asked each of them in turn to dance with him. Each, however, refused rather coldly, letting it perhaps be seen a little too plainly that he was hardly the partner for them. He turned away muttering that they would soon repent their rudeness. A minute later one of the girls said to her sister, " Oh, Marie, whatever is that crawling on your lace ? " Red with confusion, the girl killed the insect, only to see swarms more moving over her white satin skirt. The other two girls to their horror found that they also were alive with vermin. In the utmost confusion all three hurriedly left the room, and hastened home. Do what they would they were plagued for three days, when the lice vanished as suddenly as they had appeared. Mrs. Le Patourel says that in telling the story her mother-in-law always concluded : " The shame of it I can never, never forget."

Mr. John de Garis, of Les Rouvets, comments : " I have heard of too many instances of this power of giving vermin being exercised to admit of doubt. The surprising part is the removal. I have not heard of a case for more than thirty years."

Dr. A. N. Symons, of Jersey, notes : " Several times I have heard that the Witches could cover a person with lice by magic. Miss R. V., who formerly lived with her people at Coin Varin, says that one of her brothers was troubled in this way by a witch who lived in the cottage, now ruined, beside Les Luanes Hill. He took a whip and threatened to thrash the witch, whereupon the trouble was removed."

Mr. John L. Amy, the author of *Jersey Folk Lore*, relates the following incident which was told him by his mother, who had it from the widow of the man who was bewitched. Jean L. was a farmer of some wealth and influence in his parish of St. Lawrence, and much respected throughout the whole district. It happened that he had to attend at Court on a certain Saturday to pass a contract which meant £400 to him, a business country folk were wont to complete with considerable preparation and ceremony. To visit the Royal Court on such an occasion was in fact a gala day, and necessitated donning Sunday clothes and every rustic formality. A few days before the great event there came to the farm begging for a pot of cider one Collas D., a shiftless and ill reputed vagabond, to whom incidentally the farmer had always refused alms. " Be off with you," cried the goodman with some vigour on seeing the ragged rascal at his gate. " Cider or Contract," was the reply. " Either you give me the cider or you do not go to the Court on Saturday." Jean L. laughed in the beggar's face. The important morning arrived, and spruced in his smartest toggery, swinging his black malacca cane with the silver head jauntily as he strode along, Maître Jean set out on his way to the Court. All was well until he had reached the top of Mont Cochon Hill, and he had actually forgotten the threat of Collas D. It felt good to be alive with a contract for some hundred pounds in one's pocket. And he was *alive* with a vengeance ! He began to twitch and itch. He halted, tore off his collar and set about scratching his neck and face. As he looked at his clothes he turned sick with horror and dismay. He saw that he was literally swarming with filthy vermin from head to foot. No help for it. He hurried back home by the short cut across the fields keeping in the shadow of the hedges lest anyone should see him. When he opened the door of his house the lice all vanished, not a trace was there to be seen. But it proved far too late to resume his journey.

In Cornwall some half a dozen years ago two men were ill-wished with vermin. The spell was broken by standing in a church porch on Sunday morning and muttering to themselves as the congregation was leaving : " We have lost our flocks, call them home."

The sterile witch-charm known as " Tying the points ", or in French *nouer l'aiguilette* :

to starve up generation,
To strike a barrenness in men and women,

so that the sexual functions in either sex were wholly incapacitated and a complete frigidity ensued was always regarded with especial abhorrence as an abomination mortally injurious to the most intimate human relations. Yet Delrio remarks that in his day it was one of the commonest as it was one of the vilest businesses of sorcery.

Bodin adds that there were no less than fifty methods of casting this accursed spell, which indeed is still employed by witches to-day, as a modern French writer, Roland Brévannes, attests.

The bond-slave of a murderer, the witch is also a murderer, a point that has already been touched upon, and one scarcely requiring any further enlargement. In Africa the ju-ju man will " hate " his enemy to death.   The medicine doctor puts ju-ju on some person, and that person dies.   He may fall down suddenly ; he may waste inch by inch.   Only because the wizard has looked at him, has pointed towards him, and willed him to die.   That is all.

The German and Italian witches used to disinter human corpses, especially the bodies of criminals who had been hanged, to use them for the murderous slaughter of men.   From such horrid material they confected charms of especial potency.

In the Navarrese witch-trials of 1610 Juan de Echelar confessed that a candle had been used made from the arm of an infant strangled before baptism. The ends of the fingers were lit, and burned with a clear flame.

The right hand of a gibbeted felon, severed at the wrist, was employed for the ghoulish charm known as the Hand of Glory ; the Dead Man's Candle ; or, the Corpse Candlestick.   The instructions to fashion this magical taper are given at length in *Les Secrets du Petit Albert.*   The ghastly relic of mortality was mummified by being placed in an earthen pot with coarse salt, dragon-wort, black pepper, nitre, and various spices.   It was then bleached in the hottest noonday sun, or baked over a fire fed with bracken and vervain.   Certain impious incantations accompanied the process.   A candle having been moulded from the fat of a hanged murderer together with virgin wax and Lapland sesame the dead fingers were twisted so as to hold this horrible taper, which burned with a blue flame.   Whilst this was alight all those in the house became entranced in a hypnotic sleep, and rendered incapable of word or movement.   Housebreakers and assassins would purchase the Hand of Glory from witches at a high rate, and in the days when criminals were hanged in chains by the highway it was by no means impossible to procure the horrid ingredients for such a charm. There were, indeed, several recipes for it, and even to-day such practices are not unknown since it is authoritatively stated that in parts of Russia maidens have been killed in order to obtain the human fat for the manufacture of these necromantic candles. Madame de Baucé bought at a high price a Hand of Glory and a toad from the Parisian witch, La Voisin.

On the night of the 3rd January, 1831, a gang of Irish thieves broke into the house of Mr. Naper, of Loughcrew, Co. Meath. They had with them a dead man's hand with the fingers twisted round a candle. The servants, however, were alarmed and the robbers fled leaving the Hand of Glory behind them. It was suggested that it had not been exactly prepared, in which case the charm would certainly fail.

The witches, it must always be remembered, are adepts in the art of poisons, and no doubt the effect of their spells in many cases was not infrequently aided by a noxious draught. The devil, or Chief Officer of a coven, " delivers unto his *Proselite*, and so to the rest, the *Rules of his Art* instructing them in the manner of *hurting* and *helping*." Even John Webster whose *Displaying of Supposed Witchcraft* (1677), " utterly denied and disproved " " a *Corporeal League* made betwixt the Devil and the Witch ", is bound to acknowledge " secret poysoning, we grant to be too frequent and common, because those persons commonly accounted Witches are extreamly malicious and envious, and do secretly and by tradition learn strange poysons, philters and receipts whereby they do much hurt and mischief ".

Among the minor, but very active, agents concerned in the scandals that came to a climax with the notorious poisoning of Sir Thomas Overbury in 1613 was " sweet father " Forman, as the Countess of Somerset used to call him, a professed sorcerer, astrologer, and necromancer, who vended curious philtres to the more wanton court ladies, and having obtained a licence from Cambridge University to practise medicine almost openly trafficked in poison. Mrs. Anne Turner, his daughter, who was hanged at Tyburn for her share in the murder, was at her trial frankly saluted by Sir Edward Coke as a bawd, a whore, a sorcerer, a witch, a felon, and a murderer.

Of the same kidney was Dr. John Lambe, " an absolute witch, a sorcerer, a juggling person given over to lewd, wicked, and diabolical courses, an invocator and adorer of impious and wicked spirits." Practising as a physician, he sold poisonous draughts of such graduated strength that a speedy or a slow death might be arranged according to his client's convenience. There can be little doubt that had it not been for the all-powerful protection of the Duke of Buckingham the Doctor would have been brought to Tyburn. He was so hated indeed that he dare not walk abroad in the streets of London, save in disguise. One afternoon in 1628 he ventured to visit the Fortune Theatre in Golden Lane to see a new play, but being recognized on his way home, a brutal mob attacked him and with hideous yells of " Kill the Duke's devil ! Kill the wizard ! Kill the poisoner ! " they beat him to death.

The Marquise de Brinvilliers and her paramour Sainte-Croix were continually consulting astrologers and warlocks with regard to the efficacy of their drugs and the right times to administer their arsenic and lunar caustic, for there is a propriety in these things. The gangs of witches directed by the Abbé Guibourg and Catherine La Voisin numbered many poisoners of the most approved and widest experience, physicians, chemists, apothecaries, who laid claim to being artists in their profession and were mighty proud of their feats.

In Rome the witch Hieronyma Spara dispensed a wonderful elixir, clear, tasteless, and limpid, which sent those who were obstructive—an aged parent, a cruel husband,—to their long last sleep. She was hanged on 5th July, 1659. Even more famous and more enterprising was her successor La Toffania, a Neapolitan witch, who seems to have distributed her drugs wellnigh all over Europe. By a horribly profane sleight she was wont to label her vials Manna of St. Nicolas of Bari ", so that they passed as the miraculous oil which exudes from the sacred tomb of St. Nicolas, and for reverence sake were unexamined. The *Aqua Toffania* appears to have been crystallized arsenic dissolved in large quantities of water with the addition (for some unexplained reason) of the herb cymbalaria. A few drops were generally poured into coffee, chocolate, or soup, and its effects, although deadly sure, were so slow as to be almost imperceptible.

When some victim is marked for death by the witch there is made of the doomed person an image or effigy of wax, clay, marl, lead, leather, wood, or almost any material, and this being pierced with black pins, nails, thorns, or even struck through with a knife or dagger is burned or slowly melted before a great fire. As the image is pricked so the victim suffers in that part of the body ; as it is crumbled or dissolved, so he languishes ; when it is melted away or pierced to the heart, he expires. Such are the theory and practice of this " sympathetic " or " homœopathic " magic, as it is sometimes known. The image thus fashioned for purposes of sorcery has many names : figurine, puppet, moppet, doll, baby (in the obsolete sense of " doll "), effigy, maumet (the same name as given to a familiar), simulacrum, or even picture, since a painted canvas, a portrait, may be effectually employed. If a lock of hair, a piece of clothing, the nail-parings, or some other substance intimately related to the victim can be secured and moulded in or attached to the poppet the charm acquires so much the more force and propulsion. Sometimes a heart, most frequently the heart of an animal, will be used instead of a figurine. Not very many years ago some new tenants who had taken a house in Somersetshire found hidden in the chimney a big black velvet heart with pins thrust through it. They heard that the house had belonged to a witch. Other substitutes are employed. In Somersetshire, again, a sorcerer will write his enemy's name on a piece of paper and fasten this with as many black pins as possible to an onion, which must be put up the chimney. As the onion shrivels and withers so will the victim languish. An onion treated thus was found in a cottage chimney about 1880. Not long ago in a churchyard at Bradford, Yorks, a lemon was discovered stuck full of pins. The Neapolitan witches pierce a lemon, an orange, a potato, with rusty nails or pins to cast sickness upon or to kill the person who has offended them. The Sicilian *strega* transfixes an egg, an orange, or a lemon to the same end.

Sometimes the malefic charm can be directed against the witch in return, as witness an instance that came to the notice of Lady Peirse, and which happened about ten years ago. In a certain south country village in England a local farmer whose cattle ailed most mysteriously and showed every sign of having been overlooked, whilst things in general went wrong with him in every direction, consulted the witch-doctor, and was told to repeat a certain rhyme last thing at night, to nail a sheep's heart to his front door, to lock and bolt the door, to fasten every window, to sit up alone and whatever might happen on no account so much as to lift the latch until morning. He did exactly as had been prescribed. The family all went to bed, and he commenced his lonely vigil by the kitchen fire. After about half an hour there came a loud knocking at the door, and a voice shouted : "Let me in ! Let me in for a moment." The farmer, although trembling and afraid, made no answer, and did not stir from his place. After a very short interval the knocking was repeated, and a deplorable voice in plaintive accents begged for the door to be opened, but the farmer, although it was all he could do not to rise and unlock the door, remained obdurate as he thought of his suffering beasts. Lastly there was heard a very feeble knocking and a dull moaning sound. The farmer, even more alarmed, stoutly kept his post until sunrise the next morning. When he opened the door a near neighbour lay stretched across his threshold, dead. The doctor pronounced it a case of sudden heart failure. Nobody could explain why the man should have come to the farmer's house, whilst the farmer alone of his family had heard the knocks. The cattle recovered in a most extraordinary way, and all other things too began to go smoothly and well.

Mrs. Carbonell knew a case which happened in Devonshire in 1925. D. had a valuable mare which died suddenly. The veterinary surgeon was frankly puzzled, and could only say that it must have been the heat. D., however, felt sure that the mare had been overlooked, and riding over to the near market town, he decided to consult the white witch. On entering the wise man's house, he was greeted with : " I know the business upon which you have come. Go home, cut out the mare's heart, and fill it as full as you can with pins, and the one who has forspoken you will die." The farmer on his return did as he had been bid, and within a very few weeks a certain neighbour, in the flower of his age, sickened and died, nor did the doctor give his illness any name save a decline.

The magic use of actual figurines, moulded from some plastic material in human form, reaches back to remotest antiquity to Egypt, to Assyria, Babylonia, and India. It has prevailed among all peoples, savage and civilized, and admits of almost infinite variants in preparation and performance.

From ancient Egypt the magic use of wax figures passed to Greece and thence to Rome. The Anglo-Saxon Penitential incorrectly ascribed to Ecgbert, Archbishop of York, punishes this kind of sorcery, and provides for heavier penalties if the victim dies. At the Colchester Summer Assizes of 1580 there were many indictments for witchcraft and conjuration of spirits. Amongst others Nicholas Johnson of Woodham Mortimer was charged with making the portrait in wax of Her Majesty Queen Elizabeth. Elizabeth Device, the Lancashire witch, made a clay picture of John Robinson and crumbled it away, and within a week the man died. In 1900 an Italian burned a wax figure of President McKinley, quilled with pins like a hedgehog, on the steps of the American Embassy in London. Image magic is common enough to-day here in England, and in all countries of the world.

In a sentence passed upon a knot of witches at Avignon in 1582, *A Summary of All the Crimes of Witches*, one article runs thus : " that the Father of Lies should have a care to delete and obliterate you from the Book of Life you did at his direction and command with your own hands write your names in the black book there prepared, the roll of the wicked condemned to eternal death ; and that he might bind you with stouter bonds to so great a perfidy and impiety, he branded each of you with his Mark as belonging to him."

The Devil's Mark to which allusion is here made, or the Witches' Mark, as it is sometimes called, was regarded as perhaps the chief point in the identification of a witch, it was the very sign and seal of Satan upon the actual flesh of his servant and any person who bore such a mark was considered to have been convicted and proven beyond all manner of doubt of being in league with and devoted to the service of the fiend. This mark was said to be entirely insensible to pain, and when pricked, however deeply, it did not bleed. So Mr. John Bell, minister at Gladsmuir, in his tract, *The Trial of Witchcraft; or Witchcraft Arraigned and Condemned,* published early in the eighteenth century, explains : "The witch mark is sometimes like a blew spot, or a little tate, or reid spots, like flea-biting ; sometimes also the flesh is sunk in, and hollow, and this is put in secret places, as among the hair of the head, or eye-brows, within the lips, under the arm-pits, and in the most secret parts of the body." Robert Kirk, minister at Aberfoill, in his *Secret Common-wealth* (1691) writes : "A spot that I have seen, as a small mole, horny, and brown-coloured ; throw which mark when a large pin was thrust (both in buttock, nose, and rooff of the mouth), till it bowed and became crooked, the witches both men and women, nather felt a pain nor did bleed, nor knew the precise time when this was doing to them, (their eyes only being covered)."

Thus in the case of the Guernsey witches who were convicted by the Royal Court in July, 1617, Isebell Le Moigne confessed one night that, when she was at the Sabbath, the Devil marked her on the thigh. "The mark thus made having been examined by women appointed for that purpose, they certified that they had thrust pins deep into it, and that Isebell felt no pain therefrom, nor did any blood follow when the pins were withdrawn."

Whilst the notorious French wizard, Louis Gaufridi, "Lucifer's lieutenant, and Prince of all the hosts of sorcerers from Constantinople to Paris," lay in prison at Marseilles two physicians and two surgeons were directed by the judges to search him for the devil's marks. In their report which is very technical and detailed they speak of having discovered three callous marks, which when probed gave no pain, and which from this and other signs they are bound to pronounce not to be natural.

Inasmuch then as the discovery of the devil-mark was regarded as one of the most convincing indications —if not indeed an infallible proof—that the accused was guilty, it is easy to see how the searching for, the recognition and the probing of, such marks actually grew to be a profession in which not a few ingenious persons came to be recognized as experts and practical authorities. In Scotland, especially, the " prickers ", as they were called, formed a regular gild. They received a good fee for every witch whom they discovered, and, as might be expected, they did not fail to reap a golden harvest. One of the most notorious was John Kincaid of Tranent, who was acknowledged a master in his craft, although he found a serious rival in John Bain, who also showed himself a whole-hearted enthusiast. About 1630 Mr. John Balfour, of Corhouse, was feared all over the country for his exploits, and proved so ardent a publicist that he eventually came under the notice of the Lords of the Privy Council, who finding that his knowledge " has only been conjectural " put an abrupt end to his activities. Yet some twenty years later one John Dick was energetically pursuing the pricker's profession. The regular trade of these " common prickers " came to be a serious nuisance, and confessedly opened the door to all sorts of roguery. There was a Mr. Paterson, " who had run over the kingdom for trial of witches. . . . This villain gained a great deal of money, having two servants ; at last he was discovered to be a woman disguised in man's clothes." In 1649 a Scotch pricker was called in at Newcastle-upon-Tyne, but the experiment hardly proved satisfactory. He charged twenty shillings for each subject, and eventually he turned out to be a mere cheat. In 1662 the Lords of His Majesty's Secret Council forbade any sort of pricking for witchcraft save it were done by special Order in Council, and within a very few months several prickers were sentenced to terms of imprisonment.

The fleeting upon the water, or as it is generally known, the " swimming " of a witch, the water-ordeal, was popularly considered to be so supremely efficacious a test that it was still in use, albeit wholly illegal, of course, among rustics as late as the nineteenth century. The witches tied with " their thumbes and great toes . . . acrosse " and steadied by ropes—(" a roape, tyed about their middles ")—were let down into the water, some running stream, or a pond. If she sank the suspect might be cleared ; if she swam her blackest guilt was evident. For water was a holy element, it had become instinct with life whilst the earth was yet barren and uninhabited ; and as the witch had rejected the sacramental water of Baptism, so the pure lymph would refuse to receive her into its bosom. The analogy is perfectly sound, and King James is quite correct when he writes : " It appeares that God hath apoynted (for a super-naturall signe of the monstrous impietie of the Witches) that the water shall refuse to, receive them in her bosome, that have shaken off them the sacred Water of Baptisme, and ,wilfullie refused the benefite thereof." William Perkins of Cambridge, in his *Discourse of the Damned Art of Witchcraft*, posthumously published in 1608, endeavours to argue against this conclusion, by laying down that " The element out of the use of the Sacrament is no Sacrament, but returnes again to his common use ", an opinion which much commends itself to a recent writer, who thus regards Perkins as having exploded the sacred character and symbolism of Holy Water. Perkins was no doubt a very grave and earnest author, but his theology (as here) is often extremely faulty, and it is because of this that the inference seems entirely to have escaped him. Holy Water is a sacramental, and possesses a particular efficacy of its own. It has, moreover, the virtue to drive away those evil spirits whose mysterious and baleful operations can do such harm to man. Baptismal water is especially sacrosanct, for it has been mixed with the holy chrism in solemn rite. It is not necessary to labour these points in detail, sufficient to remark how Perkins and his school have mistaken and are in error in this respect.

Actually the Ordeal by Swimming was the Judgement of God, and applied for many crimes. It goes back to very early days, about the sixth or seventh century, and it is obviously related to the belief that water (in particular running water "—A running stream they darena cross "—) will dissolve all enchantment and magic glamour. During the seventeenth century swimming was much favoured in England as a test for a witch, although it was seldom countenanced by authority. In 1612 two Bedfordshire witches were swum in a mill-dam by Master Enger, a " gentleman of worship ", whom they had harmed, and they " floated like a plank ". In the same year three Northamptonshire witches were swum, and could not sink. Examples might be multiplied. In some very few instances swimming was directed or at the least permitted by the local magistracy, but Bernard in his *Guide to Grand-Jury Men* insists upon the illegality of this test, and Hopkins who certainly favoured the process was soon forced to discontinue it.

There was living in 1931 at the Essex village of Good Easter, a man who in his youth had been in trouble with the local magistrates for attempting with his friends the trial by swimming of an old hag, who was generally believed to be a witch. She was, however, rescued from their hands before they had thrown her in the pool, and the charge brought against them resolved itself into that of attempting to do grievous bodily harm.

The *Morning Post* of 28th January, 1780, has an account of two old women of Beck's Hill (Bexhill), Sussex, suspected to be witches. Many of the leading inhabitants approached the parson, the lawyer, and the mayor, requesting that these beldames should be put to the test, " to try by swearing, swimming, or weighing them if the opinion of the people was well or ill founded." As it might have fared badly with the two women if this deputation had just been scouted, " the Clerk was dispatched for the Church Bible, which the two were weighed against, and which they out-weighed, *a sure proof they were not witches.*" This is an old experiment and one that was employed from time to time in country places, but it has never been officially recognized and can hardly be regarded as more than a tradition.

It has always been held that if the victim who is overlooked can draw blood from the witch the spell will be broken. Again and again we find in the records that in order to obtain relief the witch has been scratched or blooded. This occurs as early as 1279, when John de Warham was fined 12*d*. by the Leet Court at Lynn, Norfolk, for " blood draught on Fair Alice ", whom he had (it seems) wrongly suspected. Passing down more than six centuries we may note an experience related by Mr. Walter Britten, as happening to a friend of his who was making a stay at Sidmouth in the days when the modern bicycle was still something of a novelty. The visitor, an enthusiastic devotee of the wheel, had a new machine sent down from London, and locally became known as " the flying devil ". One evening, being waylaid in a lane near Sudbury by a number of rustics, he dismounted with no small misgiving. To his surprise the leader of the party ran a sharp pin into one of his legs chanting, " Prickee wi' a pin, and draw his blood, an' ee can't hurt ee ! " After which ceremony the whole company at once appeared quite satisfied and friendly. This, of course, was nothing else than the scratching of the witch, so continually spoken of in the old trials, and recognized by the demonologists as a powerful counter-charm to malefic spells.

Writing from Plympton, on the 1st March, 1821, Lady Callcott (then Mrs. Graham) speaks of a rich baker in Plymouth, who some five years before had to pay five pounds compensation to a reputed witch. One of the baker's children being very sickly it was concluded the poor little creature had been over-looked, " and nothing but blood from the witch who had overlooked it could cure it. Accordingly, the lady of the Oven watched her opportunity ; and when the witch next came for a loaf, she and her maid flew on the old crone scratching her severely with long corking pins. The Mayor fined the baker, but it was considered extremely hard that a woman might not scratch a witch who had overlooked her child."

In August, 1927, an English lady who was walking in a wood near Travnik, in Bosnia, apparently aroused the suspicions of some peasant women, who crying out that she was a sorceress who would bewitch their children, attacked her, beating her and scratching her until the blood flowed. She escaped with difficulty, and found protection in the neighbouring village.

In 1928 a West Country smallholder was convicted of assaulting an old woman, whom he had scratched violently with a pin. The defence was that she had ill-wished him and his pig, so he had drawn blood on her to render her spells powerless to harm him for the future.

The black books or rolls of the witches carrying the names of the members of the coven were kept with great secrecy by the chief officer of the local society, or even by the Grand Master of a wider district. They would obviously have been guarded as something as precious as life itself, seeing that they contained the damning evidence of a full list of the witches of a province or county, and in addition thereto seems to have been added a number of magic formulæ, spells, charms, and probably, from time to time, a record of the doings of the various witches. The signing of such a book is continually referred to in the New England trials. So when Deliverance Hobbs had made a clean breast of her sorceries, " She now testifi'd that this *Bishop* [Bridget Bishop condemned and executed as a long-continued witch] tempted her to sign the *Book* again, and to deny what she had confess'd." The enemies of the notorious Matthew Hopkins made great capital out of the story that by some sleight of sorcery he had got hold of one of these Devil's memorandum-books, whence he copied a list of witches, and this enabled him to be so infallible in his scent.

An old Yarmouth witch in 1645 described how one night she heard a knock at her door, and peeping from her window she saw in the moonlight a tall, black man, whom she admitted. After some parley he promised to help her under certain conditions, and taking a little penknife he scratched her hand so that the blood flowed, with which she wrote her name in his book, and he guided her fingers.

Anne Bodenham, sometime servant to the notorious warlock, Dr. John Lambe, was executed at Salisbury when 80 years old. She had many books of spells, and especially a red one " written half over with blood, being the names of witches that had listed themselves under the Devil's command ". This, however, could not be recovered as it had been sent for safe keeping to a wizard named Withers, who lived near Romsey, Hants, and who absconded.

There is a somewhat vague story, no dates being given, that a Devil's book was carried off by Mr. Williamson of Cardrona (Peebles), who filched it from the witches whilst they were dancing on Minchmoor. But the whole coven at once gave chase, and he was glad to abandon it and escape alive.

Sometimes the catalogue of witches was inscribed on a separate parchment, and the book only used to write down charms and spells. Such a volume was the Red Book of Appin known to have actually been in existence a hundred years ago. Tradition said that it was stolen from the Devil by a trick. It was in manuscript, and contained a large number of magic runes and incantations for the cure of cattle diseases, the increase of flocks, the fertility of fields. This document, which must be of immense importance and interest, when last heard of was (I believe) in the possession of the now extinct Stewarts of Invernahayle. This strange volume, so the story ran, conferred dark powers on the owner, who knew what inquiry would be made even before the question was poised ; and the tome was so confected with occult arts that he who read it must wear a circlet of iron around his brow as he turned those mystic pages.

It is a strange and not very edifying chance which has popularly attached the names of great Popes and Saints to books of spells and grimoires, and some authors such as Father Delrio, Pierre Le Loyer, and Gabriel Naudé, the learned librarian of Cardinal Richelieu and Cardinal Mazarin, have been at the pains to show how absurd and indeed scandalous such attributions are. There is no need to labour the point, for of course nobody imagines that Honorius III composed an infernal grimoire or that St. Albert the Great is the author of a manual giving directions how to prepare cabbalistic talismans and a ring conferring invisibility, any more than we believe (as was once seriously asserted) that Abel wrote a treatise on judicial astrology, which he enclosed in a rock where after the Deluge it was discovered and published by the patriarch Noah.

The history with the ancillary bibliography of grimoires and books of spells is immense and immensely complicated, nor even if it were desirable to treat so dangerous a subject would it be possible to discuss it save at very considerable length. In order to illustrate the witches' library I will do no more then than mention a very few works which are so notorious that no purpose could be served by ignoring them, whilst no harm can come from so slight and guarded a notice.

Among the oldest and most terrible of the grimoires is the *Sepher Toldos Jeschu*, a Syro-chaldaic work, whose pages are happily sealed save to the very few. A book of conjurations, *Ars Notaria*, was once printed under the name of St. Jerome. Owing to a confusion between St. Cyprian, Bishop of Carthage, and St. Cyprian of Antioch the coverted sorcerer, who was martyred fifty years later, a number of mediæval spells have been ascribed to the former. Thus in Denmark and Scandinavia among the witches to-day almost any grimoire is dubbed the *Book of Cyprianus*. St. Ubald, Bishop of Gubbio in the twelfth century, who was especially famous for his powers in casting out evil spirits, is named on the title-page of a theurgical treatise which cannot be earlier than four centuries after his death. In France in the days of the Valois they were selling all sorts of alchemical and magical opuscules as being from the pen of St. Thomas Aquinas, upon whose venerable preceptor, St. Albert the Great, have been fathered perhaps the most famous, or most infamous, of all printed grimoires, *Les admirables Secrets du Grand Albert*, and the collection known by the running title *Le Petit Albert*, which two are the most extensively employed, and in some ways the most mischievous, grimoires to-day. It must be borne in mind that the numerous editions and reprints, both of

Le Grand Albert and *Le Petit Albert*, vary very widely, so much so, in fact, that a modern copy may be an entirely different book from an eighteenth century duodecimo carrying either name, whilst a third collection in its turn will present something quite new. Thus the 1668 sextodecimo, printed at Lyons, has charts of necromantic figures, talismans and pentacles, which are to be found in no other issue. (There is a facsimile, made about thirty years ago.) Add to this that for the most part the two books were clandestinely given to the Press, often without printer's name, the place incorrectly stated, a fudge imprint in fine, and it will be seen how perplexed the whole story is. Some editions are comparatively harmless ; silly maybe, and even superstitious ; others have deadly and dangerous pages.

The *Grand Albert* (as we know it) was possibly first printed about the middle of the sixteenth century, but the eighteenth century editions (of the last rarity) are considered the most complete. The *Petit Albert* was joined with the *Grand Albert* in one volume and edited (1885) by a well-known French occultist, Marius Decrespe. This is said to be the issue most prized by adepts to-day. Decrespe emphatically discredits the opinions of those who suggest that the dual work originated in any sense with St. Albert the Great, or was compiled by a student of the fifteenth century from an unedited manuscript of the learned Dominican doctor. It is almost certain that the two works as we now have them were an amalgamation of the discoveries of several individuals, and that they appeared at Lyons not earlier than the sixteenth century. Stanislas de Guaita drew attention to the fact that in spite of the many reprints both the *Grand* and the *Petit Albert* are very uncommon books.

In the Channel Islands the *Grand Albert* is known as the " Witches' Bible ", and local dialect terms it *Le Grand Mêlé*. The *Petit Albert* is *Le Petit Mêlé*, the word *Mêlé* signifying nothing more than " book ". Together they are often referred to as *Albins*, and only the sorcerer dare keep such " bad books ". There have been many cases of the two volumes appearing in various libraries which were being catalogued after the owner's decease, and such an accident is always regarded as throwing a strange light upon the character and pursuits of the defunct. The old wives say that once a man has owned the *Grand Albert* he cannot rid himself of it, do what he will. The book invariably returns to its place on the shelf, even if it be cast into a fire, thrown away at sea, torn to pieces and scattered to the winds. The only thing to do is to inter it in a grave, and read the burial service over the place, or else to get a priest to drench the accursed thing with holy water and burn it with litany and prayer.

In Jamaica when Monteul Edmond was arrested for the murder of Rupert Mapp, a boy of 12 years old, for purposes of obeah it was found that the body had been strangely mutilated and a search of the prisoner's person discovered a number of magical formulæ " copied from a work entitled *Petit Albert* the pretended author of which is claimed to be a monkish occultist of the Middle Ages ".

The Daily Gleaner, Kingston, Jamaica, on 30th January, 1934, among the police news reported that at the Sandy Bay Court, Leonard Weakley, of Cold Spring, was sentenced to six months' imprisonment for practising the black art. In his house were found the following books : *The Sixth and Seventh Books of Moses ; Albertus Magnus, or the White and Black Arts for Men and Beasts ; The Great Book of Black Magic ; The Book of Magical Art ; Hindoo Magic and Indian Occultism.*

It was stated during the John H. Blymyer trial (1928) at York, York County, Pennsylvania, that the principal " witchcraft guises " employed by the sorcerers are : The Sixth and Seventh Books of the Magical Spirit ; The Art of Moses, popularly known as The Black Art Bible ; Heaven's Letter (Himmels-brief) ; and The Long-lost Friend, which contains the necromantic rituals and the creed of pow-wowism. *The Art of Moses* is a translation, or adaptation of the *Magia divino-mosaica . . . cum nigromantia* of the sixteenth century. All these grimoires are very rare and the possession of one or two confers a certain distinction upon the witch.

The *Enchiridion* of Pope Leo III, fabled to have been presented by that great Pontiff to the Emperor Charlemagne in the year 800 is, of course, purely apocryphal. There is an early edition of 1584, and the Mainz edition of 1633 has woodcuts in black and red, but the 16mo edition " *chez le Père Angelo de Rimini* " (Paris, 1847), presents ten coloured plates of pentacles, magic circles, seals engraved with words of power, and other curious matter, such as counter-spells to divert malefic enchantments. Upon the title-page is a triangle in a double circle with Hebrew characters, *Tsabaoth Alchim*, etc., inscribed in the midst.

The grimoires need not for their contents detain us. *The Grimoire of Pope Honorius* is said to be found in manuscript at least as early as the thirteenth century.

It was printed at Rome in 1629, and has several times been reissued. The edition of 1670 has many magical and cabbalistic figures, for this volume of witchcraft is chiefly concerned with the evocation of demons.

The *Grand Grimoire* and the *Grimorium Verum* are both to a large extent derived from the famous *Clavicula Salomonis, The Key of Solomon the King*, sometimes known as the *Book of the Pentacles*. The legend of a manual of black magic written by Solomon and confided to his son Rehoboam (Roboam) is very ancient. Mr. S. L. M. Mathers, who translated *The Key of Solomon the King* in 1889, says : " I see no reason to doubt the tradition which assigns the authorship of the *Key* to King Solomon." This view, however, cannot be accepted without very considerable qualification, for it is abundantly evident that the *Key*, in any form as we now have it, must have been altered and amplified (and possibly in some particulars retrenched) by those through whose hands it passed. It is safer to allow that the *Key* is substantially based upon immemorial tradition, much of which may go back to the time of Solomon, but that it has suffered various modifications in the course of the centuries without indeed affecting its essential character and design.

It is true that *The Key of Solomon the King* has been claimed to be a work of white magic, but since (to mention no further examples) it teaches how to describe a pentacle causing ruin, utter destruction, and death, whilst another pentacle is productive of earthquakes and great storms, this pretence—for it is plainly nothing more—cannot be maintained. For obvious reasons the malefic nature of a grimoire would often have been dissembled. Moreover the manuscript grimoires are in general far more detailed and far more terrible than the printed volumes, bad enough in all conscience though the latter may be. The sorcerer dare not confide the darker secrets of his evil craft, the more potent and perilous spells to what is after all—however limited the number of copies—a certain method of publication. The compositors might be heavily bribed, nay, they might even themselves be members of the Satanic fraternity, but there would always remain the chance that by some accident a copy of a printed book might fall into hostile hands and the mine be sprung. In past centuries this must have been an even more imminent risk than to-day. Very often in the printed manuals a slight difference has been deliberately made in an exorcism, some little variant occurs in a ceremonial, lest the horrid science should be too plainly betrayed to the uninitiated and the intruder. The adept who is using the book will appreciate this policy of reticence and heed the signs of caution ; from his own training and the oral lessons he has received he can correct such divergences, and that is the reason why these mystic manuals are so often scored with manuscript emendations and so copiously annotated in their broad margins.

It has been said that wellnigh every witch of long continuance or standing possessed *The Key of Solomon the King*, and generally in a manuscript written out by himself. The advantage of this is obvious, for he could add any number of incantations and charms which he had been taught by word of mouth. In the time of Louis XIV, Duprat, a Parisian schoolmaster who was not unconnected with the Guibourg-La Vôisin gang, enjoyed a very pretty living by transcribing and wrïting out grimoires. In the eighteenth century the Marquis de Paulmy, a deep student of occultism, made a large collection of manuscript grimoires, which are now preserved in the Bibliothèque de l'Arsenal at Paris. One of the most complete of these is entitled *The Great Secret, or the Key of Solomon the King and the Ancient Grimoire*, being, as indeed is indicated by the véry name, a work combining the *Clavicula* with the *Grimoire of Pope Honorius*. Although actually it does not present a large number of figures and charts of circles it does describe many ceremonies and charms not to be found elsewhere. Dating from the early part of the eighteenth century, it is written in a very legible and elegant hand, and was evidently penned with the greatest care throughout. A note initialed by the Marquis de Paulmy says that no Hebrew manuscript of *The Key of Solomon* has ever been traced. Moreover Greek manuscripts are of the last rarity. Indeed only one was certainly known, and that reposed in the library of Charles Albert of Bavaria. Latin versions were not altogether infrequent. The manuscript actually is in French. It commences with a Preface, which does not occur in any other copy, wherein Solomon confides his *Key* to his son Rehoboam, in accordance with the old tradition. The book is supposed to have been found in Solomon's tomb, and the ivory coffer in which it was contained hence came into the possession of a Babylonian mage, who gave it to the world's philosophers. Leaving all legends aside, there is at least one salutary cautel added to the foreword. The author or transcriber, whoever he may be, is very insistent in his word of warning : " I conjure and I beseech any man into whose hands this manuscript may fall, I implore him by all that is holy, by his desire for good success in all his business and doings, that he shall never turn this book to any common use, that he shall neither publish it abroad, nor generally disclose the secrets hereof, nor translate it into the vulgar tongue, but to show it only to and to suffer it only to be seen by men who have understanding and who are well-tried and knowing in these rare secrets."

The earlier chapters of the *Key* describe in detail those preliminary ceremonies and rituals which are necessary for the successful invocation of spirits, a thing not to be embarked upon lightly or without due preparation and care. The *Key* will have it that the spirits who shall appear in these circumstances are benign influences, and but rarely evil, and these latter should be approached most circumspectly. The Christian Faith admits no such distinctions. However kindly and plausible they may seem to be we know that all such conjured spirits are demons of the pit.

As Mr. A. E. Waite has justly observed : " Much that passed current in the west as White (i.e. permissible) Magic was only a disguised goeticism, and many of the resplendent angels invoked with divine rites reveal their cloven hoofs. It is not too much to say that a large majority of past psychological experiments were conducted to establish communication with demons, and that for unlawful purposes. The popular conceptions concerning the diabolical spheres, which have all been accredited by magic, may have been gross exaggerations of fact concerning rudimentary and perverse intelligences, but the wilful viciousness of the communicants is substantially untouched thereby."

Full details of the vestments which must be donned by the charmer are supplied, and he should even wear a particular kind of buskin or shoe ; he must furnish himself with such accessories as a keen knife or whinger ; a long needle or cobbler's awl ; a ring ; a wand ; fire ; holy water ; lights ; certain sweet perfumes ; virgin parchment and a quill never yet used ; ink, and a phial of blood wherewith to write ; which things are absolutely indispensable for the operation since to summon a familiar spirit is no light and simple business as idle and silly meddling folk might suppose.

The manuscript gives an elaborate plan of the magic circle which is to be found in every manual of sorcery and in which unless he will risk the most imminent peril, even death itself, the experimenter must take his stand. This detail is emphasized in all grimoires, and the manuscript admonishes : " Note well that the mage who invokes the spirits must take his place within the circle, nor let him stir thence." The circle which was to measure nine feet in diameter, must be traced with the sharp point of the consecrated knife, and (the rubrics direct) : " having drawn this circle describe four Pentacles whereabouts are to be written the Holy Names of God, and without this circle describe yet another circle which shall be bounded by a square. Grave all these with thy knife's point."

Actually both Greek and Hebrew characters are traced about the circle and pentacles. Alpha, Omega, can be clearly distinguished ; as well as the mystic word *Agla*, which was used by the rabbis as signifying *Aieth Gadol Leolam Adonai*, Adonai (God Almighty) endureth throughout all ages. There are also written several of the seventy and two Names of God.

However, in different editions and manuscripts of *The Key of Solomon* the circle is varied, and in one ceremony the hierophant is required to have an attendance of four acolytes. Five circles are then traced, the first being greater than the rest, in which the master takes his position. The disciples stand appropriately in the smaller circles. All must be clothed in ephods of stainless white linen, and the master whilst he draws the circles recites the following psalms : II, (Why do the heathen rage,) ; LIV, (Save, me, O God, by Thy Name) ; CXII, (Praise ye the Lord) ; LXVII, (God be merciful unto us) ; XLVII, (O clap your hands, all ye people) ; and LXVIII, (Let God arise . . .). A number of other circles and pentacles having been described, the Four Great Names of God must be written around and about, to wit in the small circles, Adonai, El, Agla, and Jah, and in the larger circle Eloha, Ehie, Elijon, and the mystic Tetragrammaton, that is the Divine Name, the Name of Yahweh, which no man may pronounce (saith Rabbi Abba Shaul) and live, the separated, the hidden and mysterious Name, inscribed here in such manner as may reverently and fearfully be spoken.

Another manuscript of the *Key of Solomon*, now in the Bibliothèque de l'Arsenal, *The True and Only Key of King Solomon*, said to be translated from the Hebrew in the eighteenth century, instructs the experimenter to draw his circle in quite a different fashion. Similar names, however, are to be written, the central monogram being KIS, which stands for *Kadosh Ieve Sabaoth*, Holy Lord of Hosts.

Although as yet unpublished, there is preserved in a private English collection a manuscript translation of the *Clavicula Salomonis* by Frederick Hockley, an astrologer and occultist who died about the middle of the last century. It is entitled " Solomon's Key, by Frederick Hockley, 1828 ". Pasted inside the cover is a paper carrying the following : " Magia de Profundis, seu Clavicula Salomonis Regis, the Key of Solomon the King, or a Complete System of Profound Magical Science with a great number of coloured drawings of the Characters of the Spirits Seals, Pentacles, etc., elegant in brown calf gilt leaves." At the beginning we have : " Key of Solomon in Four books. These books were found in the Chaldee and Hebrew tongue by a Jewish Rabbi at Jerusalem & by him translated into Greek & from thence into Latin and transcribed by Fred^k Hockley the first day of Marche 1828."

The Bibliothèque de l'Arsenal has manuscripts of a yet more profoundly dangerous kind than even the more extreme examples of the group which conveniently goes under the name of *The Key of Solomon*. Thus *The True and Only Key*, to which reference has already been made, provides a curious rose-form pentacle expressly to invoke the demons of the pit. The Great Conjuration contained in another manuscript is full of horrible impiety, and may justly be styled the Dark Secret of Secrets. *The Evocation of the Seven Planetary Spirits* prescribes that certain substances, chiefly storax and benjamin are to be burned in a new censer, and I remember J. K. Huysmans saying how a devil-worshipper had once told him that the fume of these two was " agreeable to Satan our master ".

The Conjuration of Uriel and the Seraphim has the most elaborate and reticulated plans and pentacles, and among other spirits honour is paid to Alithael, Cassiel,

Sachiel, and Samael. The angel St. Uriel "Regent of the Sun"

The sharpest sighted Spirit of all in Heav'n, as Milton terms him, is mentioned in the Fourth Book of Esdras, and other ancient writings, but the names Cassiel and others too plain betray the cloven hoof.

In Francis Barrett's *The Magus ; or, Celestial Intelligencer*, 1801, is given a specimen of the Book of Spirits, being the Conjuration of Saturday in ceremonial magic ; the Ruler, Cassiel. Here then we are in the realms of demonism undisguised.

Samael is Satan, the arch-fiend, as Collin de Plancy explicitly states, whilst Stanislas de Guaita says that Samael is opposed to and fought with the Archangel, Saint Michael.

Another manuscript, entitled *Zekerboni*, was written by Pietro Mora, who describes himself as an "occult philosopher". During the Great Plague which so fearfully ravaged Milan in 1630 there was dwelling in an obscure quarter Pietro Mora, a mysterious and formidable figure, who had long been popularly accused as a vendor of poisons and a witch. A surprise visit searched his house, but the *sbirri* could trace nothing extraordinary or incriminating until almost by chance there was forced a secret panel masquing the entrance to cellars of prodigious extent, and in these vaults were discovered not only the horrid paraphernalia of sorcery, magic robes and wands, lamps, swords, tripods, thuribles, braziers, curiously graven shew-stones and crystals, together with a whole library of grimoires and Ephesian runes, but also a vast number of sealed jars and carefully labelled phials containing liquids and chemical preparations, which upon being analysed by the physicians were pronounced to be virus and poisons of the most deadly kind. Mora confessed that he was the leader of a coven of sorcerers, who had leagued themselves to spread the scourge and destroy the entire city. This they did by smearing the handles of doors and gates with a certain lethal ointment. They poisoned the springs of water, the fountains in the squares, and even the benitiers in the church porches. They distributed under the guise of charity infected clothing and foul linen from the beds of those who had died of the disease among the hospitals and the crowded warrens of the poor so that the pestilence was fearfully increased. The whole knot were apprehended and being convicted upon most plain and detailed evidence, they paid the extreme penalty of the law. The very house of Mora, as a criminal of especial atrocity, was razed to the ground, and a column erected on the spot with an inscription to commemorate his guilt.

There can be little question that Pietro Mora of Milan was the author or transcriber of *Zekerboni*, although it does not necessarily follow that the manuscript which has been preserved is his original. It may be a copy, and indeed it seems to be in a later hand. A circumstance which makes the identification more probable is that *Zekerboni* introduces into many of the spells certain terms and expressions borrowed from alchemy, and we know that Mora long sought the elixir and the philosopher's stone.

Zekerboni has a drawing of the " Great Pentacle " where four circles enclose a mesh of cryptic designs, crossing and recrossing, and scattered with Hebrew and Greek letters punctuated by curious sigils and points. The ceremony commences thus : " After the Master is come with his disciples to the appointed place of evocation he shall strike fire, and he shall exorcize the new fire wherewith he shall light the magic candle. This must be set in the lanthorn which must be held by one of the disciples so that the Master may most conveniently read the conjurations. Another disciple shall hold him ready with paper, a pen and the ink ; a third disciple shall carry the consecrated sword with naked blade. The Master shall light the charcoal for the censing and the fumigations. When he hath taken his stand within the circle, holding a lighted taper in his left hand, he shall forthwith begin the conjuration—." The formula which, it is recommended, shall be very legibly inscribed upon a fair parchment without blot or erasure differs in the various manuals. Each have certain phrases in common. The Holy Name of God is called upon, and most spells require the demon to manifest himself " in a pleasing form, without any horror of shape or size, without any loud or thunderous noise or alarum, without seeking to harm him who summons thee, and without hurting any who are of his company ".

When the spirit appears the magician must impose his commands upon him, and then give him licence to depart. The dismissal of the spirit is a very essential detail in the ceremony, for unless the demon is sent away it is possible that he may linger and great mischief may ensue. One form of concluding the rite is : " Depart then, gracious and kindly spirit, return in peace unto thy dwelling-place and unto thine own habitation, but yet do thou hold thyself ready to attend and appear before me whensoever I call upon thee and summon thee in the name of the Great Alpha, the Lord. Amen. Amen. Amen." It will be noticed how cunningly fair-spoken and even pious phrases are employed to masque the impiety of this horrid business.

Occasionally a manuscript grimoire will appear in the sale rooms. In April, 1934, part of the collection of M. Lionel Hauser was put up to auction at Sotheby's. There were many items of exceptional interest. A Treatise of Ceremonial Magic, written on vellum in cypher in French, *circa* 1750, which had belonged to and been used by the Comte de St. Germain, fetched £42 10*s.*, whilst a nineteenth century manuscript collection of spells, conjurations, and exorcisms, realized £10.

In their great Catalogue of Medicine, Alchemy, Astrology, published in 1929 (No. 520), Messrs. Maggs, the well-known London booksellers, included "A Manuscript Book of Black Magic written in Shakespeare's England", which was further very accurately described as "An Elizabethan Devil-worshipper's Prayer-Book". The date assigned is *circa* 1600, but there seems to be no clue to the identity of the compiler of the manuscript, which is written on twenty-three leaves of vellum and illustrated with thirteen crudely drawn but very powerful drawings, some of which are coloured, of the demon king Vercan, who is pictured under various forms. There are also six other drawings of demons. All of these have their several invocations on the opposite page, inscribed in Latin. The spirits to be summoned or exorcised are : Vercan, Maymon, Suth, Samax, Sarabotres, Mediac or Modiac, and Arcan. King Vercan, who is regarded as the most powerful of the demons, is called upon in thirteen prayers. He is shown as a kind of semi-human monster with a fearfully grotesque human face, horned, having a hairy body, and the feet of a bird of prey. Twice he appears with three heads, and once he is riding a bear. It should be remarked that the invocator is always surrounded by a magic circle, for indeed as a later enchanter has it, " the circles are certain fortresses," and no manifestation has power to break through these boundaries, although often the spirits will endeavour to tempt or force the operator out of the circle.

The other demons of the grimoire are : King Maymon, who appears as a black familiar with two bird-heads, and two human heads at his knees. He rides upon a dragon, and is linked with the planet Saturn. King Suth is brown. Wearing a diadem and flourishing a great sword, he bestrides a stag, and is companioned with Jupiter. King Samax is antlered, and rides a kind of panther. He is linked with Mars. King Sarabotres is green. He rides a roe, and wields a sceptre. His planet is Venus. King Mediac (or Modiac) has huge horns. Clad in red mail, he rides a bear, and is linked with Mercury. King Arcan is a black demon with flaming eyes and grinning fangs. He is hunting with bow and arrows on the back of a roebuck. His planet is the Moon.

It very infrequently happens that there is any mention of a grimoire in a contemporary trial. John Walsh, of Netherbury, Dorset, possessed a book left him by his late master, which had great circles in it, wherein he would set two wax candles and a cross of virgin wax, to raise the familiar spirit of whom he would then ask for anything stolen. When his book

THE DEMON KING MAYMON

was taken from him he could no longer summon a familiar. Rebecca West, an Essex witch, met with some other witches by appointment at the house of Elizabeth Clarke, where they all spent some time praying to their familiars, and afterwards some read in a book belonging to Elizabeth, whereupon the said familiars did appear.

A Magic book, which formerly belonged to Dr. John Caius, the famous Cambridge scholar, is preserved in the British Museum.

Dr. John Harries (1785–1839), a celebrated Welsh physician and seer who dwelt at Cŵrt-y-Cadno, a hamlet in remotest Carmarthenshire, but who was resorted to by the whole countryside, possessed a great Book of Magic which none but the wizard himself might read with impunity. The Book, indeed, was always kept locked, because (as the thaumaturge was wont to say) if any ignorant person who knew not the mystic mantra were to turn its pages he might let loose unreined influences ready to destroy him. Many wonderful stories are told of Harries, and there seems no reason to doubt that he was an occultist of extraordinary power. He openly avowed that his knowledge of future and distant things was imparted to him by familiar spirits, and his son Henry, who succeeded him, inherited his father's mysterious gifts. Henry died in 1849. He specialized in astrology, having in his youth been apprenticed to the well-known astrologer Raphael of London. Some said that the notorious Book was actually not a book at all, but a number of papers kept in an iron-bound box, which the doctor regarded as of the utmost value. So perhaps it was a manuscript grimoire. One story went that many years after the death of the Welsh wizard and his sons, the book and a magic crystal were bought from his descendants by a London barrister on a walking tour, who having heard of the fame of Harries visited the village. The family parted with the Book and the crystal at a price, but nobody in the house dare touch them or would lend a hand in their removal.

There is to-day (1933) a wise man dwelling near Llangwrig, Montgomeryshire, who is famous throughout all Wales. From near and far people come for his help. He breaks the spells of those bad folk " who have power ", that is to say witches. In a rosewood box he keeps two books, an almanac and another, whereby he can divine and cast a horoscope or map out the planets for his clients.

Upon the black roll of magicians stands no more notorious name than that of Cornelius Agrippa, and there seems little doubt that this terrible accusation is in great part due to his youthful treatise, the *Three Books of Occult Philosophy*. Even Professor Henry Morley when writing his *Life of Henry Cornelius Agrippa von Nettesheim, Doctor and Knight*, added on the title-page " Commonly known as a Magician ". Composed in 1510, not even the First Book was printed until one and twenty years later, and when after about another twelvemonth it was announced that the whole work was in the press at Cologne, Conrad Cöllin, a learned Dominican of Ulm, very justly caused the book to be thoroughly examined by the theologians before it was given to the public. So far from being an obscurantist Cöllin was the most liberal of scholars, and there was no persecution or oppression. Satisfied that it contained no heresies, he gave his formal consent to the issue of the work. " Suffer it to be printed, if they wish," he says in an extant letter. Since the *Occult Philosophy* has been analysed in some detail by Morley it will suffice to say here that the work is a commixture of Neoplatonism and the Cabbala. The last book has a long chapter on demons, and there is a good deal of angelology with some curious matters that skate on very thin ice. Indeed these *Three Books of Occult Philosophy*, or rather of Magic, for Agrippa himself confessed that his title was little more than a subterfuge, " alone constitute him a conjurer "—the phrase is Morley's.

It is all the more unfortunate that after Agrippa's death there should have appeared an abominably superstitious and profane Fourth Book of the *Occult Philosophy*, whilst in the same volume was printed a fitting companion, the *Elements of Magic* by Peter of Abano, that " vilest of vile books ", to which reference has already been made. It is significant that those responsible for seeing these grimoires through the press did not dare to give the place or the printer's name on the title-page.

In spite of his virtuous and emphatic protestations it is impossible to regard Francis Barrett's *The Magus; or, Celestial Intelligencer* as anything other than a particularly elaborate and complete grimoire. Published in 1801 by a well-known firm, James Lackington, Allen and Co., at the " Temple of the Muses ", Finsbury Square, *The Magus*, a fine quarto, is illustrated with a number of detailed designs of magic circles and pentacles, and also with several striking coloured plates, the *Powers of Evil*, being heads of

Demons, Astaroth, Abaddon, Mammon, and *Vessels of Wrath*, Theutus, Asmodeus, and the Incubus. Barrett not only sketched the heads himself with great care, but he supplies a very ample account of the familiar shapes and forms in which the spirits manifest themselves, " likewise the whole perfection of magical ceremonies is here described syllable by syllable." " The Construction and Composition of all Sorts of Magic Seals, Images, Rings, Glasses, etc.," may be found exhibited in these pages. The author, who lived at 99 Norton Street, Marylebone, in an advertisement invites those desiring to delve further into these curious matters to join his school " which will consist of no greater number than Twelve Students ", an extremely significant circumstance. The manuscript of *The Magus*, which is preserved in a private collection, enlarges upon certain particulars not altogether desirable to print, and Barrett stands forth as a magician self-confessed.

The rough woodcuts which embellish such manuals of sorcery as *Le Dragon rouge*, *La Poule Noire*, and *Le Dragon Noir* have little importance. None the less both *Le Dragon rouge* and *La Poule Noire*, which first appeared in print about 1800, have been reissued again and again, and are yet extensively consulted and employed. They are grimoires of the worst type, and even furnish necromantic evocations.

During the Helsingfors Satanist scandals of 1931, when it was discovered that a number of graves had been desecrated and bodies mutilated, upon the arrest of the cemetery caretaker, Sarrenheimo, and the search of his house it was found that he possessed a library of books dealing with the practice of the black art, and one manual in particular (said to have been printed in England) advised the use of human remains in confecting certain foul charms.

There are in use by witches to-day volumes simply entitled *Magick*, which give the full ritual for the celebration of Black Masses, with diabolic litanies, and other infernal ceremonies including the blood sacrifices on the altar. A Gnostic Mass is described, and one rubric runs, " the blood sacrifice is the critical point of the World Ceremony of the Proclamation of Horus, the Crowned and Conquering Child, as Lord of the Aeon." The Gnostics in the second century had books " full of wickedness ", and stripped of its pseudo-mystical verbiage the plain meaning of this rubric is that divine honour must be paid to the devil, Satan-Pantheus, with whom (Stanislas de Guaita says) St. Michael fought victoriously for he it is whom they salute as the Child, the Cosmic serpent who tempted Eve and by whom came death and sin.

One of these grimoires has this warning : " The student, if he attains any success in the following practices, will find himself confronted by things too glorious or too dreadful to be described. It is essential that he remain the master of all that he beholds, hears, or conceives ; otherwise he will be the slave of illusion and the prey of madness."

Éliphas Lévi, whose two great works *Dogme de la Haute Magie* (1855) and *Rituel de la Haute Magie* (1856) were together translated in 1923 as *Transcendental Magic* by Mr. Arthur Edward Waite, lays down five *Conditions of Success in Infernal Evocations* : (1) Invincible obstinacy ; (2) a conscience at once hardened to crime and not subject to remorse and fear ; (3) ignorance, affected or natural ; (4) blind faith in all that is incredible ; (5) a completely false idea of God. If these are understood in the right way they may be regarded as sufficiently summing up the essential characteristics of black magic and all goetic experiments. By *a completely false idea of God* I understand the express renunciation of God, the paying of divine honour to Satan with whom a contract (tacit or explicit) is made and whose will is done by the witch.

It must ever be borne in mind that the practice and profession of black magic are not lightly to be undertaken ; the dark mysteries are no jest, no pastime of an idle hour as many fools and empty inquirers seem to suppose. There are no dilettanti in witchcraft.

There are the mountebanks, of course, who give fatuous talks on black magic in Mayfair drawing-rooms ; there are the bright young things who try to raise the devil in a circle and do not succeed ; there is the fifth-rate novelist who peppers his trashy thrillers with occult episodes borrowed *en bloc* from some standard work. There is and there always will be plenty of humbug, and very paying humbug too, along these lines.

Before the secrets of the grimoire can be unfolded the price must be given, the terrible barter must be exchanged.

Another volume, of which mention is made—one that is often confused with, but should be distinguished from, the grimoire—is what we may term the Devil's Missal. Probably this had its origin far back in the mist of the centuries among the earliest heretics who passed down their evil traditions to their followers, the Albigenses and the Waldenses or Vaudois.

Enough has been said to show that mischief and malice were part and parcel of the witch's profession, and indeed there was required from them at their reception into this dark society a vow that they would devote themselves wholly to evil. They were moreover pledged to carry on an active Satanist propaganda, to win recruits and to use every endeavour to draw other men and women to their detestable practices and the worship of the fiend. Thus in the case of Janet Breadheid, of Auldearne, we find that her husband " enticed her into that craft ". A girl named Bellot, of Madame Bourignon's academy, confessed that her mother had taken her to the Sabbat when she was quite a child. Another girl alleged that all worshippers of the Devil " are constrained to offer him their children ". At Salem, George Burroughs, a minister, was accused by a large number of women as " the person who had Seduc'd and Compell'd them into the snares of Witchcraft ". Elizabeth Francis, of Chelmsford, a witch tried in 1566, was only about twelve years old when her grandmother taught her the art of sorcery. The Pendle beldame, Mother Demdike, " brought up her owne Children, instructed her Graund-children, and tooke great care and paines to bring them to be Witches." It is hardly to be believed that a modern writer of a certain school—fortunately at once negligible and freakish—should characterize this dedication of young children to hell and the lord of hell as " a ceremony, at once simple and touching ".

To-day the Satanists are thoroughly imbued with the missionary spirit, and are ever eager to enlar ge their ranks to the destruction of immortal souls. A very general method is for the Satanist to lure his intended proselyte into the most odious debaucheries, even to tempt him to the commission of some crime, and then if he seem laggard to subscribe his service to the demon and join the infernal gang the pressure of blackmail can be brought to bear until the poor wretch is wholly ensnared and lost. Any defection from the ranks, any attempted betrayal, or in many cases, lukewarmness even, is punished by death. Thus the members are terrorized, and many an unexplained, undiscovered murder is in truth the work of Satanists, the vengeance they have wreaked upon some traitor.

It is not necessary to do more than mention in passing the immense sums of money which have been so lavishly poured out by this dark brotherhood to corrupt and destroy whole countries and nations by their anarchy and red revolutions.

It is a commonplace of Catholic teaching that there has been a True Religion in the world ever since the creation of man—" the Universal Church began with Abel the Just "—and when Christ Himself came this existent True Religion received the designation of Christianity. Opposed to the True Religion throughout was the cult of evil, Satanism.

Witchcraft was potent—indeed more potent than ever after—and the devil had his worshippers before the coming of Christ. Not to speak of the Oriental magic of the Egyptians and the Chaldæans ; nor of Hebrew necromancies, which the Bible condemns again and again ; sorcerers flourished in Greece and Rome, and the whole body of ancient legislation clearly shows that before the dawn of Christianity, in the paynim era when a multiplicity of heathen cults prevailed throughout the Roman empire, witchcraft was as uncompromisingly prohibited as ever it was denounced and punished by the great Pontiffs, by Innocent VIII and Sixtus V; in Germany during the sixteenth and seventeenth centuries; in England by the parliaments of Elizabeth and James.

It is an empty and utterly baseless theory to suppose (as a certain type of imaginative writer has been indiscreet enough to assert) that witchcraft is the survival of some primitive cult of which nothing is known, concerning which nothing can be definitely discovered, and which is certainly not mentioned in any record or by any author. The development of such a fantasy merely leads to a wholesale wresting of historical facts, to a ludicrous perversion of evidence —probably quite unconsciously misread—and to general cheap claptrap all round.

None of the earlier religions existed with the express design and end of perpetrating evil for evil's sake. Now this constitutes the very essence of witchcraft, which is first and foremost the cult of hell. It is surely permissible to express surprise when one finds Satanism described as " a joyous religion ".

Bit with the novelty of the thing, some enterprising folklorist next asks us to look upon witchcraft " in the light of a fertility cult ", being careful, of course, for convenience sake to ignore the occult phenomena lest the issue be confused. It seems superfluous to remark that not a tittle of sound evidence can be brought forward to support such a *capriccio*.

That here and there lingered various old harmless customs and rustic festivities which had come down from pre-Christian times and which the Church had allowed, nay, had even sanctified by directing them to their right source, the Maypole dances, for example, and the Midsummer fires, which now honour St. John Baptist, is a matter of common knowledge. But there is no continuance of a pagan fertility cult.

Nor will anyone seek to argue from some extraordinary but isolated and infrequent instances of survival. In Easter week, 1282, John, the parish priest of Inverkeithing, celebrated the profane rites of Priapus, collecting young girls from the villages and compelling them to tread a measure in honour of Father Bacchus. When he had led these females forth in a troop, out of sheer wantonness he danced before carrying in front on a pole a representation of the human organs of reproduction, and singing and capering himself like a mime he viewed them all, and stirred them to lust by filthy language. The older men who being scandalized by this shameless performance rebuked him gently because they respected the dignity of his office, he violently abused, and comported himself more madly than ever. He also at dawn in Penance Week insisted that some should prick others who were stripped for penance with sharp goads, and when the graver burgesses protested he sturdily defended these indecencies. One night he was stabbed to death, nor was his assailant discovered.

About a dozen years before these pranks at Inverkeithing a cattle plague had broken out in various districts, which led to the revival of long dead mummeries. Two or three monks, it is said, advised the country folk to erect an image or terminal to Priapus, and through some ritual which involved the lighting of new fire by the friction of wood they prophesied the beasts would be relieved. At Fenton a Cistercian lay-brother actually set up this figure before the hall hearth and sprinkled the byres of the lord of the manor with holy water to which he had added " filthy matters of his own invention ". Here we have an example of a lewd and degraded superstition no doubt, but to talk of " Priapus-worship " and to describe the Cistercians as " monastic wizards " is not a trifle ridiculous, and betrays an extraordinary confusion of ideas.

In 1749 Girolamo Tartarotti (1702–1761), a minor journalist, one of the many literary *abbati* who swarmed throughout Italy at that time writing with equal elegance facile verse and fluent prose, published at Venice a large quarto volume, which he entitled *A Study of the Midnight Sabbats of Witches* (*Del Congresso Notturno delle Lammie*). His chapters are composed with an immense parade of learning—he quotes from more than three hundred and eighty authors—perhaps no such wonderful task in those days of leisure and large libraries. He shows himself, as the fashion went, a complete sceptic, and the thesis of this " member of the Republic of Letters ", for so he floridly dubs himself, is that there were never any assemblies or rendezvous of Satanists, and indeed summing it up in a few words that witchcraft is imaginary and a sick dream. *A Study of the Midnight Sabbats of Witches* is a very rare book, Tartarotti has been completely forgotten, and he would not be worth mentioning here were it not for one curious and interesting point. In the course of his excogitations he discusses the famous " Canon Episcopi ", an enactment to be considered in detail later, which speaks of certain women who seduced by the snare of the demon " believe and declare that they ride upon beasts with Diana, goddess of the pagans ", and with multitudes of women flying through the air in service and attendance upon her. From this Tartarotti evoked the fantastic idea of a " Dianic cult ", and he contends that witchcraft was nothing else than this imaginary cult. (Chapter IX : *The identity of the Dianic Cult with modern witchcraft is demonstrated and proven.*) Actually his arguments, if we may dignify unsupported statements and romancing by this name, could convince nobody, and the whole thing fell to the ground and was ignored.

A recent writer chancing upon Tartarotti's book (either, I suppose, at the British Museum or drawing from the notice in the Soldan-Heppe *Geschichte der Hexenprozesse*) promptly borrowed the idea, and came out with a new thesis concerning " the Dianic cult ", " as I propose to call it," which embraced " the religious beliefs and ritual of the people known in late mediæval times as ' Witches ' ". Of course Tartarotti was never so much as mentioned. The theory was at first mightily commended in certain quarters for its novelty, its scientific modernity, but when in the Foreword to a translation of Remy's *Demonolatry* (1930) I happened to show that Tartarotti's crochet had long since been discredited and had fallen into oblivion, the " Dianic cult " was speedily dropped, and very little (I believe) has since been heard of it.

Witchcraft does not belong to the antiquarian past ; it lives and energizes, a monstrous and fearful menace to-day, and it is perhaps only by a clear and under-standing view of the history of black magic that we can be aware of the imminent dangers which surround us.

As the Duke of Lauderdale once wrote : " It is impertinent arguing to conclude, that because there have been Cheats in the World, because there are some too credulous, and some have been put to Death for Witches, and were not, therefore all Men are deceived."

CHAPTER III

OF THE WITCH COVENS AND THEIR GRAND MASTERS; OF THE WITCHES' JOURNEY TO THE SABBAT; AND OF THE SABBAT ORGY

So vile and pestilent a superstition, whose evil and reprobate adherents the common consent of society holds as enemies to general order and, indeed, the foes of the human race.

POPE JOHN XXII.

Satan calleth them together into a Devilish Synagogue, and that he may also understand of them how well and diligently they have fulfilled their office of intoxicating committed unto them, and whom they have slain.

LAMBERT DANEAU.

The dark and secret Society of Witches spreads—a huge network of evil—over the whole world. Throughout Europe and America in particular the organization of Satanists is very thorough and very complete. In less than the span of a limited lifetime, not more than sixty years indeed after the first settlers had landed at Massachusetts Bay, Cotton Mather notes as a detail significantly dangerous in itself and worthy of particular attention the systematic and methodized federation of the Salem witches. He says, " 'Tis very Remarkable to see what an Impious and Impudent *imitation* of Divine Things is Apishly affected by the Devil," and after showing that in many striking incidents the sorceries of the native Indians might be taken to be a burlesque of the Biblical narrative, he continues : " The Devil which *then* thus imitated what was in the Church of the *Old Testament*, now among *Us* would Imitate the Affairs of the Church in the *New*. The *Witches* do say, that they form themselves much after the manner of *Congregational Churches* ; and that they have a *Baptism* and a *Supper*, and *Officers* among them, abominably Resembling those of our Lord."

There are, it is true, cases upon record and instances to be met with to-day of the solitary witch, dwelling apart and alone in some remote and unfrequented corner, apparently leading an almost isolated and eremitical life, but this is a rather rare exception.

The members of the witch society in various districts, large or small, villages, towns, great cities, or even shires and provinces, are linked up, and a correspondence is maintained between them in many mysterious ways. There is an active freemasonry of evil.

One of the oaths demanded from a novice is generally a pledge to frequent the midnight assemblies. These conventicles or *covens* are the meetings of bands or companies of witches summoned and forgathering under the discipline of an officer, who naturally was assisted in his work by other functionaries. Obviously the members of a coven would all belong as nearly as possible to the same neighbourhood, and especially was this the case in former years when the means of transit were far more slow and difficult than at the present day. It appears from the evidence at numerous trials, both at home and abroad, that those who belonged to a coven were bound to attend the weekly Esbat or rendezvous. The arrest of one member of a coven often led to the implication of many more who belonged to the same gang.

The number of witches which constituted and still

constitutes a coven has been much discussed. In a famous Scotch trial of 1662 when the revelations of Isobel Gowdie, of Auldearne, gave the fullest details concerning almost every circumstance of witchcraft, amply describing the Sabbats, the minor meetings, the ceremonies and instructions in malefic charms, she confessed " ther ar threttein persons in ilk Coeven ". In a very exhaustive investigation of this point Mr. Alexander Keiller thus sums up : " To those unaware of the probable organization of what might be termed the Witch Sect in Europe, in at any rate the sixteenth and seventeenth centuries, it may be explained that the Administrative and Executive Unit of Witchcraft customarily consisted of thirteen persons, and was usually termed a ' Coven ' or ' Coeven '." This scholar has explored in great detail " The Territorial Distribution of Witchcraft in Aberdeenshire ", and he has also set forth " The Personnel of the Aberdeenshire Witchcraft Covens in the years 1596–7 " showing that there were five distinct covens each formed of thirteen members, as well as three other covens which owing to the lack of necessary data cannot be precisely completed.

Until at least the latter part of the seventeenth century a well-organized group of witches existed between Shotley Bridge and Corbridge in the county of Northumberland. Ann Armstrong a farm servant at Burtree House, a few miles from Stocksfield-on-Tyne, was for a time partially drawn into the society and when in February, 1672–3, she voluntarily deposed before a number of magistrates her witness was most clear and detailed. Lieut.-Colonel G. R. B. Spain writes : " It is obvious from the evidence that Ann

Armstrong was closely in touch with a witchcraft organization over a large district of some fifty square miles." (" The Witches of Riding Mill, 1673 " : *Cornhill Magazine*, March, 1929.) Ann Armstrong described how the witches were divided into " coveys, consisting of thirteen persons in every covey ".

On the other hand it can be equally well shown that in many cases the local group or coven of witches did not consist of thirteen members. Sixteen witches belonged to the St. Osyth coven in 1582 ; ten witches formed the coven that infested the Waltham and Hedingham countryside five years later. The witches of Warboys who so plagued the Throgmortons and killed Lady Cromwell were three in number. No less than thirty-five witches can be traced in connexion with the famous Pendle Forest trials (1613). To attempt to divide this total into covens of thirteen is singularly futile. In the effort to do so not only has evidence been juggled, but Mother Demdike and Mother Chattox are placed in the same group, upon which Mr. L'Estrange Ewen justly comments : " This is a wild argument. Demdike and Chattox could not have been in the same coven because they were very keen rivals." Some of the London covens of Satanists to-day are composed of as many as thirty or forty men and women ; other circles again are quite small and only comprise ten initiates.

The *Officers* among the witches, of whom Cotton Mather speaks, were in the first place the local Chiefs or Masters of a coven, above whom was the Grand Master of a district.

There is very ample proof that " the Devil " of the Sabbat was not infrequently a human being, none other indeed than the Grand Master of the district, and since his officers and immediate attendants were also termed " Devils " by the witches some confusion has on occasion ensued. In Jersey the Grand Master, the Devil's deputy, was known as " Le Tchéziot ". In a few cases where sufficient details are given it is possible actually to identify " the Devil " by name.

During the trial in December, 1481, at Neuchatel, of Rolet Croschet, he confessed that when quite a lad he had been taken to a meeting of witches by Jaquet Duplan. Here he was welcomed by " the Devil ", a tall dark man, named Robin, to whom he did homage and who made much of him. The second time Croschet went to a rendezvous of sorcerers the gathering was much smaller, and the president was Captain Hanchement, evidently a well-known figure in the town, by whom he was appointed the local messenger for the society, and he used to go up and down to the various witches' houses giving notice of the assemblies and other bad businesses. At another time he attended a meeting of some other covens than his own belonging to Vauxtravers a few leagues away, and here the Provost was Etienne Goynet.

In 1579 at Windsor there used to meet " within the backside of Master Dodges in the Pittes " a coven presided over by Father Rosimond, of Farnham. It has been too ingeniously suggested that Father Rosimond *alias* Osborne, whom Mother Stiles of the coven named as her " chief", was a priest. But, no, this " wise man " (as he is termed) was a widower with a daughter who proved wellnigh as versed in sorcery as himself.

It is true that sometimes a clergyman stands revealed

as a high official among the witches. The Rev. George Burroughs, pastor at Wells, Maine, was accused by eight of the Salem witches " as being an head Actor at some of their Hellish Rendezvouses, and one who had the promise of being a King in Satan's Kingdom ". He was often heard to brag " that he was a *Conjuror*, above the ordinary Rank of Witches ", whilst several of the Satanists declared that " he was the Person who had Seduc'd, and Compell'd them into the snares of Witchcraft ". Now it is established beyond all question that George Burroughs was the Grand Master of the district. Admittedly in the wave of extreme rationalism which so inexplicably swept over Massachusetts at the beginning of the eighteenth century the General Court reversed George Burroughs' attainder and awarded damages to his heirs, but this does not in the least (as a recent historian appears to think) clear him from the guilt of witchcraft nor yet does it rebut even one particular of the charges which were proven up to the hilt again and again. Cotton Mather, for example, never altered his opinion of Burrough's culpability, and did not spare to express his sternest disapproval of the general *volte-face*.

Among a list of " confederates against Her Majesty Queen Elizabeth, who have diverse and sundry times conspired her life " we have Lord Paget, Sir George Hastings, Sir Thomas Hanmer, " Ould Birtles the great devel, Darnally the sorceror, Maude Two-good enchantresse, the ould witche of Ramsbury, several other ould witches." Full details are lacking but it seems plain that Old Birtles was the Grand Master or " Devil " of a coven of Wiltshire Witches.

The evil William, Lord Soulis, of Hermitage Castle,

often known as "Red Cap", was "the Devil" of a coven of sorcerers. He was protected by a terrible charm against any injury from rope or steel; cords could not bind nor sword pierce him. And so when he was seized by his enemies they rolled him up in sheets of lead and boiled him to death at a place called the Nine-Stane Rig.

On a circle of stones they placed the pot,
    On a circle of stones but barely nine ;
They heated it red and fiery hot,
    And the burnished brass did glimmer and shine.
They rolled him up in a sheet of lead
    A sheet of lead for a funeral pall ;
They plunged him into the cauldron red,
    And melted him body, lead, bones and all.

The chamberlain and chief counsellor of Philip IV of France, Enguerrand de Marigny, was a Grand Master of sorcerers prominent among whom were a notorious warlock, Jacobus de Lor, his wife and man-servant. Jacobus killed himself in prison whilst awaiting trial ; the witch, his wife, perished at the stake. Under Louis X, on 30th April, 1315, de Marigny was hanged at Paris.

An even more mysterious figure was Robert III d'Artois, the Grand Master of a veritable legion of witches. During the year 1333 he endeavoured to kill Philip VI, the Queen, and the Dauphin by his spells and enchantments. The design, before it could be matured, was betrayed by one of his minions, and proscription and sentence of perpetual banishment being pronounced against him, he fled to England where he proved powerful enough to stir up Edward III against France, and to his influence may be immediately ascribed the outbreak of the Hundred

Years War. He was feared and shunned everywhere as a past master of image magic, and it was also whispered that he possessed a number of most impious manuscripts of goety written by Moorish sorcerers.

From these two instances, Enguerrand de Marigny and Robert III d'Artois, we see that the activity of the Witch society was no mere piece of casual mischief wrought by doting village crones, who harmed their neighbours and scattered domestic ills and unhappiness, —bad businesses enough—but it reached further and meddled with the highest politics to the confusion of kingdoms and the ruin of dynasties. Such, as we fearfully realize when we look at the world around us is its chief business, wherein it is fatally energetic and alive to-day. To reduce the world to a chaos of blood and horror ; to stamp out and destroy all that is beautiful, all that has some reflection of God ; such are the aims and object of the Red and the Witch.

One of the most interesting identifications of " the Devil " occurs in the course of the notorious trials of Geillis Duncan, Agnes Sampson, Dr. John Fian, and their associates in 1590–1. As is well known, the whole crew was in league with Francis Stewart, Earl of Bothwell, an incendiary vehemently suspected of the black art. Long after when George Sandys was staying at Naples there came to the inn a Calabrian, an eminent scholar, who insisted on seeing the English traveller. " And he," writes Sandys, " would needs persuade me that I had insight in magick : for that Earle *Bothel* was my countryman, who lives at *Naples*, and is in these parts famous for suspected negromancie." In Scotland, Bothwell, then a young man, was almost overtly aiming at the throne, and the witch covens one and all were frantically attempting the life of King James. Agnes Sampson, "the eldest witch of them all," confessed that she had fashioned a waxen puppet, and baptized it saying : "This is King James the Sixth, ordained to be consumed at the instance of a noble man, Francis, Earl Bothwell." At the next rendezvous of witches the presiding "Devil" anxiously questioned her concerning the moulding of the image, and what effect had followed the melting of the figure at a slow fire and the piercing of it with great black pins. There can be no doubt at all that Bothwell was the moving force who energized and directed the very elaborate and numerous organization of demonolaters who were attacking the King, seeking both his crown and his life. Bothwell was in fine the Grand Master, the "Devil" of the witches, and the centre of a vast political plot.

In the nineteenth century both Albert Pike and his successor Adriano Lemmi have been identified upon abundant authority as being Grand Masters of societies practising Satanism, and as performing the hierarchical functions of "the Devil" at the modern Sabbat.

In his *Displaying of Supposed Witchcraft*, 1677, John Webster had suggested with reference to Margaret Agar and other "*deluded Haggs*" of the Brewham coven, tried at Taunton during the June Assizes of 1665, that the "little Man in black Clothes with a little band" who presided over the meeting at Hussey's Knap, a coppice near the hamlet, and who instructed the crew in moulding wax figurines and pricking them with thorns was the local Grand Master, a man-Devil, and Burns Begg points out that the witches on occasion " seem to have been undoubtedly the victims of unscrupulous and designing knaves, who personated Satan ". This, however, is no palliation of their crimes, and they are not one whit the less guilty of sorcery and devil-worship if they obey and adore a representative of Satan, rather than the demon himself. Nor do I think that the man who personated Satan at these horrid assemblies was so much an unscrupulous and designing knave as himself a demonist, believing intensely in the reality of his own dark powers, wholly and horribly dedicated and doomed to the service of evil.

Moreover sometimes the demon himself appeared whilst the rites were in full blast, as at the horrible mockery of the Last Supper attended one Good Friday by Madeleine Bavent when Mathurin Picard was the celebrant of those blasphemies, and during this abominable supper a dark familiar walked round the table at which the company were seated, crying aloud : *Not one of you shall betray me !*

God, so far as His ordinary presence and action in Nature are concerned, is hidden behind the veil of secondary causes, and when God's ape, the Demon, can work so successfully and obtain not merely devoted adherents but fervent worshippers by human agency, there is plainly no need for him to manifest himself in person either to particular individuals or at every Sabbat. None the less it is certain that he can do so, that he has done and yet does so very frequently, and the number of cases in the records of trials which are to be explained in no other way, that is to say where the devil manifests himself in some shape, appears to and has most intimate connexions with his besotted worshippers, are extremely numerous, and from what I know I am persuaded that we may safely avouch that to-day the demon is more frequently himself present at the modern sabbats than he functions through a deputy.

In the Caverne des Trois Frères, Ariège, France, there is depicted on the upper wall of the cave by some Palæolithic artist ten thousand years ago the figure of a man clothed in the skin of a stag with a horse's tail and wearing on his head huge branching antlers. This Caverne has a gallery of over four hundred pictures, but this figure " The Sorcerer " at the far end, painted high up on the rock in the " wizard's chamber ", as it has been called, dominates the whole. Here then we have a masked magician, a Grand Master of the Old Stone Age.

A whole catena of evidence from the Fathers and Doctors of the Church might be easily adduced, all sternly denunciatory of those who dress themselves in the hides of animals and don great horns, thus decked out for licentious and profane assemblies and the performance of obscenest rituals. Thus St. Cæsarius of Arles (470–542) more than once anathematizes those who dress themselves in furry pelts and who don horned helmets, completely metamorphosed into animals. He warns the faithful : " If ye abhor any participation in their sins, ye will not suffer these human stags or bull-calves or other monsters to approach you, nay, not so much as to come nigh your dwellings."

Prohibitions of these devilish mummeries and bestial vizardings are to be repeatedly found in the early Penitentials.

We are forcibly reminded, and indeed there is a most intimate and vital connexion between the two, of the fiendish masks and dresses assumed by the witch-doctors and sorcerers of Africa and Tibet.

There is complete evidence that the hierophant at the witches' Sabbat, when a human being played that rôle, generally wore this traditional disguise. Nay more, as regards the British Isles at least—and it seems clear that in other countries the habit was very similar—we possess a pictorial representation of " the Devil " as he appeared to his worshippers. During the famous Fian trials—to which reference has already been made—Agnes Sampson confessed : " The devil was clad in a black gown with a black hat upon his head. . . . His face was terrible, his nose like the beak of an eagle, great burning eyes ; his hands and his legs were hairy, with claws upon his hands and feet like the griffin." In the pamphlet *Newes from Scotland, Declaring the Damnable life and death of Doctor Fian* we have a rough woodcut, repeated twice, which shows " the Devil " preaching from the North Berwick pulpit to the whole coven of witches, and allowing for the crudity of the draughtsman and a few unimportant differences of detail—the black gown and hat are not portrayed—the demon in the picture is exactly like the description Agnes Sampson gave. It must be remembered, too, that at the Sabbat she was in a state of morbid excitation, in part due to deep cups of heady wine, the time was midnight, the place a haunted old church, the only light a few flickering, candles that burned with a ghastly blue flame.

Now " the Devil " as he is shown in the *Newes from Scotland* illustration is precisely the Devil who appears upon the title-page of Middleton and Rowley's masque *The World tost at Tennis*, 4to, 1620. This woodcut presents an episode towards the end of the masque, and here the Devil in traditional disguise, a grim black hairy shape with huge beaked nose, monstrous claws, and the cloven hoofs of a griffin, in every particular fits the details so closely observed by Agnes Sampson. I have no doubt that the drawing for this masque was actually made in the theatre, for although this kind of costly and decorative entertainment was almost always designed for court or some great nobleman's house, we know that *The World tost at Tennis* was produced with considerable success on the public stage " By the Prince his Servants ". The dress, then, of " the Devil " at the Sabbats seems frequently to have been of the nature of an elaborate theatrical costume, such as might perhaps have been found in the stock wardrobe of a rich playhouse at London, but which would have had no histrionic associations for provincial folk and even simpler rustics.

Lambert Daneau, whose *Les Sorciers* was translated in 1575 by Thomas Taylor as *A Dialogue of Witches*, says that the " witches acknowledge the Devil for their God, call upon him, pray to him, and trust in him ", and when they assemble at their Sabbats, " they repeat the oath which they have given unto him in acknowledging him as their God."

From almost every witch-trial in every land evidence to this effect might be accumulated. The matter is perfectly plain, and it is futile to attempt to conceal or confuse the issue, the God of the witches is and was the Devil, " the wicked one," " that old serpent

A Courtly Masque:

The Deuice called, The VVorld toſt at Tennis

As it hath beene diuers times Preſented to the
Contentment of many Noble and Worthy
Spectators:

By the PRINCE _his Seruants._

Inuented and ſet downe, By   Tho: _Middleton_ & _William Rowley_   Gent.

The Diuell.   Deceit.   The World.

THE WORLD TOST AT TENNIS
The First Quarto

123

called the Devil, and Satan, which deceiveth the whole world," " the Prince of the power of the air, the spirit that now worketh in the children of disobedience," who " sinneth from the beginning ", " a murderer from the beginning," " a liar, and the father of it." Be it remarked that these phrases are neither " cheap claptrap " nor " purple patches " nor swayed by colourful prejudice. I quote the simple unvarnished words of the Authorized Version of the English Bible.

On those occasions when no visible presence of discarnate evil, no demon, appeared or presided at the Sabbat orgy, divine honours were paid to Satan's deputy, the Grand Master, although it does not follow that he was in himself and of himself regarded as absolute God. It is a nice, but none the less an important distinction, and although essentially true I am not prepared to say that as such it was apprehended by the majority of the witches, assuredly not by the poorer and clownish folk from whom, in the British Isles at any rate, so many of the covens were recruited.

Among certain primitive peoples and in various savage tribes the chieftain or King was regarded as representative of and partaking in deity. He was, in fact, a man-god, and we find that very often he was ceremonially put to a violent death. As summed up by Sir James Frazer : " the motive for slaying a man-god is a fear lest with the enfeeblement of his body in sickness or old age his sacred spirit should suffer a corresponding decay, which might imperil the general course of nature and with it the existence of his worshippers who believe the cosmic energies to be mysteriously knit up with those of their human divinity." Such in brief is the theory of " The Dying God " or " The Divine Victim ", as it is conveniently known.

It is a curious and irresponsible fantasy which attempts to superimpose the hypothesis of the " Divine Victim " upon the Grand Masters of the witches. Such a figment is difficult to be approached in serious discussion, since it offers no vestige of reality, and vaguely imaginative conjectures are not easy of refutation, or rather they carry their own disproof. Yet we are assured that certain figures, both historical and legendary, as for example King Edmund, the " deed-doer ", King Edmund Ironside, King Cnut " the Great ", Bishop Walcher of Durham, William Rufus, St. Thomas of Canterbury, St. Joan of Arc, Gilles de Rais, Robin Hood, Friar Tuck, were not only Grand Masters of witch societies, but also " the Incarnate God ". Every one of these personages was ceremonially put to death, and the sacrifice was repeatedly consummated. When we venture to ask what tittle of fact exists to support this amazing assertion, we are coolly instructed that in the first place all records, all evidence from history must be swept aside as useless (a very necessary preliminary this, I am willing to admit), and " the Christian inquisitors are unanimous on this point ", which last statement is, I venture to say, wholly unfounded. It really is not worth while—even if space allowed —to enter into all these cases in detail. I would merely point out that in the instance of St. Joan of Arc these wild theories have been dealt with by scholars and historians to be exploded once and for all. Nor would it be difficult to show how preposterous such fabling is with regard to the other names. The murder of William Rufus in the New Forest was due to homosexual jealousy, and although they have been squeamishly suppressed practically the full details of the affair can be traced. If anyone likes to consider that Robin Hood and Friar Tuck were wizards I hardly suppose that any serious objection will be raised, but I submit that it is distinctly offensive to very many when St. Thomas à Becket stands thus defamed. I am only too well aware that devotion to St. Thomas is weak and anæmic enough in England. It is a matter for regret that his holy Feast is not celebrated amongst us with greater solemnity, that his secondary Feast of the Translation is observed in only one diocese. Yet there are still those who visit Canterbury " The holy blisful martir for to seke ". St. Thomas still has his clients who keep Tuesday in his honour, who have kissed the hallowed spot where he fell, who make pilgrimage and worship at his shrine.

In the case of historical figures the sole argument to show that such-an-one was a Grand Master of witches and " the Incarnate God " seems to be a violent death. I shall not be in the least surprised to be told that Jack Sheppard, Dick Turpin, Eugene Aram, George Barnwell and Sweeney Todd were " Incarnate Gods ", whilst to companion Friar Tuck let us have Grindoff the Miller, Bill Sikes, Count Fosco and Cock Robin.

To quote a shrewd saying of the famous Dr. Henry More : " *At this pitch of wit . . . is the Reason of our professed Wit-would-be's of this present Age, who will catch at any slight occasion or pretence of misbeliving those things that they cannot endure should be true.*"

The name Sabbat, the derivation of which does not appear to be exactly established, may be held to cover almost every formal assembly of devil-worshippers, and thus ranges from comparative simplicity, the secret rendezvous in the open air or in some poor hut of half-a-dozen witches devoted to the fiend and presided over by the official of the village, to a large and crowded congregation adoring the demon upon his throne and marshalled by incarnate evil intelligences, a mob outvying the angels of the pit in malice, blasphemy, and revolt, the vomit of pandemonium on earth.

The day of the week whereon the Sabbat was held varied in different localities and at several times. There is indeed an accumulation of evidence for every night, although Friday was most generally favoured. Saturday and Sunday were if possible particularly avoided, especially a Saturday. At the trial of Louis Gaufridi in May, 1614, it was proved that the Sabbats were held on every night of the week. Wednesday and Friday were the Sabbats of blasphemy and the Black Mass, whilst to the other nights were allotted the most hideous villainies which humanity can conceive or perform. In England, it was stated during the seventeenth century that the " Solemn appointments and meetings . . . are ordinarily on Tuesday or Wednesday night ". The witches of Burgundy met on Tuesday night, so we may conclude with Boguet " that there is no fixed day for the Sabbat, but that witches go to it whenever Satan so commands ". This is confirmed by Madeleine Bavent who says : " There seemed to be no fixed day for the assembly."

Antide Colas confessed that she was wont to attend

the Sabbat upon each of the greater Festivals of the year, as for example at Christmas, Easter, Corpus Christi, and Boguet gives us the reason for this too—" the wicked one celebrates his assemblies on Holy Days, and thus mockingly seduces the creatures of God from His service."

Thus we hear of Sabbats being held on the vigils of the " nine chief feasts of the year ", namely, Easter, Epiphany, Ascension Day, the Purification, Nativity and Assumption of Our Lady, Corpus Christi, All Saints, and the Nativity of St. John Baptist. In one English village the Sabbat was held on St. Bartholomew's Eve, this apostle being Patron of the Church and parish. Throughout Eastern Europe a Sabbat was held on the Eve of St. George. In Western Europe the day of one of the principal assemblies was on 30th April, the Eve of May Day, famous over all Northern Germany as Die Walpurgis-Nacht, the Night of Saint Walburga.

The Grand Sabbats were convened in a great variety of places, whilst the lesser Sabbats could be easily assembled in an even larger number of spots, as might be most convenient to the Satanists of the district, a field near a village, a wood, a tor, a valley, an open waste beneath some blasted oak, a cemetery, a ruined building, some solitary chapel or deserted church, and often in a house belonging to one of the initiates.

It was advisable that the selected locality should be remote to obviate any chance of espionage or casual interruption, and in many localities some wild ill-omened gully or the lone hill-top was shudderingly marked as the notorious haunt of witches and their fiends.

De Lancre says that in the Basque country the Grand Sabbat was invariably held near a stream, a lake, or water of some kind. Bodin confirms this to some extent, for Antoine Gandillon, a witch of long continuance, told him that there must always be water in the place of the Sabbat, and the little coven of the village of Coirières held their Sabbat near a mill-dam. The Breton witches assembled among the ancient cromlechs and ruined dolmens of their province. The market-crosses of sleepy old towns and English villages were among the favourite rendezvous of our country warlocks and witches. Mother Agar, the Brewham witch, and her company forgathered on Brewham Common, and also at Husseys-knap, a coppice just beyond the hamlet. Dr. Fian and his associates on All Hallows E'en assembled at the lonely and haunted church of North Berwick. Silvain Nevillon, who was executed at Orleans on the 4th February, 1615, confessed " that the Sabbat was celebrated in a house ", and the full details which he gave shows this to have been a large château, no doubt the home of some wealthy local magnate, a Satanist and probably the Grand Master of the district, within whose walls above 200 persons could assemble.

In Jersey the witches' rendezvous was under the shadow of a large rock south of Rocqueberg Point, St. Clement, and it is believed that at their Sabbats they often raised storms which imperilled those at sea and drowned many a fisherman.

The Guernsey witches celebrated " the Feast of the Sabbat " on Friday nights on the hill of Catiôroc, around the cromlech called " Le Trépied ". At the time of the full moon they also met near the mill which stands on the hill at Ville-ès-Pies. Their favourite spot, however, was the sands of Rocquaine Bay, where they used to perform obscene dances chanting a roundelay of which the burden ran " Qué-hou-hou ! Marie Lihou ! " words uttered in impious defiance and mockery of Notre Dame, Sainte Marie de Lihou. This was a spot of such extraordinary sanctity, that although both priory and church are but a heap of shapeless ruins even to-day the French coasting vessels as they pass salute it by lowering their topmast.

One of the most notorious meeting-places for witches was the Brocken, popularly known as the Blocksburg, the highest peak of the Hartz mountains. On Walpurgis Night huge assemblies of Satanists were wont to forgather there, some (it is said) coming from Norway and even from distant Lapland. Local Blocksburgs existed, or rather hills so called, especially in Pomerania which boasted two or three such crags.

Night was almost invariably the time for the Sabbat. Father Delrio aptly observes : " Their assemblies are generally held at dead of night when the Powers of Darkness reign ; or, sometimes, at high noon, even as the Psalmist saith, when he speaks of ' the noonday devil '." The Lancashire witches celebrated their Sabbat " about twelve of the clock in the day time ". The witches of Stoke Trister, near Wincanton, " met about nine of the Clock in the Night, in the Common near *Trister* Gate." Mother Bishop, a Somersetshire witch, confessed " That she hath been at several meetings in *Lie* Common, and at other places in the night ". On one occasion Christian Green of Brewham and other witches met the devil " in *Brewham* Forest about Noon ", but the coven more frequently used to assemble " at a place called *Husseys-knap* in the Forest in the Night time ".

The time at which the Sabbat began was generally upon the stroke of midnight. It lasted until the cock crew, when everything vanished away.

A witch named Babilla Latoma, when minutely questioned by Nicolas Remy about the nightly doing of sorcerers, confessed that nothing was more fatally obstructive to their loathsome businesses than that a cock should crow. Two other witches informed the same judge that when it was time to break up their nocturnal assemblies the officers proclaimed in stentorian voices : " Ho ! make haste and away, all ; for the cock begins to crow." That the crowing of a cock dissolves enchantments is a tradition of remotest antiquity, and the poet Prudentius very beautifully sings how the night-wandering demons, who rejoice in dunnest shades, at the crowing of the cock tremble and scatter in sore affright.

It has been quite confidently and quite erroneously stated that in England the witches' Sabbat was practically unknown, or at most, when the evidence proves overwhelming and such as is impossible to slur or set aside, it is argued that the English Sabbat " was a feeble reflection of its foreign original ", and existed only in an " attenuated " form. It is difficult in the face of facts which certainly cannot be dismissed and which one would have thought could hardly be misinterpreted to appreciate whence this fallacy arose, but since it has been so seriously put forward and maintained it becomes necessary to make specific mention of some few from the many cases in English witchcraft proving the Assemblies or " synagogues " of Satanists—and such gatherings continue very actively to-day—whereat every kind of mischief and devil's craft was hatched and ingeniously propelled.

In 1579 the Windsor coven which was presided over by Father Rosimond of Farnham were wont to assemble for their Sabbats "within the backside of Master Dodges in the Pittes", and also about eleven o'clock at night at the Pound. They were adepts in making figurines, and having moulded in red wax "pictures" of a neighbouring farmer and his maid-servant, a local butcher, and the Mayor of Windsor, they killed these four persons by sorcery, piercing the figures through and through with sharp hawthorn spines and prickles. A very important Sabbat was held by the Lancashire witches on Good Friday, 1612, at Malking Tower, the abode of old Mother Demdike, where twenty and more indulged in a gluttonous orgy, and plotted no inconsiderable amount of mischief, including the murder of Thomas Lister, of Westly, which they very effectually contrived in less than two or three months. The Salmesbury witches, three of whom were put on their trial in the same year, 1612, used to celebrate their Sabbats on Thursday and Sunday nights on the banks of the Ribble, where they met four tall black men who provided meat and wine, who danced with them and fornicated. Two of the witches who had secretly killed a small child, after the burial of the body dug it up, boiled it in a pot and ate it, seething the bones to obtain fat for the witch's ointment.

Ten years later the witches who plagued the family of that eminent poet and scholar Edward Fairfax of Fewstone, in the Forest of Knaresborough, used to meet at midnight at Timble Gill, where a table was spread with food and flagons, and the Devil sat at the upper end.

In the case of the Second Lancashire witches, 1634, Margaret Johnson confessed that on the Sunday within the octave of All Saints she attended a Sabbat at a house called Hoarestones (which was still standing in 1845) and there were present about forty witches with their familiars. She further stated that Good Friday was " one of their constant days of their general meeting ".

Matthew Hopkins relates that in 1644 when he was living at Manningtree, Essex, a number of witches, both of his own town and from neighbouring villages, " every six weeks in the night (being always on the Friday night) had their meeting close by his house, and had their several solemn sacrifices there offered to the Devil."

About the same year the Leicestershire witches used to forgather at Burton-on-the-Wolds " above four score " at a Sabbat, and at Tilbrooke bushes near Catworth " above twenty at one time " to worship and serve the demon.

In September, 1645, Goodwife Hott, a witch of Faversham, Kent, related how " there was a great meeting at Goodwife Pantery's house, and that Goodwife Dadson was there, and that Goodwife Gardner should have been there, but did not come, and the Devil sat at the upper end of the table ".

Dr. Henry More, the famous Platonist philosopher, learned that a coven of witches held their Sabbats at the house of Mother Lendall of Cambridge, a woman most ill-famed for impiety and evil, and that here late at night the " table was well furnished with guests and meat ", whilst at the head of the board there sat one in black to whom the numerous company louted low with great reverence and did obeisance. Much of the talk among the leaders of the party was carried on in a strange tongue, not understood of the humbler folk present.

The Malmesbury coven in 1671 celebrated their orgies at night in the house of one of the dark fellowship, and here they securely feasted and drank deeply and committed every kind of uncleanness, also plotting evilly enough against their enemies and planning murders with only too speedy and efficacious results.

The very dangerous and extremely well-organized society of witches who infested the Northumbrian woodlands and open moors between Shotley Bridge and Corbridge at the end of the seventeenth century had their general meeting-place at a house called Riding House, near Riding Mill Bridge End, where there was a banquet spread and " their protector whom they called their god " sat at the top of the table in a great gilt chair. One Good Friday no less than sixty-five witches attended a great feast at the house of John Newton, of the Riding, near Riding Mill, where they were served with boiled capons, rich cheeses, butter, white bread, beef, bottles of rare wine, and a vast variety of all meats. Another Sabbat was held at Allensford on the Derwent, when the whole coven danced their ritual measure. Yet another Sabbat was celebrated in the cellar of Master Francis Pye's house at Morpeth.

In Massachusetts whither the foul traditions of witchcraft had been brought from England and there could be no question of continental custom or influence, the Salem witches held their General Meetings and solemn Sabbat—"hellish Randezvouzes," Cotton Mather justly terms them—in a field not far from the village, and sometimes in a house belonging to a warlock who lived there. Here they celebrated a Sabbat on the very day a Public Fast was being kept on account of the sorceries and devilment which were so sorely plaguing the countryside. There were "Meetings, Feastings, Dancings" in other places as well, and a number of novices were baptized into this horrid society in the river at Newbury Falls.

At the risk of some slight repetition I have thought it well to give a catena extending over a century (1579–1692) to show beyond all quibble or question that the English witches assembled at set times and in set places for their formal Sabbats where every species of wickedness and devil-worship prevailed, and that there was in fine amongst them a definite and disciplined organization of the infernal cult of Satanism, which is one and the same the whole world over. It would not be difficult, moreover, to carry on the chain of evidence throughout the eighteenth and nineteenth centuries down to the London Sabbats of the present day.

I believe the point has been raised that the English Sabbats were but small gatherings in comparison with the large assemblies in Germany, in the Pyrenees, at Mohra in Sweden, in the Val Camonica, at Benevento, and other places. It is true that the witches flocked in crowds to certain notorious centres, and when a district was widely infected with Satanism naturally the covens would be more numerous. Yet we hear of no less than twenty attending a Sabbat in the second case of the Lancashire witches ; sixty-five were present at the Sabbat in John Newton's house, Riding Mill ; whilst at the notorious Sabbat at North Berwick church there assembled two hundred devil-worshippers, although, of course, strictly speaking this is not an English example. To-day also there are sometimes as many as twenty-five or thirty at a Sabbat. No doubt in villages such as Brewham the coven was few, but the Wincanton society numbered thirteen and perhaps more. Similar proportions seem to have prevailed (as we might reasonably expect) upon the continent.

The next detail which presents itself for inquiry is, how the witches reached the Sabbat ? The answer seems at first glance simple enough : they ride, they drive, they go on foot, travelling in whatever way is most convenient. When Agnes Sampson, who lived at Keith, attended the midnight Sabbat at North Berwick church, " she passed there on horseback, conveyed by her godson, called John Cooper." When the Pendle witches assembled at Malking Tower, an extremely isolated and ancient stronghold which stood on the further slope of the high conical-shaped hill which shuts in Rough Lee glen to the north-east, they " gotten on Horsebacke ", some mounting steeds of one colour, some of another. When Ann Armstrong, a servant of the Fowlers at Burtree House, near Stocksfield-on-Tyne, was taken to the Sabbat at Riding Mill Bridge End she saw the witches arrive on horseback. Their leader, whom they spoke of as " their protector ", was " a long black man riding on a bay galloway ", in other words a garran, a small stout Scotch horse.

When the orgy was over the whole crew took the saddle again for home with their protector leading the party.

Major Thomas Weir, the Edinburgh warlock, and his sister Jean Weir, used to drive to the Sabbats at Musselburgh in a coach, and for more than a hundred years after the execution of these two miserable witches it was said that the rattling and thundering of a heavy coach could be heard at midnight over the cobbles as the phantom equipage whirled along by black steeds of hell passed swiftly down the Bow to halt before Weir's horrible house and then vanish in a flame of fire. It is probable that many hauntings by spectral coaches are to be explained thus, namely that the apparitions are those of wizards who were wont thus to travel to the Sabbat and whose foul ghosts still cling to the route they covered in life on evil bent again and again. A château not far from Morlaix in Brittany is fearfully haunted in this way. On certain anniversaries the windows of the empty house are illuminated from within as by numberless candles, the old cracked bell in the turret clangs harshly, and up the long drive there speeds an ancient coach within which are seated four shadowy figures. These are said to be a certain seigneur, lord of the manor in the early decades of the eighteenth century, his son and two grandsons, all of whom were Satanists, handing down the infernal tradition from scion to scion of their accursed line.

Early in the sixteenth century a gang of Satanists made their headquarters at Yarmouth, and it is plain that they were protected by certain great persons living in that district who belonged to the evil society. In the reign of Elizabeth six Yarmouth witches, including Elizabeth Butcher, a very active devil's agent, were hanged, and under Charles I another five witches were executed. Caister Castle near Yarmouth was formerly visited by a phantom coach which drove round the courtyard of the castle and halted, whereupon a number of dark muffled figures seem to emerge silently from various doorways and corners, and enter the vehicle. The door was slammed to with a horrible noise, the crack of a whip was heard, and the six headless black horses set off at full gallop. No doubt these were the spectres of the wizards doomed endlessly to repeat their journey to the unhallowed orgies of the Sabbat.

A similar coach haunts the roads near Langley Hall, Durham. Although it is true that many cases of witchcraft have not come to light in this district it may be noted that in January, 1651–1652, two notorious warlocks were executed at Durham, and it is more than probable that the organization had secretly taken root there, whilst the boggart coach is the phantom of that which was wont to convey certain sorcerers to their diabolic rendezvous.

Witches sometimes go on foot to the Sabbat, and this usually happens when the place of their assembly is not very distant from their homes. Thus Bernard of Como, a famous Dominican scholar, remarks that when witches are to attend the Sabbat at some spot hard by their dwellings, " they proceed thither on foot conversing as they go." When a Sabbat was celebrated in the field of Longchamois, the witches of Orcieres, about a quarter of a league away, walked thither in a party. The Wincanton witches walked to the Sabbat held on the common near Trister Gate, a bare couple of miles away, whilst for Mother Style of Stoke Trister it can only have been a matter of a few hundred yards.

A young Satanist, Isaac de Queyran, told Pierre De Lancre, the Bordeaux judge, that witches who dwelt at some distance flew home from the Sabbat through the air, whilst those whose houses were not far away returned on foot. De Lancre comments : " It is truly as criminal and abominable for a Sorcerer to go to the Sabbat on foot as to be voluntarily conveyed thither by the Devil."

In all the above cases (save truly in the hints given by de Queyran) the method of proceeding to the Sabbat proves perfectly commonplace and usual, but the witches also employed other means which were extraordinary and indeed preternatural. The popular imagination has seized upon one of these and often exaggerates it into something surpassingly fantastic and bizarre, for although the witch is universally credited with the power to fly through the air mounted upon a besom or some kind of stick it is remarkable in the face of so general and picturesque a belief to find that the confessions avowing this actual mode of aerial transport are comparatively few.

None the less it is significant that the belief in the nocturnal transport through the air of sorcerers, either bent on some malefic business or to attend their assemblies, is practically universal, and exists among savage races as strongly as amongst civilized people. In the Congo, for example, members of the secret society *Bwiti* during certain wizard ceremonies rise from the ground to a height of several feet during the space of a quarter of an hour. The Indians of North America credited their pow-wows with the faculty of raising their bodies from the ground for an appreciable length of time, and a French missionary, Father Papetard told Dr. Imbert-Gourbeyre, that whilst at Oregon he had himself seen more than once native warlocks levitate themselves two or three feet from the ground and walk upon the top of the blades of long pampas grasses without bending the tender panicles. In Australia, too, the native tribes such as the Boandik, West Arunta, Kurnai, and others are perfectly familiar with the aerial transport of magicians, who are said to be conveyed by ghosts, that is to say (as we know) by demons. In one of the tribes of the Wotjobaluk group an ancient seeress not infrequently " went up aloft, being supported, as it was believed, by ghosts [devils], from whom she gleaned information as to the dead ". This is related together with many other striking examples by A. W. Howitt in his work on *The Native Tribes of South-East Australia.*

It stands to reason that Satan, the ape of God, must imitate and caricature the divine phenomenon of mystical levitation.

According to the great *Oxford English Dictionary* the word " levitation " does not date back before 1875. It was first employed in England, and in earliest use with reference to spiritualism (spiritism). Levitation means that the human body is able under certain conditions to be raised from the ground, and to remain for a longer or shorter space of time suspended in the air without any visible support, and not infrequently to move to and fro in the air without the apparent or traceable action of any physical forces.

In hagiography this is a recognized and not infrequent occurrence, and very many instances are noted by the Bollandists in their immense work on the Lives of the Saints. It is not too much to say that some hundreds of such cases have been known. There are the Scriptural examples of Enoch, Elijah, Habakkuk, S. Philip the Deacon, and the transports of Our Lord Himself, Whose earthly life was consummated in that supreme levitation we name the Ascension. There are the cases of early Saints, Saint Mary Magdalene, Saint Antony the Great, Saint Mary of Egypt. There are the modern traditions of such great names as Saint Dominic, Saint Francis, Saint Bonaventura, Saint Thomas Aquinas, Saint Catherine of Siena, Saint Peter of Alcantara, Saint Teresa, Saint Philip Neri— to name almost at random only a very few. In the nineteenth century we have that glorious visionary and mystic Anne Catherine Emmerich ; the Italian Maria Domenica Barbagli ; the Curé d'Ars ; Mary of Jesus who died in 1862, and whose levitations formed the subject of a report in a bulletin of the *Société des Sciences psychiques* ; the Carmelite Sister Mary of Jesus Crucified who died at the Carmel of Bethlehem in 1878 ; an ecstatica living near Nantes, Marie Julie Jahenny, who is still alive.

Perhaps the two most famous examples of levitation are Saint Alphonsus Liguori and Saint Joseph of Copertino. Some of the raptures and upliftings of Saint Alphonsus were experienced in public, as in the church of Foggia in December, 1745, when as he was preaching he was raised to a height from the floor in the presence of a crowded congregation who could not refrain from crying aloud : " A miracle ! a miracle ! "

With regard to the Franciscan Joseph of Copertino, who died at the Conventual house at Osimo in September,

1663, his levitations and ecstatic flights through the air from one place to another were so frequent that the Bull of canonization says no Saint can be compared to him in this respect. His raptures in saying Mass were of daily occurrence, and for no less than thirty-five years his Superiors had to exercise the greatest caution, requiring him on certain feasts, especially those of Our Lady, to say Mass in a private oratory so that the religious " should not be disturbed by the concourse of the vulgar ", many of whom came more from curiosity (it is to be feared) rather than devotion to see this marvellous mystic at the altar.

The evidence for the levitations of Saint Alphonsus and Saint Joseph (as indeed for very many other holy persons) has been sifted with the utmost thoroughness, and there is no room whatsoever left for doubt or question.

In this connexion we cannot neglect to remark upon mediumistic levitations, one of the most famous examples being the case of Daniel Dunglas Home, of whom Sir William Crookes bore witness : " On three separate occasions have I seen him raised completely from the floor of the room. . . . There are at least a hundred recorded instances of Mr. Home's rising from the ground. . . . The accumulated testimony establishing Mr. Home's levitations is overwhelming." In November, 1868, Lord Adare and Lord Lindsay saw Home raised four or five feet from the ground. At Ashley House, Home was carried out at one window and borne in through another at a height of 70 feet from the ground. Once at Adare Abbey, he floated swiftly for a space of twelve yards through the air. In a garden at Stockton he was aerially transported for more than a hundred feet.

William Stainton Moses was levitated six feet; Eusapia Palladino, on occasion from some inches to fully five feet; Mrs. French, a couple of feet; Maria Vollhart, one foot; whilst the Brazilian Carlos Mirabelli even when fastened to an armchair was levitated in the presence of several acutely observant members of the Academia Cesare Lombroso, remaining for several minutes suspended twelve feet from the ground so that the witnesses could pass and repass under the body tied to the chair. (It is by no means unusual for objects in contact with the levitated person to be similarly influenced by the phenomenon.) At Santos Mirabelli experienced levitation in the street, being uplifted from a motor car for about three minutes.

Now angels, be they blessed spirits or demons, have the power to move matter. The levitation of sorcerers is effected by the agency of evil forces, devils who bestow this favour upon an auxiliary and a companion.

Dr. John L. Nevius, of Chefoo, who was for forty years a missionary to the Chinese, in his study *Demon Possession* relates how certain Chinese wizards " are carried by invisible power from place to place. They ascend to a height of twenty or fifty feet, and are carried to a distance of four or five *li* ". (A *li* is one-third of a mile.) The same phenomenon occurs in the case of European witches, who have been and are borne by the invisible power of Satan to the Sabbat, or it may be on some other errand of mischief and destruction.

Paul Grilland in his treatise *On Witchcraft*, published in 1533, speaks of a trial of a sorceress at Rome seven years before, at which he was present, and it was asserted that she flew in the air after she had anointed her limbs with a certain magic liniment. Some witches, says Boguet, use a mysterious ointment, and others use none. " Before they go to the Sabbat," writes Guazzo, " the witches anoint themselves on some part of their bodies with an unguent made from various foul and filthy ingredients, but chiefly from murdered children ; and so anointed they are carried away on a cowl-staff, or a broom, or a reed, a cleft stick, or a distaff, or even a shovel, which things they ride."

Dr. Johann Weyer, in his treatise on witches, has transcribed certain formulæ for the magical ointment. He tells how the witches boil the fat of babes in a brazen cauldron. They scum this thickly, and make it into a kind of grease, kneading into it a commixture of hemlock, aconite, poplar leaves, and soot. Another recipe is : Cowbane, sweet flag, cinquefoil, bat's blood, belladonna, and oil. There are, Weyer adds, other ointments, but the essential ingredients remain the same in all.

Collette Dumont, a Guernsey witch, who was executed in 1617, confessed that the Devil had given her a certain black ointment, with which, having stripped, she rubbed her body all over, and then again dressed and went out of doors when she was immediately borne through the air with incredible velocity to the appointed place for the Sabbat. This was sometimes near the Torteval parish churchyard, and sometimes on the seashore hard by Rocquaine Castle.

It is related that a certain Guernsey lady of St. Pierre-du-Bois becoming very suspicious of the long hours of retirement her husband passed in his own apartments was induced by curiosity to watch him. Accordingly one day she concealed herself in the room. He entered, and stripping himself naked anointed his limbs with a certain ointment, repeating the words *va et vient*. He then seemed to disappear from sight. After a while she came forth, and went through the same ceremony, when in a twink she found herself on the summit of Pleinmont in the midst of a large company. A table was spread with costly viands, of which some who were present courteously invited her to partake. Crossing herself for her grace, she said *Au nom de Dieu soit, Amen*. No sooner had she spoken than all had disappeared, and the only signs of any beings having approached the spot were the recent marks of cloven feet which seemed to have scorched and trampled the sward in every direction.

In the *Malleus Maleficarum* it is explained at length how witches having anointed either themselves or some chair or broomstick with the devil's ointment can be and are transported up through the air about their master's business. Sometimes also they are carried on animals, which are not true animals but devils in that form. The witches too not unseldom appear to be metamorphosed into animals, especially cats. And this is merely glamour, a trick of the devil, who, Saint Thomas tells us, can entirely confuse and cheat the senses, so that a witch is persuaded she is changed into a cat, and those of her society see her as a cat, whereas it is all illusion.

" The commonest practice of all witches is to fly up through the chimney. If anyone objects that chimneys are too small and narrow, or raises any other difficulties, he must know that by virtue of that Demonolatry which makes all things monstrous and portentous, they are first bidden to exceed their natural limits ; and moreover the matter becomes more intelligible when it is remembered that the chimneys are square and wide in all peasant's cottages, and it is from this class that the vile rabble of sorcery is mostly derived." In his account of the Swedish witches of 1669–1670, who were conveyed to Blockula, the place of the Sabbat, by diabolic agencies, Anthony Horneck says that, " Being asked how they could go with their Bodies through Chimneys and broken panes of Glass, they said, that the Devil did first remove all that might hinder them in their flight, and so they had room enough to go."

During the trial of the Somersetshire witch, Julian Cox, at the Taunton assizes, 1663, a " Witness swore that she had seen *Julian Cox* fly into her own Chamber Window in her full proportion, and that she very well knew her, and was sure it was she."

From these cases it is certain that witches are levitated and carried in this way to the Sabbat. The ointment is actually of no effect *per se*, and the devil can (and often will) transport sorcerers to the Sabbat without any smearing with unguent or lotions. The ointment is employed as a sort of ceremonial subterfuge, since the demon by means of this empty ritual impresses a sense of his own power upon his worshippers, and thus he ministers to his accursed pride. Moreover the ointment is a mockery of the Holy Chrism which is used in certain Sacraments as well as at the Coronation of a King. In the same way the staff or broom is just an empty adjuvant, a common object which the devil causes to be utilized in these mysterious locomotions as a dark and infernal symbol, infusing as it were something of a ritual and liturgical nature into his beastly orgies.

In connexion with, and actually as an argument

against, the levitation and aerial journeys of witches there is often cited a document conveniently known as the Canon Episcopi, which is found in the collections *On Ecclesiastical Discipline*, a manual for the use of the bishop in the course of diocesan visitations, put together by the famous Benedictine Abbot Regino of Prüm about the year 906, but which although doubtless very much older than Regino's own day certainly does not date back to the First orthodox plenary Synod of Ancyra (now Angora, Asia Minor), which was held in 314, and to which body it was rather unaccountably referred by many older commentators and legists.

The text of this much debated and highly debatable section runs as follows : " This too must by no means be passed over that certain utterly abandoned women, turning aside to follow Satan, being seduced by the illusions and phantasmical shows of demons firmly believe and openly profess that in the dead of night they ride upon certain beasts along with the pagan goddess Diana and a countless horde of women, and that in those silent hours they fly over vast tracts of country and obey her as their mistress, whilst on certain other nights they are summoned to do her homage and pay her service." For some reason Burchard added Herodias to Diana, and the two names were maintained in later recensions. The canon continues to say that an immense number of people, deluded by this false opinion, take these things to be very true, and thus fall away from the Christian faith since they are persuaded that something having a divine nature and ineffable power exists other than the one true God. In fine they lapse into paganism.

We must not read more into the Canon Episcopi

than it precisely states. The "abandoned women" whom it so sternly censures are not witches flying to a Sabbat, but poor self-deceived creatures whose guilt consists in honouring, trusting to, obeying, and (so they deem) accompanying as her handmaids a heathen goddess in her nightly coursing through the air. They sin, moreover, in stubbornly maintaining that these evil fantasies and fables, inspired by the Father of Lies, are actual experiences and events. These delusions, no doubt, are very bad and even idolatrous. But there is no sorcery. There has been no pact with Satan. There is no working of Black Magic, no casting of malefic spells, no killing men and cattle.

Bishop Peter Binsfield treats the whole question of the Canon Episcopi at length and clearly shows that it is not aimed at witches and the midnight transvections of sorcerers to the Sabbat, but that quite another sect of deluded women is intended. His arguments are too lengthy to recapitulate here, but they are conclusive.

Later in the seventeenth century when discussing the levitation of witches the learned Jacques D'Autun openly challenged the authority of the Canon Episcopi. He pertinently inquired at what Council of Ancyra was this law laid down ? He quoted the authority of Saint Augustine to show that the historical Councils of Ancyra must be deemed irregular if they are to be regarded as having any higher status than a Synod, and some even lie under the suspicion of Arianism. In any case it was not a General Council of the Church assembled under Papal Authority, and accordingly it could not promulgate a dogma. This Canon has in fact, he concludes, come to serve as a shield for the scoffer and agnostic.

The actual ceremonies of the Sabbat at which the members of the coven have now arrived vary so much (as has indeed already been pointed out) that although the essential features of Satan's synagogue are intrinsically the same at all times and in all countries it is no easy matter to give a general account of assemblies which were marked by such confessed and multitudinous details. This has been commented upon by all the demonologists, and is especially emphasized by De Lancre who made a particular study of the Sabbat as it was held in the South of France at the beginning of the seventeenth century, and who obtained his information at first-hand from the scores of witches he examined.

The liturgy of darkness, indeed, is of its very essence opposed to the comely worship of God, wherein, as the Apostle bids, all things are to be done " decently and in order ".

The Sabbat is always conducted by a President or Chief, who is at the more important and larger meetings the Grand Master of the Satanists, at lesser assemblies the coven-master (who may, of course, be also the Grand Master) or some other official. Not infrequently an intelligence of evil, a demon, assumes corporeal form and presents himself for the adoration of his besotted followers.

The proceedings commence with the ceremonial homage paid to the President by the company, for as the witches told Remy there was always one who was invested with the chief authority on the night of their assembly.

The witches worship him by genuflections and kneeling ; by bowing the body ; by holding up their hands as in prayer; by grotesque and ridiculous gestures; by uttering aloud the most horrid blasphemies and imprecations; by calling upon the demon as god.

When they approach to adore him "Sometimes they bend their knees as suppliants, and sometimes stand with their backs turned, and sometimes kick their legs high up so that their heads are bent back and their chins point to the sky".

At the trial of Louis Gaufridi at Aix in 1611 amplest details concerning this homage were forthcoming. "The hagges and witches, who are people of a sordid and base condition, are the first that come to adore the Prince of the Synagogue, who is Lucifer's lieutenant, and he that now holdeth that place is Lewes Gaufridy," that is to say he was Grand Master of the district. "Next they goe and worship the Divell who is seated in a Throne like a Prince." This shows that not unseldom a demon in corporeal form was present at these Sabbats.

Collette Dumont, a Guernsey witch, confessed that the Sabbat commenced with the adoration of the Devil, and Isebell Le Moigne, a member of the same coven, described how the demon compelled his votaries to go down on their knees before him, adoring him and calling upon him with the words " Our great Master, help us ! "

Mention of the obscene ritual kiss, "the kiss of shame," the gage of fealty, is universal, and it is clear that this ceremony was invariably insisted upon and most scrupulously exacted. Delrio writes how the orgies are governed by a demon, Lord of the Sabbat, who often appears in some monstrous form as a great he-goat with flaming eyes and the whole

company in token of abject submission kiss his funda-
ment. As a sign of completest servitude, remarks
Ludwig Elich, at their meetings the witches kiss the
devil's posterior. Shadwell puts it bluntly enough :
All kiss the Devil's Arse. Upon this he glosses :
" Kissing the Devil's Buttocks is part of the homage
they pay the Devil, as *Bodin* says Doctor *Edlin* did,
a *Sorbon* Doctor." Guillaume Edeline, Prior of St.
Germain-en-Laye, was executed in 1453 as a wizard.
He confessed that he had done homage to Satan who
appeared in the shape of a ram by kissing his buttocks
with great reverence.

In 1393 Walter Langton, Bishop of Coventry and
treasurer of Edward I, was accused of sorcery and
of paying homage to Satan in this way. Amongst other
accusations he was commonly defamed and delated for
the crime of worshipping the Devil by kissing his posterior, and also " it is reported that he hath had frequent
colloquies with evil spirits ". A sentence passed upon
a coven of exceptionally evil and dangerous sorcerers
at Avignon in 1582 details their crimes, when amongst
other charges it is said : " You did worship the
Prince of Devils in deed and word as very God, and
(fie, for very shame !) with the greatest reverence
you did kiss with sacrilegious mouth his most foul and
beastly posterior." When the Sabbat was held at the
haunted church of North Berwick in 1590 the Devil
awaited the arrival of the witches " in the habit or
likeness of a man, and seeing that they tarried over-
long he at their coming enjoined them all to a penance
which was that they should kiss his Buttocks in sign
of duty to him, which being put over the Pulpit bare,
every one did as he had enjoined them ". Another

account has it : " Now efter that the devil had endit his admonitions he cam down out of the pulpit, and caused all the company to come and kiss his ers quhilk they said was cauld lyk yce." A French witch, Jeanne Bosdeau, in 1594, confessed to the Bordeaux judges, how at a rendezvous of more than sixty Satanists at Puy-de-Dôme a black goatish form presided. " They kiss'd his Backside, and pray'd that he would help them." A very rare tract of the fourteenth century tells how the Waldenses in their secret synagogues adored a demon cat, whom they kissed under his tail.

The ceremonial offering and burning of candles at the Sabbat is often met with, and indeed these candles were something more than symbolic and a parody of the candles blessed by the Church since they were required for the very practical purpose of affording light at these midnight rendezvous. Guazzo tells us how the witches of North Italy presented " pitch black candles " to the devil ; and Barthélemy Minguet, a French warlock, in his description of the Sabbat says that when the company went forward to adore their Master all of them were holding a pitch candle of black wax in their hands. These burned with a blue flame on account of the sulphurous material with which they were compounded. At the meeting of the Scotch witches at North Berwick round the pulpit whence the devil addressed his followers were set numbers of black tapers which burned smokily and with a blue light. Old Mother Styles told the Somersetshire magistrates that when she and her sister hags met the Man in Black " he delivers some Wax Candles like little Torches, which they give back again at parting ".

It has already been pointed out that the devil-worshippers are greedy to draw others into the snare, and ever ready by most treacherous and foulest means to proselytize and betray others to their own damnation, activities which commend them mightily in the eyes of their master. When neophytes were received into this horrid society at the Sabbat the performance was conducted with much grotesque ritual and blasphemy. There was the formal pact; the repudiation of all good; the mock baptism with the infernal sponsors; the acceptance of the duties to be engaged in all mischief; the vows of silence and secrecy; the promise to recruit with diligence.

Instructions were also given to the society; death and destruction were plotted; plans were discussed and developed. Thus we find the North Berwick devil (the Grand Master) harangues his covens from the pulpit; the Pendle witches assemble at Malking Tower to contrive the deaths of their enemies; Alice Duke, Ann Bishop, Mother Penny, and the rest of the Somersetshire gang are instructed in the art of moulding wax pictures and transfixing them with thorns and pins; spells were taught orally; sometimes drugs and poisons were confected; the witch midwives learned the practice of abortion and the quality of emmenagogic savin. If these failed they resorted to surer swifter means. A witch who was executed at Dann in Switzerland " confessed that she had killed more than forty children, by sticking a needle through the crown of their heads into their brains, as they came out of the womb." Another witch-midwife of Strassburg said that she had killed more children than she could count.

Not infrequently high politics were the question at these Sabbats, and the more powerful witches strove to decide the fate of countries and the lot of kings. It is undeniable that many of the wars which have convulsed nations, the broils and unrest, the revolutions that trouble and vex the world to-day, are in the first place organized by and energetically assisted by Satanists. For " rebellion is as the sin of witchcraft ".

Lambert Daneau writes that Satan assembles his subjects at these devilish synagogues in order that he may examine them and understand with what diligence and success they have carried out their duties of harm and hurt to man and beast, whom they have injured, and what deaths they have contrived. The witch whose deeds are vilest and most abominable is the most highly honoured and applauded. Those, on the contrary, who have done no evil, are beaten and punished.

Thus Isobel Gowdie, the Scotch witch, gave a very ample account of how the devil or Grand Master tyrannized over the local coven. " He would beat and buffet us very sore," she complained. " We were beaten if we were absent from any gathering, or if we neglected to do anything he had commanded us." When Isebell Le Moigne, the Guernsey witch, on one occasion refused to accompany the familiar to James Gallienne's house, he returned to her in the shape of a man and bruised her severely about the face and head.

Strict discipline was observed among the Vaudois witches of Arras, and when one of the coven, Jean Tacquet, a rich eschevin, was minded to withdraw his allegiance from Satan, the demon forced him to continue it by thrashing him most cruelly with a bull's pizzle. As in the days of Remy, the Satanists even now bind themselves by a solemn oath never to betray their confederates. Any possible treachery to the infernal society constitutes, of course, the gravest offence in their eyes, and the modern Satanists stop at nothing to silence a traitor. To-day many members of these hellish leagues are only prevented from breaking away through fear. It is, as we might expect, a system of terrorism. Death is the penalty for any defection from their ranks, for naturally they are extremely reluctant that any hint of their dark secrets shall be revealed to the world. Nor are those whose aim it is to engineer universal anarchy and red revolution likely to shrink from a mere casual murder.

The business (so to speak) of the Sabbat having been dispatched, there followed the pleasures, which, as may well be supposed, were of the foulest and grossest kind. They mainly consisted in dancing and feasting. Sometimes they dance before eating and sometimes after the repast. The dances are generally performed in a circle and always round to the left, withershins, nor are they graceful and elegant movements, but the most erratic and ungainly caperings, jiggings and leapings, which prove wearisome beyond words, so what is ordinarily a pastime and a source of lawful amusement becomes a labour and a toil. Nor will the demon excuse any from the dance; those who are old and torpid he drives on until perforce they endeavour to stir their limbs, awkwardly and painfully enough, no doubt. So the notorious warlock parson, Mr. Gideon Penman, showed himself particularly active during the Sabbat rites, and " was in the rear in all their dances, and beat up all those that were slow ".

The witches, according to Boguet, dance in a ring back to back, and he adds : " Sometimes too, although seldom, they dance in couples, and then one partner is here, another there, for always everything is higgledy-piggledy, in rank riot and confusion." De Lancre writes of the witches' revels that they "only dance three kinds of brawls. . . . The first is *à la Bohémienne* . . . the second with quick trippings : these are the round dances ". In the third the dancers were placed one behind another in a long straight line. The brawls (French *le bransle*) was an old French dance resembling a cotillion.

In Belgium this witches' dance was known as *Pavana*.

During the Fian trial Agnes Sampson confessed that at North Berwick church above a hundred persons " danced along the *Kirk-yard*, *Geillis Duncan* playing on a Trump [Jew's harp], and *John Fian* mussiled [masked] led the *Ring* ". As they danced, hand in hand, they were all singing with one voice,

> Cummer, go ye before, cummer, go ye,
> Gif ye will not go before, cummer, let me.

" These confessions made the King [James I, then James VI of Scotland] in a wonderful admiration, and he sent for the said Geillis Duncan, who, upon the like trump, did play the said dance before the King's Majesty."

The Capuchin Jacques D'Autun in his encyclopædic' treatise on magic (*The Folly of the Wise and the Wisdom of the Simple*) speaks of sorcerers who gyrate hand in hand in a circle as if inspired by maniac frenzy.

He further remarks that whereas a dance should be distinguished by propriety and decorum, by a certain stateliness or it may be by lively frolic, the dances of witches are uncouth and ugly, extravagant and lewd. Such are the dances of savages, and it is worth remark that among the North American Indians there is but one word to express both dancing and coitus. Meanwhile the whole company are whooping and howling, hissing and yelling, in an access of horrid rage that is akin to an absolute frenzy.

There is evidence that various instruments accompanied the dance. Violins, flutes, tambourines, citterns, hautboys, and in Scotland the pipes made music at the Sabbat. Those of the witches who had any skill were called upon to perform, and very often they obliged the company with favourite airs of a vulgar kind, but the concert always ended in hideous cacophony and bestial clamour. In North Italy the covens were wont to "sing in honour of the devil the most obscene songs to the sound of a bawdy pipe and tabor played by one seated in the fork of a tree". George Sinclar in his *Satan's Invisible World Discovered* says : "A reverend Minister told me, that one who was the Devils Piper, a wizzard confest to him, that at a Ball of dancing, the Foul spirit taught him a Baudy song to sing and play, as it were this night, and ere two days past all the Lads and Lasses of the town were lilting it throw the street. It were abomination to rehearse it." At Tranent in 1659 one man witch and eight women witches confessed that they had merry meetings with Satan, enlivened with music and dancing. John Douglas, the warlock, was the piper, and the two favourite airs of the Grand

Master 'were " Kilt thy coat, Maggie, and come thy way with me ", and " Hulie the bed will fa' ".

At Aix the witches danced " at the sound of Viols and other instruments, which are brought thither by those that were skilled to play upon them ". None the less the sorcerers and hags joined in a kind of howling music with raucous cries imitating song. The Somerset witches of the Wincanton covens said that " The Man in black, sometimes playes on a Pipe or Cittern, and the company dance ".

The music in fine was of many kinds, varying from harmonies " softly sweet, in Lydian measures ", voluptuous and venereal, to the most horrid cacophony resembling the modern jazz, wherein (be it noted) some acute observers have shrewdly scented the devil's own orchestra. Fr. Philip De Ternant, writing in *The Universe*, 18th August, 1933, justly and in good time condemns the " Voodoo Cult imported into our Dance Halls without protest ", and points out how young people are being corrupted by " the roll and the thump of the Voodoo Drum " which " responsive to subtle manipulation not far removed from black magic, plays a most hypnotic part " in the obscene, murderous, and wholly diabolical Voodoo cult. Quite unwittingly, no doubt, to-day many dancers are exercising their steps to the music of the witches. " Dreary pushing and pulling about the floor with almost aimless steps have now taken the place of dancing."

It was not without sound reason that Toussaint l'Ouverture when declaring the independence of Haiti and giving the Island a constitution forbade the Voodoo drum with its syncopation and sub-human appeal. The accursed thing has found a most profligate and tortuous entry in our midst, and unless recognized and sternly checked the poison will infect, rot, and fester, for such is its deliberate and appointed aim.

As the music of the witches, always evil, always unclean, varied in many modes so the feasts and banquetings of the witches were very dissimilar and differed widely both in their meats, their appointments, and also as regards the actual spots where they took place. According to the climate and customs of the country and the seasons of the year the Sabbat with its feast might be held under cover or in the open. Thus, as we should expect, in Italy and in France the Sabbat was frequently celebrated out of doors ; in Guernsey the feast was usually spread on the sea-shore near Rocquaine Castle ; in Sweden the witches met at a " place or house " under a roof ; the Scotch covens assembled for the junketings in outbuildings, farms, in remote and deserted chapels ; in warm weather the Riding Mill witches forgathered at the bridge end and on the moors, in colder seasons at Riding House, in a cellar or a barn ; the Somersetshire witches made their rendezvous at Anne Bishop's cottage, and in the summer on the common hard by the village, or in a clearing of Selwood Forest.

In the etching of the Sabbat orgies by Jan Ziarnko, which illustrates De Lancre's great work (1612), witches and familiars are grouped round a table, and Spranger (1710) presents the Sabbat in very similar detail. In both these the horrid banqueters are seen eagerly devouring the limbs of a roasted babe. An old woodcut (1489) shows three witches seated at a board replenished with food and wine, whilst Guazzo depicts a numerous company at tables duly covered with neat napery and heaped with all sorts of dishes, which are busily served by a retinue of inferior demons. Sometimes, indeed, the cloths appear to have been spread on the ground, picnic fashion.

The accounts of the feast vary from one extreme to the other. The Milanese witches said that " all who have sat down to such tables are bound to allow that the feasts are foul and stinking, so that they nauseate the most ravenously hungry stomach. All sorts of food may be seen, but so vile and dirty and ill-dressed that the plates were not worth eating ". Nicolas Morèle said that the taste was so dry and bad that he was fain spue out the bits he had taken. " Their wine also is black like stale blood, and is given to the company in some filthy sort of drinking horn. There is plenty of everything save only white bread and salt ".

This is all very concisely summed up in the great work of the theological school of the University of Salamanca, usually quoted as " the Salamanca doctors " : " The witches make a meal from food either furnished by themselves or by the Devil. It is sometimes most delicious and delicate, and sometimes a pie baked from babies they have slain, or disinterred corpses. A suitable grace is said before such a table". Thus when Isobel Gowdie, of Auldearne (1662), described the feast of her society which took place in Grangehill she gave fullest details : " The Devil sat at the head of the table, and all the Coven about. That night he desired Alexander Elder in Earlseat to say the grace before meat, which he did ; and is this :—

We eat this meat in the Devil's name,
With sorrow, and sighing, and mickle shame ;
We shall destroy house and hold,
Both sheep and beeves within the fold.
Little good shall come to the fore
Of all the rest of the little store.

And then we began to eat. And when we had ended eating, we looked steadfastly to the Devil, and bowing ourselves to him, we said to the Devil, We thank thee, our Lord, for this." The giving thanks to the Devil at the finish of the banquet appears to be practically a universal custom. Delrio remarks that he had actually seen and read the formulas for the " devil's grace " before and after meat. They were written out on parchment by a sorcerer constant in his attendance at Sabbats. " The grace said at this table is worthy of the infernal crew. In phrases of hideous profanity they acknowledge Beelzebub as the creator and giver and preserver of all the gifts they receive, and in the same strain do they return thanks to the foul spirit when they arise after having eaten and the tables are removed."

It has been already noticed that Ziarnko and Spranger depict the covens as feasting in cannibal fashion on human limbs, and Dominique Isabelle, a witch of Rogeville, confessed to Remy that she had seen and tasted the flesh of babes at the devil's table. At the trial of Louis Gaufridi in 1610 it came to light that the flesh of young children " which they cook and make ready in the Synagogue " was served to the witches. Madeleine Bavent also describes how on a Good Friday " the assembly performed a horrible

MAGIC, GHOSTS AND PHANTOMS
" Magica de Spectris " by Hennig Grösse

mockery of the Last Supper. They brought the body of an infant who had been roasted, and this was eaten by them all ". Sometimes human meat was eaten for magical purposes. The witches were adepts at child-stealing, or if they failed to kidnap they would not hesitate to kill their own infants. The flesh was often seethed in a caldron until it became potable, when it was regarded as a charm of surpassing power. Hence a witch busy at her caldron, confecting these horrible ingredients, so often appears in illustrations, as for example the engraved frontispiece to the rare 1656 edition (often called an Elzevir) of a work on *Magic, Ghosts, and Apparitions of all kinds,* issued by Hennig Grösse, a well-known publisher of Leipzig. Thus the Parisian witches of the Guibourg and La Voisin covens in the days of Louis XIV murdered from first to last literally hundreds of " unwanted " babies at their devilish rites, and were supplying at a high price philtres and potions of these horrible ingredients to a vast number of eager clients. A Moorish sorceress will dig up a newly-buried corpse, set it before her between her legs, and guiding the clay-cold hands stirs with them *cousscouss* (granulated flour steamed over broth) which thus acquires certain magical properties, as a love-charm, or more often when mixed with earth from a grave and certain filthy ingredients becomes the *taam*, or " accursed food ", a slow but certain poison if only but a few grains be swallowed.

Nicolas Remy and very many other authorities emphasize the fact that salt never appears at the witches' table. Bodin says that salt as an emblem of eternity is hateful to the demon ; and a German writer, Philip Ludwig Elich, is most careful to point out that salt is never seen at these evil banquets. It were easy to accumulate a mass of evidence from the witches' confessions in reference to this detail, but it will suffice to observe that in England and Scotland this taboo does not appear, the reason being that in Catholic countries salt is sanctified in solemn sacrament and ceremonial, since the ritual employs two kinds of salt for liturgical purposes, the baptismal salt and the blessed salt exorcized in the preparation of holy water from which devils flee. Salt is blessed again for the use of animals, and in honour of St. Hubert. It is used in the consecration of a church. From the earliest days indeed it has had a sacred and religious character. Protestant England knew nothing of all this.

The food furnished at Sabbats in the British Isles was for the most part seemingly of good quality and satisfying, but seldom of any extraordinary kind. The Forfar coven in 1661 at Mary Rynd's house made themselves merry with strong March ale and brandy. The Auldearne society met at a house where they had beef in plenty, ale and other good drink. The Somersetshire witches who met on Lie Common, " all sate down, a white Cloth being spread on the ground, and did drink Wine, and eat Cakes and Meat." Some ten years later the Riding Mill company were sumptuously regaled with boiled capons, cheeses, butter, flour, beef, bottles of wine and " a variety of meat ". The devil enticed the poorer sort of Swedish witches " by presenting them with Meat and Drink ", and at their rendezvous, Blockula, which was evidently a large country house, they sat down at a very long table whereon were " Broth with Colworts and Bacon in it, Oatmeal, Bread spread with Butter, Milk and Cheese. And they added that sometimes it tasted very well, and sometimes very ill ".

CHAPTER IV

OF THE BLACK MASS; AND OF THE LOVES OF THE INCUBI AND SUCCUBI

They ate the sacrifices of the dead. Yea, they sacrificed their sons and daughters unto devils. Thus were they defiled with their own works, and went a whoring with their own inventions.
Psalm CVI (Douai CV), 28, 37, 39.

It is so rash and foolish to deny the fact of these horrible connexions between the demon and human beings that in order to maintain such a position you must be prepared obstinately to reject and spurn the most weighty and carefully considered judgements of the acutest and liveliest intellects, of Saints and philosophers alike, nay, you must wage open war upon experience and common sense, whilst at the same time you are fatally exposing your ignorance of the power of the devil and the empery evil spirits can obtain over man.
FATHER PETER THYRAEUS, S.J.

" Diabolical Mysticism " includes witchcraft, diabolical possession, and the hideous stories of incubi and succubæ.
DEAN INGE.

The essential feature and climax of the Sabbat orgies was the celebration of the devil's liturgy, the Black Mass. I am of opinion that being present at a Black Mass is to join in the witches' Sabbat, and accordingly the Satanists who perform the Black Mass to-day and all who attend these vile and impious rites are actually holding a Sabbat.

A curious parallel is noted by Dr. Françoise Legey. On the night of the *Achoura*, the tenth day of Ramadan, in order to renew their magic powers, at the bidding of Eblis (the devil) the Moorish sorcerers secretly penetrate into the mosques and pollute the mat of the Imam. They make their ablutions with sour milk and urinate upon the Koran. They also foul the *tafedna*, the reservoirs of warm water in the public baths. They then hold their Sabbat with vile rites in a cemetery.

In 1324 when the Bishop of Ossory was investigating the sorceries of Dame Alice Kyteler of Kilkenny, " in rifling the closet of the ladie, they found a wafer of sacramental bread, having the divels name stamped thereon in stead of Jesus Christ, and a pipe of ointment, wherewith she greased a staffe, upon which she ambled and gallopped through thick and thin." This sacramental bread has been consecrated at a Black Mass, and it was also proved that Dame Alice, a past-mistress of goety, had sacrificed at the cross-ways nine red cocks to her familiar, Robin, son of Art. It may be observed that the sacrifice of a black cock to the demon is not infrequently mentioned in witch-trials.

The Devil's wafer of grotesque shape or impressed with strange characters was often employed by the witches. Gentien le Clerc, condemned at Orleans in 1614, frequented Sabbats, " and he had often seen the devil's priest elevate the host and the chalice, of which both were black." Thomas Boullé and l'abbé Picard were accused by Madeleine Bavent of employing blood-red hosts at their foul celebrations ; in the Mass of St. Sécaire the host is triangular with three sharp points, and black. Similar abominations are usual among the Satanists to-day, so the tradition prevails and Dame Alice Kyteler is closely linked with the twentieth century.

The Neapolitan theologian and legist, Paul Grilland, who wrote on sorcery towards the end of the sixteenth century, describes how unconsecrated wafers are inscribed with letters of blood and amorous devices and thus used at Mass, after which they are crumbled or kneaded into a paste and mingled with food or drink which is given as a love comfit or philtre. One wealthy warlock drew blood from his finger and writing therewith certain obscenities on an altar bread bribed a priest to lay it on the altar-stone under the linen cloths, so that Mass was said over it, with the addition of some secret collects and ceremonies. It may be observed that this practice is not unknown to-day. At Rome there were discovered in a prostitute's house two Hosts inscribed with curious uncials in blood, and these wafers the woman confessed she was going to give secretly to a gallant, beloved by a noble lady, who had furnished the charm. Grilland further discusses in detail the celebrations over unconsecrated breads destined for magical purposes, and also how some interpolate the very Canon of the Mass with lewd and wicked prayers to an evil end. In 1460 at a French trial it came to light that a priest seduced by a witch had actually baptized a toad, fed it with the consecrated Host, and allowed his paramour to use it for the destruction of their personal enemies. The abomination of the Black Mass is performed by some apostate or renegade priest who has abandoned himself to the service of evil and is shamefully prominent amongst the congregation of witches. It should be remarked from this fact that it is plain the witches are as profoundly convinced of the doctrines of Transubstantiation, the Totality, Permanence, and Adorableness of the Eucharistic Christ, as is the most orthodox Catholic. Indeed, unless such were the case, their revolt would be empty and meaningless, void at any rate of its material malice.

Gilles de Sillé of the diocese of St. Malo, and above all the Florentine, Antonio Francesco Prelati, who had been ordained by dispensation at an early age in the Cathedral of Pistoia by the Bishop of Arezzo, served as devil's chaplains to Gilles de Rais, and celebrated black masses in the vaults of the Chapel of St. Vincent at the Château of Tiffauges, when children were sacrificed in scores to the demon.

At Tiffauges to-day from the lonely broken arches of the Chapel one may pass through a cellar door into the crypt below, which dates from the eleventh century. Of no great size and low-sprung the solid roof is transversed by heavy yet not ungraceful semi-circular arches supported by massy pillars whose capitals are relieved with carved lozenges and croziers. The place is gloomy, and but a wan watery daylight seems to filter in, showing the rough broken floor in one corner of which gapes the naked opening of some oubliette or little well, down which no doubt were thrown the dead bodies of the children whom Prelati offered upon the altar-stone.

One can well picture the scene illumined only by two black candles, reeking of bitumen and pitch, and by the faint flicker of the rushlight set upon the ground. The silence is broken but by the hoarse blasphemy of the acolyte as he responds in a low tone to the hurried mutter of the young priest clad in the strange vestments of his infernal cult, the mock chasuble of murrey, the hue of dank clotted gore, marked with the inverse cross. The sacred words of power are spoken with a sneer. The golden chalice is raised in hideous parody ; the keen knife flashes with swift light, a moment more and the fresh blood gushes from the gaping throat of the youth lying fettered there into the sacramental cup, poor blood commingles with the saving Blood of God, and as the film of death closes over the agonizing eyes of his victim the Italian calls aloud upon Apollyon, the prince of darkness, to accept the sacrifice, to manifest himself and show himself gracious unto his faithful worshippers granting their desire.

It was commonly rumoured that Charles IX of France employed an apostate monk to celebrate the eucharist of hell before himself and his intimates. Bodin at any rate describes how he summoned to his presence a condemned sorcerer named Trois-eschelles du Mayne, who was pardoned on condition that he should give the king an ample account of the Sabbat orgies and all the horrid mystery of witchcraft. This the warlock proved very ready to do, and not only vividly painted Satan's bacchanalia in glowing phrase, but had no scruples about naming a large number of those whom he had recognized at these infernal synagogues.

That the assassination of Henri III, the younger brother and successor of Charles IX, was largely the outcome of constant reports which were assiduously circulating throughout the north of France accusing him of Satanism is now fairly well established. The murder of the Cardinal of Lorraine on the 23rd December, 1588, and the subsequent denunciation of the king from a hundred flaming pulpits as a heretic, deposed, excommunicate, had so incensed popular feeling that a' mere mob revolt blazed forth in civil war, but the charges of devil worship determined his death. A contemporary pamphlet of fifteen pages, octavo, published at Paris in 1589 and entitled *The Horrid Sorceries of Henry de Valois, and the Oblations which he offered to the Demon in the Wood of Vincennes. Together with an engraving of the figures of two devils in silver gilt to whom he sacrificed* openly arraigns the monarch's homosexuality and sorceries in terms of sternest condemnation. It is said that in a grove of the forest of Vincennes there were discovered two silver statues of satyrs, curiously gilded, and about four feet high. In his left hand each held a stout club upon which he leaned, in his right was a small bowl of purest shining crystal. Each stood upon a round base, richly wrought, and supported by four feet chased in the baroque fashion. In the crystal bowls were thin grey ashes, as if a handful of unknown herbs or some sort of incense had been burned. What proved more significant than all was that the satyrs had their back turned to a golden cross, some $3\frac{1}{2}$ feet in length, in the midst of which was set a piece of wood, believed to be a Relic of the True Cross.

The enemies of the king created a resounding scandal out of this mysterious discovery, whilst his friends laughed at the whole business, lightly remarking that the two satyrs were nothing more or less than candle-sticks of the antique form. To this it was answered that the figures had no sort of pricket to hold a candle, and the fact that they were placed with their backs to the Holy Cross smelt of sorcery. Nor might this be considered an accidental gesture, since the obscenity of the satyrs betrayed them, and if two tapers should be lit to honour the Relic were not angel-bearers or at any rate plain sconces more appropriate and more decent than lewd heathen goat-men ?

Yet another contemporary pamphlet *A Sharp Remonstrance addressed to Henri de Valois* gives fantastic stories of schools for necromancy being established at the Louvre, of the celebration of Black Masses, of the invocation of demons, and how the King maintained a familiar, named Terragon, to whose embraces he compelled a public prostitute to submit herself. Whether Henri III dabbled in occult arts or no can only be regarded as "not proven", for it must be remembered that the evidence is violently prejudiced and inimical, and it is well known that at the very time these and other equally ribald pasquils were pouring from the press and rabid accusations of black magic filled the air the prominent Leaguers were attempting the king's death by fashioning his image in wax and piercing it to the heart with long pins and bodkins, whilst scarcely a day went by that they did not call to consultation some astrologer to read the heavens' face for the royal doom or some foul diviner to cast the runes.

Pierre De Lancre describes in some detail the Black Mass as it was celebrated by the witch covens of the Pyrenees at the beginning of the seventeenth century. The demon or the Grand Master vests himself in the usual robes to say Mass, which is to say (one supposes) he wears the amice, alb, girdle, stole, maniple and chasuble. The words are spoken with a thousand glib sneers and mocking accents. The altar was erected on four supports, sometimes under a sheltering tree, at others upon a flat rock or some naturally convenient place. No *Confiteor* was said, and *Alleluia* was strictly avoided, but the officiant who held in his hand a book of which he frequently turned the leaves began to mutter in a low voice prayers, epistle and gospel, so that it was hardly in this respect to be distinguished from the Mass itself. At the Offertory he drew back a little from the altar and on occasion seated himself, whilst the assembly approached in order, kissed his left hand and presented each one a candle. When the Queen of the Sabbat—the witch who ranked first after the Grand Master, the oldest and vilest of the crew—was present she sat on the left of the altar and received the offerings, loaves, eggs, any meat or country produce, and money, so long as the coins were not stamped with a cross. In her hand she held a small flat disc or plate, technically known as the " pax " or " pax-brede ". This was engraved with a figure of the demon, which the whole congregation devoutly kissed.

At this point the Grand Master or some warlock appointed for that purpose preached a sermon, haranguing the assembly in a strain of the most rancid blasphemy and inciting them to every crime.

The ceremonies continued, and the Host which was elevated was seen to be round and black, stamped with a figure of the demon in red. The words, *Hoc est enim corpus meum*, were spoken. The chalice was also elevated. The congregation prostrated themselves upon the earth, and with loud clamours adored. A second discourse or sermon was pronounced and then the mock communion followed. All present were given a particle of the Host, and they drank twice of the chalice, a brew so infect, so stinking, so cold that it seemed to freeze the very marrow of their bones. None the less each one was compelled to swallow the nauseous draught however ill they might stomach it.

This description appears to point to some potent drug being mingled in Satan's chalice.

It may be remarked that the use of incense at the Black Mass is very rarely noticed, but Silvain Nevillon, a French witch, spoke of a fume which "smelled abominably foul, not sweet and odorous as is the incense burned in churches". At the modern Black Mass the rough tang of acrid herbs often fills the air, for the Satanists to-day during their hellish liturgy burn in braziers, chafing-dishes and thuribles rue, henbane, deadly nightshade, lumps of resin and rotting leaves, a smoke and stench which, as one of the gang declared, " is fragrant and grateful to the nostrils of our Master." Boguet speaks of the Black Mass as sung by a priest vested in an old and dirty black cope with no cross on it. " And to make Holy Water the Devil urinates in a hole in the ground, and the worshippers are sprinkled with his filthy stale by the celebrant who has a black asperge."

When Louis Gaufridi, the wizard-priest of Accoules (Marseilles) was brought to trial in February, 1611, a tale of almost unheard-of abomination was ripped open, and Madeleine de la Palud described in amplest detail the countless Sabbats she had attended, where Lucifer's lieutenant, the Prince of the Synagogue (in effect Gaufridi himself), was worshipped with divine honours. The Black Mass was said in Satan's name, either by Gaufridi or by some other miserable wretch, when " the Host was really and truly consecrated and offered to the demon ", whilst the Precious Blood was sprinkled from the chalice over the vile crew who shouted and yelled : " His Blood be on us, and on our children ! "

Horrible as is the story of Madeleine de la Palud it may be paralleled, and is indeed exceeded, by the narrative of Madeleine Bavent, a Franciscan sister of the Third Order, attached to the convent of St. Louis and St. Elizabeth at Louviers, a little old-world Norman town some twenty-six miles from Rouen.

Mathurin Picard, the evil chaplain of the community, a warlock deeply versed in black magic, was wont to celebrate the infernal eucharist in a midnight vault. Around the altar in this den of devils were set great candelabra, and these alone gave the required light. Mass from the " Book of Blasphemy " was said by Picard, by his assistant Thomas Boullé, and by other wizard-priests who often brought with them Hosts and chalices to be fearfully defiled by the coven. The Host used at these celebrations is described as resembling the usual Altar Bread, but of a slightly reddish hue. At the elevation the whole gang shrieked out the vilest profanities. It was customary for all present to communicate at the eucharist of hell. " Every action I saw performed at the Sabbat," says Madeleine Bavent, " was indescribably loathsome."

In addition to the Black Mass other rites took place —processions, renunciations, liturgical cursings and maledictions, the stabbing and lancing with knives of consecrated Hosts, the throttling of little babes who were sacrificed to the demon. On one Good Friday a woman brought her new-born infant to the Sabbat, and it was decided the child should be crucified, which was done under conditions of peculiar horror. Part of the bleeding body was employed to confect their charms, and the rest they buried.

During the reign of Louis XIV a veritable epidemic

of sacrilege seemed to rage through Paris, and indeed the investigations conducted by the Lieutenant of Police, Gabriel-Nicolas de la Reynie, let loose such an avalanche of scandal and crime implicating not only persons of low degree but the highest and most powerful names in France that at the last the King in his absolute authority was of necessity compelled to quash the whole business. Poisons had been brewed, Black Masses said, necromancy practised, abortions procured, murders contrived, plots laid for the death of court favourite and political foe, and all these abominations seemed to centre round two figures of the blackest underworld of Paris, the abbé Guibourg and La Voisin.

Catherine Montvoisin—La Voisin as she was commonly called—had long been known to the criminal and the curious as midwife, poisoner, bawd and witch. There was no infamy which might not be purchased in the secret chambers of her house, No. 25 Rue Beauregard. She was assisted in the many branches of her mysterious and obscene profession by numerous satellites and lovers, chief amongst whom Romani, a handsome young Italian boy and an actor of great talent, filled many a curious rôle. The two executioners of Paris, M. Guillaume and M. Larivière, contended for her favours, gallants who could bring her fine presents of the limbs and fat of murderers who had swung on the gibbet or been broken on the wheel, whence she made tall black tapers for her secret ceremonies. A wanton hermaphrodite, exotic and perverse, La Trianon dwelt in that awful house, to which also daily resorted some curious old women, whose calling no one rightly knew, La Gallet,

La Lepère, La Joly, La Filastre, La Bosse, La Thomas. As a matter of fact they were one and all, and a score beside, adepts in the art of poisoning and abortionists of no mean skill and practice. A wit called 25 Rue Beauregard " the centre of the city ", and it is no exaggeration to say that all Paris from duchess to drab, from marshal to muckman, crowded La Voisin's doors.

The Abbé Guibourg, known among the witches as M. le Prieur, the illegitimate son of Henri de Mont-morency, was a man of some seventy years, who is described as tall and heavy-limbed with a malign and sensual face. " He can be compared with no one else," wrote de la Reynie, " for the tale of his poisonings, and his traffic in drugs and witchcraft. He is familiar with every form of villainy, guilty of a large number of horrible crimes and suspected of complicity in many more." It was M. le Prieur who celebrated innumer-able Satanic Masses at the instance of Madame de Montespan in order to secure for her supreme power and the eternal fidelity of the King. Even before Louis had separated from de La Vallière the vicar of St.-Séverin, the Abbé Mariette, had been reciting erotic charms over the hearts of two pigeons consecrated during Mass in the names of Louis de Bourbon and Athénais de Montespan, and apparently the spell had succeeded. But Louis was fickle and apt to be pro-miscuous in his amours, so his love must be fixed on her alone and the aid of the Abbé Guibourg was requested. In the chapel of the Château de Villebousin near Montlhéry, at Saint-Denis, a long black velvet pall was spread over the altar, and upon this the royal mistress laid herself in a state of perfect nudity. Six black candles were lit, the celebrant robed himself in a chasuble thickly embroidered with esoteric characters wrought in silver, the gold paten and chalice were placed upon the naked belly of the living altar to whose warm flesh the horrible old priest pressed his bloated lips each time the rubrics directed him to kiss the place of sacrifice. All was hushed save for the low monotonous murmur of the blasphemous liturgy. The Host was consecrated, and then the Precious Blood. An assistant crept forward bearing an infant in her arms. The child was held over the altar, a sharp swift gash across the neck, a stifled cry, and warm red drops fell into the chalice whilst the full tide streamed upon the white figure beneath. The corpse was handed to La Voisin, who flung it callously into an oven fashioned for that purpose, which glowed white-hot.

It was proved that a regular traffic had been carried on for years with beggar-women and the lowest prostitutes, who sold their children for this purpose. At her trial La Voisin confessed that no less than 2,500 babies had been disposed of in this manner, for the Black Mass was continually being celebrated not only by Guibourg but by other priests. The figures are so startling that some incredulity has been expressed by those who do not know the Paris of Louis XIV, but there appears no reason to doubt the sum. We may bear in mind that a whole pack of venal and utterly unscrupulous midwives was actively at work ; that when the impostume of filth and crime was ripe to bursting no less than 319 warrants were issued, whilst there were very many more whose names were suppressed so deeply did they implicate the highest in the land, nay, the very Throne itself ; that six and thirty witches, poisoners and abortionists were executed ; that 147, Guibourg, Lesage, Romani, De Vanens, and others were sentenced to close confinement in the remotest fortresses ; that many, such as the magician Blessis, went to the galleys for life ; and many, again, were conducted by the police over the frontier, condemned to perpetual exile. Several persons died in prison, and others again (of noble and unblemished lineage) committed suicide in agonies of shame lest they should be involved, however remotely, or even as witnesses, in such scandalous and abominable proceedings.

Perhaps the most sad circumstance that came to light during the investigation of these orgies of witchcraft was the large number of priests concerned. Not to mention the mere panders and poisoners—and Éliphas Lévi says that Black Magic is " above all the science of poisoning "—amongst those who habitually celebrated the Black Mass were the Abbé Brigallier, almoner to Mlle de Montpensier, who married the Duc de Lauzun ; the Abbé Cotton who offered in sacrifice to Satan a child baptized with Holy Oils used in the Sacrament of Extreme Unction, and then strangled, and whose speciality was " La Messe du Saint Esprit ", which is said over a piece of goat's skin sprinkled with holy water and which is intended to cure certain illnesses, to induce love or hate, even to conjure up the demon, all of which Dr. Jean-Baptiste Thiers in his great work denounces as a most pestilent superstition, nay, more, he roundly condemns this practice as a " Witch's Mass ", and profane in the highest degree ; the Abbé Davot, assistant priest at Notre Dame de Bonne-Nouvelle only a few doors from La Voisin's house, whose custom it was to lay under the corporal at Mass a piece of paper inscribed with the name of the person who should be brought to love, or if hated, damned to die, a practice eagerly pursued to-day—if a priest may be found ; the Abbé Deshayes, who demanded exorbitant fees for his Black Masses and who was also a most skilful coiner ; Father Gabriel, a Capuchin, who with the Abbé Seysson, was wont to say Masses at La Voisin's house over women's after-births and children's cauls to confect charms of particular potency ; the Abbé Lepreux, a school-master, deep in the most shameful court secrets, who dedicated infants to the demon, and consecrated snakes and toads to mingle with poisons for their greater efficacy ; the Abbé Mabile, who celebrated the sacrifice of the Death's Head ; the Abbé Maléscot, who had entered into a sort of partnership with the witch and abortionist, La Gallet, for whom he touted with very considerable success ; the Abbé Mariette, who whilst still young had been banished from Paris for his sorceries (it is clear that he was only saved from the stake owing to family interest, for he was of a wealthy and good house), but who returned almost openly to place himself at the service of Madame de Montespan ; the Abbé Olivier, who consecrated an altar for Black Masses in a brothel ; the Abbé Rebours, who said Black Masses on the body of his mistress ; the Abbé Tournet, who said Masses in order to kill the child in the womb, and who was in great request among the evil sisterhood. This catalogue of a dozen wizard-priests drawn from the archives of the Bastille could easily be multiplied four or five times. There was also Jean-Baptiste Sébault, of the diocese of Bourges, who whilst lodging in Paris at the house of a doctor, named

Charmillon, seduced Marianne Charmillon, a girl of twenty-two, his host's daughter, and continually brought her to the Black Mass. The Abbé Guignard celebrated a Satanic Mass in a cellar over her body, and was served by Sébault in a state of complete nudity. An aphrodisiac was brewed at this orgy. The Abbé Lemaignan sacrificed young children, and possessed whole sets of rich vestments in which to celebrate the eucharist of hell.

It is only too much to be feared that the evil science of Guibourg and his company was handed down throughout the eighteenth century. The Duc de Richelieu, who was born in 1696 and died at the age of ninety-two in 1788, was much suspected of studying goety and the worst kinds of occult science. It was said that whilst quite a young man he had formed too close an intimacy with an Austrian noble whose tastes lay in the same direction, and whose wealth enabled him to purchase the secrets of those who had known the Abbé Guibourg and had been instructed by him in every dark secret of magic. Two Capuchins, who were his chaplains, celebrated Black Masses, at which the devotees assisted, in the old deserted chapel of a lone country-house. After this the Duke and his friend defiled the Hosts, in the hope that thereon Satan would appear to crown and reward their blasphemy.

Under the Regency, necromancers and wizards and traffickers in Satanic eucharists abounded, for Philippe d'Orléans was notoriously addicted to occultism of every kind. As might be expected there are revolting pictures of the Black Mass in the lewd pages of de Sade. In *Justine* such a Mass celebrated in a cloister is described in filthy detail. When Juliette is initiated into the " Society of the Friends of Crime " the Host and Crucifix are desecrated. Again, a little later, two Satanic orgies are exhibited, when the High Altar is the scene of every defilement. There are other and even more obscene descriptions of the Black Mass in the work, but these it is unnecessary to particularize.

Upon the night of the execution of King Louis XVI, 21st January, 1793, a number of French devil-worshippers formed themselves into a definite society to foster revolution and propagate their cult of evil. The third chief of this organization died at Florence about 1905. He was believed to be nearly a hundred years old. This particular Society of Satanists spread very rapidly into Italy and soon penetrated Germany. A little later it had established itself very secretly in England, and there can be no question that it has proved one of the most potent forces for evil since its very inception. It has developed and flourished exceedingly and flung out its poisonous tentacles in all directions. It would be no exaggeration to say that much of the world's misery and unrest is due to this foul conspiracy against God and humanity.

Nowhere in France during the first half of the nine-teenth century was religious life more fervent and more zealous than throughout the diocese of Agen. Under such saintly Bishops as de Bonnac (the first to refuse the constitutional oath of 1792), and Jean Aimé de Levezon de Vezins pious associations, communities and confraternities were warmly encouraged, not the least of these devout fellowships being the Children of Mary founded by Adèle de Trenquelléon and the widow of a physician, Madame Belloc. This latter

THE WITCHES' SYNAGOGUE
Goya

lady employed a housekeeper, Virginie (whose surname curiously has not been recorded), and to her horror this woman one day revealed to her pious mistress that she was a Satanist of long continuance, the member of an infernal society which had its headquarters under the very shadow of St. Caprasius, the pro-cathedral. Virginie stated that when about twelve years old she had been taken to a house in the city were was an altar dedicated to the devil, at which an aged priest celebrated a Mass of blasphemy during which there occurred a fearful manifestation of corporeal evil. Moreover she was taught that each Communion she must retain the Host in her mouth, and then eject it secretly so that she might bring it to the midnight Sabbats to be horribly profaned by the impious crew, whose necromancies and conjurations were of the vilest and most abominable description. Madame Belloc hastened to call in the assistance of the Abbé Degans, to whom Virginie confessed that she would sometimes attend as many as five or six early Masses in different churches to obtain the Host. Upon her resolution to repent she fell a prey to an unclean spirit which the Abbé Degans expelled with difficulty and after many exorcisms. One curious feature of the case was the continual apports of Hosts, many of which were marked with bloody characters. Much scandal ensued, and an ecclesiastical inquiry followed. Many suspicious circumstances came to light concerning Virginie when she formed a connexion with the pseudo-prophet Eugène Vintras and his followers, in whose private chapel at Tilly-sur-Seulles (as one of the sect, Gozzoli, quite unequivocally testified) the most horrible obscenities were practised during the celebration of sacrilegious eucharists. It is significant that in 1845 Vintras came to England and established himself in London as the Master of a dark and evil cult which has never died.

Virginie declared that the Grand Master of the Agen Satanists became truly penitent, and made his peace with Heaven. There can be little doubt, however, that many of the latter statements she made were untrue. It is probable that after her first revelations the Satanists so threatened and terrified her that she lied freely to conceal their identities and their rendezvous. That their chapel was never discovered is no occasion for surprise. They very well know how to cover their tracks.

About the same time 1830–1850 a band of devil worshippers were carrying on their foul witchcrafts at Bordeaux, and numberless Hosts were stolen from the churches, especially from Saint-André and Sainte-Eulalie. In 1852 there burst forth a resounding scandal owing to the celebration of Black Masses in Paris by a band of most impious and malevolent Satanists.

To retail the sacrilege of Black Masses down the years would be weary repetition. Suffice that Satanism in every country yet has its votaries and is extensively practised. It is a matter of notoriety that in 1924 two ciboria, containing 100 consecrated Hosts, were carried off by an old woman from Notre Dame in circumstances which clearly indicated that the holy vessels were not the objects of the larceny. In 1895 a particularly revolting instance of defilement of the Host occurred in the Island of Mauritius. Rome, Salerno, Naples, Florence, Lyons, London, York,

Brighton, Brussels, Bruges, and many other towns have all suffered from these abominations. In more than one quarter of London—on the northern heights, in a south-west suburb, in the East End, in the City, by the riverside—have the Satanists made a den, a chapel and altar to the demon they worship with rites of the most horrid lewdness and impiety.

It is very well known that the terrible picture of the black mass drawn by Jorris Karl Huysmans in his masterpiece *Là-Bas* (1891) is true in every detail, and all the characters are taken from life, and have indeed been precisely identified. Thus Madame Chantelouve is (in large part at least) Madame Berthe Courrière, and Docre is named by Mons. Léon Deffoux and other authorities as l'abbé Roca, although Mons. Pierre Dufay, whose opinion carries weight, argues that he is rather Canon Van Ecke (or Van Arche), sometime a chaplain of the sanctuary of the Precious Blood at Bruges.

That extraordinary and erratic visionary the Abbé J.-A. Boullan in a letter to Huysmans, dated 10th February, 1890, says : "Amongst ecclesiastics Satanism is more widely practised and ardently pursued than even in the Middle Ages. It is to be found at Rome ; and above all at Paris, Lyons, and Châlons, so far as France is concerned ; in Belgium Bruges is their headquarters." Perhaps it should not be forgotten that the orthodoxy of Boullan himself was more than suspect, and whilst there was much open gossip of strange masses by which evil charms and enchantments were dissolved,—the Eucharist of Glory,—there were also darker hints which pointed to plain Satanism. Boullan asserted that he employed White Magic ;

his opponents—and he had many enemies—declared that he was an adept in Black Magic.

In May, 1895, when the legal representatives of the Borghese family visited the Palazzo Borghese, which had been rented for some time in separate floors or suites, they found some difficulty in obtaining admission to certain apartments on the first floor, the occupant of which seemed unaware that the lease was about to expire. By virtue of the terms of the agreement, however, he was obliged to allow them to inspect the premises to see if any structural repairs or alterations were necessary, as Prince Scipione Borghese, who was about to be married, intended immediately to take up his residence in the ancestral home with his bride. One door the tenant obstinately refused to unlock, and when pressed he betrayed the greatest confusion. The agents finally pointed out that they were within their rights to employ actual force, and that if access was longer denied they would not hesitate to do so forthwith. When the keys had been produced, the cause of the reluctance was soon plain. The room within was inscribed with the words *Templum Palladicum.* The walls were hung all round from ceiling to floor with heavy curtains of silk damask, scarlet and black, excluding the light ; at the further end there stretched a large tapestry upon which was woven in more than life-size a figure of Lucifer, colossal, triumphant, dominating the whole. Exactly beneath an altar had been built, amply furnished for the liturgy of hell ; candles, vessels, rituals, missal, nothing was lacking. Cushioned prie-dieus and luxurious chairs, crimson and gold, were set in order for the assistants ; the chamber being lit by electricity, fantastically arrayed so as to glare from an enormous human eye. The visitors soon quitted the accursed spot, the scene of devil-worship and blasphemy, nor had they any desire more nearly to examine the appointments of this infernal chapel.

A writer of authority has said : " Turning to English accounts, little or nothing of the Black Mass is to be traced," and we find this echoed more than once. The point of the matter lies here. In 1559 Queen Elizabeth initiated her religious settlement by the enactment of Penal Laws, which in a very few years were greatly increased in severity, and since the Act of Uniformity of this year was designed to compel the use of the Anglican Book of Common Prayer it punished by deprivation and imprisonment all clerics who followed any other service. A little later the Mass was prohibited, and in effect the punishment for saying Mass was death. Even in the reign of George III, in 1767, upon the delation of a common informer, the Rev. Mr. Maloney was tried at Croydon for having said Mass and condemned to perpetual imprisonment, but after three or four years the Government commuted the sentence to perpetual banishment. In 1769 the Hon. James Talbot, a brother of the fourteenth Earl of Shrewsbury, and Bishop of Birtha, was tried for his life at the Old Bailey and only escaped owing to a conflict of evidence as the informers obviously did not know what a Mass was and it was urged that the Bishop might have been conducting some other service. The famous . Lord Mansfield utilized every technicality and loophole (not to say quibble) of the law to prevent the conviction of priests accused of saying Mass. One point he was wont to urge turned on the fact that the Protestant informers could not be aware in what a Mass consisted and that even if a man were in vestments at an altar using certain ceremonies this might not be the Mass. At any rate it is clear that in Protestant England the Mass had no place, although in certain villages the tradition of the sanctity of the Sacrifice and its mysterious power lingered until the very time of the Oxford Movement. It can, however, be clearly shown, both in England and in Scotland, that the witches celebrated a mock-sacrament.

Before the upheaval under Henry VIII the Black Mass was certainly known in the British Isles. In the twelfth century Gerald de Barry laments those wizard-priests who corrupt the very Sacrament of the Altar to black magic by celebrating Masses over wax images in order to lay a spell on some person, as also others who sing a Solemn Requiem ten times and apply it to some living man that he may die on the tenth day or very soon after, and go down to the tomb. In 1286 an apostate monk, a Cistercian of Rievaulx Abbey, Godfrey Darel, was commonly defamed as a celebrant of Black Masses, and reported to the Archbishop of York.

There is very definite evidence for a mock-sacrament in Scotland as late as the end of the seventeenth century. In August, 1678, the devil convened " a great meeting of witches in Lothian ", where amongst others appeared a hideous figure who had once been admitted to the ministry, and had served the parish of Crichton, about six miles from Dalkeith. This warlock parson, Mr. Gideon Penman, was of notoriously evil life and stood in high favour with the devil who spoke of him as " Mr. Gideon, my chaplain ". He had turned under the devil a preacher of hellish sermons, for he was reputed very eloquent in the pulpit. In mockery of Christ and His holy ordinance of the Sacrament of His Supper, the devil gave a sacrament to the witches, bidding them eat it, and to drink in remembrance of himself. The villain, Penman, used very readily to assist Satan in these ceremonies, and in preaching. Lord Fountainhall, the famous Scottish lawyer (who was incidentally an extreme Protestant), when describing the same assembly of witches says that the Devil " adventured to give them the communion or holy sacrament, the bread was like wafers, the drink was sometimes blood, sometimes black moss-water. He preached, and most blasphemously ".

In New England we find the same tradition of what may be termed the Protestant equivalent of a black mass. The Rev. George Burroughs, a pastor at Wells, Maine, and Grand Master of the coven, preached to the witches at their meetings, " and there they had a Sacrament " with a woman, Martha Carrier, as Deacon. One member of the gang confessed how " the Witches had a *Sacrament* that day at an house in the Village, and they had *Red Bread* and *Red Drink* ". According to Madeleine Bavent the Host at the Mass of blasphemies was red, and there are many references to the Red Drink in the chalice with which the Abbé Guibourg even mingled blood. At Salem the traditional rites of this foul travesty of worship were strictly observed, and these practices must have been carefully handed down and exactly taught to the New England representatives of the witch society.

During the reign of George I the riots of the " Hell-Fire Clubs ", which were simply Sabbats of Satanists, had grown to such a height that in 1721 a proclamation was issued for the suppression of " certain scandalous Clubs or Societies of young persons who meet together, and in the most impious and blasphemous manner insult the most sacred principles of our Holy Religion, affront Almighty God Himself, and corrupt the minds and morals of one another ". The inquiry was strict, and for a time these Clubs or covens were driven underground. Generally they met in the lowest taverns, where the Satanists of to-day are often wont to forgather to celebrate the Black Mass.

In 1745 the well-known wit, George Selwyn, was sent down from Oxford for celebrating (or at least participating in—the details are not clear) a mock-communion. A terrific scandal ensued, which Selwyn's friend attempted to meet by swearing that the whole business was but a drunken orgy. It is pretty plain, however, that there was a good more in it than that, and the fact that we find Selwyn enrolled a member of the " Monks of Medmenham " is doubly significant.

Medmenham Abbey a Cistercian foundation, is near Marlow, Bucks, on the banks of the River Thames. It was occupied by a notorious profligate, Sir Francis Dashwood, who having converted it into a most luxurious retreat, built or restored a chapel on the model he had seen of the monasteries in France and Italy, and in 1732 here inaugurated " the Order of St. Francis ", so dubbed after his own name, also termed " the Franciscans " or " the Franciscan Monks ". (It may be remarked that there is an inexactitude here. A Franciscan is a friar, and cannot be a monk.) It seems that only later was this Society known as the " Hell-Fire Club ". The original number of members, besides the Superior, was twelve—a witch's coven, and each was baptized with the name of an apostle. It is hardly necessary to give the list in full, more especially as from time to time the numbers varied, but many of the " Order " were in their day famous and influential names, as for example John Wilkes, Charles Churchill, Paul Whitehead, Robert Lloyd, the Earl of Sandwich, George Bubb-Dodington, and Selwyn. A certain young Sir John d'Aubrey also attended the secret meetings. The " monks " or rather Satanists met twice a year for the space of a week. " The cellars were stored with the choicest wines; the larders with the delicacies of every climate ; and the *cells* were fitted up, for all the purposes of lasciviousness, for which proper objects were also provided."

There were novices, whose probationary office " was to attend upon their superiours in the celebration of their mysteries, which were all performed in the chapel of the monastery, when no other servants were ever permitted to enter, on the most common occasion, as the very *decorations* of it would in a great measure have betrayed their secrets ". The various members of this company were bound to secrecy by oaths and imprecations, since " so outrageous an insult upon the laws was liable to punishment from the secular power ".

The initiate clad in a robe of white linen was led to the Chapel at the tolling of a bell, and when at his knock the door opened to the sound of soft and solemn music he had to advance to the communion rails and there make a profession of his principles " nearly in the words, but with the most gross perversion of the sense of the articles of faith of the religion established in the country ". The brotherhood knelt round the altar whilst the superior repeated a prayer in the same strain and manner with the *profession* of the candidate *to the Being whom they served.* The novice was elected with mimic ceremonial, and next in a manner not proper to be described, followed their eucharist, every most sacred rite and observance of Religion being profaned, and all the prayers and hymns of praise appointed for the worship of the Deity burlesqued by a perversion to the horrid occasion.

Little wonder that " a formal story was propagated over the whole country, that the end of their meeting was to worship the Devil, to whom this chapel was dedicated, and who had *often* been seen among them, in variety of shapes ".

The truth had leaked out, for it is plain from this contemporary account that the Monks of Medmenham were Satanists, who at their Sabbats carried on and perpetuated the foul and blasphemous traditions of the witch.

I have been quoting from Charles Johnstone's key-novel " *Chrysal* : or the Adventures of a Guinea, wherein are exhibited Views of several striking Scenes with Curious and interesting Anecdotes, of the most Noted Persons in every Rank of Life, whose Hands it passed through, in America, England, Holland, Germany, and Portugal ", 1760–65. Johnstone in this remarkable book has painted contemporary life with unflinching exactness, and it is certain that either in some way he managed to be present at the mysteries of Medmenham, or else he gained most detailed information from one of the members of that horrid society.

About the middle of the eighteenth century, on the borderland of Germany and the Low Countries, the devil-worshippers joined themselves into a body, a vast secret organization called " Buxen ". This grew to be a most formidable gang, terrorizing the whole of the Limburg district and the province of Treves, until a state of appalling anarchy ensued. The custom of the Buxen was to meet after nightfall in some lonely spot and to commence proceedings by the celebration of the Black Mass when Hosts, stolen from the tabernacle were foully desecrated. This was the time for the initiation of recruits. It is said that their obscene ceremonies were generally conducted in one of three ruined sanctuaries, the church of St. Rose near Sittardt, the oratory of St. Leonard hard by Roldyck, and a haunted chapel at Oermond on the Meuse. Afterwards, hideously masqued and disguised, they sallied forth—sometimes to the number of two or three hundred—and raided farms, small holdings, country houses, even attacking villages. If they passed a church on the way they invariably burst open the doors, robbed the tabernacle, and gutted the whole building leaving it in flames. A veritable reign of terror ruled, for so carefully was the secret of membership guarded that no man knew whether his neighbour, nay, his brother or his son might not be a Bux. Any attempt at resistance, any suspicion of treachery, met with the most terrible reprisals. The society was only broken up and crushed after the sternest measures had been taken, a permanent gallows being set up in many places, and some hamlets having two gibbets apiece. Leopold Leeuwerk, dubbed their chaplain, a Satanist who had offered hundreds of Black Masses to the demon, was caught at last, whilst another of their leaders was hanged in 1772 on the moor of Graed, and a few years later the Buxen had come to an end.

Closely connected with the Black Mass of the Satanists and a plain survival from the Middle Ages is that grim superstition of the Gascon peasant, the Mass of St. Sécaire. Few priests know the awful ritual, and of those who are learned in such dark lore fewer yet would dare to perform the monstrous ceremonies and utter the prayer of blasphemy. No confessor, no bishop, not even the Archbishop of Auch, may shrive the celebrant; he can only be absolved at Rome by the Holy Father himself. The Mass is said upon a broken and desecrated altar in some ruined or deserted church where owls hoot and mope and bats flit through the crumbling windows, where toads spit their venom upon the sacred stone. The priest must make his way thither late attended only by an acolyte of impure and evil life. At the first stroke of eleven he begins; the liturgy of hell is mumbled backward, the canon said with a mow and a sneer; he ends just as midnight tolls. The Host is triangular, with three sharp points and black. No wine is consecrated but foul brackish water drawn from a well wherein has been cast the body of an unbaptized babe. The holy sign of the cross is made with the left foot upon the ground. And the man for whom that mass is said will slowly pine away, nor doctor's skill nor physic will avail him aught, but he will suffer, and dwindle, and surely drop into the grave.

When the blasphemous liturgy of the Sabbat was done all present gave themselves up to the most promiscuous debauchery without respect of age, dignity, relationship, or sex. There is no obscenity, says Boguet, which is not practised and eagerly pursued in these assemblies. It is true that the sworn confessions of such witches as Madeleine de la Palud and Madeleine Bavent reveal a veritable abysm of turpitude. Gentien le Clerc, a young Satanist of Orleans, whose mother presented him to the devil when he was but three years old, related how he had assisted at innumerable Sabbats held in a meadow near, or sometimes even in the very market square of Olivet, a village on the left bank of the Loiret, about two and a half miles from Orleans.

The ceremony commenced with an asperges of filthy water or even urine. After this the Devil (the Grand Master) celebrated the Mass. He wore a chasuble of the usual form but embroidered with a broken cross, and after he had elevated the Host and the Chalice, both of which were black, he turned his back to the altar in contempt, as is done in the Satanists' liturgy to-day. The infamous Marie de Sains spoke of a diabolical litany, which commenced—

Lucifer, miserere nobis,
Belzebuth, miserere nobis.

The Mass was read from a great book, which seemed to have scarlet letters on the white vellum, and some pages of which appeared all black. It had a rough, furry cover as though made of a wild beast's pelt. The pax was given in the accustomed place, but all present kissed some obscene or grotesque object. After this was done, Gentien avowed that the worshippers, one and all, abandoned themselves to a very riot of lust and spintrian pollutions. To accumulate details were superfluous. The same story is told throughout the centuries. In *Chrysal* Johnstone writes how the Monks of Mendenham after their mock communion service sat down to a banquet " at which nothing that the most refined luxury, the most lascivious imagination could suggest to kindle loose desire, and provoke and gratify appetite was wanting both the superiours and the inferiours vying with each other in loose songs and dissertations of such gross lewdness, and daring impiety, as despair may be supposed to dictate to the damn'd ". To-day the meetings of Satanists invariably end in unspeakable orgies of filth and the most hideous debauchery.

The learned authors of the *Malleus Maleficarum* write at length " *Concerning Witches who copulate with Devils* ", and it is obvious that there is no question here of animal familiars, but rather of evil intelligences who are, it is believed, able to assume a body of flesh. As Saint Augustine says, it is beyond all doubt proven that certain devils do continually practise this uncleanness, and tempt others to it, which is affirmed by such grave persons and with such confidence that it were impudence to deny it. A whole catena of authorities from the earliest times until the present day might be cited, but the matter may be summed up as by Delrio who writes : " So many sound authors and theologians have upheld this belief that to differ from them is mere obstinacy and foolhardiness ; for the Saints, the Fathers and Doctors, and all the wisest writers on philosophy agree upon this matter, the truth of which is furthermore proved by the experience of all ages and people."

Above all sounds the solemn thunder of the Bull of Innocent VIII announcing in no ambiguous phrase :

" It has indeed come to our knowledge and deeply grieved are we to hear it that many persons of both sexes, utterly forgetful of their souls' salvation and straying far from the Catholic Faith have (had commerce) with evil spirits, both incubi and succubi."

The incubus (the word derives from post-classical Latin and literally means *one who lies upon* anything) is the demon who assumes a male form, the succubus or succuba (from late Latin, literally meaning *one who lies under* anything, a harlot) is the demon when assuming a female form, and the famous Dominican Charles Réné Billuart in his *Treatise upon the Angelic Hosts* explicitly informs us : " The same evil spirit may serve as a succubus to a man, and as an incubus to a woman."

Commenting upon the passage in the Book of Genesis (vi, 4), " the sons of God came in unto the daughters of men, and they bare children to them," Pope Benedict XIV explains : " This passage has reference to those Demons who are known as incubi and succubi."

Dom Dominic Schram, a celebrated Benedictine theologian, emphatically lays down : " It is certain that—whatever doubters may say—there exist such demons, incubi and succubi. . . . Wherefore the men or women who suffer these impudicities are sinners who either invite demons . . . or who freely consent to demons when the evil spirits tempt them to commit such abominations."

From these great names, and it were an easy matter to quote a hundred more, it will be seen that the Fathers and Saints, and all scholars and theologians of importance affirm the possibility of commerce with incarnate evil intelligences. The question rises and must be briefly answered how demons or familiars, seeing that they are pure spiritual beings, can not only assume human flesh but thus perform the peculiarly carnal acts of coition and generation.

Following the opinion of Guazzo, who is supported not only by Plato, Philo, Josephus, and other ancient writers, but also by St. Augustine, St. Jerome, and the consensus of all theologians, Lodovico Maria Sinistrari, in his famous treatise *Demoniality* answers that the Demon assumes the corpse of another human being, male or female, as the case may be, or else that from a commixture of other materials he shapes for himself a body endowed with motion by means of which it is possible for the evil spirit to have sexual intercourse with human beings. In this latter instance advantage might be taken, no question, of a person in a mediumistic trance or hypnotic sleep. Jacopo de Voragine relates how once when a priest was sorely tempted by a beautiful woman who entered his chamber in a state of nudity he took his stole and threw it round her neck. With a shriek she fell to the ground, and there lay the rotting corpse of a harlot who had been many days dead.

There is yet another explanation which seems equally possible. Can we not look to the phenomena observed in connexion with ectoplasm as an explanation of this? Again and again in materializing séances physical forms which may be touched and freely handled are built up and presently disintegrate in a few moments of time. In a symposium *Survival* Miss Felicia Scatcher relates certain of her own experiences that go far to prove the partial re-materialization of the dead by the utilizing of the material substance and ectoplasmic emanations of the living. Mr. Godfrey Raupert in his *Modern Spiritism* describes in considerable detail how at these experiments and sittings an entire human form " is fully and immediately ' materialized ', . . . The solidity and life-likeness of these forms would seem to depend very largely upon the sensitive and the sitters. If the conditions are very favourable they may have all the characteristics of real human beings with all the functions of a human body in full working order. The pulse or the heart may be felt to be beating, and the organs of sight or of speech or of hearing to be acting to perfection. . . . The forms have been known to remain materialized for a considerable time, to have apported flowers and other light articles, to have carried on prolonged and interesting conversations, and to have acted in other respects like ordinary human beings, possessing and operating in an ordinary human body ".

Here then we have an ample solution of the activities of the incubi and succubi, and although neither of these explanations precludes the other, I take this latter to be the more general from the fact that the incubus can assume the shape of some person whose embraces the witch may desire. There are many recorded instances of this, and it is alluded to by the dramatist Middleton in his play *The Witch* when Hecate says :—

> What young man can we wish to pleasure us,
> But we enjoy him in an incubus ?

Thus when the young gallant Almachildes visits her abode, she exclaims :—

> 'Tis Almachildes—the fresh blood stirs in me—
> The man that I have lusted to enjoy :
> I've had him thrice in incubus already.

o

That is the early seventeenth century, and at the end of the nineteenth we find that Huysmans in *Là-Bas* introduces the occultist Ledos under the name Gévingey who discusses in some detail the question of incubi and succubi, relating instances which have come under his own knowledge. I do not hesitate to refer to the pages of Huysmans as it is well known that he had deeply studied the whole subject and he has actual documentation for what he relates. The following conversation takes place between Durtal, who is Huysmans himself, and Madame Chantelouve. This demoniacal woman in a scene of closest intimacy cries to her lover : " You must know then that I can possess you when and how I please, in the same way as I have possessed Byron, Baudelaire, Gérard de Nerval, all the men I love . . ." " What can you mean ? " " I tell you that I only have to desire their embrace, a you are longing for me at this moment, and then be ore I fall asleep . . ." " Well, what then ? " " Yo , your real self, will—I know it—prove a mere weakling to the Durtal who visits me at nights, whom I adore, and whose burning kisses drive me mad ! " He looked at her in amaze. Then in a flash he realized the truth of those foul incubus lusts of which Ledos had spoken.

We have seen that the Grand Master of a district often presided over and directed the Sabbat orgies, and then it was he, an apostate priest, who celebrated the Black Mass. Sometimes also the familiar assigned to a new witch was in the first place and under certain conditions a man, one of the assembly, who either approached her in some infernal disguise or else embraced her without any attempt at concealment of his individuality, some lusty varlet who would afterwards minister to her pleasure. For we must bear in mind that throughout these witch-trials there is often much in the evidence which may be explained by the agency of human beings, not that this essentially meliorates their offences, for the whole band of sorcerers are acting under Satanic inspiration and are the slaves of the devil. At the same time too we meet those connexions and other dark businesses which admit of no explanation save that of the materialization of evil intelligences of power. Detailed and full as is the evidence we possess, it frequently becomes a most difficult matter when we are studying a particular case to decide whether it be an instance of a witch having had actual commerce and communion with the fiend, or whether she was herself cheated by devils, who mocked her, and persuading her to deem herself in overt union with them, thus led the wretch on to misery and death, duped as she was by the father of lies, sold for a delusion and by profitless endeavour in evil.

It is probable too that a witch would sometimes be served by an incubus or succubus as the case might be, and sometimes by another member of the coven. There are, doubtless, also many cases which stand on the border-line, half hallucination, half reality.

The confessions of the pupils who were in the charge of Antoinette Bourignon afford extraordinary details of these matters. They " declared that they had daily carnal Cohabitation with the Devil ; that they went to the Sabbaths or Meetings, where they Eat, Drank, Danc'd, and committed other Whoredom and Sensualities ". To repeat the several particular accounts were superfluous. One may suffice for the rest, that of a girl, named Bellot, then aged fifteen. She said that her mother had taken her to a Sabbat whilst she was still very young, "and that being a little Wench, this Man-Devil was then a little Boy too, and grew up as she did, having been always her Love, and Caressed her Day and Night." A young sorcerer from Lorraine, Dominic Petrone, was only twelve years old when his mother enticed him into an abominable marriage of this kind, in which he had much delight.

Remy observes that the demons and witches even simulate marriages, and he records the avowals of sorcerers who had been present at such ceremonies. De Lancre describes how at the Sabbats the Devil performs marriages between warlocks and witches, joining their hands with a sneering benediction. Colette Fischer of Mainz acknowledged that it was no unusual thing for witches to wed demons, who (it is related) feign hot jealousy and carefully watch over their spouses. The Rev. John Gaule in his *Select Cases of Conscience touching Witches and Witchcraft*, published in 1646, mentions that the same customs prevailed in England : "Oft times he marries them ere they part, either to himself, or their Familiar, or to one another ; and that by the Book of Common Prayer (as a pretender to Witch finding lately told me in the Audience of Many)." The Capuchin, Jacques D'Autun, writing in 1678, has a chapter upon "The horrid blasphemy and beastliness of these mock-marriages which are celebrated at the witches' Sabbat".

Rebecca West, a witch of Lawford, Essex, and the daughter of a witch, related how the devil came to her " as she was going to bed, and told her, he would marry her, and that she could not deny him ; she said he kissed her, but was as cold as clay, and married her that night ". He promised to be her loving husband, and swore that her enemies were thenceforth his enemies. " Then she promised him to be his obedient wife till death, and to deny God and Christ Jesus." A young sorcerer, Pétrone of Armentières, declared that when he approached a succuba so intensely cold and gelid did she appear that his own limbs seemed frozen and nipped as with arctic snows. Another warlock, Hennezel, acknowledged that he could not accomplish any venereal act with his succuba, Schwartzburg, who was he verily believed hewn from ice. A Suffolk witch, the widow Bush of Barton, said that the Devil, who appeared to her as a dark swarthy youth, " was colder than man." Isobel Gowdie and Janet Breadheid of the Auldearne coven, 1662, both asserted that the Devil was " a meikle, blak, roch man, werie cold ; and I fand his nature als cold within me as spring-well-water ".

This unnatural physical coldness of the Demon is commented upon again and again by witches at their trials in every country in Europe throughout the centuries. Now ectoplasm is described as being to the touch a cold and viscous mass comparable to contact with a reptile, and it may be that here we have the solution to the whole mystery.

It is extremely significant too as the pages of Boguet, Remy, De Lancre, and many other demonologists show this coupling with the demon was not accomplished without physical pain. Thus Thievenne Paget declared that the act caused her as keen agony as if she had been in travail. Jeanne Bosdeau who was tried by the

Parliament of Bordeaux in 1594 said that the demon " had carnal knowledge of her which was with great pain ". The Pyrenean witches acknowledged that this fornication with the devil caused them untold sufferings. Temperance Lloyd, a Devonshire witch, confessed that the Devil had carnal knowledge of her body thrice, and always with great pain.

Moreover it is evident from the several accounts of the Sabbat which agree in various countries that the Devil or President of the assembly was wont to have connexion with every one or at least with very many of the women present. The Grand Master and Officer also exercised the right to select first for his own pleasure such witches as he chose, as appears from a passage in De Lancre who writes that after sorcerer and sorceress had been joined in mock marriage by the Devil he first took the bride's maidenhead.

Obviously no one human being could serve so many women, and it follows that use must have been made of an instrument ; the artificial phallus was employed. This is quite clear too from the extremely detailed description of the genital organs of the President of the Sabbat given by the Lorraine witches to Nicolas Remy. Nicole Morèle, Claude Fellet, Alexée Drigie, and indeed the whole infernal sisterhood spoke of these as monstrous beyond all conception. It will not escape notice either that the Devil as drawn from the life—for the sketch was doubtless made at the actual performance—on the title-page of Middleton and Rowley's masque *The World tost at Tennis* is abundantly and indeed grotesquely supplied in this respect. He is pictured in exactly similar fashion in more than one old chap-book, whilst a phallus, to which reference is made

THE DEVIL-CHASTISING THE WITCHES
George Cruikshank

in the text, was worn by the actor dressed up as the monkey (*Bavian*) in the May-dance scene in Shakespeare and Fletcher's *The Two Noble Kinsmen*. Troops of phallic demons formed a standing characteristic of the old German carnival comedy. Moreover, several of the fantastic types of the Commedia dell'arte in the second decade of the seventeenth century were traditionally equipped in like manner.

The artificial penis was a commonplace among the erotica of ancient civilizations ; it was very generally utilized in Egypt, Assyria, India, Mexico, all over the world. It has been found in tombs ; frequently was it to be seen as an ex-voto ; in a slightly modified form it is yet the favourite mascot of Southern Italy. Often enough they do not even trouble to disguise the thing. It is mentioned by the Greek writers, by Aristophanes, Herodas, and others. Among the Latins it is spoken of by Petronius and Tibullus. It was familiar in the brothels of Byzantium. It was employed by the Galli, priests of Cybele ; in the worship of Bacchus ; in the debauched ritual of Priapus. A later historian speaks of phallic ceremonies and the use of ithyphalli in the tenth century. "A sterile lust, common in the earliest times," says the *Erotic Glossary of the Latin Tongue*. The Councils, the Fathers, the Doctors of the Church ; Clement of Alexandria, Arnobius, Nicetas, Theodoret, Lactantius, the great St. Augustine, and many a prohibition of West and East have spoken of these practices in terms of severest condemnation. It is demonstrable then that artificial methods of coition, common in pagan antiquity, have been unblushingly practised throughout all the ages, as indeed they are at the present day, and that they have been repeatedly, ay and vehemently, banned and reprobated by the voice of the Church, a malison and an injunction which would doubtless recommend them to the favour of the Satanists, whose dark debaucheries of lust take an additional thrill, a new glamour if they can add to obscenity disobedience. Yet we have also to face the fact that there are darker and fouler mysteries still, hideous copulations of hell, which neither human intercourse nor the employ of a mechanical property can explain.

It is the universal opinion that children are born of these horrible unions. These are either demoniac monsters or prodigies of wickedness. They are always in some way hideously deformed, although of course the blemish may be concealed from sight. In any case their odious and malignant nature inevitably betrays the fiendish origin. At Toulouse in 1275, Angèle de la Barthe, a hag of some sixty, was condemned for having had intercourse with an evil spirit from which conjunction she brought forth a vilely misshapen creature whom she nourished with the flesh of infants, slain by her or dug up from their graves in remote churchyards. Towards the end of the seventeenth century an Essex witch, Sarah Smith, from her commerce with a familiar " was brought to Bed of a Strange Monster, the Body of it like a Fish with Scales thereon, it had no Legs but a pair of great Claws. . . . Which eat and fed for some time. Which Monster . . . was by Command of the Magistrates knock'd on the Head, and several Surgeons were there to dissect it ". Sinistrari gives the names of several persons who made a noise in the world and were shrewdly suspected of being the offspring of the demon and a witch. Thomas Malvenda, a famous Dominican writer, says that children thus begotten are often tall, very hardy and bloodily bold, arrogant beyond words, and desperately wicked. Both Malvenda and St. Robert Bellarmine hold that Antichrist will be the progeny of a demon and a witch. Others indeed have it that Antichrist will be the Devil in the flesh in awful mockery of the Incarnation. Be that as it may, the appalling wickedness, the power and infinite capacity for evil of certain prominent figures to-day can only be explained if we realize that such must verily be the children of Satan and witches.

A candid consideration will show that for every detail of the Sabbat, however fantastically presented and exaggerated in the witch-trials of so many centuries, there is amplest warrant and unimpeachable evidence. There is some hallucination no doubt ; there is lurid imagination, and coarse vanity which paints the colours thick ; but there is a solid stratum of fact, and very terrible fact throughout. And to-day the Satanist is as tirelessly active in our midst as ever he was in bygone ages. Nay, actually the Devil is massing his forces on every side.

Generally the Sabbat orgies lasted till cock-crow, before which time none of the assembly was suffered to withdraw. It is true that in the avowal of Louis Gaufridi, executed at Aix in 1610, he speaks of remaining at the Sabbat two or three hours, just as he felt inclined, but this seems altogether exceptional, and he was moreover the Grand Master of the coven. That the crowing of a cock dissolves enchantments is a tradition of extremest antiquity. The Jews believed that the clapping of a cock's wings will render the power of demons ineffectual and dissolve all magic spells. The poet Prudentius sang : " They say that the foul night-wandering spirits, who rejoice in dunnest night, at the crowing of the cock tremble and scatter in sore dismay." In the time of St. Benedict Matins and Lauds were recited at dawn, and were often known as *Gallicinium*, Cock-crow. The rites of Satan ceased when the Office of Holy Church began.

At the hour of the Nativity, that most blessed time, the cocks crew all night long. A cock crew lustily at the Resurrection. A witch named Babilla Latoma confessed to Nicolas Remy that the cock was the most hateful of all birds to sorcerers. Johann Bulmer and his wife Desirée, who belonged to a coven of Le Mans district, said that the synagogue of sorcerers was usually disbanded by the President and the familiars proclaiming : " Ho ! Speed all and away—away ! For the cocks begin to crow ! "

The sound of bells also is most detested by the hellish crew, and Bishop Binsfeld in a fine passage compares the music of church bells to the hoisting of the royal standard of our King. Not only can they subdue tempests but they put to instant flight devils and witches, they breathe benediction and peace. It is recorded by an Italian writer that on a certain occasion when the debauchery of the Sabbat had been prolonged the horrid crew were surprised to hear the Angelus ringing out its early salutation to the Virgin Mother from a village steeple hard by. The demons fled howling and disappeared with a most noisome stench abandoning their besotted worshippers to fare as best they might. Bishop Peter Binsfeld says that the charm was broken, the glamour dissipated, and the Sabbat vanished if one pronounced with devotion the Sacred Names of Jesus or Mary.

The Sabbat ends. As the dawn breaks the unhallowed crew separate in haste, and hurry each one on his way homewards, pale, weary, and haggard after the night of taut hysteria, of frenzied evil, hate, and vilest excess.

The cock crows ; the Sabbat ends ; the sorcerers scatter and flee away.

CHAPTER V

Thou shalt not suffer a witch to live.
Exodus, xxii, 18.

The word Witchcraft itself belongs to Anglo-Saxon days, and even if we possessed no other evidence of the fearful prevalence in the centuries before the Norman Conquest of wellnigh every kind of traffic with the darker powers throughout all England the fact that these horrid businesses were only too wide-spread might indeed be considered amply proven when we are able to recognize and enumerate no less than some forty native terms denoting all kinds of black magic and the various professors of that evil craft. Actually the wealth of witness from laws, both ecclesiastical and secular, from sermons and homilies, from leechdoms, chronicles and legend, is overwhelming.

It was in the spring of the year 597 that the Apostle of the English, Saint Augustine, with his little company landed on the Isle of Thanet, presently to be welcomed by King Æthelbert, himself still a pagan, although his wife and dear queen, Bertha of Paris, enjoyed the free exercise of her religion. It will be readily remembered how the King fearing some possible incantations on the part of the strangers insisted that their first interview should take place in the open air under the shadow of a sacred oak, the tree worshipped by the Druids, by the ancient Celts and Teutons, by Slavs and Lithuanians, at Nemi, in Syria, the tree whose majesty was revered by the whole Aryan race. The King's apprehensions, however, were speedily set at rest, and he forthwith invited the missionaries to his royal city of Canterbury, a barbarous and squalid place enough, to which, however, they gladly came, as the Venerable Bede describes, bearing the Holy Cross together with a picture of the Sovereign King, Our Lord Jesus Christ, and chanting in unison sweet psalms and litanies as they went on their way.

After the death of Æthelbert in 616 great reverses befell Christianity, and witchcraft notably increased throughout the land. The dark opposing powers were not easily to be driven from the fair realm of Britain, and in 633 it seemed as if the Faith would be wholly extinguished throughout the North of England on account of the fierce persecutions of Penda, the pagan King of Mercia, whose court was thronged with wizards, diviners, and cunning women.

Rædwald, King of the East-Angles, a most powerful monarch who died about 627, and was fourth Bretwalda, erected (as the Venerable Bede tells us) in one and the same temple a high altar at which Mass was said, and a side altar at which sacrifices were offered to the devil.

In 747 was convened at the behest of Pope Zachary the Second Council of Clovesho, which forbade all abominations and vain pagan practices, " wizardry, sorcery, divinings, fortune-telling, periapts, spells, conjurations, and incantations, which are the very filth of the wicked, yea, heathen falsehood and deceit."

Continuous legislation, the codes of Ælfred, of

Edward and Guthrum, of Æthelstan, and many more ban witchcraft, demanding the supreme penalty for those who slay others by their spells. The Secular Laws of Cnut denounce those who " love witchcrafts to ensue them, or contrive secret murder in anywise ; or offer evil sacrifice or by soothsaying, or perform anything pertaining to such abominable illusions ". By secret murder is intended any killing through a charm or some kind of witchcraft. The " evil sacrifice " is the Black Mass.

The Christian Council of the Gold Coast, of which the Anglican Bishop of Accra is chairman, published in January, 1932, a lengthy memorandum dealing with African sorceries. Among the powers which a wizard is supposed to possess is " The power to inflict disease and death upon a human victim without physical contact or physical medium (popular belief distinguishes between witchcraft and poisoning) ". The Christian Council includes representatives of the English Church Mission, of the Methodist and Presbyterian bodies. [1] It appears that some of the members were disinclined to believe in witchcraft, but be that as it may the warning of the *Vox Populi* of Accra which commented adversely upon the documents is soundest of all : " Our sincere advice to the churches of the Gold Coast is to leave the Devil alone . . . Of some meek strangers in Palestine it was once reported, ' We would see Jesus '. A Christian Council to-day would see the Devil and his works and pay for it."

Writing in the *Daily Express* on 3rd June, 1933, Mr. Arthur Hudson, K.C., former Attorney-General of the Gold Coast, mentions several instances of homicide by witchcraft. One of the earliest complaints that came before him was that of a man whose father had been killed by a wizard. The wizard had been angry with the deceased, had declared that he should die on a certain day, and on that day the victim died. In the present sad state of the law the murderer could not be convicted, and Mr. Hudson wisely attempted to frighten him by threats of punishment if any more complaints were made concerning his activities. In another instance a warlock told a man who had given offence that as he walked home to his farm a snake would come out of the bush and bite him, and that he would die. The man was bitten exactly in this way, and died. Here again the warlock could only be intimidated in hopes that he would for the future for very fear eschew his sorceries.

It would be easy to give many more quotations from and references to Anglo-Saxon and pre-Norman documents and writings of all kinds, but enough has been said to show that witchcraft, known in all its aspects throughout England long before the Conquest, was ever forbidden by the Law and banned by the Church.

After the Conquest the Anglo-Saxon statutes against witchcraft and all ecclesiastical censures and excommunications were in practice continued. William I in a summary of his legislation assigns perpetual exile as the punishment for any murder by black magic. (The technical word in the first instance implies the use of poison, but poison and spells were so invariably intermingled that the terms became synonymous.) It was soon found necessary to make the penalty more severe. Thus the code known as the Laws of Henry I, which may be dated about 1110, decrees that any murder, whether it be by poisoning or by witchcraft, is punishable with death. If, however, the victim has not been killed but has been injured in body or lies sick the offender may make compensation by payment of a heavy fine. The code specifies one particular form of malefic magic which was regarded as especially heinous, the piercing of an image or poppet to slay the man in whose likeness it was moulded.

In 1071 when William I was attacking Hereward the Wake and had abandoned all hope of capturing the Isle of Ely, a Norman knight ventured to suggest that as a last resource they should avail themselves of the help of an old woman, who (as he said) by her mysterious art was able to sap the defenders of their manhood and drive them pell-mell in a panic from their strongholds. The crone was brought to the camp under cover of darkness, but not so secretly that the news reached Hereward by means of a spy. The Saxon chief, disguising himself very adroitly in rags, obtained a lodging at the cottage of a widow where the witch dwelt. He overheard the two hags conversing in French, a language they, of course, deemed a vagrom wayfarer could not understand. At midnight the women went down to a spring of water which ran at the end of the garden, and concealed among the trees he watched whilst they invoked the " guardian of the springs ", a demon who answered in a hoarse and horrible voice. In consequence he was able to employ a counter-spell. When the enemy with great confidence made their next sally, the witch was stationed in a high chariot in their midst to ply her art whilst they fought. The Normans, however, were routed with heavy loss, and the sorceress being cast to the ground was slain in the *mêlée*.

That such foul creatures, ever ready to work harm, literally swarmed throughout England in those centuries cannot be doubted, even as it is certain that Satanists infest the country in our own time. Again and again the laws—silent to-day—forbade and penalized sorcery and enchantments. Nor can we be surprised that on occasion persons tormented by some sorceress have suddenly and violently avenged themselves, as when John of Kerneslawe was surprised one evening by a hideous hag who entering his cottage struck him smartly with her staff, and in a moment all his limbs were writhen and racked with pain. In self-defence, as against the devil, he snatched up a javelin and struck her through so that she died. But John fell into a delirium and ran lunatic, nor did he recover his wits until the clergy of the district very properly ordered that the body of the witch should be burned to ashes.

There was a terrific scandal in 1303 when one of the chief men in the realm, Walter Langton, Bishop of Coventry and treasurer of Edward I, was delated before Pope Boniface VIII as a notorious warlock and of worshipping the Demon with obscene ceremonies. After a most searching inquiry the incriminated prelate proved able successfully to clear himself of the crime.

There seems little doubt that politics were mixed up in this case, as they most certainly were the motive of the famous trials of 1324 when no less than twenty-seven defendants were brought before the King's Bench for murder by fashioning and tormenting a wax image. Upon All Hallows E'en, 1323, a number of Coventry men went privately to the house of a notorious " nigromauncer ", John of Nottingham, who was then living in their town, and having bound him and his man, Robert Marshall from Leicester, to closest secrecy, paid him a large sum of money to undertake the slaying of King Edward II, the royal favourite young Hugh le Despenser, and other great men of quality. The old warlock and his servant forthwith set to work. A remote and ancient manor, some half a league from Coventry, was the scene of their operations. In this horrible haunted house they set about their work. They were well feed, and provided with seven pounds of fair white wax and two ells of superfine canvas to fashion the mommets, the King with a gilded crown on his head, Monsieur Hugh, and the rest. Long and thoroughly they laboured at their modelling. It was resolved that first they would make an experiment upon Richard de Sowe, a courtier whom they hated. Accordingly they moulded their figurine, and at midnight on the Friday before the Feast of Holy Rood (3rd May) Master John gave Marshall a long leaden pin bidding him thrust boldly two inches deep into the forehead of the doll. The next morning the servant went to de Sowe's house upon some casual errand to learn that he was writhing on his bed in agony, uttering piercing cries with burning pains in the head and frantically delirious whilst the physicians were at their wits' end to diagnose the mysterious malady. And so he lingered until some days later the warlock drew the pin from the brow and struck it featly into the heart of the image. Whereupon de Sowe expired, and Marshall panicky and dithering with fear rushed off to the Sheriff, one Simon Crozier, before whom he confessed all that had been going on, which immediately resulted in the arrest of Master John and the whole gang of conspirators. Shame to say the wealthy burgesses greased the palm of justice and escaped, but Master John was not so lucky for he died in durance on the very eve of the trial, whilst the unfortunate wight who blabbed was sent back to prison to abide there.

In the forty-fifth year of Edward III, that is to say 1371, a Southwark man was brought before the King's Bench upon a charge of sorcery. He was found to have in his wallet the mummified head and embalmed hands of a dead man, a skull, and a grimoire. In spite of such damning evidence the Chief Justice, Sir John Knyvet, only required him to take solemn oath that he would never practise any kind of witchcraft nor cast a spell for good or ill, whilst the book and the loathly relics of mortality were burned in Tothill Fields.

In 1376 the so-called " Good Parliament " openly charged Alice Perrers, the fascinating mistress of Edward III with witchcraft, and declared that she maintained in her house a mysterious Dominican, " who in outward show professed physic " but by whose experiments Alice had allured the King to her unlawful love. He had fashioned a rare ring of memory the virtue whereof was to keep the doting monarch ever mindful of the lady.

Under Richard II and Henry IV there were constant prosecutions of conjurors and traffickers in black magic, whilst Henry V was plainly very much perturbed about the increase of sorcerers in his realms. He even prosecuted his stepmother, Joan of Navarre, for attempting his life by witchcraft, and her confessor, a Franciscan, John Randolf, an admitted adept, was lodged in the Tower. There seems little doubt that the friar had moulded wax figurines after the traditional manner.

Dames of high degree indeed seem to have been particularly implicated in accusations of witchcraft employed for political motives, and we frequently have very full details of such cases chronicled of course owing to their notoriety and importance, hundreds of similar instances in the lower walks of life passing unrecorded. Thus in 1441 Eleanor Cobham, Duchess of Gloucester, wife of "the Good Duke Humphrey", "sometime Protector of England," was "arrested and put in hold, for she was suspect of treason". It was found that she was deeply implicated in the witchcrafts and sorceries of a learned astrologer, Roger Bolingbroke, with whom also were concerned Thomas Southwell, a canon of St. Stephen's ; Sir John Hume a priest ; William Woodham ; and Margery Jourdemain, a witch of the vilest antecedents. Bolingbroke asserted that he had "wrought the said necromancy" at the duchess' command but it was with a view to ascertain "to what estate she should come ", (in other words her chance of succeeding to the throne) and not to plot any treason against the king. There can be little doubt, however, that the death of Henry VI was being attempted according to the orthodox mode of piercing and melting wax images. Bolingbroke was hanged at Tyburn, beheaded and quartered ; Canon Southwell died in prison ; whilst Mother Jourdemain, "the Witch of Eye" (the Manor of Eye-next-Westminster), who had been imprisoned on a charge of sorcery eleven years before but afterwards discharged, was burned at the stake in Smithfield, since she was guilty of high treason as well as malefic magic. The Duchess of Gloucester was compelled to do public penance, walking the streets of London barefoot and bareheaded, in a white shift, and carrying a lighted taper of two pounds weight. She was then confined for life at Peel Castle in the Isle of Man, a fastness yet horribly haunted by her unquiet ghost.

Before his execution Bolingbroke was set on a high platform outside St. Paul's, whilst a rousing sermon was preached to the crowd. He was dressed in his magic robes, holding a huge scimitar in his right hand and a great gilt sceptre in his left, " arrayed in that marvellous array he was wont to don when about his magic." Upon the scaffold was also placed his necromantic throne, a chair of subtle wizardry, curiously painted, wherein he used to sit when he wrought his dark craft, and on the four corners of the chair stood four swords and from every sword there hung an image of a foul fiend graven in copper. Such chairs are still occasionally to be found. In 1929 I saw a very fine specimen then in the possession of Mr. John Jennings. This was of mahogany, and inserted in the back showed the painting of a magician, holding his wand of power, and surrounded by demons. The picture was covered by an elegantly shaped shield of bevelled Vauxhall glass. On the arms and seat were various mystic devices inlaid and *piqués* in brass. Other instruments appertaining to Bolingbroke's craft and which had been found in his closet were displayed, stars, pentacles, cups, censers, images of silver and other metals, together with waxen mommets not a few. Thomas Southwell used to say Mass at an altar in the Lodge of Hornsey Park over " certain instruments fit for the craft of necromancy ". He had celebrated a requiem for the living king, and had also baptized a wax figurine of Henry, piercing it with a sharp bodkin. The case not being proved against Sir John Hume and Woodham, they were acquitted.

Even Jacquette de Luxembourg, Duchess of Bedford, and mother-in-law of Edward IV was attacked by evil tongues who declared that she had fashioned two puppets to compel the king to love her daughter. There were also rumours of a mysterious figure, the image of a soldier, about a finger's length, but broken in the midst and mended with wire which the lady used for purposes of magic. The Duchess made her plaint to the Privy Council, and the whole thing broke down utterly, which did not, however, hinder Richard of Gloster some years later when he was aiming at the throne reviving the scandals, and declaring that his brother's marriage with Elizabeth was invalid as having been contrived " by sorcery and witchcraft, committed by the said Elizabeth and her mother ". He also charged them together with that other witch of their counsel, Shore's wife, with wasting his body by their spells, and did not hesitate to pull up his sleeve and show his shrunken withered arm to the Privy Council, swearing that thus " yonder sorceress, my brother's wife " and her company had plagued him, whereas all present knew well that he had been deformed from birth. And so Jane Shore must do public penance therefor, and walk the London streets clad only in a shift, barefoot, and carrying a lighted taper.

Throughout the fifteenth century there were prosecutions of the smaller fry; and an almost continuous list of cases, year after year, might be recorded. Thus Richard Walker, a chaplain, is accused by the Prior of Winchester of sorcery, and is found to have in his closet a beryl stone for divining, two grimoires, and two dolls of wax. In 1444 there was publicly punished in London a man " the which wrought by a wicked spirit the which was called Oberycom, and the manner of his process and working was written and hanged about his neck when he was in the pillory ". In 1500 Thomas Wright, a Premonstratensian Canon of Sulby Abbey, near Market Harborough, came under grave suspicion for " using books of experiments ", and for having bribed a mysterious " vagabond " to teach him the way of occult science.

At the trial of the Duke of Buckingham, twenty-one years later, an accusation of sorcery supported the capital charge of high treason. He had consulted with Dom Nicholas Hopkins, a monk of the Hinton Charterhouse, of whom he inquired concerning the King's death—a fatal question, if true. It was also alleged that the Duke had been heard to say that Cardinal Wolsey was an idolater and sorcerer, nourishing a familiar, who advised him how to keep the royal favour.

When Henry VIII was beginning to grow a little weary of the gospel light that gleamed from Boleyn's eyes he whispered to some convenient friend that unquestionably he had " made the marriage seduced by witchcraft ", a self-evident fact since God denied him a son. Before the birth of Elizabeth indeed a whole horde of occultists had been consulted to determine the sex of the child. All plumped for a boy, and when the royal mistress was delivered of a girl it was felt to be to " the great reproach of the astrologers, sorcerers, and sorceresses ".

The very comprehensive " Bill against conjurations and witchcrafts ", 1542, by which all using occult arts, were it even to discover stolen goods, are adjudged guilty of felony with pain of death, was short-lived enough, being repealed in the first year of Edward VI, 1547.

It was at the beginning of the reign of Elizabeth that drastic measures were taken against the black art. Although drafted soon after her accession it was not until 1563 that the measure passed on to the statute-book and became English law. In 1604 this act was repealed under James I, and a new act passed. It may be convenient very briefly to sum up the provisions of the two acts. Both prescribe the death penalty for Employing or Exercising Witchcraft with the intent to kill or destroy. To hurt persons in body or to waste and destroy goods under Elizabeth for the first offence was punished with a year's imprisonment and the pillory " by the space of six hours " each quarter ; for a second offence imprisonment for life. Under James the first offence in this kind was punishable with death. To employ witchcraft to find treasure or stolen goods both Acts punished with a year's imprisonment and the pillory. A second offence of this nature meant perpetual imprisonment under Elizabeth ; under James, death. The same penalties were attached to the felony of provoking persons to unlawful love by witchcraft, or indeed to employing witchcraft for any ends whatsoever. By the Act of James the consulting, covenanting with, entertaining, employing, feeding or rewarding any evil spirit was punishable with death.

The same penalty was prescribed for invocation or conjurations of demons, as also for taking up any dead body from the grave, or securing any skin, bone, or part of a corpse to employ in any manner of witchcraft or enchantment. Such is the main tenor of these Acts. There are ancillary penalties ; forfeiture of property, loss of clergy. The Act of Elizabeth was automatically repealed by the Act of James I. The Act of James I remained law until the reign of George II, 1736.

It should be remarked that the death sentence for a witch was " to be hanged by the neck until he or she be dead ". It is generally, but most erroneously supposed, that in England the stake was the doom of a witch and that she was burned alive. Some few witches such as Margery Jourdemain under Henry VI and Mother Lakeland of Ipswich in 1645 were burned at the stake, but this was because they were guilty of treason. The former was convicted of high treason against the King ; the latter of petty treason, she had killed her husband by sorcery. In Scotland the witch was burned, sometimes alive, and sometimes after being strangled at the stake. This too was the general custom on the Continent. Sometimes also (but infrequently) witchcraft was combined with heresy, for which the penalty was fire. By an Act of Henry VIII poisoning was punishable by " death by boiling ", and the witches were adepts in the art of poisoning, but no case has been quoted (so far as I am aware) in English records where a witch was thus executed.

Statistics which have been very carefully investigated and compared show that there were more trials for . witchcraft during the two and forty years of Elizabeth than throughout the entire seventeenth century. It may be remarked that during the whole reign of James I, twenty-two years, not more than forty executions for witchcraft have been traced. The popular tradition which so confidently affirms that the most responsible and prominent figure in the history of English witchcraft is King James I, whose accession from Scotland to the English throne fanned expiring embers into a blazing flame and fearfully energized a furious and long unbated flood of persecution sending literally thousands of crazy gaffers and doting beldames to torture and to death is, be it said once and for all, the merest figment of ignorance.

Under James there was only one material change in the existing law which could be termed more rigid, and it is significant that in 1622 when Edward Fairfax, the translator of Tasso, accused six women who were duly brought before the York Assizes of bewitching his two daughters, although the evidence seems conclusive and the jury found a true bill, the Judge after hearing several witnesses pronounced that the matter " reached not to the point of the statute ", stopped the trial and discharged the prisoners.

One of the most notorious of Elizabethan cases was that of the Witches of St. Osyth. This little village stands on a creek of the River Colne, fitly described as " the lonely waters of St. Osyth Creek with its derelict quay of rotting timber ". It is situated some four miles from Clacton-on-Sea, and a dozen miles from Colchester. St. Osyth, which derives its name from the daughter of an English prince, a pious maid who preserved her virginity even in the marriage state and who founded a nunnery in this place erstwhile called Chick, where.

she was martyred by Danish pirates in 653—her feast is kept on the 7th October—is one of the oldest inhabited spots in the country, having been a Royal demesne of King Cnut. To-day there is a population of between fourteen and fifteen hundred.

Here at the end of the sixteenth century dwelt in a wretched cottage with her eight-year-old bastard son, Thomas Rabbet, a woman of ill repute, Ursula Kemp *alias* Grey, who eked out a scanty maintenance by acting as midwife, nursing children, harlotry, and various kinds of magic, both black and white, which included "unwitching" the sick. Davy, the son of a neighbour, Grace Thurlow, a poor and needy woman, fell sick, and amongst other gossips Ursula Kemp came to see the child. Taking him by the hand she muttered some mysterious words, and the lad was almost immediately restored to health. Her suspicions confirmed, Grace Thurlow refused to allow Ursula Kemp to nurse a newly born baby girl. Soon afterwards the infant fell out of the cradle and broke its neck, an accident the mother pretty plainly attributed to the vengeance of the witch. Hereupon Ursula Kemp threatened her with lameness, to which she made sharp reply : " Take heed, Ursley, thou hast a naughty name." But soon enough Grace Thurlow was crippled with pain, so that she could scarcely drag herself about the room on her hands and knees. Complaint was made to Mr. Brian Darcy, high sheriff of the county, who promptly examined young Thomas Rabbet, and there was soon unripped a whole coven of Satanists. At length Ursula confessed the crimes of witchcraft and murder. The death of Grace Thurlow's baby would have been easy enough to accomplish, and it seems quite plain that Ursula Kemp, who was the chief of the St. Osyth's witches, had been initiated into all the secrets of poisoning, which horrid art was so universally practised by the wise-women and conjurers of the day, both at home and abroad.

Ursula Kemp herself entertained four puckrels or familiars; two other members of the gang, Alice Hunt and Margery Salmon, the daughters of old Mother Barnes, a notorious witch, had two spirits, bequeathed them by their mother; Elizabeth Bennett also had two familiars; whilst Annis Herd nourished no less than six small imps. Terrible was the mischief the coven had wrought before they were discovered. Five murders lay to the count of Ursula Kemp; Elizabeth Bennett killed two farmers and their wives and much cattle; Elizabeth Eustace had slain seven cows and a number of pigs, wellnigh ruining their owner; Joan Robinson overlooked geese and a litter of pigs, drowned cows, struck horses with spavins, and men with a wasting sickness; Cecilia Celles, a labourer's wife of Clacton, and Alice Mansfield had burned ricks, standing corn, and a barn stored with grain. And so the trial proceeded with guilty confessions, accusations, bitter recriminations, and counter-accusations until sixteen persons were involved. Thirteen witches were convicted, ten at least of whom were guilty of murder by sorcery and were executed. The accounts are a little confused, and it may be that the whole thirteen suffered.

In a chapel of the south aisle belonging to the parish church of St. Peter and St. Paul, St. Osyth, is a mural tablet to Brian Darcy, High Sheriff of Essex, who died on 25th December, 1587. Outside one of the old cottages is affixed a notice " Step Right In Here to

See the Genuine Skeleton of a Witch. Admission Three Pence ". In a deep pit at the end of the garden, protected by timber rails and a wooden cover lies the skeleton of a woman, a horrid sight ! Great iron nails have been driven through the knees and ankles. They were fixed years ago lest the unhappy soul should reanimate those bleaching bones and send the terror walking abroad in the night.

It must not be forgotten that in the days of Elizabeth, and the two kings her successors there lived wise men and seers whose practices very nearly trenched upon witchcraft, if indeed they were not entirely necromantical, but who were consulted and protected by the great ones at court, aristocratic ladies and men of the first quality. Such were the famous Dr. John Dee, who was employed by Leicester as a conjurer and figure-caster, and who was " continually busied about one thing and another at the fancy " of Elizabeth herself. It was he who named the 14th January, 1559, as a happy day for her coronation. There were also his scryers, Barnabas Saul, and the enigmatical Edward Kelley, in whose story sober fact and wild romance are so inextricably blended that it is hard to know what to believe. There was Dr. Simon Forman who set up in London as an astrologer in 1583, and obtained a large practice amongst the amatory court gallants and light wanton ladies, who was frequently imprisoned at the instance of medical and other authorities, but who was granted a licence as a physician by Cambridge University in 1603. He was a magician professed, and one who knew the guilty secrets of Somerset and the Countess of Essex. The all-powerful favourite, Buckingham, protected Dr. John Lambe, who was even more notorious as a sorcerer than Forman. The " Duke's devil " they dubbed him. William Lilly and John Booker were in some sort of the same line as these occultists, and one remembers the trick of the scapegrace Earl of Rochester who masqueraded as Alexander Bendo professing *inter alia* " Astrological Predictions, Divination by Dreams ", and whose lodging " in *Tower-Street*, next door to the sign of the *Black Swan*, at a Goldsmith's House " was crowded by the wits and lovely cyprians of the Whitehall of Charles II. Even the celebrated Oxford mathematician, Thomas Allen, of Gloucester Hall (Worcester College) who died in 1632 was commonly reputed to command familiars, and to have learned his science from the astral spirits he could evoke at will.

I am inclined to believe that the case of the Lancashire witches—perhaps the most celebrated case in the history of English witchcraft—may have gone far to bolster the false idea that King James' reign was a period of fanatical malevolence when " the judges and magistrates, the constables and the mob began to hunt up as their lawful prey " old women from every nook and chimney corner.

The first trial of the Lancashire witches took place in 1612. Some five and twenty years before that date Elizabeth Sowtherns, better known as old Mother Demdike, encountered in Pendle Forest an evil spirit (whom she had probably invoked) to whom she sold her soul. At once she became an active missionary for the Satanists, and although at first the way was slow about five years later she persuaded Anne Whittle or Chattox " to condescend and agree to become subject unto that devilish abominable profession of witchcraft ". Henceforward these two wretches and all their families practised witchcraft. Mother Demdike brought in her married daughter Elizabeth Device, and her grandchildren, Alison and James Device ; Mother Chattox proselytized to evil her daughter, Anne Redfearn. The infection spread, and even a woman of some degree, Mrs. Elizabeth Nutter, joined the coven. Later a violent quarrel took place between the Devices and the Chattox family, each party endeavouring to harm the friends and relations of the other. Terrible mischief ensued, and the coven became bolder and bolder, almost openly holding their Sabbats at the lonely Malking Tower on the further slope of the high hill which shuts in Rough Lee glen, not far from the old road to Gisburn.

> Malkin's Tower . . . where
> Report makes caitiff witches meet to swear
> Their homage to the devil, and contrive
> The deaths of men and beasts.

A veritable reign of terror oppressed the whole country-side and everyone went in mortal fear of the witches. At length towards the end of March, 1612, Mr. Roger Nowell, a Justice of the Peace, caused old Demdike and Alison Device, Mother Chattox and her daughter to be brought before him. Their confessions were such that he committed them to Lancaster Castle. Even during their imprisonment the rest of the coven proved so audacious as to hold a Sabbat at Malking Tower on the following Good Friday. This led to further arrests. At the Assizes no less than nineteen prisoners were put on their trial, of which number ten were executed, murder by witchcraft having been clearly proved against them. Old Demdike had died in gaol. They were shown to be guilty of every circumstance of sorcery, and were as dangerous a gang of Satanists as very well could be. As Dr. G. B. Harrison says : " the Lancaster trial reveals the practice of the witch-cult in its full horror . . . There seems, in short, to have been little injustice in the sentences passed at Lancaster in August, 1612."

The case of the Second Lancashire Witches occurred in 1633–34, and was to a large extent a recrudescence of the former Pendle scandals. The affair, which presents several interesting features, came to an end when, as many as seventeen suspected persons having been tried and condemned, all upon further investigation were pardoned by Charles I.

Towards the end of the reign of this monarch, almost immediately upon the outbreak of the Rebellion, a veritable epidemic of witchcraft swept through the Eastern Counties, and there emerges the extraordinary figure of Matthew Hopkins " commonly call'd Witch Finder Generall ". The Holy Scripture tells us that Rebellion and Witchcraft go hand in hand, and it is not surprising to find that during those troublous years the land was corrupt to the core with sorcery. Hopkins, the son of James Hopkins, minister of Wenham, Suffolk, had practised the law at Ipswich first, and then at Manningtree, Essex. It was in his own town that his attention was drawn to witchcraft for a whole coven, " seven or eight of that horrible sect of Witches living in the Town where he lived . . . with divers other adjacent Witches of other Towns " on Friday nights held their Sabbat close by his house, and " had their several solemn sacrifices offered to the Devil ". He at once proceeded

A YORKSHIRE WITCH AND HER IMPS
From a contemporary drawing, 1622

237

to inquire into these mysterious doings with the result that numerous arrests were made. This was in March, 1645. His campaign once begun, Hopkins who had got great glory from the business, zealously extended his operations and was eager to smell out witches in every direction. Accordingly he commenced a kind of visitation in which he was accompanied by his lieutenant—so to speak—John Stearne, who strenuously aided and abetted him, and also by an assistant Goody Phillips whose special province lay in discovering the witch-mark on the bodies of the accused. It was a very profitable concern, and it has been calculated that between them the trio must have netted far more than a thousand pounds, a very considerable sum in those days. The usual methods employed by Hopkins were searching for the devil's mark ; watching the witch, which meant that the suspected person tied with cords in an uneasy posture was kept without food or drink for twenty-four hours and not allowed to sleep, since it was believed that then her imps, in the shape of spiders or a fly or a wasp were bound to appear ; walking the witch, that is to say compelling a person to hurry up and down a room at a great rate until of very weariness and pain a confession was extorted ; and swimming the witch. This last ordeal was greatly favoured by Hopkins and his satellites, but so notoriously illegal was such a test that he was at last compelled to relinquish it. The old story that Hopkins himself was seized by the irate people, accused of being a wizard, and swum in a pond where he was drowned has no sort of foundation in fact. He died peaceably at Manningtree " after a long sickness of a Consumption

. . . without any trouble of conscience for what he had done, as was falsely reported of him ". The Church Registers record his burial, 12th August, 1647. From 1645 to 1647 he had brought at least a couple of hundred to the gallows. This is shown by Stearne, who in his *Confirmation and Discovery of Witch-craft*, published the year after Hopkins' death, writes how he was himself in part an agent in searching out witches, " being about two hundred in number, in Essex, Suffolk, Northamptonshire, Huntingdonshire, Bedfordshire, Norfolk, Cambridgeshire, and the Isle of Ely in the County of Cambridge, besides other places, justly and deservedly executed upon their legal trials."

It is not at all to be wondered at that during the Rebellion and under the Commonwealth the evil weed of witchcraft spread so rapidly throughout England and that sorcerers fouled the whole land since, as is now proved beyond any shadow of doubt, Oliver Cromwell was a Satanist, intimately leagued with the powers of darkness to whom he had sold his soul for temporal success. After 1642, indeed, as the historian Eachard has well remarked : " Blasphemies, Heresies, Enthusiasms, and Witchcrafts were in a full tide." In my *Geography of Witchcraft*, published ten years ago, I drew attention to the pact which Cromwell had made with the devil, and related his interview with the fiend before the battle of Worcester. In *The Occult Review*, April, 1936, Mr. S. Everard has an article " Oliver Cromwell and Black Magic " in which he presents irrefutable evidence that Cromwell derived his power from the exercise of black magic. Mr. Everard whose investigations are very thorough treats the whole subject with great fairness. He comments upon the quite unequivocal expression of Denzil Holles, after first Baron Holles of Ifield, who when addressing Cromwell and Oliver St. John speaks of the " Sabbaths " when " you imparted to your fellow witches the bottom of your designs, . . . all your falsehoods, villainies and cruelties with your full intention to ruin three kingdoms ". Even more damning is a letter in which Cromwell unbosoms himself to that impious wretch Hugh Peter and writes how the day after he received his commission " walking in the evening in Hyde Park the Devil appear'd to me in human shape and upon promises of assuring the always success over my enemies, the honour thereof tempted me to sell my soul and body to him ". The infernal pact was for thirty-nine years. And when Cromwell died at three of the clock on the 3rd September, 1658, there had raged for many hours a fearful storm round Whitehall ; the Devil had come for his own, folk said.

Mr. Everard makes a good point when he emphasizes the horrible sacrileges and blasphemies which were so common under the rule of Cromwell, and as is well known actively encouraged and incited by him. Churches were polluted and profaned in the most revolting manner, since " the essence of Satanism is desecration ".

The admirers of Cromwell have been absolutely unable to answer these charges. At best they have been forced to content themselves with sharp but not very relevant reflections upon scholars who " burrow among the lampoons of the Restoration ". I think I may venture to claim some acquaintance with Restoration literature and I can safely assert that the occult practices of Cromwell are not a theme with Restoration satirists, high or low. His witchcrafts are proved not by the censure and detraction of any opponent, but by historical documents whose genuineness cannot be called in doubt. It is commonly reported that either (as I hope) in bitter jest, or in earnest, all members of the House of Commons were advised to make a daily bow to the statue of Cromwell. This would be plain idolatry, and something worse. It is sad and shameful enough that a statue of Cromwell should ever have been erected, sadder still that it should be allowed to remain. Cromwell was a Satanist, and to my mind it is extremely significant that the Reds should carry a banner of Cromwell in procession.

The case of the Drummer of Tedworth which caused so great a stir shortly after the Restoration of King Charles II, the knockings and the sound of a drum which disturbed the household of Mr. Mompesson may more properly be said to belong to poltergeist hauntings than to witchcraft, although it is not disputed that sorcery played its part in the phenomena.

In Somerset during the year 1664 a coven of Satanists was discovered by Robert Hunt, a magistrate of the Wincanton district. Julian Cox, a fearful crone, who had signed a written pact with the devil, who had attended countless Sabbats in Brewham Forest, and who had wrought terrible mischiefs during her threescore years and ten was hanged. We are fortunate in having very full details of the Somerset coven since Robert Hunt entrusted Glanvil with his Book of Examinations of Witches. " It contains," says that learned divine, " the discovery of such an hellish Knot of them, and that discovery so clear and plain, that perhaps there hath not yet any thing appeared to me with stronger Evidence to confirm the belief of Witches."

The charges of witchcraft being proven up to the hilt two sorceresses, Amy Duny and Rose Cullender of Lowestoft, were hanged at Bury St. Edmunds in March, 1664. The trial is famous, largely owing to the fact that Sir Matthew Hale was the presiding judge who pronounced sentence, and Sir Thomas Browne, then Dr. Browne, testified to the undeniable truth of witchcraft, and gave it as his opinion that the victims of these evil crones were clearly bewitched.

In August, 1682, Temperance Lloyd, Mary Trembles, and Susanna Edwards were hanged at Exeter. All three had wasted and killed their neighbours by their malefic charms. All three had entertained familiars in filthy commerce.

The last execution for witchcraft which has been traced in England is that of Alice Molland, sentenced at the Exeter Lent Assizes of 1685.

The two cases which are still sometimes quoted, that of " two notorious witches " Elinor Shaw and Mary Phillips, said to have been burned at Northampton in March, 1705, and that of Mary Hicks and her little daughter, aged nine, supposed to have been hanged at Huntingdon in 1716, are purely fictitious. The pamphlets which profess to give details of these executions are mere catchpenny invention, the Northampton incident being nothing else than a hash-up of a Chelmsford witch-trial of 1645.

The last execution of a witch in Scotland took place at Dornock in 1722. The last witch-trial in Ireland, the Island-Magee Witch Trial, when five sorceresses were sentenced to a year's imprisonment and the pillory was in 1711. It is true that Mary Butters, the Carnmoney witch, was put forward for trial in 1808, but no bill was found. It should be emphasized that to quote the Clonmel case of 1895 as a "witch-burning" is altogether inaccurate. The woman was put on the fire in the belief that she was a fairy changeling, and that she would instantly vanish in the flames, whilst the real wife, kidnapped by the little people, would then return. The last execution in France appears to have been that of a warlock condemned by the Parliament of Bordeaux in 1718. At Kempten in Bavaria Anna Maria Schwägelin, who was perhaps lunatic, was beheaded for sorcery in 1775. The last time the law burned a witch in Spain was at Seville in 1781. In the Swiss Protestant canton of Glarus, Anna Göldi was hanged as a witch in 1782. Two carrion hags, notorious and rampant Satanists, were sent to the stake in Poland in 1793.

It is perhaps worth recording that the burning alive of five witches by the Alcade Ignacio Castello of San Jacopo in Mexico on 20th August, 1877, " with consent of the whole population " is a myth having no sort of foundation in fact.

Even to-day there are instances when the populace maddened by the malice of some witch take the law into their own hands, and sometimes with very deplorable results. Thus in November, 1929, six natives were sentenced to death by a special court in Swaziland. Their crime was the murder, with his three wives and three children, of an elderly *induna* (tribal leader), who had been " smelt out " by the witch doctors as a wizard. The accused avowed their guilt, but pleaded that the deceased was a black magician, and that he had cast a spell on many of their friends, who languished and died. They had set fire to the *induna's* hut, and when the seven occupants endeavoured to escape they were assegaied and flung back into the flames.

In November, 1932, ten people were arrested at Bogota, Columbia. The cottage of an old witch living in the village of Sativa Norte had been set on fire whilst she was asleep and she and her daughter burned to death. In May, 1935, a beldame of seventy-five, commonly believed to be a sorceress, was rescued by the Mexican police from being burned at the stake. Neighbours had seized her, and the faggots were beginning to crackle and blaze when the authorities arrived on the scene.

Towards the end of the seventeenth century and during the first decade of the eighteenth cases of witch-craft still came before the English courts, but the judges for the most part refused to convict. Sir John Holt, Chief Justice of the King's Bench (1689–1710), showed himself a notorious sceptic in these matters and secured acquittal after acquittal. When Richard Hathaway, the 'prentice to a Southwark blacksmith, accused Sarah Morduck of having bewitched him much trouble ensued. In the end, however, Hathaway found himself charged with rank imposture and Sir John Holt sentenced him to a year's imprisonment and the pillory thrice.

The case of Jane Wenham, the " Wise Woman of Walkerne " caused an immense sensation in 1711–12, and became " the discourse of London town ". At the trial in March the Hertford Assizes were thronged ; opinions were almost equally divided, and rivers of ink flowed. In spite of Mr. Justice Powell's direction and efforts to secure an acquittal the jury brought in a verdict of guilty of witchcraft. Jane Wenham was formally condemned, only to be reprieved and very shortly set at liberty. She lived until 1730 upon a small pension allowed by certain charitable people of quality.

The last witch-trial proper in England—or rather commitment for trial—was that of an old woman and her son at Leicester Assizes in September, 1717, before Lord Parker. The trial did not come on since the bill was not found.

The Act of James I was repealed in the ninth year of George II, 1736, and witchcraft ceased to be a statutory or (under English law) an ecclesiastical offence. This new Act also repealed the Act " Anentis Witchcrafts " of the Ninth Parliament of Queen Mary of Scotland, 1563. It was provided " That from and after the said Twentyfourth Day of June, [1736], no Prosecution, Suit, or Proceeding, shall be commenced or carried on against any Person or Persons for Witchcraft, Sorcery, Inchantment, or Conjuration, or for charging another with any such Offence, in any Court whatsoever in Great Britain ". To prevent and punish " any Pretences to such Arts or Powers " whereby ignorant persons are frequently deluded and defrauded, any Person who shall " pretend to exercise or use any kind of Witchcraft, Sorcery, Inchantment, or Conjuration, or undertake to tell Fortunes, or pretend, from his or her Skill or Knowledge in any occult or crafty Sciences, to discover where or in what

Manner any Goods or Chattels, supposed to have been stolen or lost, may be found ", is liable to a year's imprisonment and to be publicly pilloried once a quarter for the space of one hour.

I quote from the *Daily Mail*, Friday, 31st May, 1935. " Sorcery Charge Fails. For only the second time in the last 100 years a charge of sorcery was brought under the Witchcraft Act of 1736 at Carlisle Assizes yesterday.

" The accused woman, Mrs. Katie McGee, aged 35, who was alleged to have undertaken to tell the fortune of Mrs. Alice Rothesay, of Beckermet, was acquitted.

" Mr. Glynn Blackledge, for the prosecution, said that the last charge under the Act was brought in 1904, and Mr. Justice Singleton interposed : ' So this jury may be making history.' "

It may be observed that proceedings against professional fortune-tellers, palmists, and consulting mediums of any kind, are now generally taken under the Vagrancy Act of 1824, which includes : " Every person pretending or professing to tell fortunes, or using any subtle craft, means, or device, by palmistry or otherwise, to deceive and impose on any of His Majesty's subjects." From the wording of the Act it cannot apply to anyone having no intention to deceive, none the less it has been held by the divisional court that a person " telling fortunes ", however honestly, commits an offence within the Statute. Such an interpretation, it might well be argued, opens up the widest issues, yet although there is obviously need for a drastic reform of these vague and indeterminate Statutes one cannot but hope that, lest a worse thing happen, they will be left untouched until better conditions prevail and a saner outlook is reached.

Well might the Associate Presbytery in their annual Confession of National and Personal Sins lament " the Penal Statutes against Witches having been repealed by Parliament, contrary to the express Law of God ".

To estimate the number of executions for witchcraft in England from the accession of Queen Elizabeth in 1558 until the Repeal of 1736 is almost an impossible task. What can with perfect confidence be said is that nearly all writers have grossly exaggerated the figures, and multiplied by tens, even by hundreds. In his annotations on *Hudibras* (1744), the Cambridge antiquary Dr. Zachary Grey remarks : " I have somewhere seen an account of betwixt three and four thousand [witches] that suffered in the King's dominions, from the year 1640 to the King's restoration." Daines Barrington computes that a couple of centuries saw 30,000 executions ; Robert Steele in *Social England* says that 70,000 witches were hanged under the Act of James I. All these figures are grotesquely inflated and utterly unreasonable. Mr. L'Estrange Ewen, who speaks with greater authority, writes : " actually the number of executions for witchcraft in England from 1542–1736 may be guessed at less than 1,000."

CHAPTER VI

> *I would yet have it plainly known that I am a sworn enemy to
> witches, and that I shall never spare them, for their execrable abomina-
> tions, and for the countless numbers of them which are seen to increase
> every day so it seems that we are now in the times of Antichrist, since,
> among the many signs that are given of his advent, this is one of the
> chief, namely, that witchcraft shall then be rife throughout the world.*
>
> HENRI BOGUET.

Not many years ago a well-known writer inquired
of me in the public press if I could inform him when
and where the last Sabbat was celebrated. I did not
reply, because my answer must have been " yesterday
night " or " the night before yesterday " since, of
course, Sabbats are continually being celebrated by
Satanists at the present time. As to the place, it might
be London or any other of the cities or small towns
or even villages in England which are the centres of
devil-worshippers.

On Wednesday, 10th September, 1930, there
appeared in *The Times* an article entitled " The Last
Witch. A Question for the Antiquary ", a question,
moreover, which wisely enough the writer did not
attempt to answer. We are informed that " there were
many parts of the British Isles where belief in and
reprisals for witchcraft still existed when " Sir Walter
Scott's *Letters on Demonology and Witchcraft* " was
published in 1830 for Murray's respectable Family

Library ". Evidently *The Times* correspondent knew nothing of witchcraft in England at a later date, and from one point of view the article, however interesting, was extremely futile and a full hundred years out-of-date. Accidentally it proved valuable, none the less, since it provoked a number of letters very conclusively showing that witchcraft is no mere historical fact of the past, but that it is active and malignant to-day. To talk of " The Last Witch " is absurd. Satanism, in some cases scarcely veiled, is rampant in our midst. Satanist and witch are identical terms.

To suppose, again, as with some almost seems to be the case that the crass materialism of the Act of George II (1736) killed witchcraft is folly. Rather it protected the warlock and the sorceress. The only result of this fatuous legislation was that those who had been injured in body or in property by a witch took the law into their own hands, and during the eighteenth century there are recorded from every part of England a large number of examples of witches being swum by the populace. In June, 1736, the very year that the statute was passed certain witches were swum at Twyford in Leicestershire, an affair which gave the cue to the Rev. Joseph Juxon to preach " A Sermon upon Witchcraft. Occasion'd by the Late Illegal Attempt to Discover Witches by Swimming ". The scepticism, one might say the rationalism of the eighteenth century clergy is, of course, notorious. In July, 1737, a witch was swum in a Bedfordshire village. She floated like a cork three times, but subsequently when weighed against the Church Bible outbalanced it. At Monk's Sleigh, Norfolk, a witch was swum on the 19th December, 1748.

On 22nd April, 1751, occurred the notorious Hertfordshire swimming ordeal. John Osborne and Ruth his wife, witches of long continuance, who had destroyed a neighbouring farmer's stock and afflicted him with a strange sickness, were seized by an incensed mob and swum in Marston mere. Souse they flung the pair into the water, and Mother Osborne did not sink. The wretched couple, however, expired through exposure and ill-treatment, and Thomas Colley, the prime mover of this business, was arrested, tried for murder at Hertford Assizes, on Tuesday, 20th July, 1751, found guilty and hanged in chains on the following 24th August. A very shocking and deplorable outbreak, no doubt, but the statute is wholly responsible. The villagers could not be expected for their own safety sake to tolerate witches among them to rot and blast the whole community, and the infidels who framed the law are to blame in the first place for these riots and disorders which seem an almost inevitable consequence of their imprudence and presumption.

Witches were swum in Suffolk in 1752 ; in Leicestershire in 1760 ; in Cambridgeshire in 1769. Two witches who had forspoken and maimed cattle were swum by a number of irate farmers in the Hundreds of Essex in 1774. Two years later there was a case of swimming in Leicestershire.

In 1785 a poor woman, Sarah Bradshaw of Mears Ashby, who was suspected of being a witch in order to prove her innocence, voluntarily submitted to be dipped. She immediately plumped to the bottom of the pond, and this her neighbours took to be an incontestable proof she was clear of the accusation.

Ten years later a case of swimming is reported from Suffolk.

In February, 1808, a girl named Alice Brown, who lived at Great Paxton, Hunts, whilst endeavouring to cross the Ouse on thin ice fell through into the water and with great difficulty scrambled back to the bank where a friend, Fanny Amey, awaited her. As might be expected Alice Brown became exceedingly ill, and owing to the fright Fanny Amey was in little better state. A neighbour at once proclaimed that the pair had been overlooked. He told a story of a town in Bedfordshire where he had recently been staying. There a doting crone was more than suspected of causing a man to languish away by her evil spells. Accordingly the victim filled a vessel with his urine and heated it in a corked bottle. The result was that the old woman was seen to enter the room ; she hurried wildly to and fro grimacing and convulsed as if racked with pain ; and then vanished with a horrid yell. After a few days the witch died, when the sick man was completely cured.

This story was repeated with immense effect. Shortly it was bruited in Great Paxton that Alice Brown, Fanny Amey, and Mary Fox were bewitched and rumour pointed to Mrs. Anne Izzard, a farmer's wife some sixty years of age as the sorceress. In vain the Rev. Isaac Nicholson sternly rebuked his congregation from the pulpit. Two or three accidents seeming to confirm their accusations, one Sunday evening of May a crowd broke into the Izzards' house. They scratched the unfortunate woman, pricked her with pins, pelted her, and threatened her with ducking. With difficulty she escaped their hands, only to be assaulted the following day. The result was that a number of her neighbours were brought up before Mr. Justice Grose on a charge of assault. Several were sent to prison, and others were bound over to find security for their good behaviour, failing which they were remanded in custody. Even this did not entirely end the matter, for in the autumn of the same year a local magistrate committed two women, a mother and daughter, to Huntingdon jail for assaulting Anne Izzard and calling her witch.

A rousing " Sermon against Witchcraft " was preached in the Parish Church of Great Paxton on the 17th July, 1808, by Mr. Nicholson, who did not spare his language in his denunciation of the " Two atrocious attacks on the Person of Ann Izzard as a reputed witch ".

In 1825 a poor old man, Isaac Stebbings, aged 67, was " swum for a wizard " at Wickham Skeith, Suffolk, and all but killed by an angry mob—*The Suffolk Chronicle* quoted in *The Times*, 19th July, 1825.

Two years later, at the Monmouth Assizes, four persons were found guilty of assaulting an old trot of ninety, Mary Nicolas, commonly accused of being a witch. She was alleged to have overlooked cattle so that the beasts died. They had scratched her with a briar to draw blood ; searched for the devil's teat, which they swore they had found ; and threatened to swim her in a pool.

Writing in 1861, Mrs. Lynn Linton spoke of an " old gentleman who died at Polstead not so long ago, and who, when a boy, had seen a witch swum in Polstead Ponds, ' and she went over the water like a cork ' ; who had also watched another witch feeding her three imps like blackbirds ; and who only wanted five pounds to have seen all the witches in the parish dance on a knoll together ".

A magistrate who wrote anonymously to *The Times* on 3rd April, 1857, related how in the previous November application was made to him by a farmer whose wife had been overlooked by old Mrs. C., demanding that the police might be instructed to swim her or at least search her for the devil's mark. When the magistrate remonstrated the man explained that urine had been warmed in a hermetically sealed bottle, and sure enough as it grew hot Mrs. C., tormented in her bladder, has come to their kitchen window and stood there grinning and mowing at them through the casement. He added that only a few years before a witch, Mother Pointer, had been swum in the village pond, and it was found she could not sink. One woman told the magistrate of a witch whom she had known when she was a girl. It was never denied that Betsy Norris had bewitched cows, pigs, geese, and people. The hag was swum more than once but could never sink. Place-names are not given in the letter.

In 1864 Emma Smith, the wife of a beer-shop keeper at Ridgwell, Essex, and Samuel Stammers, a carpenter, were convicted at the Chelmsford Assizes of common assault for swimming in the previous year an old Frenchman, called " Dummy ", who was generally reputed to be a wizard, and who had over-looked the female defendant. " Dummy," a deaf and dumb gaffer of nearly ninety, at least pretended to sorcery, and eked out a miserable living by fortune-telling and the sale of charms. On the night of

3rd August Mrs. Smith, who had been anæmic and ill for many months, encountered "Dummy" in the taproom of the Swan at Sible Hedingham when she loudly accused him of being the cause of her failing health. The crowd, led by Stammers, egged her on until she seized a stick and began to belabour the warlock, shouting : "You old Devil, you served me out, and I'll serve you out." Eventually the unfortunate wretch was dragged to a brook which ran down the side of Watermill Lane, and Stammers flung him into the water at a spot where it was particularly deep. The next day he died from shock and exposure. At their trial Stammers pleaded not guilty, whilst for her defence Emma Smith kept reiterating that she was bewitched. The bench of magistrates who committed them to the Assizes remarked that "the whole disgraceful transaction arose out of a deep belief in witchcraft which possesses to a lamentable extent the tradespeople and lower orders of the district".

At Dunmow on the 23rd June, 1880, two men were convicted of assault for attempting to throw an old witch into a pond.

In 1931 there was living at Good Easter, Essex, a villager who in his youth had been before the magistrates charged together with several of his friends with an attempt to do grievous bodily harm. They had attempted to duck an old woman who was a notorious witch.

A parish doctor, who elected to remain anonymous, gives an account in *All the Year Round*, 5th January, 1867, of a witch living in his district, a village "two miles from a populous borough town", within an hour's railway journey from London. Old Mother

Redburn, a hag of seventy-two, "was accredited with all the recognized powers of curse and spell and evil eye. She has bewitched pigs, and they have refused to fatten ; she has bewitched cows, and they have become dry or died ; children under her baneful influence have wasted away to mere skeletons ; young women have gone into decline ; young men have been lamed ; old men and women have become blind, deaf, bedridden, palsied, a prey to every human woe, all owing—in the popular belief—to the ill-will of Old Mother Redburn. Cabbages, corn, turnips, and potatoes have all in their turn withered and rotted before her curse." Shortly after he commenced practice in the place the doctor was called in to see Mrs. Smith, who was blind with cataract in both eyes, deaf, and bedridden. He could discover no reason why she should not be able to stand and walk, but a neighbour shrewdly hinted : "Ah ! *we* all think that Mother Redburn has most to say to it." At last Mr. Smith decided to leave the neighbourhood, " to give the missus a chance by movin' of her " to another place. " I suppose," queried the doctor, " you think Mother Redburn prevents her getting well ? " " No one else, sir, darn her ! " was the reply. " Many years ago Mrs. Redburn, sir, came to our back-door to borrow some taters which my wife refused. Words ensued, and a day or two after the wife's eyesight began to fail. There was another dispute over some cabbages, and then my old woman became blind, deaf and bedridden, all through offending Mrs. Redburn." Certain it is that from the very night of settling in their new home, Mrs. Smith improved in an astonishing manner. She was at once able to sit up, and shortly began to walk about briskly enough, whilst her hearing returned. The cataract, however, remained.

The Daily Chronicle, 15th February, 1879, records a case of witchcraft at Caergwrle. Mrs. Braithwaite supplied a Mrs. Williams with milk, but suddenly refused to serve her. The reason was that Mrs. Braithwaite had always been very successful with her butter until she offended Mrs. Williams, when her butter would not come try as she might. She declared Mrs. Williams had overlooked the churn, and called after her, " Out, witch ! witch ! If you don't leave the place, I'll shoot you." Mrs. Williams applied to the bench for protection as everyone in the district believed her to be a witch. The magistrates directed an officer to caution Mrs. Braithwaite against repeating the threats.

Writing in *The Times*, 20th September 1930, Mr. Andrew Innes, of High Tenter Fell, Kendal, relates several recent exploits of a Caithness witch. On one occasion when a farmer refused to sell her a young cow, saying he needed the milk himself, the witch charmed the animal so that she could yield no more milk, but remained dry.

The Leigh Chronicle, 19th April, 1879, reports the case of William Bulwer, of Etling Green, who was charged at the East Dereham Petty Sessions with assaulting Christiana Martins, a girl of eighteen. Recriminations of the filthiest description passed between the two and from words they came to blows. The defendant stated : " Mrs. Martins is an old witch, gentlemen, that is what she is and she charmed me, and I got no sleep for her for three nights, and one night at half-past eleven o'clock, I got up because I could not sleep, and went out and found a ' walking toad ' under a clod which had been dug up with a three-pronged fork. That is why I could not rest ; she is a bad old woman ; she put this toad under there to charm me, and her daughter is just as bad, gentlemen. She would bewitch anyone ; she charmed me, and I got no rest day or night for her, till I found this ' walking toad ' under the turf. She dug a hole and put it there to charm me, gentlemen, that is the truth. I got the toad out and put it in a cloth, and took it upstairs and showed it to my mother, and ' throwed ' it into the pit in the garden. She went round this here ' walking toad ' after she had buried it, and I could not rest by day or sleep by night till I found it."

Mrs. Martins also bewitched by a curious look or side-glance, a form of spell noticed in the *Malleus Maleficarum*. I have no doubt that Bulwer's story, clumsily told, was entirely accurate, and that the toad was one of the woman's imps.

In 1886 there happened to be found hidden away in the belfry of an English country church a long cord tied in elaborate strands and interwoven with the feathers of a black hen. Obviously it had been made for some definite purpose and presently an old woman in the village identified it as a " witch's ladder ", proof positive that some persons in the neighbourhood knew something of the traditional occult lore and were endeavouring to cast a spell.

In 1911 a poor woman was tried in Ireland for killing an old witch, who by means of a familiar, a rat, had tormented her to madness. *The Irish Times*, 14th June, 1911.

At the Glamorgan Assizes on the 27th July, 1920,

before Mr. Justice Avory, William Davies, a hawker, and his wife Mary Jane Davies, were sentenced to terms of imprisonment with hard labour for obtaining sums of money and articles of value from various persons " by pretending to exercise witchcraft ". David James, an old farmer living at Twynygarreg Farm, near Treharris, said that he and his family had been suffering from a skin disease. Mary Jane Davies told him that they were bewitched and the cattle also were overlooked. She undertook to cure the household, but first demanded a number of articles she scented as having been " cursed ". They also paid her considerable sums in cash. A neighbouring farmer, James Williams, who likewise had illness in his family was warned by the female Davies that his house was under malign influences. He gave her money to avert the working of the charm. The two families fully believed that some witch had cast an evil spell upon them, and it was contended for the defence that the accused had been called in to remove the ban and that no false pretences were used. It is, of course, quite possible that the Davies, witches, had in the first instance brought disaster upon the two households and then cunningly contrived that they should be summoned actually to undo their own mischief.

In July, 1929, Eugene Burgess, a taxicab driver, was arrested at Kalamazoo, Michigan, for the murder of Mrs. Etta Fairchild, aged seventy-five. This woman, who was undoubtedly a witch, bragged of the numbers of people (including her own husband) whom she had killed by her foul enchantments. Burgess invited the woman who was the inmate of a charity home to his house and then brained her with a piece of lead piping and a hammer. Mrs. Burgess, who had been overlooked by the witch, said : " I stagger lots of times and have pains and aches and trouble in breathing. It was either her life or ours." Mrs. Fairchild had also bewitched the seventeen year old daughter of Burgess, and intended to waste her to death.

Thus in the *Daily Express*, 22nd January, 1934, there is an account of a man in a remote Dorset hamlet who has been bewitched and is dying slowly although physically there is nothing the matter with him. " Doctors have examined him from head to toe. They pronounced him perfectly healthy in wind and limb. Yet they are powerless to save him." The local physician said : " The man is doomed. We can do nothing for him, as he is determined to die." The victim is described as a tall, gaunt man of middle age. His cheeks were sunken and pasty ; he was so weak he could scarcely stand. For about two and a half years he had been ailing. A gipsy came to the door, and when he asked her if she could suggest a remedy, she told him that someone, a woman, had " looked over " him. Yet since the repeal of the law of James I the witch must go scathless and scot-free.

In July, 1935, a man who lived near Taunton committed suicide because he had been " overlooked " by a witch.

Witches are as numerous, as malign and mischievous in England to-day, as ever they were in the sixteenth and seventeenth centuries, and legislation is as much needed now as then.

In one part of the Empire, at least, in Jamaica the laws against witchcraft (obeah) are happily in full force.

By the *Encyclopedia Americana* (1829–1833 ; vol. iv, 1832), the word Obeah is thus defined : " a species of witchcraft practised among the Negroes, the apprehension of which, operating upon the superstitious fears, is frequently attended with disease and death." We remark then that the result of Jamaican and English witchcraft is the same. Fr. Joseph J. Williams, S.J., the eminent authority upon voodoo and obeah, observes that " real obeah must be regarded as a form of Devil-worship " since the agent (the witch) is the servant of the Sasabonsan or the Devil invoked and relied upon to produce the desired effect. Obeah " is professedly a projection of spiritual power with the harm of an individual as an objective. Practically, its end is attained through fear, supplemented if needs be by secret poisoning ". This might well stand for a definition of European witchcraft, for the two things are one and the same.

The obeah-man fears the priest as one who can exercise a more powerful influence. In their own fashion the coloured folk think that the Catholic Church controls the strongest obeah. The devotees of the obeah cult, says Fr. Williams, believe that a priest can give evidence of his dominance by " lighting a candle on them ". " Fadder take pin and Fadder take candle, and him stick der pin in der candle ; and him light der candle on you. Der candle him burn and him burn and him burn. And you waste and you waste and you waste. And when der flame touch dat pin—you die." The threat made in jest by a priest " I think I'll have to light a candle on you " will bring the stoutest black to his knees.

Fr. Williams quotes a number of reports from *The*

Daily Gleaner of Kingston to show that witchcraft (obeah) is widely prevalent and most obstinately practised throughout the island. Moreover the majority of cases that come before the Court are mixed up with a deal of imposture, low money-grubbing, and gain. In his real professional practice the obeah-man is as secret and close as the witch of three centuries ago. A little gamble with luck he will chance. He will help in love affairs or effect a cure or clear a haunted house, and if he is caught at any of these games he pays the penalty, and then returns to his trade exercising a trifle more caution, asking his clients for a rather higher fee. But when it is a question of real obeah he will take good care to assure himself of inviolable secrecy, for he will never run the risk of having a capital offence proved against him.

Thus on 24th November, 1933, Vitelleus Brown was charged with practising obeah. He said he could cure a swollen knee, which he attributed to obeah in the first instance. Someone " had set hand " on the sufferer, who was to be healed for three pounds. On the following day Alexander Brown was charged with the same offence. A man and woman consulted him, declaring they were very sick. He informed the woman that a policeman had put a ghost upon her, and asked a fee of three pounds to " take off the duppy ". On 14th December of the same year at Spanish Town there was " Six Months for Obeahman ". David Simon was convicted of contracting to remove the duppies from Ada Bogle's house, which she swore was beset with spirits who scratched and rapped and pelted the place with stones. Simon's job was to drive away the unruly ghosts.

On the 9th January, 1934, George Washington Pitt was fined £12 10s. for practising obeah. He had been heard to boast that : " He could cure ; he could kill ; he could get his clients good positions." This vaunt betrays a knowledge of the darkest secrets of obeah, the art of dealing out death and decay.

In *Chambers's Journal*, 11th January, 1902, an article entitled " Obeah To-day in The West Indies " points out that " In many countries superstitious rites are practised to bring good luck ; but that is not the case as a rule with *obeah*. Its root idea is the worship and propitiation of the Evil One : it is essentially malevolent. A Negro usually goes to the obeah-man to harm his neighbour, not to do any good to himself ; and that is why the law regards the matter so seriously ". The Jamaican legislation of 1760 provides against " the Wicked Art of Negroes going under the Apellation of obeah-men and obeah-women pretending to have Communication with the Devil and other Evil Spirits " and enacts that " any Negro or other Slave who shall pretend to any Supernatural Power and be detected in making use of any . . . materials related to the practice of Obeah or Witchcraft in order to delude or impose upon the Minds of others shall upon Conviction thereof before two Magistrates and three Freeholders suffer Death or Transportation ". *The Times* of London, 5th December, 1818, quotes " a recent Act of the house of Assembly (Barbados) " which punishes negroes or slaves wilfully, maliciously and unlawfully pretending to any magical or supernatural charm or power, or who use and carry on the wicked and unlawful practice of obeah, with death, transportation, or such other penalty as the

Court may decide. Obeah, European witchcraft in the past, Satanism in England to-day, are all one and the same thing, essential evil, malignant, destructive, accursed by God, hateful to man, the cult of the Devil.

The Daily Express, 20th January, 1937, says that " Voodooism, with its strange, awful rites, is still flourishing in Michigan ", and reports how a negro woman and her child sought the protection of the police, since her husband, Verlen McQueen, was going to sacrifice them to Satan in a huge jar of boiling water. The man, when arrested, was found stirring a great cauldron of water set over a fierce fire. In 1932, a voodoo magician, Robert Harris, beheaded another negro upon an altar. Harris was confined in an asylum. Negro children are actually being sent to secret voodoo schools.

The Church Times, 21st December, 1928, quoting the latest number of the diocesan magazine of the Bishop of Mauritius, says : " I wonder how many people in Mauritius realize what a strong hold sorcery in some form or another has on quite a large number of persons in Mauritius, by no means all of whom are of the uneducated classes, and all of whom profess some form of Christianity. Although prosecutions for witchcraft *qua* witchcraft have ceased, indirectly it is still dealt with under other names by the penal codes of every civilized country. In Mauritius those involved are prosecuted for swindling. I am assured by those qualified to give accurate information that witchcraft or Petit Albert is practised by many thousands of persons in Mauritius. No one professing the Christian Faith can, without mortal sin, have anything to do with any form of witchcraft. Petit Albert is nothing less than the cult of the Devil." Here the Bishop gives three examples of invocations.

"The petitions are for personal gain or injury to enemies, and are often of an erotic or obscene character. Sacred names and phrases are used in a blasphemous way. These intercessions are accompanied by various ceremonies, in which a skull, a dagger, camphor, and flowers figure. Engravings of saints have pins stuck in various parts of the figure ; I have seen a picture of the Sacred Heart covered with such pins. A crucifix is also frequently used in these blasphemous rites. It has been known in Mauritius for a newly-interred female corpse to be dug up and used for horrible purposes. To take part in such practices, and at the same time to pose as a Christian, is, in my opinion, perilously near committing unforgivable sin."

Not without reason has Rumania definitely banned magic in every form. *The Daily Mail*, Wednesday, 1st April, 1936.

In *The Times* of Thursday, 21st January, 1932, was published an extraordinary—and to my mind a disturbing—article entitled " A Satanist Picture ". There was at Burlington House an Exhibition of French Art, including a picture of " The Annunciation " loaned from Aix-en-Provence. The writer stated that this was locally acknowledged to be the work of a Satanist painter. It hangs in a " dark chapel " in the Church of the Madeleine. " It has always been there. Who painted it ? " A Satanist who concealed his name through fear of the Inquisition ? " Did the picture enter the church under the auspices of that Robert Mauvoisin, Archbishop of Aix, who, accused of sorcery and convicted of having celebrated Black Masses with

the blood of little children was condemned at Avignon by Pope John XXII ?   Or was it offered to the parish by Rodrigue de Lune, nephew of the Antipope Benedict XIII, who vowed himself to the devil ? "
" This is quite conceivable ! "

Better still ; " Is it not possible that it was surreptitiously hung in its niche by the Abbé Gaufridi, who, during the minority of Louis XIII, was burnt alive in the Place des Prêcheurs for having convoked a whole convent of Ursulines to Witches' Sabbaths ? "

All this is very alarming. The picture is examined in detail.   " Here the announcing angel has owl's wings ; the ray of light emanating from God the Father, before reaching Mary, falls on a monkey crouching on the edge of a lectern. In the groining, instead of doves and larks, flutter bats and vampires. From the trefoils of the arches horned devils peep. In the vase beside the lily stand three evil herbs, basil, foxglove, and belladonna, and, indubitable sign of Satanic consecration, both God the Father and the angel, instead of raising fingers in the orthodox attitude of benediction, advance the thumb between the third and middle fingers according to the obscene and malefic gesture which Spanish wizards termed *hacer figa*, and with which, according to mediæval demonologists, the devil often opened Sabbaths.

" In the shutters of the triptych two pious figures are standing beneath shelves laden with books. These will keep their secret, and we shall never know their titles. Let us wager, however, that they spell Cabal, and that the priest and deacon keeping vigil in this singular sanctuary were reading, not the Breviary, but the ' Malleus Maleficarum ', the ' Daemonomania ', or the ' Livre des Charmes, Sorcelages et Enchantements ' " [sic].

This is a regular thrill. Unfortunately some details in the very picturesque description are a trifle inaccurate. The announcing Angel, St. Gabriel, has not owl's wings. The rays of light do not more than pass over the lectern of which the finial is a monkey. The bats and vampires instead of fluttering in the groining, flutter only in the writer's imagination. A fluttering vampire is a novelty, to be sure. There are no evil herbs beside the lily, no foxglove, no belladonna. What may be clearly seen has been identified as the blue columbine, which obtains its name from a pretty fancy as resembling a nest of doves, and a red flower which is either the rose or the poppy. The thumb of the Father is not " advanced between His third and middle fingers ", in fact it is scarcely visible, nor indeed is that of the Angel who is not blessing at all. One would be glad to know which mediæval demonologists state that the Devil opened the Sabbath with the gesture, *hacer figa*. Reference, please. The " two pious figures " will not and do not desire to keep their secret. The name of one, *Jeremias propheta*, is quite legibly inscribed beneath him. The name *Isaias propheta* is by chance out of sight. We are told of two possible donors of the fourteenth century. In this case it is hardly likely that the " pious figures " would be reading works written respectively at the end of the fifteenth and sixteenth centuries. Nor is it probable that the picture " entered the church under the auspices " of an Archbishop condemned by a Pope who was ,dead more than a hundred years before it was painted. True, an alternative is suggested.

But is there the slightest reason for supposing that the sorcerer Louis Gaufridi, executed in 1611, has any connexion whatsoever with the picture?

I may remark that it is impious—although doubtless no offence was intended—to speak of a Saint, St. Sara, as the " patroness of fairies, witches ".

The whole article " A Satanist Picture " is—to use the mildest terms—founded upon a complete misapprehension, but such a mistake may leave a very ugly impression. There are " Satanist Pictures ", but not such as this, and my late friend, the Provost of Eton, Dr. M. R. James, both in a private letter to myself and in a letter published in *The Times*, 25th January, 1932, expressed himself as aggrieved that the Mystery of the Annunciation should have been made the subject of such an imputation.

Satanism is alive to-day. It is a power in the land. Mysterious, unseen, wholly evil.

I myself have been shown two ancient candlesticks of great value upon which in a secret place was inscribed in Hebrew characters the Most Holy Name of God,—but inverted. They had been used at the hideous celebration of a diabolic Eucharist.

In 1899 Mons. Serge Basset, a well-known French journalist, who unhappily fell in the Great War, was present at a Black Mass, and his account of the ceremony appeared in *Le Matin* of 27th May of that year. The circumstances were peculiar. Mons. Basset had contributed an article to *L'Éclair* expressing himself entirely sceptical concerning the practice of Satanic Masses to-day, whereupon he received a letter requesting him in very plain terms to meet the writer at 9 o'clock on the following Thursday in the Place Saint-

Sulpice, whence he would be conducted to a Black Mass and see for himself. Suspecting a practical joke he did not reply, and even ignored a second and more pressing communication. A few evenings later there called at his flat a lady, heavily veiled, who told him that it was she who had been his correspondent, and who invited him, if really in earnest, to accompany her—unless indeed he were afraid. " You do not believe in us," she said. " Very well, I will convince you." A car was waiting, and full of curiosity he agreed to go. Such precautions were taken that he was unable to gather their route, nor could he guess the name of the lonely street where they stopped, as he was immediately hurried into a large house, which seemed in complete darkness. Here he was ushered into a lofty room of some size, fitted up as a chapel. About twenty or a couple of dozen persons were present, of whom seven or eight were women. Amongst the men several appeared quite young, almost boys. At the far end of the room, dimly lighted by one faint lamp, he could half-discern an altar, and when six black candles were presently lit he saw that they were equally ranged on either side of a monstrous figure, a hideous goat, squatting on its haunches, bearded and lewd, with great red staring eyes. It butted with its huge protudent horns the tips of which glowed with a dull crimson flame. The walls of the room were painted with esoteric designs, curious triangles of gold within silver circles, pentacles, many-rayed stars, Hebrew and Greek characters, all intermingled with vividly designed scenes of the most shameless obscenity. A sombre chant was heard in low, mournful tones *Gloria in profundis Satano ! In profundis Satano Gloria !*

More candles were lit, and there approached the altar a tall man vested in a richly laced alb and a cope of flaming scarlet embroidered with gilt cones and pomegranates. The server was a woman, a horrible hag, raddled and scarred with villainy. From unseen braziers the fume of heady incense mixed with pungent herbs began to load the heated air. The voices of celebrant and server alternated in low muttered tones : *Introibo ad altare dei nostri Satanis. Ad Deum qui nunc oppressus resurget et triumphabit.* Suddenly a girl, hardly beyond her teens, darted forward, and stripping off her clothes knelt stark naked before the altar. *Quid velis?* (What would you?) asked the celebrant. *Ad sacrificium corpus meum offero* (I present my body as the place of sacrifice), she cried. He bowed his head silently, and at his gesture she mounted on the altar where she lay at full length covered with a black veil. In hideous parody of the Offertory a jewelled ciborium was presented whence the celebrant drew a large black host and elevated it with the ritual prayer. *Accipe etiam sanguinem nostrum* (Receive also our blood), clamoured the frenzied worshippers. The ceremony continued. From time to time the woman stretched on the altar uttered hysterical screams and moans. Suddenly the celebrant turned and scattered a number of black hosts to the devotees who rushed towards him with mænad fury. By this time all, or nearly all, were in a state of nudity. It seemed as if worse horrors were to follow, and Mons. Basset clapped his hands before his eyes with a cry of disgust. At that moment two men who had been standing in the shadow intently watching his every movement sprang forward and caught him by either arm. " Get out of here," they shouted, hustling him towards the door. "Get out. You've seen too much already."

He was hurried down a long dark passage, up some stairs across a garden, and through a door which was slammed and bolted behind him. He found himself in a narrow back street, whence it was with difficulty that he made his way to a district he recognized and knew. At the time his story was questioned in some quarters, but although he steadily refused to give further particulars—he was undoubtedly bound by an oath of secrecy—Mons. Basset pledged his word that the details he related were in every respect exactly true. Nor would it be at all hard closely to parallel this scene in London and in many another English city to-day.

The following experience which,—with the suppression of actual names, an obvious precaution—I am allowed to relate, happened less than ten years ago to the sister of a personal friend of mine. This lady who is a Catholic and a medical doctor was persuaded by two acquaintances to accompany them to a "fortune-teller" in Merthyr Tydfil. They made their way to a little house in a poor street and were admitted by a woman who seemed obviously demented, so wild-eyed was she and so eccentric in her gestures and behaviour. An old grey-headed man appeared from within, ready to interview them. He promptly denied that he was a "fortune-teller". "I am not a Christian," he said, "nor a Jew. I belong to the oldest religion in the world." He then fastened his attention upon my friend's sister and accused her of being his enemy. "You are carrying a rosary with you," he cried, and such was in fact the case. He next invited all three of his visitors downstairs to a basement. My friend's sister at first refused to go, but when she found herself left alone with the woman who had admitted them and who began to laugh and mutter in a menacing fashion she preferred to descend, and joined the rest who were in a chapel, the altar of which blazed with candles. Above in the centre was suspended a pair of horns, and queer objects were ranged on the altar-table. This lady had no knowledge and little suspicion of the truth. The old man spoke to her for a few minutes and asked her to lay her hand on the altar and say : " In the Name of the Father." This she refused to do, and she forthwith insisted upon her companions leaving the place with her. The warlock had already told her several things concerning herself and her family. He cried : " I cannot prevent you going for you are protected by the constant prayers of an old man whom I see reclining in a chair and telling his beads." This, no doubt, referred to the lady's father, an invalid who spent his day in a chair, and was extremely devout, passing the hours in prayer and intercession.

Up and down England there is hardly a village without a witch. In our great cities, our larger towns, our seats of learning, Satanists abound and are organized (as of old) into covens of wickedness. Black Masses are celebrated in Mayfair and Chelsea ; in Wapping and Shoreditch ; in Brighton ; in Birmingham ; in Liverpool ; in Edinburgh. Under conditions of peculiar horror a Black Mass was celebrated in the ruins of Godstow Nunnery near Oxford. A band of Satanists have their rendezvous not far from the city of Cambridge.

During the Helsingfors scandals of 1931, a veritable

outburst of Satanism and necromancy, it was commonly bruited (and stated in the newspapers) that the Finnish police had called in the help of Scotland Yard since London was believed to be the headquarters of the infernal society, the Black International.

Who shall say that the statute of James I was severe ? Rather did it not incline to clemency.

The Divine Law has spoken : " Thou shalt not suffer a Witch to live."

" Certain London cults practise the Black Mass, where black bread, black wine, and black candles are used, worshippers confess every good deed as a sin, and do penance."—*The Daily Mail*, 14th April, 1934.

Lady Peirse has well written : " They may call it psychism or occultism ; they may learn to cast curses or spells ; they may invoke the help of the powers of evil, but it is practically the same thing, and its lure to mankind is as old and mysterious as the wind that blows over the earth, urging them with strange elusive thrills to recapture and use the old powers of the Serpent."

" I am perfectly certain that there are witches to-day —both men and women who do a great deal of harm by their foul practices and bring ill-luck to people. I do not consider this is superstition at all but just common sense." I spoke those words at a public meeting in February, 1933. The next day the newspapers blazoned their headlines : " Modern Faith in Witches. Clergyman thinks they Exist." " Priest believes in Witches. Common Sense ! "

Now and again some gang of devil-worshippers may be—almost by accident—broken up and dispersed, but there are (I fear) few persons who realize how far-spread and how cunningly organized are these Societies of Evil. To the ordinary man Satanism often seems incredible, or at any rate a myth of the remote Dark Ages. He does not realize, and he is happy in his ignorance, the devil's fires that burn just a very little way beneath the thin and crumbled crust of our boasted modern civilization.

The Witch of Eye

François Baculard D'Arnaud
(1716-1805)

'Fear me not, fear me not, good Sir John: the stout heart of Eleanor Cobham will not fail her; albeit that as yet I do not choose to be present at these orgies. How sayest thou, Margaret Jourdmain is there, and assisted by Roger Bolinbroke?'

The person by whom this question was asked was a female; who, although somewhat declined into the vale of years, was still remarkable for her stately and majestic gait, and the symmetry and beauty of her features. Her stature seemed to be above six feet; her long, flowing, and once jet black, but now grey, tresses, fell in rich ringlets down her back; and her high, pale forehead was singularly contrasted with her dark and fiery eye. Her rank and wealth were sufficiently indicated by the splendour of her dress. She wore a long flowing robe of silk; her hair was plaited with jewels, whence pendant drops, composed of precious stones of great value and size, hung upon her forehead; and a collar of gold, from which hung a chain of the same costly material, was fastened round her neck. She sat in a massive oaken chair, curiously carved, and placed in the midst of a large Gothic chamber, through whose windows the moonbeams poured a flood of many-coloured light, as they took the tinge of the painted glass through which they streamed.

The walls of the apartment were hung with rich tapestry, and the floor was strewed with rushes. A large silver candelabra, bearing lighted waxen tapers, descended from the ceiling and illuminated the whole apartment. A small table, of similar workmanship to the chair in which she sat, stood before the lady, and on it was spread, wide open, a large parchment volume, in the perusal of which she appeared to have been very recently occupied.

Opposite to her stood a man, whose shaven crown, the beads and cross dependent from his neck, his white cassock, and his narrow scapulary, proclaimed him to be a monk of the Cistercian order. He was a short and meagre figure, with small red eyes, a sharp aquiline nose, black beard and brows, and extraordinarily intelligent, but at the same time somewhat repulsive and malignant, expression of countenance.

'They have been busily engaged, madam,' he said, in answer to the lady's question, 'in your Grace's service, since the hour of noon. At that hour the waxen image was completed and the fatal fire was lighted; and *from that hour* did Henry, marrow, bones, an all, begin to waste and wither away; and shall continue so to do, until the throne of England shall be left vacant for a worthier occupant.'

'Thanks, good Sir John,' said the lady, unclasping the collar of gold round her neck, and placing it, with the chain attached to it, in the priest's hands; 'A thousand thanks! Do I not well, Sir John? Heaven knows that it is not for the sake of gratifying any ambitious thoughts of my own that I enter upon this seemingly unhallowed work; but in compassion of the miseries which the unhappy people of England endure under the sway of the feeble and incapable Henry, who is the unresisting instrument of all their ill, in the hands of that she-wolf of France, and this newly created Duke of York, Richard Plantagenet.'

'Your Grace is but to blame,' said the obsequious priest, 'for having so long delayed to avail yourself of that knowledge, and those arts, into the mysteries of which your poor servant has been the unworthy means of initiating you, for the purpose of putting an end to the evils with which our country is overwhelmed. How will the loyal heart of your servant Hume rejoice, when he hears the welcome shouts of "God save King Humphrey!" "God save Queen Eleanor!"'

'Peace, peace, good Hume!' said the lady; 'thou talkest idly.' But a smile of hope brightened her features at the same time, and belied the expression of her lips. 'Heaven knows that there is no one in this realm would pray more fervently for the welfare of Henry of Lancaster than Eleanor Cobham; but that, while he lives, England must lie at the mercy of Margaret of Anjou, and Richard of Plantagenet. Yet, Hume, I would fain receive some more certain assurance as to my future destiny. When wilt thou invoke to my presence the spirit who is to answer such questions as I shall propound ?'

'Madam,' answered Hume, 'it is by severe and painful penance, anxious watching, and long fasting, alone, that I can prevail upon that invisible power whom I serve, to gratify your Grace's desire. Neither can Margaret Jourdmain nor Roger Bolinbroke assist me; for they have not attained such proficiency in the occult sciences as to be able to command spirits to do their bidding. Time, a short but carefully spent time, will empower me to call one before you who shall reveal to your Grace the secrets of futurity.'

Had the Duchess at that moment fixed her eye upon her chaplain, she would have detected, in his changing colour and trembling limbs, the hypocrite and the impostor. Whatever might have been the reality of the pretensions to occult lore on the part of Jourdmain and Bolinbroke, the only magic of which Hume was master, was the ascendancy of a strong mind over a weak one. The Duchess knew him to be a man of vast and various learning and acquirements; and had been initiated by him into the study of languages, and of the natural sciences. She therefore readily credited his pretensions to knowledge of a more profound and mysterious character; and he, by flattering her ambitious hopes, and pretending to minister to their gratification, continued to store his own purse at her expense, and to indulge himself in such pleasures as his straitened means, and not his sacerdotal oath, alone debarred him from. He had accordingly promised to raise a spirit who should reveal her future destiny to her, being deficient in the science of Astrology (which was then, as it is now, the only *lawful* means made use of for decyphering futurity, without the imputation of crime). He had, for this purpose, hired two professors of the black art, or witchcraft, to construct a waxen image of the King, who, they pretended, would waste away under the influence of a strange disease, as that image melted before a fire which they had kindled. Hume knew him own pretensions to occult knowledge to be unfounded, and believed those of his associates to be the same. The death of the King, and the elevation of dame Eleanor, were not the objects which the crafty priest had in view; but the multiplication of his own wealth and pleasures, by means of the well-stored purse of the Duchess of Gloucester.

'Hume!' said the lady, 'hasten the period at which my desires may be gratified. In the mean time, receive my thanks for the services which thou hast already rendered me. But, give us leave awhile, good Sir John; my Lord approaches.'

The priest made a lowly reverence, and left the apartment, almost at the same moment that the Duke of Gloucester entered. This was the son of King Henry the Fourth, who, by his virtues, had acquired the appellation of 'the good Duke Humphrey'. He entered with a hurried and agitated step: his face was pale; his lips quivered; and his eye rolled wildly and fearfully.

'My gracious Lord,' said the Duchess, 'what has happened? I fear some strange and unlooked for misfortune.'

'Eleanor,' said the Duke, 'the young King is taken suddenly and dangerously ill. His physicians can neither divine the nature of his malady, nor devise any cure.'

'Ha!' said the Duchess; her eyes sparkling, and her cheek glowing as she spoke; – 'suddenly, Duke Humphrey, sayest thou, that the King was thus attacked? And at what hour, I pray thee?'

'At the hour of noon;' answered the Duke.

'At noon – at noon!' repeated the Duchess to herself, clasping her hands, and pacing the apartment in a state of mental abstraction. 'It was *at that hour*, as Hume informed me, that the wise woman's labours were completed. Humphrey,' she added, turning towards the Duke, 'the King will die.'

'Now heaven forefend!' replied Duke Humphrey; 'so young – so good – so pious!'

'The fitter for heaven!' interrupted the Duchess. 'For this world, and especially for the station he fills, *he* is, of all men, most unfit. The monk's cloister, or the hermit's cell, indeed, might have found in him a fitting occupant; but the throne of

France and England suits him not; and the sceptre of Henry the Fifth is not adapted to his puny grasp.'

'Alas, alas!' said the Duke of Gloucester; 'he will neither fill the one nor grasp the other long.'

'The will of heaven must be submitted to,' said Eleanor; 'and the people of England, when they are obliged to exchange King Henry for King Humphrey, must learn to yield in patience to so fearful a visitation.'

'Now, by heaven, Nell!' said the Duke; and an expression of indignation and anger succeeded that of deep distress which had clouded his fine features – 'thou maddest me. Is ours an age at which to nurse the idle dreams of ambition? and is the malady of a young and virtuous prince, like Henry, a fitting subject of exultation to his nearest relatives? I fear, Eleanor, that pride and ambition have dried up the milk of human charity in thy bosom. I fear, too,' – here he spoke in a low and stifled tone, while cold big drops stood upon his temples, – 'that thou pursuest unholy and unlawful studies. Beware! Eleanor Cobham, beware! – the public suspicion is awakened against thee; the Queen loves thee not; the Duke of York thirsts for thy blood; and Humphrey of Gloucester's power to defend and protect thee is becoming smaller and weaker with each waning moon.'

The consciousness of her guilt, and the abruptness and suddenness of the accusation, struck the Duchess of Gloucester mute; while her cheek changed from a fiery red to an ashy paleness, her breath came short and thick, and her limbs trembled under her. 'Humphrey,' she at length said, as with a violent effort she recovered her self-possession, drew her stately figure up to its utmost height, and laid her hand upon the arm of the Duke; 'this is cruel and unkind; and, from thee, most unexpected. Because I have devoted myself to study, the ignorant vulgar have charged me with the practice of magic; and the malignity of those, my foes whose superior education and station prevent them from being themselves the dupe of so idle an accusation, has nevertheless given sanction and confirmation to it; but, that the Duke of Gloucester, – the most accomplished and learned prince in Christendom, in whose well-stored library I have acquired that knowledge which is now imputed to me as a crime, – that *he* should join in the senseless outcry of the vulgar and malignant, is a calamity against the occurrence of which I confess that I was not sufficiently prepared. Go! Duke Humphrey; denounce me to the King! offer up your wife as an expiatory sacrifice to the wrath of Margaret of Anjou, and Richard Plantagenet! Suffolk will smile upon you – your good uncle Beaufort will once more admit you to his paternal embrace; and rare and jocund will be the dance and the wassailing over the grave of Eleanor Cobham.'

Thus saying, she rushed out of the apartment, leaving the Duke, over whose feelings she well knew the extent of her influence, penetrated with uneasiness and sorrow at having given her pain or offence; although he could not entirely banish from his mind the suspicions which had been awakened in it.

To the wonder and joy of the Duchess, and the consternation of Hume, day after day brought news to the Duke of Gloucester's palace of the increasing malady of the King, and of the futility of *every* effort which had been made to stop its fatal progress. The chaplain, who had believed that the associates whom he had engaged to assist him in his attack on the Duchess's purse were no more able to effect the King's death by magic than he was to raise a spirit, began to fear that their diabolical learning was no vain pretension – so strangely coincident was the progress of the King's disease with the work on which the Witch of Eye and Bolinbroke were engaged.

Dissolute and avaricious as he was, his heart sunk within him at the idea of being an accomplice in the murder of his sovereign, especially by such means. Remorse for his crime was also mingled with no small portion of fear as to its consequences to himself; for it was by no means certain, that amidst the contentions of parties which would necessarily follow the death of the King, his patroness would rule the ascendant. To add to his perplexity, Eleanor had become importunate with him to raise the spirit who, he had promised, should reveal to her her future destiny; and, on his repeated excuses and postponements, had rated him in terms which his wounded pride could ill brook. Moodily and dejectedly pondering over these circumstances, Hume was pacing the great hall of the ducal palace. He had just received an intimation from Bolinbroke, that their work was proceeding most auspiciously; that in less than twelve hours the waxen image would entirely melt away; and that within that time, therefore, King Henry must sink under the influence of his disease.

'Save me! save me, gracious heaven!' he exclaimed; 'wherefore have I sold myself, body and soul, to this diabolical confederacy? I will break the hellish trammels in which I am bound. I will hasten to the Duke of York, reveal all, and while there is yet time, save the King from the machinations of his enemies. And yet,' he added, after a short pause, 'this is but an idle fear by which I am suffering myself to be unmanned. Strange as it is that the King's illness should happen at the same time that these idle mummeries are practising, it does not therefore follow that it is caused by them; neither do I yet know that any symptoms have today appeared to render the near approach of death probable.' -

At that moment the Duke of Gloucester, with several attendants, passed through the hall. As he passed Hume, the priest made a lowly reference. 'To your prayers, to your prayers, good Sir John,' said the Duke; 'pray for our pious King, whose mortal career is fast drawing to its close.'

'I trust,' said Hume, crossing himself, 'that his Highness will yet live many years to rule over a happy and loyal people.'

'That hope is vain, Hume,' said the Duke. 'I have just received a message from Queen Margaret, commanding my immediate attendance; and informing me, that *the King has not twelve hours' life in him*. Fare thee well, reverend father! and forget not to pray for good King Henry's soul.'

Hume gazed on the Duke without answering him, astounded and dismayed. 'Twelve hours!' he exclaimed, after Humphrey and his followers had disappeared. 'It is the very period which Bolinbroke mentioned, as that at which his hellish purpose would be achieved. I will wash my hands of this unhallowed deed. The Duke of York shall know the fiend-like purpose of the Duchess. Yet would I not willingly lead to destruction the woman to whom I owe my rank and fortune. I would not lead to the scaffold or to the stake —'

At that moment he felt his arm wrung forcibly, and, turning round, beheld the very person who principally occupied his thoughts, standing before him. There was an unusual flush on the cheek of the Duchess; her eye seemed to flash fire, and her stately form appeared to dilate to still more majestic proportions. She looked as though she already grasped the sceptre of France and England, and wore the regal diadem upon her brow.

'So moody and contemplative, Sir John Hume?' she said; 'and at the hour when all our labours are about to be crowned with success?'

'I understand your Grace's meaning,' said the priest: 'the King is dying?'

'*Even so,*' said the Duchess; 'thanks to thy powerful arts!'

Hume shuddered; and, lifting his sleeve to his brow, wiped away the drops which had started there. 'Gracious madam, say not so!' he exclaimed. 'I trust that his Highness will yet – will at least for a time; – pardon me, pardon me! I know not what I say; yet, were it not well that these proceedings should be stayed for a time? The King's disorder may be natural; and then –'

'Peace, peace!' said Eleanor; 'thou talkest childishly. It was the will of fate that Margaret of Anjou's crown should be transferred to these brows of mine. But, Hume,' she added, in a determined and somewhat angry tone, 'I must see and converse with this spirit immediately. I will not be delayed longer; and if thy art cannot raise him, I must seek the aid of others who are greater proficients.'

'Not yet, gracious madam, not yet,' said Hume: 'and I pray thee again consider whether we are not somewhat too sudden in our machinations for the death of the King. Command the Witch of Eye and Bolinbroke to suspend their operations for the present. If the King's illness is so speedily followed by *death*, the public will suspect –'

'Peace, man!' said the Duchess, whose haughty and imperious temper for a moment got the better of her discretion, and smiting the priest violently on his cheek — 'peace, doting prattler! counsel me not, but obey me. Raise me the spirit, or by heaven —'

At that moment the Duchess's eye caught the expression of Hume's features, and she was startled and awed at the mingled malignity, contempt, and triumph, which she read there. Eleanor Cobham although noted for the violence and impetuosity of her passions, was equally remarkable for the swiftness and adroitness with which she could master and disguise them. In an instant, the flush of anger passed from her face, her lip curled with a smile, and her whole countenance seemed lighted up with gaiety.

'Why Hume, man,' she said, 'thou lookest as if thou believedst us in earnest offended, and forgetful of the services which our good chaplain has performed on our behalf. But in truth, Sir John, I *must* converse with this spirit. Gratify the wish of thy Duchess —'

'Of my Queen!' said Hume, sinking on his knee, and taking the opportunity of his prostration to mask his features in an expression of becoming reverence and humility.

'Whether Duchess or Queen,' said the lady, 'the reward bestowed by Eleanor Cobham on those who obey her will shall be princely.'

'Your Grace's will,' said Hume, 'is your lowly servant's law. This night, if it so please ye, your wish shall be gratified.'

'Ha!' said the Duchess; 'at what hour?'

'At the hour of eleven, which is just one hour before the charm which is to work King Henry's death will be complete, will I conduct you to my apartment, where the Witch of Eye and Bolinbroke are busily at work. There you shall see and hear the spirit which will reveal to you your future destiny.'

- 'I will not fail thee, good Sir John,' said Eleanor, thrusting a purse into his hand. 'At the hour of eleven thou shalt find we are ready to accompany thee.' Thus saying, and waving her hand to the priest, she hurried from his presence.

'And at the hour of eleven, proud Eleanor Cobham,' said Hume, following her slowly with his eye till she disappeared from the hall, 'I will raise thee such a spirit as thou wouldst give the wealth of England to *lay*. There needed but this,' he added, while his features assumed an expression of demoniacal ferocity – 'there needed but this dishonest blow to wind my spirit to its purpose.' – He paused a moment; but, in that moment, his flashing eye, his changing brow, and his heaving breast, seemed to indicate thoughts sufficient to occupy his mind for a century. At length, wrapping his cloak closely round him, drawing his cowl over his brow, and exclaiming, 'I have it ! I have it ! ' he rushed out of the hall.

This conversation took place at about the hour of noon; and the bell had just tolled the eleventh hour, when the Duchess of Gloucester, leaning on the arm of Hume, entered the chamber in which her emissaries were performing, or pretending to perform, their wicked ceremonies.

It was a lofty and spacious apartment, which the Duke of Gloucester had specially appropriated to the use of the chaplain, and which was held sacred from the intrusion of every other person. Here, therefore, Hume had an opportunity of pursuing, without interruption or discovery, his studies in those occult sciences to which he had devoted himself. The Duchess started as she entered; for the pale lurid flame by which alone the chamber was illuminated, cast a fearful and preternatural light over every object on which it glanced. Eleanor, however, soon suppressed the feeling of fear by which she had at first been overpowered, and advanced into the apartment.

The fire from which this ghastly and melancholy light proceeded, glowed on the hearth, at the eastern end of the room. Over it cowered two figures, whose squalid dresses, misshapen forms, and wan and emaciated features, were in fearful unison with the whole scene. One was a woman, bent nearly double with age and infirmity; a very few tufts, or patches, of white hair were upon her head; but the scantiness of hair there was compensated by the profusion with which it grew above her lip and chin. Her cheek was sunken and hollow, her lips dry and withered, and, as they moved up and down, while she seemed to be mumbling some diabolical prayer or incantation, they showed that the hag could not boast of the possession of a single tooth. Her right hand rested on a stick, while her left was elevated, and moved to and fro in accompaniment to the spell which she was muttering. Her companion was a lean and shrivelled old man, whose grey beard swept his breast, and who, with a large volume in his hand, which he was attentively perusing, knelt by the fire, and seemed to be examining, by his book, the accuracy of the lesson which the old woman was repeating.

The Duchess, bold of heart as she was, could not help shuddering, and clasped more firmly the arm of Hume, as she gazed upon these two fearful beings; especially as she perceived, that although they stood in the full blaze of the fire, their figures cast no shadow on the floor of the apartment. But an object of still more intense interest to *her*, soon diverted her gaze another way.

At the opposite end of the apartment stood a large waxen image, which needed not the crown upon its head, or the sceptre in its hand, to tell her that it was intended to represent King Henry; so perfect and faithful a portraiture did it present of that monarch. For nearly a month had this image been stationed opposite the fire which we have described, and which had been kept incessantly burning, night and day.

During that time, the figure had melted and wasted beneath the influence of the heat; and it now presented the appearance of a man emaciated by illness, and fast sinking into the grave. The Duchess, who had on the previous day seen the King, gave a smile of grim delight, as she saw the evidence of the success of her magical practices before her. The most intense silence reigned in the apartment, interrupted only by the faint mumbling of the hag, and the crackling of the faggots in the blaze. The Duchess, however, soon broke this portentous silence, by advancing towards the fire, and saying to the unearthly-looking beings who stood beside it – 'Rare artists! accept the thanks of Eleanor Cobham; and doubt not, as soon as the work is accomplished, that your recompense shall be far more substantial.'

The people whom she addressed, were Margaret Jourdain, or Jourdmain, who was better known as 'The Witch of Eye,' from the place of her birth; and Roger Bolinbroke, who was, like Hume, a priest, but had devoted his learning and talents to the study of sorcery. These persons had long been employed by Hume, and paid him the utmost respect and deference; not only on account of the liberal gifts by which he repaid their services, but because they believed him to be a greater proficient in the arts of magic than themselves, and to be able even to raise spirits – a degree of proficiency in those diabolical arts to which they did not pretend. They answered the address of the Duchess by directing their eyes slowly towards her, making the sign of the cross, not upon their foreheads, but their backs, and then sinking upon their knees before her, exclaiming, 'God save *Queen* Eleanor!'

'Thanks, gentle friends; thanks for your unshaken loyalty and unremitting services!' said the Duchess. 'But tell me, I pray ye, when the work shall be accomplished?'

'*When the bell*,' said the witch, in a discordant tone, or rather shriek, '*shall have tolled the midnight hour!*'

At that moment the bell of the ducal palace drowned all other sounds, by tolling heavily and solemnly the first quarter after the hour of eleven.

'Ha! sayest thou so?' said the Duchess; and as the lurid blaze brightened her features, it showed them still more brightened by the hope of approaching grandeur and sovereignty.

'Even so,' said the hag; 'then will yonder image sink to the ground, destroyed and dissolved in that flame; *and then will the spirit of Henry of Windsor melt beneath the influence of his disease, dissolve, and mingle with the elements.*'

'Then look to it, Margaret of Anjou! look to it, Richard Plantagenet!' said the Duchess; 'for Eleanor Cobham has been injured, and will be revenged. But still I am troubled; doubt and uncertainty *yet* hang over my future fate. Henry may cease to be King, and yet Eleanor not become Queen. These signs and symbols may be delusions. Hume, I claim the performance of thy promise. Call up a spirit who shall make answer to such questions as I shall propound.'

'Your Grace,' said Hume, 'shall be obeyed; yet, pardon me, but I fear your courage may fail.'

'Nay, nay, dotard!' said the Duchess, impatiently; 'I mean,' she added, eager to retract the offensive epithet, 'my good Sir John – fear not my courage; I have gone too far to recede.'

The chaplain then bowed reverentially, and, drawing a white wand from beneath his cloak, advanced into the midst of the apartment. With this wand he described a circle on the floor, which he perambulated three times, pouring from a phial which he held in his hand a blood-red liquor, and chanting, in a low and solemn tone, something which appeared to be a metrical composition, but was in a language unintelligible to the Duchess. He then threw himself on the floor, and remained in a posture apparently of adoration, and groaning bitterly for several minutes; then, starting up, he rushed towards the fire, seized the volume which Bolinbroke held in his hand, and, returning to the circle, began to read loudly and rapidly from it; but still in a language which the Duchess did not understand.

At length he closed the volume, bowed reverently three times, and retreated backwards out of the circle. At that moment, the bell tolled the second quarter after eleven. A noise like the sound of distant thunder was heard, the floor of the apartment opened, and a figure which could not be distinctly seen, but appeared to be tall, and wrapped in a black mantle, stood before them.

A shriek burst from the lips of the Duchess and even from those of Bolinbroke and the Witch. 'For the love of heaven, be silent!' said Hume, in a whisper to the former: 'waste not these precious moments in idle alarms: demand what ye will of the spirit; but, be courageous, and be brief.'

'Tell me,' said Eleanor, advancing towards the circle, but trembling in every limb – 'tell me what fate awaits King Henry?'

She gazed with dim, but anxiously straining eyes, on the being whom she interrogated; as, in a sullen feeble voice the spirit answered:

> 'When yonder image melts in yonder blaze,
> Henry shall number out his mortal days.'

'Why, that is well!' exclaimed the Duchess, forgetting her alarm in the confirmation which this prediction gave to her wildest hopes. 'But, Henry,' she added, 'is not the only person whose existence gives me uneasiness. Tell me, too, what fate awaits the Duke of York?'

The spirit answered, in the same tone —

> 'Plantagenet from earth shall fly,
> Swiftly and speedily as *I*.'

'Why that,' said Eleanor, 'is better tidings still: *thou* wilt vanish in an instant, when my bidding is performed. And shall the residue of Plantagenet on this earth be no more permanent than thy own? Happy, happy Eleanor!'

'For heaven's sake, madam,' said Hume, gazing anxiously on a dial on which the rays of the fire at that moment fell, telling him that the midnight hour was fast approaching — 'this is idle and inauspicious delay. Would you demand ought further of the spirit?'

'One, one more question!' she exclaimed. 'Tell me,' she said; and then hesitating for a moment, seemed anxious yet fearful to put the question — 'tell me my own future fate — the fate of Eleanor Cobham?'

The answer was not given to this question so speedily as before; but, when it was pronounced, it was in a peculiarly emphatic and impressive tone:

> 'The secrets of thy future fate
> Let my attending spirits state;
> Tell the Dame of Gloucester's doom;
> Come, attending spirits, come!'

The spirit, as he finished his prediction, was seen to apply something to his lips; and presently afterwards, no unearthly and aerial sound was heard to proceed from them, but the loud and distinct blast of a bugle. A responsive shout was heard to follow it, and then the doors of the apartment were burst open, and a band of soldiers, carrying drawn swords and lighted torches in their hands, rushed in. The pretended spirit advanced towards them, and, throwing away the black mantle in which his form and face had been enveloped, discovered to the terrified and astonished Duchess the features of the Duke of York!

'The fire! the fire!' said Hume, darting a look of agony at the dial.

'Ha! I did indeed forget!' said the Duke of Buckingham, who was the leader of the soldiers. 'Fellows, extinguish that accursed light!'

The soldiers immediately advanced to the fire; and, trampling upon the now faint and decaying embers, speedily succeeded in extinguishing it. The last spark, however, had scarcely been trodden out, before the bell tolled the hour of midnight.

'Heaven be praised!' said Hume; 'the accursed deed has been prevented. Had yonder spark retained a gleam of light for an instant *longer*, the spirit of good King Henry had passed away for ever.'

'Peace, double traitor!' said the Duke of York. 'Good King Henry is doubtless indebted to thee for his life; but he has to thank not thy loyalty, but thy malignity and avarice. Both, however, shall be gratified, agreeably to the promise which I made thee. The woman, Duchess though she be, who insulted thee, shall be brought to a terrible expiation of her crimes; and the reward which she promised thee for aiding and concealing her damnable practices, shall be more than doubled for having revealed them.'

Eleanor gazed in sullen silence on the scene that had terminated all her hopes, and probably her life. She saw herself too completely in the hands of her enemies for any effort at resistance or escape to be availing; and was too proud to expose the bitterness and humiliation of her feelings, by tears or idle upbraidings. One scornful and malignant smile, which she glanced at Hume, was the only expression of her sentiments in which she indulged, and then she left the apartment, with her arms fettered to those of Bolinbroke and the Witch of Eye, in the custody of Buckingham and the soldiers.

The events which followed are matter of history, and too well known to require more than a brief recital. The Duchess of Gloucester, Hume, the Witch of Eye, and Bolinbroke, were tried and condemned, on the clearest evidence, for the crimes of conspiring the death of the King, and practising the arts of magic and witchcraft.

The Witch was burned in Smithfield, Bolinbroke was hanged at Tyburn, and the Duchess sentenced to do open penance in four public places within the city of London, and afterwards to imprisonment for life in the Isle of Man. Hume was not only pardoned, but liberally rewarded. This man did not appear really to have possessed any knowledge of the occult sciences; but seems to have imposed on the credulity of the Duchess.

That Margaret Jourdmain and Roger Bolinbroke were *really* magicians and wizards, was religiously believed by all, and the *fact* that the King, at the very moment that the magical fire was extinguished in the house of the Duke of Gloucester, recovered his full and perfect health, at his palace at Westminster, gave support and confirmation to such a belief, however irrational it may *now* appear.

The Duke of Gloucester, whatever might be his feelings at the disgrace and punishment of his Duchess, did not attempt any exercise of his authority for their prevention; but, to use the language of an old chronicler, 'toke all these thynges paciently, and saied little.'

J. Sheridan Le Fanu

CARMILLA

PROLOGUE

Upon a paper attached to the Narrative which follows, Doctor Hesselius has written a rather elaborate note, which he accompanies with a reference to his Essay on the strange subject which the MS. illuminates.

This mysterious subject he treats, in that Essay, with his usual learning and acumen, and with remarkable directness and condensation. It will form but one volume of the series of that extraordinary man's collected papers.

As I publish the case, in this volume, simply to interest the " laity," I shall forestall the intelligent lady, who relates it, in nothing ; and, after due consideration, I have determined, therefore, to abstain from presenting any *précis* of the learned Doctor's reasoning, or extract from his statement on a subject which he describes as " involving, not improbably, some of the profoundest arcana of our dual existence, and its intermediates."

I was anxious, on discovering this paper, to re-open the correspondence commenced by Doctor Hesselius, so many years before, with a person so clever and careful as his informant seems to have been. Much to my regret, however, I found that she had died in the interval.

She, probably, could have added little to the Narrative which she communicates in the following pages, with, so far as I can pronounce, such a conscientious particularity.

CHAPTER I

AN EARLY FRIGHT

In Styria, we, though by no means magnificent people, inhabit a castle, or schloss. A small income, in that part of the world, goes a great way. Eight or nine hundred a year does wonders. Scantily enough ours would have answered among wealthy people at home. My father is English, and I bear an English name, although I never saw England. But here, in this lonely and primitive place, where everything is so marvellously cheap, I really don't see how ever so much more money would at all materially add to our comforts, or even luxuries.

My father was in the Austrian service, and retired upon a pension and his patrimony, and purchased this feudal residence, and the small estate on which it stands, a bargain.

Nothing can be more picturesque or solitary. It stands on a slight eminence in a forest. The road, very old and narrow, passes in front of its drawbridge, never raised in my time, and its moat, stocked with perch, and sailed over by many swans, and floating on its surface white fleets of water-lilies.

Over all this the schloss shows its many-windowed front ; its towers, and its Gothic chapel.

The forest opens in an irregular and very picturesque glade before its gate, and at the right a steep Gothic bridge carries the road over a stream that winds in deep shadow through the wood.

I have said that this is a very lonely place. Judge whether I say truth. Looking from the hall door towards the road, the forest in which our castle stands extends fifteen miles to the right, and twelve to the left. The nearest inhabited village is about seven of your English miles to the left. The nearest inhabited schloss of any historic associations, is that of old General Spielsdorf, nearly twenty miles away to the right.

I have said "the nearest *inhabited* village," because there is, only three miles westward, that is to say in the direction of General Spielsdorf's schloss, a ruined village, with its quaint little church, now roofless, in the aisle of which are the mouldering tombs of the proud family of Karnstein, now extinct, who once owned the equally-desolate château which, in the thick of the forest, overlooks the silent ruins of the town.

Respecting the cause of the desertion of this striking and melancholy spot, there is a legend which I shall relate to you another time.

I must tell you now, how very small is the party who constitute the inhabitants of our castle. I don't include servants, or those dependants who occupy rooms in the buildings attached to the schloss. Listen, and wonder ! My father, who is the kindest man on earth, but growing old ; and I, at the date of my story, only nineteen. Eight years have passed since then. I and my father constituted the family at the schloss. My mother, a Styrian lady, died in my infancy, but I had a good-natured governess, who had been with me from, I might almost say, my infancy. I could not remember the time when her fat, benignant face was not a familiar picture in my memory. This was Madame Perrodon, a native of Berne, whose care and good nature in part supplied to me the loss of my mother, whom I do not even remember, so early I lost her. She made a third at our little dinner party. There was a fourth, Mademoiselle De Lafontaine, a lady such as you term, I believe, a " finishing governess." She spoke French and German, Madame Perrodon French and broken English, to which my father and I added English, which, partly to prevent its becoming a lost language among us, and partly from patriotic motives, we spoke every day. The consequence was a Babel, at which strangers used to laugh, and which I shall make no attempt to reproduce in this narrative. And there were two or three young lady friends besides, pretty nearly of my own age, who were occasional visitors, for longer or shorter terms ; and these visits I sometimes returned.

These were our regular social resources ; but of course there were chance visits from " neighbours " of only five or six leagues' distance. My life was, notwithstanding, rather a solitary one, I can assure you.

My gouvernantes had just so much control over me as you might conjecture such sage persons would have in the case of a rather spoiled girl, whose only parent allowed her pretty nearly her own way in everything.

The first occurrence in my existence, which produced a terrible impression upon my mind, which, in fact, never has been effaced, was one of the very earliest incidents of my life which I can recollect. Some people will think it so trifling that it should not be recorded here. You will see, however, by-and-by, why I mention it. The nursery, as it was called, though I had it all to myself, was a large room in the upper story of the castle, with a steep oak roof. I can't have been more than six years old, when one night I awoke, and looking round the room from my bed, failed to see the nursery-maid. Neither was my nurse there ; and I thought myself alone. I was not frightened, for I was one of those happy children who are studiously kept in ignorance of ghost stories, of fairy tales, and of all such lore as makes us cover up our heads when the door creaks suddenly, or the flicker of an expiring candle makes the shadow of a bed-post dance upon the wall, nearer to our faces. I was vexed and insulted at finding myself, as I conceived, neglected, and I began to whimper, preparatory to a hearty bout of roaring ; when to my surprise, I saw a solemn, but very pretty face looking at me from the side of the bed. It was that of a young lady who was kneeling, with her hands under the coverlet. I looked at her with a kind of pleased wonder, and ceased whimpering. She caressed me with her hands, and lay down beside me on the bed, and drew me towards her, smiling ; I felt immediately delightfully soothed, and fell asleep again. I was wakened by a sensation as if two needles ran into my breast very deep at the same moment, and I cried loudly. The lady started back, with her eyes fixed on me, and then slipped down upon the floor, and, as I thought, hid herself under the bed.

I was now for the first time frightened, and I yelled with all my might and main. Nurse, nursery-maid, housekeeper, all came running in, and hearing my story, they made light of it, soothing me all they could meanwhile. But, child as I was, I could perceive that their faces were pale with an unwonted look of anxiety, and I saw them look under the bed, and about the room, and peep under tables and pluck open cupboards ; and the housekeeper whispered to the nurse : " Lay your hand along that hollow in the bed ; some one *did* lie there, so sure as you did not ; the place is still warm."

I remember the nursery-maid petting me, and all three examining my chest, where I told them I felt the puncture, and pronouncing that there was no sign visible that any such thing had happened to me.

The housekeeper and the two other servants who were in charge of the nursery, remained sitting up all night ; and from that time a servant always sat up in the nursery until I was about fourteen.

I was very nervous for a long time after this. A doctor was called in, he was pallid and elderly. How well I remember his long saturnine face, slightly pitted with small-pox, and his chestnut wig. For a good while, every second day, he came and gave me medicine, which of course I hated.

The morning after I saw this apparition I was in a state of terror, and could not bear to be left alone, daylight though it was, for a moment.

I remember my father coming up and standing at the bedside, and talking cheerfully, and asking the nurse a number of questions, and laughing very heartily at one of the answers ; and patting me on the shoulder, and kissing me, and telling me not to be frightened, that it was nothing but a dream and could not hurt me.

But I was not comforted, for I knew the visit of the strange woman was *not* a dream ; and I was *awfully* frightened.

I was a little consoled by the nursery-maid's assuring me that it was she who had come and looked at me, and lain down beside me in the bed, and that I must have been half-dreaming not to have known her face. But this, though supported by the nurse, did not quite satisfy me.

I remember, in the course of that day, a venerable old man, in a black cassock, coming into the room with the nurse and house-keeper, and talking a little to them, and very kindly to me ; his face was very sweet and gentle, and he told me they were going to pray, and joined my hands together, and desired me to say, softly, while they were praying, " Lord, hear all good prayers for us, for Jesus' sake." I think these were the very words, for I often repeated them to myself, and my nurse used for years to make me say them in my prayers.

I remember so well the thoughtful sweet face of that white-haired old man, in his black cassock, as he stood in that rude, lofty, brown room, with the clumsy furniture of a fashion three hundred years old, about him, and the scanty light entering its shadowy atmosphere through the small lattice. He knelt, and the three women with him, and he prayed aloud with an earnest quavering voice for, what appeared to me, a long time. I forget all my life preceding that event, and for some time after it is all obscure also ; but the scenes I have just described stand out vivid as the isolated pictures of the phantasmagoria surrounded by darkness.

CHAPTER II

A GUEST

I am now going to tell you something so strange that it will require all your faith in my veracity to believe my story. It is not only true, nevertheless, but truth of which I have been an eye-witness.

It was a sweet summer evening, and my father asked me, as he sometimes did, to take a little ramble with him along that beautiful forest vista which I have mentioned as lying in front of the schloss.

" General Spielsdorf cannot come to us so soon as I had hoped," said my father, as we pursued our walk.

He was to have paid us a visit of some weeks, and we had expected his arrival next day. He was to have brought with him a young lady, his niece and ward, Mademoiselle Rheinfeldt, whom I had never seen, but whom I had heard described as a very charming girl, and in whose society I had promised myself many happy days. I was more disappointed than a young lady living in a town, or a bustling neighbourhood can possibly imagine. This visit, and the new acquaintance it promised, had furnished my day dream for many weeks.

" And how soon does he come ? " I asked.

" Not till autumn. Not for two months, I dare say," he answered. " And I am very glad now, dear, that you never knew Mademoiselle Rheinfeldt."

" And why ? " I asked, both mortified and curious.

" Because the poor young lady is dead," he replied. " I quite forgot I had not told you, but you were not in the room when I received the General's letter this evening."

I was very much shocked. General Spielsdorf had mentioned in his first letter, six or seven weeks before, that she was not so well as he would wish her, but there was nothing to suggest the remotest suspicion of danger.

" Here is the General's letter," he said, handing it to me. " I am afraid he is in great affliction ; the letter appears to me to have been written very nearly in distraction."

We sat down on a rude bench, under a group of magnificent lime trees. The sun was setting with all its melancholy splendour behind the sylvan horizon, and the stream that flows beside our home, and passes under the steep old bridge I have mentioned, wound through many a group of noble trees, almost at our feet, reflecting in its current the fading crimson of the sky. General Spielsdorf's letter was so extraordinary, so vehement, and in some places so self-contradictory, that I read it twice over—the second time aloud to my father—and was still unable to account for it, except by supposing that grief had unsettled his mind.

It said, " I have lost my darling daughter, for as such I loved her. During the last days of dear Bertha's illness I was not able to write to you. Before then I had no idea of her danger. I have lost her, and now learn *all*, too late. She died in the peace of innocence, and in the glorious hope of a blessed futurity. The fiend who betrayed our infatuated hospitality has done it all. I thought I was receiving into my house innocence, gaiety, a charming companion for my lost Bertha. Heavens ! what a fool have I been ! I thank God my child died without a suspicion of the cause of her sufferings. She is gone without so much as conjecturing the nature of her illness, and the accursed passion of the agent of all this misery. I devote my remaining days to tracking and extinguishing a monster. I am told I may hope to accomplish my righteous and merciful purpose. At present there is scarcely a gleam of light to guide me. I curse my conceited incredulity, my despicable affectation of superiority, my blindness, my obstinacy —all—too late. I cannot write or talk collectedly now. I am distracted. So soon as I shall have a little recovered, I mean to devote myself for a time to enquiry, which may possibly lead me as far as Vienna. Some time in the autumn, two months hence, or earlier if I live, I will see you—that is, if you permit me ; I will then tell you all that I scarce dare put upon paper now. Farewell. Pray for me, dear friend."

In these terms ended this strange letter. Though I had never seen Bertha Rheinfeldt, my eyes filled with tears at the sudden intelligence ; I was startled, as well as profoundly disappointed.

The sun had now set, and it was twilight by the time I had returned the General's letter to my father.

It was a soft clear evening, and we loitered, speculating upon the possible meanings of the violent and incoherent sentences which I had just been reading. We had nearly a mile to walk before reaching the road that passes the schloss in front, and by that time the moon was shining brilliantly. At the drawbridge we met Madame Perrodon and Mademoiselle De Lafontaine, who had come out, without their bonnets, to enjoy the exquisite moonlight.

We heard their voices gabbling in animated dialogue as we approached. We joined them at the drawbridge, and turned about to admire with them the beautiful scene.

The glade through which we had just walked lay before us. At our left the narrow road wound away under clumps of lordly trees, and was lost to sight amid the thickening forest. At the right the same road crosses the steep and picturesque bridge, near which stands a ruined tower, which once guarded that pass ; and beyond the bridge an abrupt eminence rises, covered with trees, and showing in the shadow some grey ivy-clustered rocks.

Over the sward and low grounds, a thin film of mist was stealing like smoke, marking the distances with a transparent veil ; and here and there we could see the river faintly flashing in the moon-light.

No softer, sweeter scene could be imagined. The news I had just heard made it melancholy ; but nothing could disturb its character of profound serenity, and the enchanted glory and vagueness of the prospect.

My father, who enjoyed the picturesque, and I, stood looking in silence over the expanse beneath us. The two good governesses, standing a little way behind us, discoursed upon the scene, and were eloquent upon the moon.

Madame Perrodon was fat, middle-aged, and romantic, and talked and sighed poetically. Mademoiselle De Lafontaine—in right of her father, who was a German, assumed to be psycho-logical, metaphysical, and something of a mystic—now declared that when the moon shone with a light so intense it was well known that it indicated a special spiritual activity. The effect of the full moon in such a state of brilliancy was manifold. It acted on dreams, it acted on lunacy, it acted on nervous people ; it had marvellous physical influences connected with life. Mademoiselle related that her cousin, who was mate of a merchant ship, having taken a nap on deck on such a night, lying on his back, with his face full in the light of the moon, had awakened, after a dream of an old woman clawing him by the cheek, with his features horribly drawn to one side ; and his countenance had never quite recovered its equilibrium.

" The moon, this night," she said, " is full of odylic and magnetic influence—and see, when you look behind you at the front of the schloss, how all its windows flash and twinkle with that silvery splendour, as if unseen hands had lighted up the rooms to receive fairy guests."

There are indolent states of the spirits in which, indisposed to talk ourselves, the talk of others is pleasant to our listless ears ; and I gazed on, pleased with the tinkle of the ladies' con-versation.

"I have got into one of my moping moods to-night," said my father, after a silence, and quoting Shakespeare, whom, by way of keeping up our English, he used to read aloud, he said :—

" I forget the rest. But I feel as if some great misfortune were hanging over us. I suppose the poor General's afflicted letter has had something to do with it."

At this moment the unwonted sound of carriage wheels and many hoofs upon the road, arrested our attention.

They seemed to be approaching from the high ground overlooking the bridge, and very soon the equipage emerged from that point. Two horsemen first crossed the bridge, then came a carriage drawn by four horses, and two men rode behind.

It seemed to be the travelling carriage of a person of rank ; and we were all immediately absorbed in watching that very unusual spectacle. It became, in a few moments, greatly more interesting, for just as the carriage had passed the summit of the steep bridge, one of the leaders, taking fright, communicated his panic to the rest, and, after a plunge or two, the whole team broke into a wild gallop together, and dashing between the horsemen who rode in front, came thundering along the road towards us with the speed of a hurricane.

The excitement of the scene was made more painful by the clear, long-drawn screams of a female voice from the carriage window.

We all advanced in curiosity and horror ; my father in silence, the rest with various ejaculations of terror.

Our suspense did not last long. Just before you reach the castle drawbridge, on the route they were coming, there stands by the roadside a magnificent lime tree, on the other stands an ancient stone cross, at sight of which the horses, now going at a pace that was perfectly frightful, swerved so as to bring the wheel over the projecting roots of the tree.

I knew what was coming. I covered my eyes, unable to see it out, and turned my head away ; at the same moment I heard a cry from my lady-friends, who had gone on a little.

Curiosity opened my eyes, and I saw a scene of utter confusion. Two of the horses were on the ground, the carriage lay upon its side, with two wheels in the air ; the men were busy removing the traces, and a lady, with a commanding air and figure had got out, and stood with clasped hands, raising the handkerchief that was in them every now and then to her eyes. Through the carriage door was now lifted a young lady, who appeared to be lifeless. My dear old father was already beside the elder lady, with his hat in his hand, evidently tendering his aid and the resources of his schloss. The lady did not appear to hear him, or to have eyes for anything but the slender girl who was being placed against the slope of the bank.

I approached ; the young lady was apparently stunned, but she was certainly not dead. My father, who piqued himself on being something of a physician, had just had his fingers to her wrist and assured the lady, who declared herself her mother, that her pulse, though faint and irregular, was undoubtedly still distinguishable. The lady clasped her hands and looked upward, as if in a momentary transport of gratitude ; but immediately she broke out again in that theatrical way which is, I believe, natural to some people.

She was what is called a fine-looking woman for her time of life, and must have been handsome ; she was tall, but not thin, and dressed in black velvet, and looked rather pale, but with a proud and commanding countenance, though now agitated strangely.

" Was ever being so born to calamity ? " I heard her say, with clasped hands, as I came up. " Here am I, on a journey of life and death, in prosecuting which to lose an hour is possibly to lose all. My child will not have recovered sufficiently to resume her route for who can say how long. I must leave her ; I cannot, dare not, delay. How far on, sir, can you tell, is the nearest village ? I must leave her there ; and shall not see my darling, or even hear of her till my return, three months hence."

I plucked my father by the coat, and whispered earnestly in his ear, " Oh ! papa, pray ask her to let her stay with us—it would be so delightful. Do, pray."

" If Madame will entrust her child to the care of my daughter and of her good gouvernante, Madame Perrodon, and permit her to remain as our guest, under my charge, until her return, it will confer a distinction and an obligation upon us, and we shall treat her with all the care and devotion which so sacred a trust deserves."

" I cannot do that, sir, it would be to task your kindness and chivalry too cruelly," said the lady, distractedly.

" It would, on the contrary, be to confer on us a very great kindness at the moment when we most need it. My daughter has just been disappointed by a cruel misfortune, in a visit from which she had long anticipated a great deal of happiness. If you confide this young lady to our care it will be her best consolation. The nearest village on your route is distant, and affords no such inn as you could think of placing your daughter at ; you cannot allow her to continue her journey for any considerable distance without danger. If, as you say, you cannot suspend your journey, you must part with her to-night, and nowhere could you do so with more honest assurances of care and tenderness than here."

There was something in this lady's air and appearance so distinguished, and even imposing, and in her manner so engaging, as to impress one, quite apart from the dignity of her equipage, with a conviction that she was a person of consequence.

By this time the carriage was replaced in its upright position, and the horses, quite tractable, in the traces again.

The lady threw on her daughter a glance which I fancied was not quite so affectionate as one might have anticipated from the beginning of the scene ; then she beckoned slightly to my father and withdrew two or three steps with him out of hearing ; and talked to him with a fixed and stern countenance, not at all like that with which she had hitherto spoken.

I was filled with wonder that my father did not seem to perceive the change, and also unspeakably curious to learn what it could be that she was speaking, almost in his ear, with so much earnestness and rapidity.

Two or three minutes at most, I think, she remained thus employed, then she turned, and a few steps brought her to where her daughter lay, supported by Madame Perrodon. She kneeled beside her for a moment and whispered, as Madame supposed, a little benediction in her ear ; then hastily kissing her, she stepped into her carriage, the door was closed, the footmen in stately liveries jumped up behind, the outriders spurred on, the postilions cracked their whips, the horses plunged and broke suddenly into a furious canter that threatened soon again to become a gallop, and the carriage whirled away, followed at the same rapid pace by the two horsemen in the rear.

CHAPTER III

We followed the *cortège* with our eyes until it was swiftly lost to sight in the misty wood ; and the very sound of the hoofs and wheels died away in the silent night air.

Nothing remained to assure us that the adventure had not been an illusion for a moment but the young lady, who just at that moment opened her eyes. I could not see, for her face was turned from me, but she raised her head, evidently looking about her, and I heard a very sweet voice ask complainingly, " Where is mamma ? "

Our good Madame Perrodon answered tenderly, and added some comfortable assurances.

I then heard her ask :

" Where am I ? What is this place ? " and after that she said, " I don't see the carriage ; and Matska, where is she ? "

Madame answered all her questions in so far as she understood them ; and gradually the young lady remembered how the misadventure came about, and was glad to hear that no one in, or in attendance on, the carriage was hurt ; and on learning that her mamma had left her here, till her return in about three months, she wept.

I was going to add my consolations to those of Madame Perrodon when Mademoiselle De Lafontaine placed her hand upon my arm, saying :

" Don't approach, one at a time is as much as she can at present converse with ; a very little excitement would possibly overpower her now."

As soon as she is comfortably in bed, I thought, I will run up to her room and see her.

My father in the meantime had sent a servant on horseback for the physician, who lived about two leagues away ; and a bedroom was being prepared for the young lady's reception.

The stranger now rose, and leaning on Madame's arm, walked slowly over the drawbridge and into the castle gate.

In the hall the servants waited to receive her, and she was conducted forthwith to her room.

The room we usually sat in as our drawing-room is long, having four windows, that looked over the moat and drawbridge, upon the forest scene I have just described.

It is furnished in old carved oak, with large carved cabinets, and the chairs are cushioned with crimson Utrecht velvet. The walls are covered with tapestry, and surrounded with great gold frames, the figures being as large as life, in ancient and very curious costume, and the subjects represented are hunting, hawking, and generally festive. It is not too stately to be extremely comfortable ; and here we had our tea, for with his usual patriotic leanings he insisted that the national beverage should make its appearance regularly with our coffee and chocolate.

We sat here this night, and with candles lighted, were talking over the adventure of the evening.

Madame Perrodon and Mademoiselle De Lafontaine were both of our party. The younger stranger had hardly lain down in her bed when she sank into a deep sleep ; and those ladies had left her in the care of a servant.

" How do you like our guest ? " I asked, as soon as Madame entered. " Tell me all about her ? "

" I like her extremely," answered Madame, " she is, I almost think, the prettiest creature I ever saw ; about your age, and so gentle and nice."

" She is absolutely beautiful," threw in Mademoiselle, who had peeped for a moment into the stranger's room.

" And such a sweet voice ! " added Madame Perrodon.

" Did you remark a woman in the carriage, after it was set up again, who did not get out," inquired Mademoiselle, " but only looked from the window ? "

No, we had not seen her.

Then she described a hideous black woman, with a sort of coloured turban on her head, who was gazing all the time from the carriage window, nodding and grinning derisively towards the ladies, with gleaming eyes and large white eye-balls, and her teeth set as if in fury.

" Did you remark what an ill-looking pack of men the servants were ? " asked Madame.

" Yes," said my father, who had just come in, " ugly, hang-dog looking fellows, as ever I beheld in my life. I hope they mayn't rob the poor lady in the forest. They are clever rogues, however ; they got everything to rights in a minute."

" I dare say they are worn out with too long travelling," said Madame. " Besides looking wicked, their faces were so strangely lean, and dark, and sullen. I am very curious, I own ; but I dare say the young lady will tell us all about it to-morrow, if she is sufficiently recovered."

" I don't think she will," said my father, with a mysterious smile, and a little nod of his head, as if he knew more about it than he cared to tell us.

This made me all the more inquisitive as to what had passed between him and the lady in the black velvet, in the brief but earnest interview that had immediately preceded her departure.

We were scarcely alone, when I entreated him to tell me. He did not need much pressing.

" There is no particular reason why I should not tell you. She expressed a reluctance to trouble us with the care of her daughter, saying she was in delicate health, and nervous, but not subject to any kind of seizure—she volunteered that—nor to any illusion ; being, in fact, perfectly sane."

" How very odd to say all that ! " I interpolated. " It was so unnecessary."

" At all events it *was* said," he laughed, " and as you wish to know all that passed, which was indeed very little, I tell you. She then said, ' I am making a long journey of *vital* importance '— she emphasized the word— 'rapid and secret ; I shall return for my child in three months ; in the meantime, she will be silent as to who we are, whence we come, and whither we are travelling.' That is all she said. She spoke very pure French. When she said the word ' secret,' she paused for a few seconds, looking sternly, her eyes fixed on mine. I fancy she makes a great point of that. You saw how quickly she was gone. I hope I have not done a very foolish thing, in taking charge of the young lady."

For my part, I was delighted. I was longing to see and talk to her ; and only waiting till the doctor should give me leave. You who live in towns, can have no idea how great an event the intro-duction of a new friend is, in such a solitude as surrounded us.

The doctor did not arrive till nearly one o'clock ; but I could no more have gone to my bed and slept, than I could have overtaken, on foot, the carriage in which the princess in black velvet had driven away.

When the physician came down to the drawing-room, it was to report very favourably upon his patient. She was now sitting up, her pulse quite regular, apparently perfectly well. She had sus-tained no injury, and the little shock to her nerves had passed away quite harmlessly. There could be no harm certainly in my seeing her, if we both wished it ; and, with this permission, I sent, forthwith, to know whether she would allow me to visit her for a few minutes in her room.

The servant returned immediately to say that she desired nothing more.

You may be sure I was not long in availing myself of this permission.

Our visitor lay in one of the handsomest rooms in the schloss. It was, perhaps a little stately. There was a sombre piece of tapestry opposite the foot of the bed, representing Cleopatra with the asp to her bosom ; and other solemn classic scenes were displayed, a little faded, upon the other walls. But there was gold carving, and rich and varied colour enough in the other decorations of the room, to more than redeem the gloom of the old tapestry.

There were candles at the bed side. She was sitting up ; her slender pretty figure enveloped in the soft silk dressing-gown, embroidered with flowers, and lined with thick quilted silk, which her mother had thrown over her feet as she lay upon the ground.

What was it that, as I reached the bed side and had just begun my little greeting, struck me dumb in a moment, and made me recoil a step or two from before her ? I will tell you.

I saw the very face which had visited me in my childhood at night, which remained so fixed in my memory, and on which I had for so many years so often ruminated with horror, when no one suspected of what I was thinking.

It was pretty, even beautiful ; and when I first beheld it, wore the same melancholy expression.

But this almost instantly lighted into a strange fixed smile of recognition.

There was a silence of fully a minute, and then at length *she* spoke ; *I* could not.

" How wonderful ! " she exclaimed. " Twelve years ago, I saw your face in a dream, and it has haunted me ever since."

" Wonderful indeed ! " I repeated, overcoming with an effort the horror that had for a time suspended my utterances. " Twelve years ago, in vision or reality, *I* certainly saw you. I could not forget your face. It has remained before my eyes ever since."

Her smile had softened. Whatever I had fancied strange in it, was gone, and it and her dimpling cheeks were now delightfully pretty and intelligent.

I felt reassured, and continued more in the vein which hospitality indicated, to bid her welcome, and to tell her how much pleasure her accidental arrival had given us all, and especially what a happiness it was to me.

I took her hand as I spoke. I was a little shy, as lonely people are, but the situation made me eloquent, and even bold. She pressed my hand, she laid hers upon it, and her eyes glowed, as, looking hastily into mine, she smiled again, and blushed.

She answered my welcome very prettily. I sat down beside her, still wondering ; and she said :

" I must tell you my vision about you ; it is so very strange that you and I should have had, each of the other so vivid a dream, that each should have seen, I you and you me, looking as we do now, when of course we both were mere children. I was a child about six years old, and I awoke from a confused and troubled dream, and found myself in a room, unlike my nursery, wainscoted clumsily in some dark wood, and with cupboards and bedsteads, and chairs, and benches placed about it. The beds were, I thought, all empty, and the room itself without any one but myself in it ; and I, after looking about me for some time, and admiring especially an iron candlestick, with two branches, which I should certainly know again, crept under one of the beds to reach the window ; but as I got from under the bed, I heard someone crying ; and looking up, while I was still upon my knees, I saw *you* —most assuredly you—as I see you now ; a beautiful young lady, with golden hair and large blue eyes, and lips—your lips—you, as you are here. Your looks won me ; I climbed on the bed and put my arms about you, and I think we both fell asleep. I was aroused by a scream ; you were sitting up screaming. I was frightened, and slipped down upon the ground, and, it seemed to me, lost consciousness for a moment ; and when I came to myself, I was again in my nursery at home. Your face I have never forgotten since. I could not be misled by mere resemblance. You *are* the lady whom I then saw."

It was now my turn to relate my corresponding vision, which I did, to the undisguised wonder of my new acquaintance.

" I don't know which should be most afraid of the other," she said, again smiling. " If you were less pretty I think I should be very much afraid of you, but being as you are, and you and I both so young, I feel only that I have made your acquaintance twelve years ago, and have already a right to your intimacy ; at all events, it does seem as if we were destined, from our earliest childhood, to be friends. I wonder whether you feel as strangely drawn towards me as I do to you ; I have never had a friend— shall I find one now ? " She sighed, and her fine dark eyes gazed passionately on me.

Now the truth is, I felt rather unaccountably towards the beautiful stranger. I did feel, as she said, " drawn towards her," but there was also something of repulsion. In this ambiguous feeling, however, the sense of attraction immensely prevailed. She interested and won me ; she was so beautiful and so indescribably engaging.

I perceived now something of languor and exhaustion stealing over her, and hastened to bid her good-night.

" The doctor thinks," I added, " that you ought to have a maid to sit up with you to-night ; one of ours is waiting, and you will find her a very useful and quiet creature."

" How kind of you, but I could not sleep, I never could with an attendant in the room. I shan't require any assistance—and, shall I confess my weakness, I am haunted with a terror of robbers. Our house was robbed once, and two servants murdered, so I always lock my door. It has become a habit—and you look so kind I know you will forgive me. I see there is a key in the lock."

She held me close in her pretty arms for a moment and whispered in my ear, " Good-night, darling, it is very hard to part with you, but good-night ; to-morrow, but not early, I shall see you again."

She sank back on the pillow with a sigh, and her fine eyes followed me with a fond and melancholy gaze, and she murmured again, " Good-night, dear friend."

Young people like, and even love, on impulse. I was flattered by the evident, though as yet undeserved, fondness she showed me. I liked the confidence with which she at once received me. She was determined that we should be very dear friends.

Next day came and we met again. I was delighted with my companion ; that is to say, in many respects.

Her looks lost nothing in daylight—she was certainly the most beautiful creature I had ever seen, and the unpleasant remembrance of the face presented in my early dream, had lost the effect of the first unexpected recognition.

She confessed that she had experienced a similar shock on seeing me, and precisely the same faint antipathy that had mingled with my admiration of her. We now laughed together over our momentary horrors.

CHAPTER IV

HER HABITS—A SAUNTER

I told you that I was charmed with her in most particulars.

There were some that did not please me so well.

She was above the middle height of women. I shall begin by describing her. She was slender, and wonderfully graceful. Except that her movements were languid—*very* languid—indeed, there was nothing in her appearance to indicate an invalid. Her complexion was rich and brilliant ; her features were small and beautifully formed ; her eyes large, dark, and lustrous ; her hair was quite wonderful, I never saw hair so magnificently thick and long when it was down about her shoulders ; I have often placed my hands under it, and laughed with wonder at its weight. It was exquisitely fine and soft, and in colour a rich very dark brown, with something of gold. I loved to let it down, tumbling with its own weight, as, in her room, she lay back in her chair talking in her sweet low voice, I used to fold and braid it, and spread it out and play with it. Heavens ! If I had but known all !

I said there were particulars which did not please me. I have told you that her confidence won me the first night I saw her ; but I found that she exercised with respect to herself, her mother, her history, everything in fact connected with her life, plans, and people, an ever-wakeful reserve. I dare say I was unreasonable, perhaps I was wrong ; I dare say I ought to have respected the solemn injunction laid upon my father by the stately lady in black velvet. But curiosity is a restless and unscrupulous passion, and no one girl can endure, with patience, that her's should be baffled by another. What harm could it do anyone to tell me what I so ardently desired to know ? Had she no trust in my good sense or honour ? Why would she not believe me when I assured her, so solemnly, that I would not divulge one syllable of what she told me to any mortal breathing.

There was a coldness, it seemed to me, beyond her years, in her smiling melancholy persistent refusal to afford me the least ray of light.

I cannot say we quarrelled upon this point, for she would not quarrel upon any. It was, of course, very unfair of me to press her, very ill-bred, but I really could not help it ; and I might just as well have let it alone.

What she did tell me amounted, in my unconscionable estimation—to nothing.

It was all summed up in three very vague disclosures.

First.—Her name was Carmilla.

Second.—Her family was very ancient and noble.

Third.—Her home lay in the direction of the west.

She would not tell me the name of her family, nor their armorial bearings, nor the name of their estate, nor even that of the country they lived in.

You are not to suppose that I worried her incessantly on these subjects. I watched opportunity, and rather insinuated than urged my enquiries. Once or twice, indeed, I did attack her more directly. But no matter what my tactics, utter failure was invariably the result. Reproaches and caresses were all lost upon her. But I must add this, that her evasion was conducted with so pretty a melancholy and deprecation, with so many, and even passionate declarations of her liking for me, and trust in my honour, and with so many promises, that I should at last know all, that I could not find it in my heart long to be offended with her.

She used to place her pretty arms about my neck, draw me to her, and laying her cheek to mine, murmur with her lips near my ear, " Dearest, your little heart is wounded ; think me not cruel because I obey the irresistible law of my strength and weakness ; if your dear heart is wounded, my wild heart bleeds with yours. In the rapture of my enormous humiliation I live in your warm life, and you shall die—die, sweetly die—into mine. I cannot help it ; as I draw near to you, you, in your turn, will draw near to others, and learn the rapture of that cruelty, which yet is love ; so, for a while, seek to know no more of me and mine, but trust me with all your loving spirit."

And when she had spoken such a rhapsody, she would press me more closely in her trembling embrace, and her lips in soft kisses gently glow upon my cheek.

Her agitations and her language were unintelligible to me.

From these foolish embraces, which were not of very frequent occurrence, I must allow, I used to wish to extricate myself ; but my energies seemed to fail me. Her murmured words sounded like a lullaby in my ear, and soothed my resistance into a trance, from which I only seemed to recover myself when she withdrew her arms.

In these mysterious moods I did not like her. I experienced a strange tumultuous excitement that was pleasurable, ever and anon, mingled with a vague sense of fear and disgust. I had no distinct thoughts about her while such scenes lasted, but I was conscious of a love growing into adoration, and also of abhorrence. This I know is paradox, but I can make no other attempt to explain the feeling.

I now write, after an interval of more than ten years, with a trembling hand, with a confused and horrible recollection of certain occurrences and situations, in the ordeal through which I was unconsciously passing ; though with a vivid and very sharp remembrance of the main current of my story. But, I suspect, in all lives there are certain emotional scenes, those in which our passions have been most wildly and terribly roused, that are of all others the most vaguely and dimly remembered.

Sometimes after an hour of apathy, my strange and beautiful companion would take my hand and hold it with a fond pressure, renewed again and again ; blushing softly, gazing in my face with languid and burning eyes, and breathing so fast that her dress rose and fell with the tumultuous respiration. It was like the ardour of a lover ; it embarrassed me ; it was hateful and yet overpowering ; and with gloating eyes she drew me to her, and her hot lips travelled along my cheek in kisses ; and she would whisper, almost in sobs, " You are mine, you *shall* be mine, and you and I are one for ever." Then she has thrown herself back in her chair, with her small hands over her eyes, leaving me trembling.

" Are we related," I used to ask ; " what can you mean by all this ? I remind you perhaps of some one whom you love ; but you must not, I hate it ; I don't know you—I don't know myself when you look so and talk so."

She used to sigh at my vehemence, then turn away and drop my hand.

Respecting these very extraordinary manifestations I strove in vain to form any satisfactory theory—I could not refer them to affectation or trick. It was unmistakably the momentary breaking out of suppressed instinct and emotion. Was she, notwithstanding her mother's volunteered denial, subject to brief visitations of insanity ; or was there here a disguise and a romance ? I had read in old story books of such things. What if a boyish lover had found his way into the house, and sought to prosecute his suit in masquerade, with the assistance of a clever old adventuress. But here were many things against this hypothesis, highly interesting as it was to my vanity.

I could boast of no little attentions such as masculine gallantry delights to offer. Between these passionate moments there were long intervals of common-place, of gaiety, of brooding melancholy, during which, except that I detected her eyes so full of melancholy fire, following me, at times I might have been as nothing to her. Except in these brief periods of mysterious excitement her ways were girlish ; and there was always a languor about her, quite incompatible with a masculine system in a state of health.

In some respects her habits were odd. Perhaps not so singular in the opinion of a town lady like you, as they appeared to us rustic people. She used to come down very late, generally not till one o'clock, she would then take a cup of chocolate, but eat nothing ; we then went out for a walk, which was a mere saunter, and she seemed, almost immediately, exhausted, and either returned to the schloss or sat on one of the benches that were placed, here and there, among the trees. This was a bodily languor in which her mind did not sympathise. She was always an animated talker, and very intelligent.

She sometimes alluded for a moment to her own home, or mentioned an adventure or situation, or an early recollection, which indicated a people of strange manners, and described customs of which we knew nothing. I gathered from these chance hints that her native country was much more remote than I had at first fancied.

As we sat thus one afternoon under the trees a funeral passed us by. It was that of a pretty young girl, whom I had often seen, the daughter of one of the rangers of the forest. The poor man was walking behind the coffin of his darling ; she was his only child, and he looked quite heartbroken. Peasants walking two-and-two came behind, they were singing a funeral hymn.

I rose to mark my respect as they passed, and joined in the hymn they were very sweetly singing.

My companion shook me a little roughly, and I turned surprised.

She said brusquely, " Don't you perceive how discordant that is ? "

" I think it is very sweet, on the contrary," I answered, vexed at the interruption, and very uncomfortable, lest the people who composed the little procession should observe and resent what was passing.

I resumed, therefore, instantly, and was again interrupted. " You pierce my ears," said Carmilla, almost angrily, and stopping her ears with her tiny fingers. " Besides, how can you tell that your religion and mine are the same ; your forms wound me, and I hate funerals. What a fuss ! Why, *you* must die—*everyone* must die ; and all are happier when they do. Come home."

" My father has gone on with the clergyman to the churchyard. I thought you knew she was to be buried to-day."

" *She* ? I don't trouble my head about peasants. I don't know who she is," answered Carmilla, with a flash from her fine eyes.

" She is the poor girl who fancied she saw a ghost a fortnight ago, and has been dying ever since, till yesterday, when she expired."

" Tell me nothing about ghosts. I shan't sleep to-night if you do."

" I hope there is no plague or fever coming ; all this looks very like it," I continued. " The swineherd's young wife died only a week ago, and she thought something seized her by the throat as she lay in her bed, and nearly strangled her. Papa says such horrible fancies do accompany some forms of fever. She was quite well the day before. She sank afterwards, and died before a week."

" Well, *her* funeral is over, I hope, and *her* hymn sung ; and our ears shan't be tortured with that discord and jargon. It has made me nervous. Sit down here, beside me ; sit close ; hold my hand ; press it hard—hard—harder."

We had moved a little back, and had come to another seat.

She sat down. Her face underwent a change that alarmed and even terrified me for a moment. It darkened, and became horribly livid ; her teeth and hands were clenched, and she frowned and compressed her lips, while she stared down upon the ground at her feet, and trembled all over with a continued shudder as irrepressible as ague. All her energies seemed strained to suppress a fit, with which she was then breathlessly tugging ; and at length a low convulsive cry of suffering broke from her, and gradually the hysteria subsided. " There ! That comes of strangling people with hymns ! " she said at last. " Hold me, hold me still. It is passing away."

And so gradually it did ; and perhaps to dissipate the sombre impression which the spectacle had left upon me, she became unusually animated and chatty ; and so we got home.

This was the first time I had seen her exhibit any definable symptoms of that delicacy of health which her mother had spoken of. It was the first time, also, I had seen her exhibit anything like temper.

Both passed away like a summer cloud ; and never but once afterwards did I witness on her part a momentary sign of anger. I will tell you how it happened.

She and I were looking out of one of the long drawing-room windows, when there entered the court-yard, over the draw-bridge, a figure of a wanderer whom I knew very well. He used to visit the schloss generally twice a year.

It was the figure of a hunchback, with the sharp lean features that generally accompany deformity. He wore a pointed black beard, and he was smiling from ear to ear, showing his white fangs. He was dressed in buff, black, and scarlet, and crossed with more straps and belts than I could count, from which hung all manner of things. Behind, he carried a magic-langern, and two boxes, which I well knew, in one of which was a salamander, and in the other a mandrake. These monsters used to make my father laugh. They were compounded of parts of monkeys, parrots, squirrels, fish, and hedgehogs, dried and stitched together with great neatness and startling effect. He had a fiddle, a box of conjuring apparatus, a pair of foils and masks attached to his belt, several other mysterious cases dangling about him, and a black staff with copper ferrules in his hand. His companion was a rough spare dog, that followed at his heels, but stopped short, suspiciously at the drawbridge, and in a little while began to howl dismally.

In the meantime, the mountebank, standing in the midst of the court-yard, raised his grotesque hat, and made us a very cere-monious bow, paying his compliments very volubly in execrable French, and German not much better. Then, disengaging his fiddle, he began to scrape a lively air, to which he sang with a merry discord, dancing with ludicrous airs and activity, that made me laugh, in spite of the dog's howling.

Then he advanced to the window with many smiles and salutations, and his hat in his left hand, his fiddle under his arm, and with a fluency that never took breath, he gabbled a long advertisement of all his accomplishments, and the resources of the various arts which he placed at our service, and the curiosities and entertainments which it was in his power, at our bidding to display.

"Will your ladyships be pleased to buy an amulet against the oupire, which is going like the wolf, I hear, through these woods," he said, dropping his hat on the pavement. "They are dying of it right and left, and here is a charm that never fails ; only pinned to the pillow, and you may laugh in his face."

These charms consisted of oblong slips of vellum, with cabalistic ciphers and diagrams upon them.

Carmilla instantly purchased one, and so did I.

He was looking up, and we were smiling down upon·him, amused ; at least, I can answer for myself. His piercing black eye, as he looked up in our faces, seemed to detect something that fixed for a moment his curiosity.

In an instant he unrolled a leather case, full of all manner of odd little steel instruments.

"See here, my lady," he said, displaying it, and addressing me, " I profess, among other things less useful, the art of dentistry. Plague take the dog ! " he interpolated. " Silence, beast ! He howls so that your ladyships can scarcely hear a word. Your noble friend, the young lady at your right, has the sharpest tooth—long, thin, pointed, like an awl, like a needle ; ha, ha ! With my sharp and long sight, as I look up, I have seen it distinctly ; now if it happens to hurt the young lady, and I think it must, here am I, here are my file, my punch, my nippers ; I will make it round and blunt, if her ladyship pleases ; no longer the tooth of a fish, but of a beautiful young lady as she is. Hey ? Is the young lady displeased ? Have I been too bold ? Have I offended her ? "

The young lady, indeed, looked very angry as she drew back from the window.

"How dares that mountebank insult us so ? Where is your father ? I shall demand redress from him. My father would have had the wretch tied up to the pump, and flogged with a cart-whip, and burnt to the bones with the castle brand ! "

She retired from the window a step or two, and sat down, and hardly lost sight of the offender, when her wrath subsided as suddenly as it had risen, and she gradually recovered her usual tone, and seemed to forget the little hunchback and his follies.

My father was out of spirits that evening. On coming in he told us that there had been another case very similar to the two fatal ones which had lately occurred. The sister of a young peasant on his estate, only a mile away, was very ill, had been, as she described it, attacked very nearly in the same way, and was now slowly but steadily sinking.

"All this," said my father, "is strictly referable to natural causes. These poor people infect one another with their superstitions, and so repeat in imagination the images of terror that have infested their neighbours."

"But that very circumstance frightens one horribly," said Carmilla.

"How so?" inquired my father.

"I am so afraid of fancying I see such things; I think it would be as bad as reality."

"We are in God's hands; nothing can happen without His permission, and all will end well for those who love Him. He is our faithful creator; He had made us all, and will take care of us."

"Creator! *Nature!*" said the young lady in answer to my gentle father. "And this disease that invades the country is natural. Nature. All things proceed from Nature—don't they? All things in the heaven, in the earth, and under the earth, act and live as Nature ordains? I think so."

"The doctor said he would come here to-day," said my father, after a silence. "I want to know what he thinks about it, and what he thinks we had better do."

"Doctors never did me any good," said Carmilla.

"Then you have been ill?" I asked.

"More ill than ever you were," she answered.

"Long ago?"

"Yes, a long time. I suffered from this very illness; but I forget all but my pain and weakness, and they were not so bad as are suffered in other diseases."

"You were very young then?"

"I dare say; let us talk no more of it. You would not wound a friend?" She looked languidly in my eyes, and passed her arm round my waist lovingly, and led me out of the room. My father was busy over some papers near the window.

"Why does your papa like to frighten us?" said the pretty girl, with a sigh and a little shudder.

"He doesn't, dear Carmilla, it is the very furthest thing from his mind."

"Are you afraid, dearest?"

" I should be very much if I fancied there was any real danger of my being attacked as those poor people were."

" You are afraid to die ? "

" Yes, every one is."

" But to die as lovers may—to die together, so that they may live together. Girls are caterpillars while they live in the world, to be finally butterflies when the summer comes ; but in the meantime there are grubs and larvæ, don't you see—each with their peculiar propensities, necessities and structure. So says Monsieur Buffon, in his big book, in the next room."

Later in the day the doctor came, and was closeted with papa for some time. He was a skilful man, of sixty and upwards, he wore powder, and shaved his pale face as smooth as a pumpkin. He and papa emerged from the room together, and I heard papa laugh, and say as they came out :

" Well, I do wonder at a wise man like you. What do you say to hippogriffs and dragons ? "

The doctor was smiling, and made answer, shaking his head—

" Nevertheless, life and death are mysterious states, and we know little of the resources of either."

And so they walked on, and I heard no more. I did not then know what the doctor had been broaching, but I think I guess it now.

CHAPTER V

A WONDERFUL LIKENESS

This evening there arrived from Gratz the grave, dark-faced son of the picture-cleaner, with a horse and cart laden with two large packing-cases, having many pictures in each. It was a journey of ten leagues, and whenever a messenger arrived at the schloss from our little capital of Gratz, we used to crowd about him in the hall, to hear the news.

This arrival created in our secluded quarters quite a sensation. The cases remained in the hall, and the messenger was taken charge of by the servants till he had eaten his supper. Then with assistants, and armed with hammer, ripping chisel, and turnscrew he met us in the hall, where we had assembled to witness the unpacking of the cases.

Carmilla sat looking listlessly on, while one after the other the old pictures, nearly all portraits, which had undergone the process of renovation, were brought to light. My mother was of an old Hungarian family, and most of these pictures, which were about to be restored to their places, had come to us through her.

My father had a list in his hand, from which he read, as the artist rummaged out the corresponding numbers. I don't know that the pictures were very good, but they were, undoubtedly very old, and some of them very curious also. They had, for the most part, the merit of being now seen by me, I may say, for the first time ; for the smoke and dust of time had all but obliterated them.

"There is a picture that I have not seen yet," said my father. "In one corner, at the top of it, is the name, as well as I could read, ' Marcia Karnstein,' and the date ' 1698 ' ; and I am curious to see how it has turned out."

I remembered it ; it was a small picture, about a foot and a half high, and nearly square, without a frame ; but it was so blackened by age that I could not make it out.

The artist now produced it, with evident pride. It was quite beautiful ; it was startling ; it seemed to live. It was the effigy of Carmilla !

"Carmilla, dear, here is an absolute miracle. Here you are, living, smiling, ready to speak, in this picture. Isn't it beautiful, papa ? And see, even the little mole on her throat."

My father laughed, and said "Certainly it is a wonderful likeness," but he looked away, and to my surprise seemed but little struck by it, and went on talking to the picture-cleaner, who was also something of an artist, and discoursed with intelligence about the portraits or other works, which his art had just brought into light and colour, while *I* was more and more lost in wonder the more I looked at the picture.

"Will you let me hang this picture in my room, papa ?" I asked.

"Certainly, dear," said he, smiling, "I'm very glad you think it so like. It must be prettier even than I thought it, if it is."

The young lady did not acknowledge this pretty speech, did not seem to hear it. She was leaning back in her seat, her fine eyes under their long lashes gazing on me in contemplation, and she smiled in a kind of rapture.

"And now you can read quite plainly the name that is written in the corner. It is not Marcia ; it looks as if it was done in gold. The name is Mircalla, Countess Karnstein, and this is a little coronet over it, and underneath A.D. 1698. I am descended from the Karnsteins ; that is, mamma was."

" Ah ! " said the lady, languidly, " so am I, I think, a very long descent, very ancient. Are there any Karnsteins living now? "

" None who bear the name, I believe. The family were ruined, I believe, in some civil wars, long ago but the ruins of the castle are only about three miles away."

" How interesting ! " she said, languidly. " But see what beautiful moonlight ! " She glanced through the hall door, which stood a little open. " Suppose you take a little ramble round the court and look down at the road and river."

" It is so like the night you came to us," I said.

She sighed, smiling.

She rose, and each with her arm about the other's waist, we walked out upon the pavement.

In silence, slowly we walked down to the drawbridge, where the beautiful landscape opened before us.

" And so you were thinking of the night I came here ? " she almost whispered. " Are you glad I came ? "

" Delighted, dear Carmilla," I answered.

" And you ask for the picture you think like me, to hang in your room," she murmured with a sigh, as she drew her arm closer about my waist, and let her pretty head sink upon my shoulder.

" How romantic you are, Carmilla," I said. " Whenever you tell me your story, it will be made up chiefly of some one great romance."

She kissed me silently.

" I am sure, Carmilla, you have been in love ; that there is, at this moment, an affair of the heart going on."

" I have been in love with no one, and never shall," she whispered, " unless it should be with you."

How beautiful she looked in the moonlight !

Shy and strange was the look with which she quickly hid her face in my neck and hair, with tumultuous sighs, that seemed almost to sob, and pressed in mine a hand that trembled.

Her soft cheek was glowing against mine. " Darling, darling," she murmured, " I live in you ; and you would die for me, I love you so."

I started from her.

She was gazing on me with eyes from which all fire, all meaning had flown, and a face colourless and apathetic.

" Is there a chill in the air, dear ? " she said drowsily. " I almost shiver ; have I been dreaming ? Let us come in. Come, come ; come in."

" You look ill, Carmilla ; a little faint. You certainly must take some wine," I said.

" Yes, I will. I'm better now. I shall be quite well in a few minutes. Yes, do give me a little wine," answered Carmilla, as we approached the door. " Let us look again for a moment ; it is the last time, perhaps, I shall see the moonlight with you."

" How do you feel now, dear Carmilla ? Are you really better ? " I asked.

I was beginning to take alarm, lest she should have been stricken with the strange epidemic that they said had invaded the country about us.

" Papa, would be grieved beyond measure," I added, " if he thought you were ever so little ill, without immediately letting us know. We have a very skilful doctor near this, the physician who was with papa to-day."

" I'm sure he is. I know how kind you all are ; but, dear child, I am quite well again. There is nothing ever wrong with me, but a little weakness. People say I am languid ; I am incapable of exertion ; I can scarcely walk as far as a child of three years old ; and every now and then the little strength I have falters, and I become as you have just seen me. But after all I am very easily set up again ; in a moment I am perfectly myself. See how I have recovered."

So, indeed, she had ; and she and I talked a great deal, and very animated she was ; and the remainder of that evening passed without any recurrence of what I called her infatuations. I mean her crazy talk and looks, which embarrassed, and even frightened me.

But there occurred that night an event which gave my thoughts quite a new turn, and seemed to startle even Carmilla's languid nature into momentary energy.

CHAPTER VI

A VERY STRANGE AGONY

When we got into the drawing-room, and had sat down to our coffee and chocolate, although Carmilla did not take any, she seemed quite herself again, and Madame, and Mademoiselle

De Lafontaine, joined us, and made a little card party, in the course of which papa came in for what he called his " dish of tea."

When the game was over he sat down beside Carmilla on the sofa, and asked her, a little anxiously, whether she had heard from her mother since her arrival.

She answered " No."

He then asked her whether she knew where a letter would reach her at present.

" I cannot tell," she answered, ambiguously, " but I have been thinking of leaving you ; you have been already too hospitable and too kind to me. I have given you an infinity of trouble, and I should wish to take a carriage to-morrow, and post in pursuit of her ; I know where I shall ultimately find her, although I dare not yet tell you."

" But you must not dream of any such thing," exclaimed my father, to my great relief. " We can't afford to lose you so, and I won't consent to your leaving us, except under the care of your mother, who was so good as to consent to your remaining with us till she should herself return. I should be quite happy if I knew that you heard from her ; but this evening the accounts of the progress of the mysterious disease that has invaded our neighbour-hood, grow even more alarming ; and my beautiful guest, I do feel the responsibility, unaided by advice from your mother, very much. But I shall do my best ; and one thing is certain, that you must not think of leaving us without her distinct direction to that effect. We should suffer too much in parting from you to consent to it easily."

" Thank you, sir, a thousand times for your hospitality," she answered, smiling bashfully. " You have all been too kind to me ; I have seldom been so happy in all my life before, as in your beautiful château, under your care, and in the society of your dear daughter."

So he gallantly, in his old-fashioned way, kissed her hand, smiling, and pleased at her little speech.

I accompanied Carmilla as usual to her room, and sat and chatted with her while she was preparing for bed.

" Do you think," I said, at length, " that you will ever confide fully in me ? "

She turned round smiling, but made no answer, only continued to smile on me.

" You won't answer that ? " I said. " You can't answer pleasantly ; I ought not to have asked you."

" You were quite right to ask me that, or anything. You do not know how dear you are to me, or you could not think any confidence too great to look for. But I am under vows, no nun half so awfully, and I dare not tell my story yet, even to you. The time is very near when you shall know everything. You will think me cruel, very selfish, but love is always selfish ; the more ardent the more selfish. How jealous I am you cannot know. You must come with me, loving me, to death ; or else hate me, and still come with me, and *hating* me through death and after. There is no such word as indifference in my apathetic nature."

" Now, Carmilla, you are going to talk your wild nonsense again," I said hastily.

" Not I, silly little fool as I am, and full of whims and fancies ; for your sake I'll talk like a sage. Were you ever at a ball ? "

" No ; how you do run on. What is it like ? How charming it must be."

" I almost forget, it is years ago."

I laughed.

" You are not so old. Your first ball can hardly be forgotten yet."

" I remember everything about it—with an effort. I see it all, as divers see what is going on above them, through a medium, dense, rippling, but transparent. There occurred that night what has confused the picture, and made its colours faint. I was all but assassinated in my bed, wounded *here*," she touched her breast, " and never was the same since."

" Were you near dying ? "

" Yes, very—a cruel love—strange love, that would have taken my life. Love will have its sacrifices. No sacrifice without blood. Let us go to sleep now ; I feel so lazy. How can I get up just now and lock my door ? "

She was lying with her tiny hands buried in her rich wavy hair, under her cheek, her little head upon the pillow, and her glittering eyes followed me wherever I moved, with a kind of shy smile that I could not decipher.

I bid her good-night, and crept from the room with an uncomfortable sensation.

I often wondered whether our pretty guest ever said her prayers. *I* certainly had never seen her upon her knees. In the morning she never came down until long after our family prayers were over, and at night she never left the drawing-room to attend our brief evening prayers in the hall.

If it had not been that it had casually come out in one of our careless talks that she had been baptised, I should have doubted her being a Christian. Religion was a subject on which I had never heard her speak a word. If I had known the world better, this particular neglect or antipathy would not have so much surprised me.

The precautions of nervous people are infectious, and persons of a like temperament are pretty sure, after a time, to imitate them. I had adopted Carmilla's habit of locking her bed-room door, having taken into my head all her whimsical alarms about midnight invaders, and prowling assassins. I had also adopted her precaution of making a brief search through her room, to satisfy herself that no lurking assassin or robber was " ensconced."

These wise measures taken, I got into my bed and fell asleep. A light was burning in my room. This was an old habit, of very early date, and which nothing could have tempted me to dispense with.

Thus fortified I might take my rest in peace. But dreams come through stone walls, light up dark rooms, or darken light ones, and their persons make their exits and their entrances as they please, and laugh at locksmiths.

I had a dream that night that was the beginning of a very strange agony.

I cannot call it a nightmare, for I was quite conscious of being asleep. But I was equally conscious of being in my room, and lying in bed, precisely as I actually was. I saw, or fancied I saw, the room and its furniture just as I had seen it last, except that it was very dark, and I saw something moving round the foot of the bed, which at first I could not accurately distinguish. But I soon saw that it was a sooty-black animal that resembled a monstrous cat. It appeared to me about four or five feet long, for it measured fully the length of the hearth-rug as it passed over it ; and it continued to-ing and fro-ing with the lithe sinister restlessness of a beast in a cage. I could not cry out, although as you may suppose, I was terrified. Its pace was growing faster, and the room rapidly darker and darker, and at length so dark that I could no longer see anything of it but its eyes. I felt it spring lightly on the bed. The two broad eyes approached my face, and suddenly I felt a stinging pain as if two large needles darted, an inch or two apart, deep into my breast. I waked with a scream. The room was lighted by the candle that burnt there all through the night, and I saw a female figure standing at the foot of the bed, a little at the right side. It was in a dark loose dress, and its hair was down and covered its shoulders. A block of stone could not have been more still. There was not the slightest stir of respiration. As I stared at it, the figure appeared to have changed its place, and was now nearer the door ; then, close to it, the door opened, and it passed out.

I was now relieved, and able to breathe and move. My first thought was that Carmilla had been playing me a trick, and that I had forgotten to secure my door. I hastened to it, and found it locked as usual on the inside. I was afraid to open it—I was horrified. I sprang into my bed and covered my head up in the bed-clothes, and lay there more dead than alive till morning.

CHAPTER VII

DESCENDING

It would be vain my attempting to tell you the horror with which, even now, I recall the occurrence of that night. It was no such transitory terror as a dream leaves behind it. It seemed to deepen by time, and communicated itself to the room and the very furniture that had encompassed the apparition.

I could not bear next day to be alone for a moment. I should have told papa, but for two opposite reasons. At one time I thought he would laugh at my story, and I could not bear its being treated as a jest ; and at another, I thought he might fancy that I had been attacked by the mysterious complaint which had invaded our neighbourhood. I had myself no misgivings of the kind, and as he had been rather an invalid for some time, I was afraid of alarming him.

I was comfortable enough with my good-natured companions, Madame Perrodon, and the vivacious Mademoiselle Lafontaine. They both perceived that I was out of spirits and nervous, and at length I told them what lay so heavy at my heart.

Mademoiselle laughed, but I fancied that Madame Perrodon looked anxious.

" By-the-by," said Mademoiselle, laughing, " the long lime tree walk, behind Carmilla's bedroom window, is haunted ! "

" Nonsense ! " exclaimed Madame, who probably thought the theme rather inopportune, " and who tells that story, my dear ? "

" Martin says that he came up twice, when the old yard-gate was being repaired before sunrise, and twice saw the same female figure walking down the lime tree avenue."

" So he well might, as long as there are cows to milk in the river fields," said Madame.

" I dare say ; but Martin chooses to be frightened, and never did I see a fool *more* frightened."

" You must not say a word about it to Carmilla, because she can see down that walk from her room window," I interposed, " and she is, if possible, a greater coward than I."

Carmilla came down rather later than usual that day.

" I was so frightened last night," she said, so soon as we were together, " and I am sure I should have seen something dreadful if it had not been for that charm I bought from the poor little hunchback whom I called such hard names. I had a dream of something black coming round my bed, and I awoke in a perfect horror, and I really thought, for some seconds, I saw a dark figure near the chimney piece, but I felt under my pillow for my charm, and the moment my fingers touched it, the figure disappeared, and I felt quite certain, only that I had it by me, that something frightful would have made its appearance, and perhaps, throttled me, as it did those poor people we heard of."

" Well, listen to me," I began, and recounted my adventure, at the recital of which she appeared horrified.

" And had you the charm near you ? " she asked, earnestly.

" No, I had dropped it into a china vase in the drawing-room, but I shall certainly take it with me to-night, as you have so much faith in it."

At this distance of time I cannot tell you, or even understand, how I overcame my horror so effectually as to lie alone in my room that night. I remember distinctly that I pinned the charm to my pillow. I fell asleep almost immediately, and slept even more soundly than usual all night.

Next night I passed as well. My sleep was delightfully deep and dreamless. But I wakened with a sense of lassitude and melancholy which, however, did not exceed a degree that was almost luxurious.

" Well, I told you so," said Carmilla, when I described my quiet sleep, " I had such delightful sleep myself last night ; I pinned the charm to the breast of my nightdress. It was too far away the night before. I am quite sure it was all fancy, except the dreams. I used to think that evil spirits made dreams, but our doctor told me it is no such thing. Only a fever passing by, or some other malady, as they often do, he said, knocks at the door, and not being able to get in, passes on, with that alarm."

"And what do you think the charm is ? " said I.

"It has been fumigated or immersed in some drug, and is an antidote against the malaria," she answered.

"Then it acts only on the body ? "

"Certainly ; you don't suppose that evil spirits are frightened by bits of ribbon, or the perfumes of a druggist's shop ? No, these complaints, wandering in the air, begin by trying the nerves, and so infect the brain ; but before they can seize upon you, the antidote repels them. That I am sure is what the charm has done for us. It is nothing magical, it is simply natural."

I should have been happier if I could quite have agreed with Carmilla, but I did my best, and the impression was a little losing its force.

For some nights I slept profoundly ; but still every morning I felt the same lassitude, and a languor weighed upon me all day. I felt myself a changed girl. A strange melancholy was stealing over me, a melancholy that I would not have interrupted. Dim thoughts of death began to open, and an idea that I was slowly sinking took gentle, and, somehow, not unwelcome possession of me. If it was sad, the tone of mind which this induced was also sweet. Whatever it might be, my soul acquiesced in it.

I would not admit that I was ill, I would not consent to tell my papa, or to have the doctor sent for.

Carmilla became more devoted to me than ever, and her strange paroxysms of languid adoration more frequent. She used to gloat on me with increasing ardour the more my strength and spirits waned. This always shocked me like a momentary glare of insanity.

Without knowing it, I was now in a pretty advanced stage of the strangest illness under which mortal ever suffered. There was an unaccountable fascination in its earlier symptoms that more than reconciled me to the incapacitating effect of that stage of the malady. This fascination increased for a time, until it reached a certain point, when gradually a sense of the horrible mingled itself with it, deepening, as you shall hear, until it discoloured and perverted the whole state of my life.

The first change I experienced was rather agreeable. It was very near the turning point from which began the descent of Avernus.

Certain vague and strange sensations visited me in my sleep. The prevailing one was of that pleasant, peculiar cold thrill which we feel in bathing, when we move against the current of a river. This was soon accompanied by dreams that seemed interminable, and were so vague that I could never recollect their scenery and persons, or any one connected portion of their action. But they left an awful impression, and a sense of exhaustion, as if I had passed through a long period of great mental exertion and danger. After all these dreams there remained on waking a remembrance of having been in a place very nearly dark, and of having spoken to people whom I could not see ; and especially of one clear voice, of a female's, very deep, that spoke as if at a distance, slowly, and producing always the same sensation of indescribable solemnity and fear. Sometimes there came a sensation as if a hand was drawn softly along my cheek and neck. Sometimes it was as if warm lips kissed me, and longer and more lovingly as they reached my throat, but there the caress fixed itself. My heart beat faster, my breathing rose and fell rapidly and full drawn ; a sobbing, that rose into a sense of strangulation, supervened, and turned into a dreadful convulsion, in which my senses left me, and I became unconscious.

It was now three weeks since the commencement of this unaccountable state. My sufferings had, during the last week, told upon my appearance. I had grown pale, my eyes were dilated and darkened underneath, and the languor which I had long felt began to display itself in my countenance.

My father asked me often whether I was ill ; but, with an obstinacy which now seems to me unaccountable, I persisted in assuring him that I was quite well.

In a sense this was true. I had no pain, I could complain of no bodily derangement. My complaint seemed to be one of the imagination, or the nerves, and, horrible as my sufferings were, I kept them, with a morbid reserve, very nearly to myself.

It could not be that terrible complaint which the peasants call the oupire, for I had now been suffering for three weeks, and they were seldom ill for much more than three days, when death put an end to their miseries.

Carmilla complained of dreams and feverish sensations, but by no means of so alarming a kind as mine. I say that mine were extremely alarming. Had I been capable of comprehending my condition, I would have invoked aid and advice on my knees. The narcotic of an unsuspected influence was acting upon me, and my perceptions were benumbed.

I am going to tell you now of a dream that led immediately to an odd discovery.

One night, instead of the voice I was accustomed to hear in the dark, I heard one, sweet and tender, and at the same time terrible, which said, " Your mother warns you to beware of the assassin." At the same time a light unexpectedly sprang up, and I saw Carmilla, standing, near the foot of my bed, in her white night-dress, bathed, from her chin to her feet, in one great stain of blood.

I wakened with a shriek, possessed with the one idea that Carmilla was being murdered. I remember springing from my bed, and my next recollection is that of standing on the lobby, crying for help.

Madame and Mademoiselle came scurrying out of their rooms in alarm ; a lamp burned always on the lobby, and seeing me, they soon learned the cause of my terror.

I insisted on our knocking at Carmilla's door. Our knocking was unanswered. It soon became a pounding and an uproar. We shrieked her name but all was vain.

We all grew frightened, for the door was locked. We hurried back, in panic, to my room. There we rang the bell long and furiously. If my father's room had been at that side of the house, we would have called him up at once to our aid. But, alas ! he was quite out of hearing, and to reach him involved an excursion for which we none of us had courage.

Servants, however, soon came running up the stairs ; I had got on my dressing-gown and slippers meanwhile, and my com-panions were already similarly furnished. Recognising the voices of the servants on the lobby, we sallied out together ; and having renewed, as fruitlessly, our summons at Carmilla's door, I ordered the men to force the lock. They did so, and we stood, holding our lights aloft, in the doorway, and so stared into the room.

We called her by name ; but there was still no reply. We looked round the room. Everything was undisturbed. It was exactly in the state in which I left it on bidding her good night. But Carmilla was gone.

CHAPTER VIII

SEARCH

At sight of the room, perfectly undisturbed except for our violent entrance, we began to cool a little, and soon recovered our senses sufficiently to dismiss the men. It had struck Mademoiselle that possibly Carmilla had been wakened by the uproar at her door, and in her first panic had jumped from her bed, and hid herself in a press, or behind a curtain, from which she could not, of course, emerge until the major-domo and his myrmidons had withdrawn. We now recommenced our search, and began to call her by name again.

It was all to no purpose. Our perplexity and agitation increased. We examined the windows, but they were secured. I implored of Carmilla, if she had concealed herself, to play this cruel trick no longer—to come out, and to end our anxieties. It was all useless. I was by this time convinced that she was not in the room, nor in the dressing-room, the door of which was still locked on this side. She could not have passed it. I was utterly puzzled. Had Carmilla discovered one of those secret passages which the old housekeeper said were known to exist in the schloss, although the tradition of their exact situation had been lost. A little time would, no doubt, explain all—utterly perplexed as, for the present, we were.

It was past four o'clock, and I preferred passing the remaining hours of darkness in Madame's room. Daylight brought no solution of the difficulty.

The whole household, with my father at its head, was in a state of agitation next morning. Every part of the château was searched. The grounds were explored. Not a trace of the missing lady could be discovered. The stream was about to be dragged ; my father was in distraction ; what a tale to have to tell the poor girl's mother on her return. I, too, was almost beside myself, though my grief was quite of a different kind.

The morning was passed in alarm and excitement. It was now one o'clock, and still no tidings. I ran up to Carmilla's room, and found her standing at her dressing-table. I was astounded. I could not believe my eyes. She beckoned me to her with her pretty finger, in silence. Her face expressed extreme fear.

I ran to her in an ecstasy of joy ; I kissed and embraced her again and again. I ran to the bell and rang it vehemently, to bring others to the spot, who might at once relieve my father's anxiety.

" Dear Carmilla, what has become of you all this time ? We have been in agonies of anxiety about you," I exclaimed. " Where have you been ? How did you come back ? "

" Last night has been a night of wonders," she said.

" For mercy's sake, explain all you can."

" It was past two last night," she said, " when I went to sleep as usual in my bed, with my doors locked, that of the dressing-room' and that opening upon the gallery. My sleep was uninterrupted, and, so far as I know, dreamless ; but I awoke just now on the sofa in the dressing-room there, and I found the door between the rooms open, and the other door forced. How could all this have happened without my being awakened ? It must have been accompanied with a great deal of noise, and I am particularly easily wakened ; and how could I have been carried out of my bed without my sleep having been interrupted, I whom the slightest stir startles ? "

By this time, Madame, Mademoiselle, my father, and a number of the servants were in the room. Carmilla was, of course, overwhelmed with enquiries, congratulations, and welcomes. She had but one story to tell, and seemed the least able of all the party to suggest any way of accounting for what had happened.

My father took a turn up and down the room, thinking. I saw Carmilla's eye follow him for a moment with a sly, dark glance.

When my father had sent the servants away, Mademoiselle having gone in search of a little bottle of valerian and sal-volatile, and there being no one now in the room with Carmilla except my father, Madame, and myself, he came to her thoughtfully, took her hand very kindly, led her to the sofa, and sat down beside her.

" Will you forgive me, my dear, if I risk a conjecture, and ask a question ? "

" Who can have a better right ? " she said. " Ask what you please, and I will tell you everything. But my story is simply one of bewilderment and darkness. I know absolutely nothing. Put any question you please. But you know, of course, the limitations mamma has placed me under."

" Perfectly, my dear child. I need not approach the topics on which she desires our silence. Now, the marvel of last night consists in your having been removed from your bed and your room without being wakened, and this removal having occurred apparently while the windows were still secured, and the two doors locked upon the inside. I will tell you my theory, and first ask you a question."

Carmilla was leaning on her hand dejectedly ; Madame and I were listening breathlessly.

" Now, my question is this. Have you ever been suspected of walking in your sleep ? "

" Never since I was very young indeed."

" But you did walk in your sleep when you were young ? "

" Yes ; I know I did. I have been told so often by my old nurse."

My father smiled and nodded.

" Well, what has happened is this. You got up in your sleep, unlocked the door, not leaving the key, as usual, in the lock, but taking it out and locking it on the outside ; you again took the key out, and carried it away with you to some one of the five-and-twenty rooms on this floor, or perhaps upstairs or downstairs. There are so many rooms and closets, so much heavy furniture, and such accumulations of lumber, that it would require a week to search this old house thoroughly. Do you see, now, what I mean ? "

" I do, but not all," she answered.

" And how, papa, do you account for her finding herself on the sofa in the dressing-room, which we had searched so carefully ? "

" She came there after you had searched it, still in her sleep, and at last awoke spontaneously, and was as much surprised to find herself where she was as any one else. I wish all mysteries were as easily and innocently explained as yours, Carmilla," he said, laughing. " And so we may congratulate ourselves on the certainty that the most natural explanation of the occurrence is one that involves no drugging, no tampering with locks, no burglars, or poisoners, or witches—nothing that need alarm Carmilla, or any one else, for our safety."

Carmilla was looking charmingly. Nothing could be more beautiful than her tints. Her beauty was, I think enhanced by that graceful languor that was peculiar to her. I think my father was silently contrasting her looks with mine, for he said :—

" I wish my poor Laura was looking more like herself " ; and he sighed.

So our alarms were happily ended, and Carmilla restored to her friends.

CHAPTER IX

THE DOCTOR

As Carmilla would not hear of an attendant sleeping in her room, my father arranged that a servant should sleep outside her door so that she could not attempt to make another such excursion without being arrested at her own door.

That night passed quietly ; and next morning early, the doctor, whom my father had sent for without telling me a word about it, arrived to see me.

Madame accompanied me to the library ; and there the grave little doctor, with white hair and spectacles, whom I mentioned before, was waiting to receive me.

I told him my story, and as I proceeded he grew graver and graver.

We were standing, he and I, in the recess of one of the windows, facing one another. When my statement was over, he leaned with his shoulders against the wall, and with his eyes fixed on me earnestly with an interest in which was a dash of horror.

After a minute's reflection, he asked Madame if he could see my father.

He was sent for accordingly, and as he entered, smiling, he said :

" I dare say, doctor, you are going to tell me that I am an old fool for having brought you here ; I hope I am."

But his smile faded into shadow as the doctor, with a very grave face, beckoned him to him.

He and the doctor talked for some time in the same recess where I had just conferred with the physician. It seemed an earnest and argumentative conversation. The room is very large, and I and Madame stood together, burning with curiosity, at the further end. Not a word could we hear, however, for they spoke in a very low tone, and the deep recess of the window quite concealed the doctor from view, and very nearly my father, whose foot, arm, and shoulder only could we see ; and the voices were, I suppose, all the less audible for the sort of closet which the thick wall and window formed.

After a time my father's face looked into the room ; it was pale, thoughtful, and, I fancied, agitated.

" Laura, dear, come here for a moment. Madame, we shan't trouble you, the doctor says, at present."

Accordingly I approached, for the first time a little alarmed ;

for, although I felt very weak, I did not feel ill ; and strength, one always fancies, is a thing that may be picked up when we please.

My father held out his hand to me as I drew near, but he was looking at the doctor, and he said :

" It certainly *is* very odd ; I don't understand it quite. Laura, come here, dear ; now attend to Doctor Spielsberg, and recollect yourself."

" You mentioned a sensation like that of two needles piercing the skin, somewhere about your neck, on the night when you experienced your first horrible dream. Is there still any soreness ? "

" None at all," I answered.

" Can you indicate with your finger about the point at which you think this occurred ? "

" Very little below my throat—*here,*" I answered.

I wore a morning dress, which covered the place I pointed to.

" Now you can satisfy yourself," said the doctor. " You won't mind your papa's lowering your dress a very little. It is necessary, to detect a symptom of the complaint under which you have been suffering."

I acquiesced. It was only an inch or two below the edge of my collar.

" God bless me !—so it is," exclaimed my father, growing pale.

" You see it now with your own eyes," said the doctor, with a gloomy triumph.

" What is it ? " I exclaimed, beginning to be frightened.

" Nothing, my dear young lady, but a small blue spot, about the size of the tip of your little finger ; and now," he continued, turning to papa, " the question is what is best to be done ? "

" Is there any danger ? " I urged, in great trepidation.

" I trust not, my dear," answered the doctor. " I don't see why you should not recover. I don't see why you should not begin *immediately* to get better. That is the point at which the sense of strangulation begins ? "

" Yes," I answered.

" And—recollect as well as you can—the same point was a kind of centre of that thrill which you described just now, like the current of a cold stream running against you ? "

" It may have been ; I think it was."

" Ay, you see ? " he added, turning to my father. " Shall I say a word to Madame ? "

" Certainly," said my father.

He called Madame to him, and said :

" I find my young friend here far from well. It won't be of any great consequence, I hope ; but it will be necessary that some steps be taken, which I will explain by-and-by ; but in the meantime, Madame, you will be so good as not to let Miss Laura be alone for one moment. That is the only direction I need give for the present. It is indispensable."

" We may rely upon your kindness, Madame, I know," added my father.

Madame satisfied him eagerly.

" And you, dear Laura, I know you will observe the doctor's direction."

" I shall have to ask your opinion upon another patient, whose symptoms slightly resemble those of my daughter, that have just been detailed to you—very much milder in degree, but I believe quite of the same sort. She is a young lady—our guest ; but as you say you will be passing this way again this evening, you can't do better than take your supper here, and you can then see her. She does not come down till the afternoon."

" I thank you," said the doctor. " I shall be with you, then, at about seven this evening."

And then they repeated their directions to me and to Madame, and with this parting charge my father left us, and walked out with the doctor ; and I saw them pacing together up and down between the road and the moat, on the grassy platform in front of the castle, evidently absorbed in earnest conversation.

The doctor did not return. I saw him mount his horse there, take his leave, and ride away eastward through the forest. Nearly at the same time I saw the man arrive from Dranfeld with the letters, and dismount and hand the bag to my father.

In the meantime, Madame and I were both busy, lost in conjecture as to the reasons of the singular and earnest direction which the doctor and my father had concurred in imposing. Madame, as she afterwards told me, was afraid the doctor apprehended a sudden seizure, and that, without prompt assistance, I might either lose my life in a fit, or at least be seriously hurt.

This interpretation did not strike me ; and I fancied perhaps luckily for my nerves, that the arrangement was prescribed simply to secure a companion, who would prevent my taking too much exercise, or eating unripe fruit, or doing any of the fifty foolish things to which young people are supposed to be prone.

About half-an-hour after, my father came in—he had a letter in his hand—and said :

" This letter had been delayed ; it is from General Spielsdorf. He might have been here yesterday, he may not come till to-morrow, or he may be here to-day."

He put the open letter into my hand ; but he did not look pleased, as he used when a guest, especially one so much loved as the General, was coming. On the contrary, he looked as if he wished him at the bottom of the Red Sea. There was plainly something on his mind which he did not choose to divulge.

" Papa, darling, will you tell me this ? " said I, suddenly laying my hand on his arm, and looking, I am sure, imploringly in his face.

" Perhaps," he answered, smoothing my hair caressingly over my eyes.

" Does the doctor think me very ill ? "

" No, dear ; he thinks, if right steps are taken, you will be quite well again, at least on the high road to a complete recovery, in a day or two," he answered, a little drily. " I wish our good friend, the General, had chosen any other time ; that is, I wish you had been perfectly well to receive him."

" But do tell me, papa," I insisted, " *what* does he think is the matter with me ? "

" Nothing ; you must not plague me with questions," he answered, with more irritation than I ever remember him to have displayed before ; and seeing that I looked wounded, I suppose, he kissed me, and added, " You shall know all about it in a day or two ; that is, all that *I* know. In the meantime, you are not to trouble your head about it."

He turned and left the room, but came back before I had done wondering and puzzling over the oddity of all this ; it was merely to say that he was going to Karnstein and had ordered the car-riage to be ready at twelve, and that I and Madame should accompany him ; he was going to see the priest who lived near those picturesque grounds, upon business, and as Carmilla had never seen them, she could follow, when she came down, with Mademoiselle, who would bring materials for what you call a pic-nic, which might be laid for us in the ruined castle.

At twelve o'clock, accordingly, I was ready, and not long after, my father, Madame and I set out upon our projected drive. Passing the drawbridge we turn to the right, and follow the road over the steep Gothic bridge westward, to reach the deserted village and ruined castle of Karnstein.

No sylvan drive can be fancied prettier. The ground breaks into gentle hills and hollows, all clothed with beautiful wood, totally destitute of the comparative formality which artificial planting and early culture and pruning impart.

The irregularities of the ground often lead the road out of its course, and cause it to wind beautifully round the sides of broken hollows and the steeper sides of the hills, among varieties of ground almost inexhaustible.

Turning one of these points, we suddenly encountered our old friend, the General, riding towards us, attended by a mounted servant. His portmanteaus were following in a hired waggon, such as we term a cart.

The General dismounted as we pulled up, and, after the usual greetings, was easily persuaded to accept the vacant seat in the carriage, and send his horse on with his servant to the schloss.

CHAPTER X

BEREAVED

It was about ten months since we had last seen him ; but that time had sufficed to make an alteration of years in his appearance. He had grown thinner ; something of gloom and anxiety had taken the place of that cordial serenity which used to characterise his features. His dark blue eyes, always penetrating, now gleamed with a sterner light from under his shaggy grey eyebrows. It was not such a change as grief alone usually induces, and angrier passions seemed to have had their share in bringing it about.

We had not long resumed our drive, when the General began to talk, with his usual soldierly directness, of the bereavement, as he termed it, which he had sustained in the death of his beloved niece and ward ; and he then broke out in a tone of intense bitterness and fury, inveighing against the " hellish arts " to which she had fallen a victim, and expressing with more exasperation than piety, his wonder that Heaven should tolerate so monstrous an indulgence of the lusts and malignity of hell.

My father, who saw at once that something very extraordinary had befallen, asked him, if not too painful to him, to detail the circumstances which he thought justified the strong terms in which he expressed himself.

"I should tell you all with pleasure," said the General, "but you would not believe me."

"Why should I not?" he asked.

"Because," he answered testily, "you believe in nothing but what consists with your own prejudices and illusions. I remember when I was like you, but I have learned better."

"Try me," said my father; "I am not such a dogmatist as you suppose. Besides which, I very well know that you generally require proof for what you believe, and am, therefore, very strongly predisposed to respect your conclusions."

"You are right in supposing that I have not been led lightly into a belief in the marvellous—for what I have experienced *is* marvellous—and I have been forced by extraordinary evidence to credit that which ran counter, diametrically, to all my theories. I have been made the dupe of a preternatural conspiracy."

Notwithstanding his professions of confidence in the General's penetration, I saw my father, at this point, glance at the General, with, as I thought a marked suspicion of his sanity.

The General did not see it, luckily. He was looking gloomily and curiously into the glades and vistas of the woods that were opening before us.

"You are going to the Ruins of Karnstein?" he said. "Yes, it is a lucky coincidence; do you know I was going to ask you to bring me there to inspect them. I have a special object in exploring. There is a ruined chapel, isn't there, with a great many tombs of that extinct family?"

"So there are—highly interesting," said my father. "I hope you are thinking of claiming the title and estates?"

My father said this gaily, but the General did not recollect the laugh, or even the smile, which courtesy exacts for a friend's joke; on the contrary, he looked grave and even fierce, ruminating on a matter that stirred his anger and horror.

"Something very different," he said, gruffly. "I mean to unearth some of those fine people. I hope, by God's blessing, to accomplish a pious sacrilege here, which will relieve our earth of certain monsters, and enable honest people to sleep in their beds without being assailed by murderers. I have strange things to tell you, my dear friend, such as I myself would have scouted as incredible a few months since."

My father looked at him again, but this time not with a glance of suspicion—with an eye, rather, of keen intelligence and alarm.

" The house of Karnstein," he said, " has been long extinct : a hundred years at least. My dear wife was maternally descended from the Karnsteins. But the name and title have long ceased to exist. The castle is a ruin ; the very village is deserted ; it is fifty years since the smoke of a chimney was seen there ; not a roof left."

" Quite true. I have heard a great deal about that since I last saw you ; a great deal that will astonish you. But I had better relate everything in the order in which it occurred," said the General. "You saw my dear ward—my child, I may call her. No creature could have been more beautiful and only three months ago none more blooming."

" Yes, poor thing ! when I saw her last she certainly was quite lovely," said my father. " I was grieved and shocked more than I can tell you, my dear friend ; I knew what a blow it was to you."

He took the General's hand, and they exchanged a kind pressure. Tears gathered in the old soldier's eyes. He did not seek to conceal them. He said :

" We have been very old friends ; I knew you would feel for me, childless as I am. She had become an object of very dear interest to me, and repaid my care by an affection that cheered my home and made my life happy. That is all gone. The years that remain to me on earth may not be very long ; but by God's mercy I hope to accomplish a service to mankind before I die, and to subserve the vengeance of Heaven upon the fiends who have murdered my poor child in the spring of her hopes and beauty ! "

" You said, just now, that you intended relating everything as it occurred," said my father. " Pray do ; I assure you that it is not mere curiosity that prompts me."

By this time we had reached the point at which the Drunstall road, by which the General had come, diverges from the road which we were travelling to Karnstein.

" How far is it to the ruins ? " enquired the General, looking anxiously forward.

" About half a league," answered my father. " Pray let us hear the story you were so good as to promise."

CHAPTER XI

"With all my heart," said the General, with an effort ; and after a short pause in which to arrange his subject, he commenced one of the strangest narratives I ever heard.

" My dear child was looking forward with great pleasure to the visit you had been so good as to arrange for her to your charming daughter." Here he made me a gallant but melancholy bow. " In the meantime we had an invitation to my old friend the Count Carlsfeld, whose schloss is about six leagues to the other side of Karnstein. It was to attend the series of fêtes which, you remember, were given by him in honour of his illustrious visitor, the Grand Duke Charles."

" Yes ; and very splendid, I believe, they were," said my father.

" Princely ! But then his hospitalities are quite regal. He has Aladdin's lamp. The night from which my sorrow dates was devoted to a magnificent masquerade. The grounds were thrown open, the trees hung with coloured lamps. There was such a display of fireworks as Paris itself had never witnessed. And such music—music, you know, is my weakness—such ravishing music ! The finest instrumental band, perhaps, in the world, and the finest singers who could be collected from all the great operas in Europe. As you wandered through these fantastically illuminated grounds, the moon-lighted château throwing a rosy light from its long rows of windows, you would suddenly hear these ravishing voices stealing from the silence of some grove, or rising from boats upon the lake. I felt myself, as I looked and listened, carried back into the romance and poetry of my early youth.

" When the fireworks were ended, and the ball beginning, we returned to the noble suite of rooms that was thrown open to the dancers. A masked ball, you know, is a beautiful sight ; but so brilliant a spectacle of the kind I never saw before.

" It was a very aristocratic assembly. I was myself almost the only ' nobody ' present.

" My dear child was looking quite beautiful. She wore no mask. Her excitement and delight added an unspeakable charm to her features, always lovely. I remarked a young lady, dressed magnificently, but wearing a mask, who appeared to me to be observing my ward with extraordinary interest. I had seen her, earlier in the evening, in the great hall, and again, for a few minutes, walking near us, on the terrace under the castle windows, similarly employed. A lady, also masked, richly and gravely dressed, and with a stately air, like a person of rank, accompanied her as a chaperon. Had the young lady not worn a mask, I could, of course, have been much more certain upon the question whether she was really watching my poor darling. I am now well assured that she was.

" We were now in one of the *salons*. My poor dear child had been dancing, and was resting a little in one of the chairs near the door ; I was standing near. The two ladies I have mentioned had approached, and the younger took the chair next my ward ; while her companion stood beside me, and for a little time addressed herself, in a low tone, to her charge.

" Availing herself of the privilege of her mask she turned to me, and in the tone of an old friend, and calling me by my name, opened a conversation with me, which piqued my curiosity a good deal. She referred to many scenes where she had met me—at Court, and at distinguished houses. She alluded to little incidents which I had long ceased to think of, but which, I found, had only lain in abeyance in my memory, for they instantly started into life at her touch.

" I became more and more curious to ascertain who she was, every moment. She parried my attempts to discover very adroitly and pleasantly. The knowledge she showed of many passages in my life seemed to me all but unaccountable ; and she appeared to take a not unnatural pleasure in foiling my curiosity, and in seeing me flounder, in my eager perplexity, from one conjecture to another.

" In the meantime the young lady, whom her mother called by the odd name of Millarca, when she once or twice addressed her, had, with the same ease and grace, got into conversation with my ward.

" She introduced herself by saying that her mother was a very old acquaintance of mine. She spoke of the agreeable audacity which a mask rendered practicable ; she talked like a friend ; she admired her dress, and insinuated very prettily her admiration of her beauty. She amused her with laughing criticisms upon the people who crowded the ballroom, and laughed at my poor child's fun. She was very witty and lively when she pleased, and after a time they had grown very good friends, and the young stranger lowered her mask, displaying a remarkably beautiful face. I had never seen it before, neither had my dear child. But though it was new to us, the features were so engaging, as well as lovely, that it was impossible not to feel the attraction powerfully. My poor girl did so. I never saw anyone more taken with another at first sight, unless indeed, it was the stranger herself, who seemed quite to have lost her heart to her.

" In the meantime, availing myself of the licence of a masquerade, I put not a few questions to the elder lady.

" ' You have puzzled me utterly,' I said, laughing. ' Is that not enough ? won't you, now, consent to stand on equal terms, and do me the kindness to remove your mask ? '

" ' Can any request be more unreasonable ? ' she replied. ' Ask a lady to yield an advantage ! Beside, how do you know you should recognise me ? Years make changes.'

" ' As you see,' I said, with a bow, and, I suppose, a rather melancholy little laugh.

" ' As philosophers tell us,' she said ; ' and how do you know that a sight of my face would help you ? '

" ' I should take chance for that,' I answered. ' It is vain trying to make yourself out an old woman ; your figure betrays you.'

" ' Years, nevertheless, have passed since I saw you, rather since you saw me, for that is what I am considering. Millarca, there, is my daughter ; I cannot then be young, even in the opinion of people whom time has taught to be indulgent, and I may not like to be compared with what you remember me. You have no mask to remove. You can offer me nothing in exchange.'

" ' My petition is to your pity, to remove it.'

" ' And mine to yours, to let it stay where it is,' she replied.

" ' Well, then, at least you will tell me whether you are French or German ; you speak both languages so perfectly.'

" ' I don't think I shall tell you that, General ; you intend a surprise, and are meditating the particular point of attack.'

" ' At all events, you won't deny this,' I said, ' that being honoured by your permission to converse, I ought to know how to address you. Shall I say Madame la Comtesse ! '

" She laughed, and she would, no doubt, have met me with another evasion—if, indeed, I can treat any occurrence in an interview every circumstance of which was pre-arranged, as I now believe, with the profoundest cunning, as liable to be modified by accident.

" ' As to that,' she began ; but she was interrupted, almost as she opened her lips, by a gentleman, dressed in black, who looked particularly elegant and distinguished, with this drawback, that his face was the most deadly pale I ever saw, except in death. He was in no masquerade—in the plain evening dress of a gentleman ; and he said, without a smile, but with a courtly and unusually low bow :—

" ' Will Madame la Comtesse permit me to say á very few words which may interest her ? '

" The lady turned quickly to him, and touched her lip in token of silence ; she then said to me, ' Keep my place for me, General ; I shall return when I have said a few words.'

" And with this injunction, playfully given, she walked a little aside with the gentleman in black, and talked for some minutes, apparently very earnestly. They then walked away slowly together in the crowd, and I lost them for some minutes.

" I spent the interval in cudgelling my brains for conjecture as to the identity of the lady who seemed to remember me so kindly, and I was thinking of turning about and joining in the conversation between my pretty ward and the Countess's daughter, and trying whether, by the time she returned, I might not have a surprise in store for her, by having her name, title, château, and estates at my fingers' ends. But at this moment she returned, accompanied by the pale man in black, who said :

" ' I shall return and inform Madame la Comtesse when her carriage is at the door.'

" He withdrew with a bow."

CHAPTER XII

A PETITION

" ' Then we are to lose Madame la Comtesse, but I hope only for a few hours,' I said, with a low bow.

" ' It may be that only, or it may be a few weeks. It was very unlucky his speaking to me just now as he did. Do you now know me ? ' '

" I assured her I did not.

" ' You shall know me,' she said, ' but not at present. We are older and better friends than, perhaps, you suspect. I cannot yet declare myself. I shall in three weeks pass your beautiful schloss about which I have been making enquiries. I shall then look in upon you for an hour or two, and renew a friendship which I never think of without a thousand pleasant recollections. This moment a piece of news has reached me like a thunderbolt. I must set out now, and travel by a devious route, nearly a hundred miles, with all the dispatch I can possibly make. My perplexities multiply. I am only deterred by the compulsory reserve I practise as to my name from making a very singular request of you. My poor child has not quite recovered her strength. Her horse fell with her, at a hunt which she had ridden out to witness, her nerves have not yet recovered the shock, and our physician says that she must on no account exert herself for some time to come. We came here, in consequence, by very easy stages—hardly six leagues a day. I must now travel day and night, on a mission of life and death—a mission the critical and momentous nature of which I shall be able to explain to you when we meet, as I hope we shall, in a few weeks, without the necessity of any concealment.'

" She went on to make her petition, and it was in the tone of a person from whom such a request amounted to conferring, rather than seeking a favour. This was only in manner, and, as it seemed, quite unconsciously. Than the terms in which it was expressed, nothing could be more deprecatory. It was simply that I would consent to take charge of her daughter during her absence.

" This was, all things considered, a strange, not to say, an audacious request. She in some sort disarmed me, by stating and admitting everything that could be urged against it, and throwing herself entirely upon my chivalry. At the same moment, by a fatality that seems to have predetermined all that happened, my poor child came to my side, and, in an undertone, besought me to invite her new friend, Millarca, to pay us a visit. She had just been sounding her, and thought, if her mamma would allow her, she would like it extremely.

" At another time I should have told her to wait a little, until, at least, we knew who they were. But I had not a moment to think in. The two ladies assailed me together, and I must confess the refined and beautiful face of the young lady, about which there was something extremely engaging, as well as the elegance and fire of high birth, determined me ; and quite overpowered, I submitted, and undertook, too easily, the care of the young lady, whom her mother called Millarca.

" The Countess beckoned to her daughter, who listened with grave attention while she told her, in general terms, how suddenly and peremptorily she had been summoned, and also of the arrangement she had made for her under my care, adding that I was one of her earliest and most valued friends.

"I made, of course, such speeches as the case seemed to call for, and found myself, on reflection, in a position which I did not half like.

"The gentleman in black returned, and very ceremoniously conducted the lady from the room.

"The demeanour of this gentleman was such as to impress me with the conviction that the Countess was a lady of very much more importance than her modest title alone might have led me to assume.

"Her last charge to me was that no attempt was to be made to learn more about her than I might have already guessed, until her return. Our distinguished host, whose guest she was, knew her reasons.

"'But here,' she said, 'neither I nor my daughter could safely remain for more than a day. I removed my mask imprudently for a moment, about an hour ago, and, too late, I fancied you saw me. So I resolved to seek an opportunity of talking a little to you. Had I found that you *had* seen me, I should have thrown myself on your high sense of honour to keep my secret for some weeks. As it is, I am satisfied that you did not see me ; but if you now *suspect*, or, on reflection, *should* suspect, who I am, I commit myself, in like manner, entirely to your honour. My daughter will observe the same secrecy, and I well know that you will, from time to time, remind her, lest she should thoughtlessly disclose it.'

"She whispered a few words to her daughter, kissed her hurriedly twice, and went away, accompanied by the pale gentleman in black, and disappeared in the crowd.

"'In the next room,' said Millarca, 'there is a window that looks upon the hall door. I should like to see the last of mamma, and to kiss my hand to her.'

"We assented, of course, and accompanied her to the window. We looked out, and saw a handsome old-fashioned carriage, with a troop of couriers and footmen. We saw the slim figure of the pale gentleman in black, as he held a thick velvet cloak, and placed it about her shoulders and threw the hood over her head. She nodded to him, and just touched his hand with hers. He bowed low repeatedly as the door closed, and the carriage began to move.

"'She is gone,' said Millarca, with a sigh.

"'She is gone,' I repeated to myself, for the first time—in the hurried moments that had elapsed since my consent—reflecting upon the folly of my act.

" ' She did not look up,' said the young lady, plaintively.

" ' The Countess had taken off her mask, perhaps, and did not care to show her face,' I said ; ' and she could not know that you were in the window.'

" She sighed and looked in my face. She was so beautiful that I relented. I was sorry I had for a moment repented of my hospitality, and I determined to make her amends for the unavowed churlishness of my reception.

" The young lady, replacing her mask, joined my ward in persuading me to return to the grounds, where the concert was soon to be renewed. We did so, and walked up and down the terrace that lies under the castle windows. Millarca became very intimate with us, and amused us with lively descriptions and stories of most of the great people whom we saw upon the terrace. I liked her more and more every minute. Her gossip, without being ill-natured, was extremely diverting to me, who had been so long out of the great world. I thought what life she would give to our sometimes lonely evenings at home.

" This ball was not over until the morning sun had almost reached the horizon. It pleased the Grand Duke to dance till then, so loyal people could not go away, or think of bed.

" We had just got through a crowded saloon, when my ward asked me what had become of Millarca. I thought she had been by my side, and she fancied she was by mine. The fact was, we had lost her.

" All my efforts to find her were vain. I feared that she had mistaken, in the confusion of a momentary separation from us, other people for her new friends, and had, possibly, pursued and lost them in the extensive grounds which were thrown open to us.

" Now, in its full force, I recognised a new folly in my having undertaken the charge of a young lady without so much as knowing her name ; and fettered as I was by promises, of the reasons for imposing which I knew nothing, I could not even point my enquiries by saying that the missing young lady was the daughter of the Countess who had taken her departure a few hours before.

" Morning broke. It was clear daylight before I gave up my search. It was not till near two o'clock next day that we heard anything of my missing charge.

" At about that time a servant knocked at my niece's door, to say that he had been earnestly requested by a young lady, who appeared to be in great distress, to make out where she could find the General Baron Spielsdorf and the young lady, his daughter, in whose charge she had been left by her mother.

" There could be no doubt, notwithstanding the slight inaccuracy, that our young friend had turned up ; and so she had. Would to Heaven we had lost her !

" She told my poor child a story to account for her having failed to recover us for so long. Very late, she said, she had got into the housekeeper's bedroom in despair of finding us, and had then fallen into a deep sleep which, long as it was, had hardly sufficed to recruit her strength after the fatigues of the ball.

" That day Millarca came home with us. I was only too happy, after all, to have secured so charming a companion for my dear girl."

CHAPTER XIII

THE WOOD-MAN

" There soon, however, appeared some drawbacks. In the first place, Millarca complained of extreme languor—the weakness that remained after her late illness—and she never emerged from her room till the afternoon was pretty far advanced. In the next place, it was accidentally discovered, although she always locked her door on the inside, and never disturbed the key from its place, till she admitted the maid to assist at her toilet, that she was undoubtedly sometimes absent from her room in the very early morning, and at various times later in the day, before she wished it to be understood that she was stirring. She was repeatedly seen from the windows of the schloss, in the first faint grey of the morning, walking through the trees, in an easterly direction, and looking like a person in a trance. This convinced me that she walked in her sleep. But this hypothesis did not solve the puzzle. How did she pass out from her room, leaving the door locked on the inside. How did she escape from the house without unbarring door or window ?

" In the midst of my perplexities, an anxiety of a far more urgent kind presented itself.

" My dear child began to lose her looks and health, and that in a manner so mysterious, and even horrible, that I became thoroughly frightened.

"She was at first visited by appalling dreams ; then, as she fancied, by a spectre, something resembling Millarca, sometimes in the shape of a beast, indistinctly seen, walking round the foot of the bed, from side to side. Lastly came sensations. One, not unpleasant, but very peculiar, she said, resembled the flow of an icy stream against her breast. At a later time, she felt something like a pair of large needles pierce her, a little below the throat, with a very sharp pain. A few nights after, followed a gradual and convulsive sense of strangulation ; then came unconsciousness."

I could hear distinctly every word the kind old General was saying, because by this time we were driving upon the short grass that spreads on either side of the road as you approach the roofless village which had not shown the smoke of a chimney for more than half a century.

You may guess how strangely I felt as I heard my own symptoms so exactly described in those which had been experienced by the poor girl who, but for the catastrophe which followed, would have been at that moment a visitor at my father's château. You may suppose, also, how I felt as I heard him detail habits and mysterious peculiarities which were, in fact, those of our beautiful guest, Carmilla !

A vista opened in the forest ; we were on a sudden under the chimneys and gables of the ruined village, and the towers and battlements of the dismantled castle, round which gigantic trees are grouped, overhung us from a slight eminence.

In a frightened dream I got down from the carriage, and in silence, for we had each abundant matter for thinking ; we soon mounted the ascent, and were among the spacious chambers, winding stairs, and dark corridors of the castle.

"And this was once the palatial residence of the Karnsteins ! " said the old General at length, as from a great window he looked out across the village, and saw the wide, undulating expanse of forest. " It was a bad family, and here its blood-stained annals were written," he continued. " It is hard that they should, after death, continue to plague the human race with their atrocious lusts. That is the chapel of the Karnsteins, down there."

He pointed down to the grey walls of the Gothic building, partly visible through the foliage, a little way down the steep. " And I hear the axe of a woodman," he added, " busy among the trees that surround it ; he possibly may give us the information of which I am in search, and point out the grave of Mircalla, Countess of Karnstein. These rustics preserve the local traditions of great families, whose stories die out among the rich and titled so soon as the families themselves become extinct."

" We have a portrait, at home, of Mircalla, the Countess Karnstein ; should you like to see it ? " asked my father.

" Time enough, dear friend," replied the General. "I believe that I have seen the original ; and one motive which has led me to you earlier than I at first intended, was to explore the chapel which we are now approaching."

" What ! see the Countess Mircalla," exclaimed my father ; " why, she has been dead more than a century ! "

" Not so dead as you fancy, I am told," answered the General.

" I confess, General, you puzzle me utterly," replied my father, looking at him, I fancied, for a moment with a return of the suspicion I detected before. But although there was anger and detestation, at times, in the old General's manner, there was nothing flighty.

" There remains to me," he said, as we passed under the heavy arch of the Gothic church—for its dimensions would have justified its being so styled—" but one object which can interest me during the few years that remain to me on earth, and that is to wreak on her the vengeance which, I thank God, may still be accomplished by a mortal arm."

" What vengeance can you mean ? " asked my father, in increasing amazement.

" I mean, to decapitate the monster," he answered, with a fierce flush, and a stamp that echoed mournfully through the hollow ruin, and his clenched hand was at the same moment raised, as if it grasped the handle of an axe, while he shook it ferociously in the air.

" What ! " exclaimed my father, more than ever bewildered.

" To strike her head off."

" Cut her head off ! "

" Aye, with a hatchet, with a spade, or with anything that can cleave through her murderous throat. You shall hear," he answered, trembling with rage. And hurrying forward he said :

" That beam will answer for a seat ; your dear child is fatigued ; let her be seated, and I will, in a few sentences, close my dreadful story."

The squared block of wood, which lay on the grass-grown pavement of the chapel, formed a bench on which I was very glad to seat myself, and in the meantime the General called to the woodman, who had been removing some boughs which leaned upon the old walls ; and, axe in hand, the hardy old fellow stood before us.

He could not tell us anything of these monuments ; but there was an old man, he said, a ranger of this forest, at present sojourning in the house of the priest, about two miles away, who could point out every monument of the old Karnstein family and, for a trifle, he undertook to bring him back with him, if we would lend him one of our horses, in little more than half-an-hour.

" Have you been long employed about this forest ? " asked my father of the old man.

" I have been a woodman here," he answered in his *patois*, " under the forester, all my days ; so has my father before me, and so on, as many generations as I can count up. I could show you the very house in the village here, in which my ancestors lived."

" How came the village to be deserted ? " asked the General.

" It was troubled by *revenants*, sir ; several were tracked to their graves, there detected by the usual tests, and extinguished in the usual way, by decapitation, by the stake, and by burning ; but not until many of the villagers were killed.

" But after all these proceedings according to law," he continued—" so many graves opened, and so many vampires deprived of their horrible animation—the village was not relieved. But a Moravian nobleman, who happened to be travelling this way, heard how matters were, and being skilled—as many people are in his country—in such affairs, he offered to deliver the village from its tormentor. He did so thus : There being a bright moon that night, he ascended, shortly after sunset, the tower of the chapel here, from whence he could distinctly see the churchyard beneath him ; you can see it from that window. From this point he watched until he saw the vampire come out of his grave, and place near it the linen clothes in which he had been folded, and glide away towards the village to plague its inhabitants.

" The stranger, having seen all this, came down from the steeple, took the linen wrappings of the vampire, and carried them up to the top of the tower, which he again mounted. When the vampire returned from his prowlings and missed his clothes, he cried furiously to the Moravian, whom he saw at the summit of the tower, and who, in reply beckoned him to ascend and take them. Where-upon the vampire, accepting his invitation, began to climb the steeple, and so soon as he had reached the battlements, the Moravian, with a stroke of his sword, clove his skull in twain, hurling him down to the churchyard, whither, descending by the winding stairs, the stranger followed and cut his head off, and next day delivered it and the body to the villagers, who duly impaled and burnt them.

"This Moravian nobleman had authority from the then head of the family to remove the tomb of Mircalla, Countess Karnstein, which he did effectually, so that in a little while its site was quite forgotten."

"Can you point out where it stood?" asked the General, eagerly.

The forester shook his head and smiled.

"Not a soul living could tell you that now," he said; "besides they say her body was removed; but no one is sure of that either."

Having thus spoken, as time pressed, he dropped his axe and departed, leaving us to hear the remainder of the General's strange story.

CHAPTER XIV

THE MEETING

"My beloved child," he resumed, "was now growing rapidly worse. The physician who attended her had failed to produce the slightest impression upon her disease, for such I then supposed it to be. He saw my alarm, and suggested a consultation. I called in an abler physician, from Gratz. Several days elapsed before he arrived. He was a good and pious, as well as a learned man. Having seen my poor ward together, they withdrew to my library to confer and discuss. I, from the adjoining room, where I awaited their summons, heard these two gentlemen's voices raised in some-thing sharper than a strictly philosophical discussion. I knocked at the door and entered, I found the old physician from Gratz maintaining his theory. His rival was combating it with undis-guised ridicule, accompanied with bursts of laughter. This un-seemly manifestation subsided and the altercation ended on my entrance.

"'Sir,' said my first physician, 'my learned brother seems to think that you want a conjuror, and not a doctor.'

"'Pardon me,' said the old physician from Gratz, looking displeased, ' I shall state my own view of the case in my own way another time. I grieve, Monsieur le Général, that by my skill and science I can be of no use. Before I go I shall do myself the honour to suggest something to you.'

" He seemed thoughtful, and sat down at a table, and began to write. Profoundly disappointed, I made my bow, and as I turned to go, the other doctor pointed over his shoulder to his companion who was writing, and then, with a shrug, significantly touched his forehead.

" This consultation, then, left me precisely where I was. I walked out into the grounds, all but distracted. The doctor from Gratz, in ten or fifteen minutes, overtook me. He apologised for having followed me, but said that he could not conscientiously take his leave without a few words more. He told me that he could not be mistaken ; no natural disease exhibited the same symptoms ; and that death was already very near. There remained, however, a day, or possibly two, of life. If the fatal seizure were at once arrested, with great care and skill her strength might possibly return. But all hung now upon the confines of the irrevocable. One more assault might extinguish the last spark of vitality which is, every moment, ready to die.

"'And what is the nature of the seizure you speak of ?' I entreated.

"'I have stated all fully in this note, which I place in your hands, upon the distinct condition that you send for the nearest clergyman, and open my letter in his presence, and on no account read it till he is with you ; you would despise it else, and it is a matter of life and death. Should the priest fail you, then, indeed, you may read it.'

" He asked me, before taking his leave finally, whether I would wish to see a man curiously learned upon the very subject, which, after I had read his letter, would probably interest me above all others, and he urged me earnestly to invite him to visit him there ; and so took his leave.

" The ecclesiastic was absent, and I read the letter by myself. At another time, or in another case, it might have excited my ridicule. But into what quackeries will not people rush for a last chance, where all accustomed means have failed, and the life of a beloved object is at stake ?

" Nothing, you will say, could be more absurd than the learned man's letter. It was monstrous enough to have consigned him to a madhouse. He said that the patient was suffering from the visits of a vampire ! The punctures which she described as having occurred near the throat, were, he insisted, the insertion of those two long, thin, and sharp teeth which, it is well known, are peculiar to vampires ; and there could be no doubt, he added, as to the well-defined presence of the small livid mark which all concurred in describing as that induced by the demon's lips, and every symptom described by the sufferer was in exact conformity with those recorded in every case of a similar visitation.

" Being myself wholly sceptical as to the existence of any such portent as the vampire, the supernatural theory of the good doctor furnished, in my opinion, but another instance of learning and intelligence oddly associated with some hallucination. I was so miserable, however, that, rather than try nothing, I acted upon the instructions of the letter.

" I concealed myself in the dark dressing-room, that opened upon the poor patient's room, in which a candle was burning, and watched there till she was fast asleep. I stood at the door, peeping through the small crevice, my sword laid on the table beside me, as my directions prescribed, until, a little after one, I saw a large black object, very ill-defined, crawl, as it seemed to me, over the foot of the bed, and swiftly spread itself up to the poor girl's throat, where it swelled, in a moment, into a great, palpitating mass.

" For a few moments I had stood petrified. I now sprang forward, with my sword in my hand. The black creature suddenly contracted toward the foot of the bed, glided over it, and, standing on the floor about a yard below the foot of the bed, with a glare of skulking ferocity and horror fixed on me, I saw Millarca. Speculating I know not what, I struck at her instantly with my sword ; but I saw her standing near the door, unscathed. Horrified, I pursued, and struck again. She was gone ! and my sword flew to shivers against the door.

" I can't describe to you all that passed on that horrible night. The whole house was up and stirring. The spectre Millarca was gone. But her victim was sinking fast, and before the morning dawned, she died."

The old General was agitated. We did not speak to him. My father walked to some little distance, and began reading the inscriptions on the tombstones ; and thus occupied, he strolled into the door of a side chapel to prosecute his researches. The General leaned against the wall, dried his eyes, and sighed heavily. I was relieved on hearing the voices of Carmilla and Madame, who were at that moment approaching. The voices died away.

In this solitude, having just listened to so strange a story, connected, as it was, with the great and titled dead, whose monuments were mouldering among the dust and ivy round us, and every incident of which bore so awfully upon my own mysterious case—in this haunted spot, darkened by the towering foliage that rose on every side, dense and high above its noiseless walls—a horror began to steal over me, and my heart sank as I thought that my friends were, after all, not about to enter and disturb this triste and ominous scene.

The old General's eyes were fixed on the ground, as he leaned with his hand upon the basement of a shattered monument.

Under a narrow, arched doorway, surmounted by one of those demoniacal grotesques in which the cynical and ghastly fancy of old Gothic carving delights, I saw very gladly the beautiful face and figure of Carmilla enter the shadowy chapel.

I was just about to rise and speak, and nodded smiling, in answer to her peculiarly engaging smile ; when, with a cry, the old man by my side caught up the woodman's hatchet, and started forward. On seeing him a brutalised change came over her features. It was an instantaneous and horrible transformation, as she made a crouching step backwards. Before I could utter a scream, he struck at her with all his force, but she dived under his blow, and unscathed, caught him in her tiny grasp by the wrist. He struggled for a moment to release his arm, but his hand opened, the axe fell to the ground, and the girl was gone.

He staggered against the wall. His grey hair stood upon his head, and a moisture shone over his face, as if he were at the point of death.

The frightful scene had passed in a moment. The first thing I recollect after, is Madame standing before me, and impatiently repeating again and again, the question, " Where is Mademoiselle Carmilla ? "

I answered at length, " I don't know—I can't tell—she went there," and I pointed to the door through which Madame had just entered ; " only a minute or two since."

" But I have been standing there, in the passage, ever since Mademoiselle Carmilla entered ; and she did not return."

She then began to call " Carmilla " through every door and passage and from the windows, but no answer came.

"She called herself Carmilla?" asked the General, still agitated.

"Carmilla, yes," I answered.

"Aye," he said ; that is Millarca. That is the same person who long ago was called Mircalla, Countess Karnstein. Depart from this accursed ground, my poor child, as quickly as you can. Drive to the clergyman's house, and stay there till we come. Begone ! May you never behold Carmilla more ; you will not find her here."

CHAPTER XV

ORDEAL AND EXECUTION

As he spoke one of the strangest-looking men I ever beheld, entered the chapel at the door through which Carmilla had made her entrance and her exit. He was tall, narrow-chested, stooping, with high shoulders, and dressed in black. His face was brown and dried in with deep furrows ; he wore an oddly-shaped hat with a broad leaf. His hair, long and grizzled, hung on his shoulders. He wore a pair of gold spectacles, and walked slowly, with an odd shambling gait, and his face sometimes turned up to the sky, and sometimes bowed down toward the ground, seemed to wear a perpetual smile ; his long thin arms were swinging, and his lank hands, in old black gloves ever so much too wide for them, waving and gesticulating in utter abstraction.

"The very man !" exclaimed the General, advancing with manifest delight. "My dear Baron, how happy I am to see you, I had no hope of meeting you so soon." He signed to my father, who had by this time returned, and leading the fantastic old gentleman, whom he called the Baron, to meet him. He introduced him formally, and they at once entered into earnest conversation. The stranger took a roll of paper from his pocket, and spread it on the worn surface of a tomb that stood by. He had a pencil case in his fingers, with which he traced imaginary lines from point to point on the paper, which from their often glancing from it, together, at certain points of the building, I concluded to be a plan of the chapel. He accompanied, what I may term his lecture, with occasional readings from a dirty little book, whose yellow leaves were closely written over.

They sauntered together down the side aisle, opposite to the spot where I was standing, conversing as they went ; then they began measuring distances by paces, and finally they all stood together, facing a piece of the side-wall, which they began to examine with great minuteness ; pulling off the ivy that clung over it, and rapping the plaster with the ends of their sticks, scraping here, and knocking there. At length they ascertained the existence of a broad marble tablet, with letters carved in relief upon it.

With the assistance of the woodman, who soon returned, a monumental inscription, and carved escutcheon, were disclosed. They proved to be those of the long lost monument of Mircalla, Countess Karnstein.

The old General, though not I fear given to the praying mood, raised his hands and eyes to heaven, in mute thanksgiving for some moments.

" To-morrow," I heard him say ; " the commissioner will be here, and the Inquisition will be held according to law."

Then turning to the old man with the gold spectacles, whom I have described, he shook him warmly by both hands and said :

" Baron, how can I thank you ? How can we all thank you ? You will have delivered this region from a plague that has scourged its inhabitants for more than a century. The horrible enemy, thank God, is at last tracked."

My father led the stranger aside, and the General followed. I knew that he had led them out of hearing, that he might relate my case, and I saw them glance often quickly at me, as the discussion proceeded.

My father came to me, kissed me again and again, and leading me from the chapel, said :

" It is time to return, but before we go home, we must add to our party the good priest, who lives but a little way from this ; and persuade him to accompany us to the schloss."

In this quest we were successful : and I was glad, being unspeakably fatigued when we reached home. But my satisfaction was changed to dismay, on discovering that there were no tidings of Carmilla. Of the scene that had occurred in the ruined chapel, no explanation was offered to me, and it was clear that it was a secret which my father for the present determined to keep from me.

The sinister absence of Carmilla made the remembrance of the scene more horrible to me. The arrangements for that night were singular. Two servants and Madame were to sit up in my room that night ; and the ecclesiastic with my father kept watch in the adjoining dressing-room.

The priest had performed certain solemn rites that night, the purport of which I did not understand any more than I comprehended the reason of this extraordinary precaution taken for my safety during sleep.

I saw all clearly a few days later.

The disappearance of Carmilla was followed by the discontinuance of my nightly sufferings.

You have heard, no doubt, of the appalling superstition that prevails in Upper and Lower Styria, in Moravia, Silesia, in Turkish Servia, in Poland, even in Russia ; the superstition, so we must call it, of the vampire.

If human testimony, taken with every care and solemnity, judicially, before commissions innumerable, each consisting of many members, all chosen for integrity and intelligence, and constituting reports more voluminous perhaps than exist upon any one other class of cases, is worth anything, it is difficult to deny, or even to doubt the existence of such a phenomenon as the vampire.

For my part I have heard no theory by which to explain what I myself have witnessed and experienced, other than that supplied by the ancient and well-attested belief of the country.

The next day the formal proceedings took place in the Chapel of Karnstein. The grave of the Countess Mircalla was opened ; and the General and my father recognized each his perfidious and beautiful guest, in the face now disclosed to view. The features, though a hundred and fifty years had passed since her funeral, were tinted with the warmth of life. Her eyes were open ; no cadaverous smell exhaled from the coffin. The two medical men, one officially present, the other on the part of the promoter of the enquiry, attested the marvellous fact, that there was a faint but appreciable respiration, and a corresponding action of the heart. The limbs were perfectly flexible, the flesh elastic ; and the leaden coffin floated with blood, in which to a depth of seven inches, the body lay immersed. Here then, were all the admitted signs and proofs of vampirism. The body, therefore, in accordance with the ancient practice, was raised, and a sharp stake driven through the heart of the vampire, who uttered a piercing shriek at the moment, in all respects such as might escape from a living person in the last agony. Then the head was struck off, and a torrent of blood flowed from the severed neck. The body and head were next placed on a pile of wood, and reduced to ashes, which were thrown upon the river and borne away, and that territory has never since been plagued by the visits of a vampire.

My father has a copy of the report of the Imperial Commission, with the signatures of all who were present at these proceedings, attached in verification of the statement. It is from this official paper that I have summarised my account of this last shocking scene.

CHAPTER XVI

CONCLUSION

I write all this you suppose with composure. But far from it ; I cannot think of it without agitation. Nothing but your earnest desire so repeatedly expressed, could have induced me to sit down to a task that has unstrung my nerves for months to come, and re-induced a shadow of the unspeakable horror which years after my deliverance continued to make my days and nights dreadful, and solitude insupportably terrific.

Let me add a word or two about that quaint Baron Vordenburg, to whose curious lore we were indebted for the discovery of the Countess Mircalla's grave.

He had taken up his abode in Gratz, where, living upon a mere pittance, which was all that remained to him of the once princely estates of his family, in Upper Styria, he devoted himself to the minute and laborious investigation of the marvellously authenticated tradition of vampirism. He had at his fingers' ends all the great and little works upon the subject. *Magia Posthuma, Phlegon de Mirabilibus, Augustinus de curâ pro Mortuis, Philosophicæ et Christianæ Cogitationes de Vampiris*, by John Christofer Herenberg ; and a thousand others, among which I remember only a few of those which he lent to my father. He had a voluminous digest of all the judicial cases, from which he had extracted a system of principles that appear to govern—some always, and others occasionally only—the condition of the vampire. I may mention, in passing, that the deadly pallor attributed to that sort of *revenants*, is a mere melodramatic fiction. They present, in the grave, and when they show themselves in human society, the appearance of healthy life. When disclosed to light in their coffins, they exhibit all the symptoms that are enumerated as those which proved the vampire-life of the long-dead Countess Karnstein.

How they escape from their graves and return to them for certain hours every day, without displacing the clay or leaving any trace of disturbance in the state of the coffin or the cerements, has always been admitted to be utterly inexplicable. The amphibious existence of the vampire is sustained by daily renewed slumber in the grave. Its horrible lust for living blood supplies the vigour of its waking existence. The vampire is prone to be fascinated with an engrossing vehemence, resembling the passion of love, by particular persons. In pursuit of these it will exercise inexhaustible patience and stratagem, for access to a particular object may be obstructed in a hundred ways. It will never desist until it has satiated its passion, and drained the very life of its coveted victim. But it will, in these cases, husband and protract its murderous enjoyment with the refinement of an epicure, and heighten it by the gradual approaches of an artful courtship. In these cases it seems to yearn for something like sympathy and consent. In ordinary ones it goes direct to its object, overpowers with violence, and strangles and exhausts often at a single feast.

The vampire is, apparently, subject, in certain situations, to special conditions. In the particular instance of which I have given you a relation, Mircalla seemed to be limited to a name which, if not her real one, should at least reproduce, without the omission or addition of a single letter, those, as we say, anagrammatically, which compose it. *Carmilla* did this ; so did *Millarca*.

My father related to the Baron Vordenburg, who remained with us for two or three weeks after the expulsion of Carmilla, the story about the Moravian nobleman and the vampire at Karnstein churchyard, and then he asked the Baron how he had discovered the exact position of the long-concealed tomb of the Countess Millarca. The Baron's grotesque features puckered up into a mysterious smile ; he looked down, still smiling on his worn spectacle-case and fumbled with it. Then looking up, he said :

" I have many journals, and other papers, written by that remarkable man ; the most curious among them is one treating of the visit of which you speak, to Karnstein. The tradition, of course, discolours and distorts a little. He might have been termed a Moravian nobleman, for he had changed his abode to that territory, and was, beside, a noble. But he was, in truth, a native of Upper Styria. It is enough to say that in very early youth he had been a passionate and favoured lover of the beautiful Mircalla, Countess Karnstein. Her early death plunged him into inconsolable grief. It is the nature of vampires to increase and multiply, but according to an ascertained and ghostly law.

" Assume, at starting, a territory perfectly free from that pest. How does it begin, and how does it multiply itself ? I will tell you. A person, more or less wicked, puts an end to himself. A suicide, under certain circumstances, becomes a vampire. That spectre visits living people in their slumbers ; *they* die, and almost invariably, in the grave, develop into vampires. This happened in the case of the beautiful Mircalla, who was haunted by one of those demons. My ancestor, Vordenburg, whose title I still bear, soon discovered this, and in the course of the studies to which he devoted himself, learned a great deal more.

" Among other things, he concluded that suspicion of vampirism would probably fall, sooner or later, upon the dead Countess, who in life had been his idol. He conceived a horror, be she what she might, of her remains being profaned by the outrage of a posthumous execution. He has left a curious paper to prove that the vampire, on its expulsion from its amphibious existence, is projected into a far more horrible life ; and he resolved to save his once beloved Mircalla from this.

" He adopted the stratagem of a journey here, a pretended removal of her remains, and a real obliteration of her monument. When age had stolen upon him, and from the vale of years he looked back on the scenes he was leaving, he considered, in a different spirit, what he had done, and a horror took possession of him. He made the tracings and notes which have guided me to the very spot, and drew up a confession of the deception that he had practised. If he had intended any further action in this matter, death prevented him ; and the hand of a remote descendant has too late for many, directed the pursuit to the lair of the beast."

We talked a little more, and among other things he said was this :

" One sign of the vampire is the power of the hand. The slender hand of Mircalla closed like a vice of steel on the General's wrist when he raised the hatchet to strike. But its power is not confined to its grasp ; it leaves a numbness in the limb it seizes, which is slowly, if ever, recovered from."

The following Spring my father took me a tour through Italy. We remained away for more than a year. It was long before the terror of recent events subsided ; and to this hour the image of

Carmilla returns to memory with ambiguous alternations—sometimes the playful, languid, beautiful girl ; sometimes the writhing fiend I saw in the ruined church ; and often from a reverie I have started, fancying I heard the light step of Carmilla at the drawing-room door.

———————

THE CONFESSION OF THE WITCHES OF ELFDALE

*

In 1669 the people of the villages of Mohra and Elfdale in Sweden, believing that they were troubled by witches, were visited by a royal commission, the result of whose investigations was the execution of twenty-three adults and fifteen children; running of the gauntlet by thirty-six between the ages of nine and sixteen years; the lashing on the hand of twenty children for three Sundays at the church-door, and similar lashing of the aforesaid thirty-six once a week for a year. Portions of the confessions of the witches are given below from the Public Register.

We of the province of Elfdale do confess that we used to go to a gravel pit which lay hard by a cross-way (Hecate), and there we put on a vest (Wolf-girdle) over our heads, and then danced round, and after this ran to the cross-way, and called the Devil thrice, first with a still voice, the second time somewhat louder, and the third time very loud, with these words – *Antecessor, come and carry us to Blockula*. Whereupon immediately he used to appear, but in different habits; but for the most part we saw him in a grey coat and red and blue stockings: he had a red beard (Barbarossa), a high-crowned hat

(Turncap), with linen of divers colours wrapt about it, and long garters upon his stockings.

Then he asked us whether we would serve him with soul and body. If we were content to do so, he set us upon a beast which he had there ready, and carried us over churches and high walls; and after all we came to a green meadow where Blockula lies. We must procure some scrapings of altars, and filings of church clocks; and then he gives us a horn with a salve in it, wherewith we do anoint ourselves (chrism); and a saddle with a hammer (Thor's), and a wooden nail, thereby to fix the saddle (Walkyr's); whereupon we call upon the Devil and away we go.

For their journey, they said they made use of all sorts of instruments, of beasts, of men, of spits, and posts, according as they had opportunity: if they do ride upon goats (Azazel) and have many children with them, that all may have room, they stick a spit into the backside of the Goat, and then are annointed with the aforesaid ointment. What the manner of their journey is, God only knows. Thus much was made out, that if the children did at any time name the names (Egyptian spells) of those that had carried them away, they were again carried by force either to Blockula, or to the cross-way, and there miserably beaten, insomuch that some of them died of it.

A little girl of Elfdale confessed that, naming the name of JESUS as she was carried away, she fell suddenly upon the ground, and got a great hole in her side, which the Devil presently healed up again, and away he carried her; and to this day the girl confessed she had exceeding great pain in her side.

They unanimously confessed that Blockula is situated in a delicate large meadow, whereof you can see no end. The place or house they met at had before it a gate painted with divers colours; through this gate they went into a little meadow distinct from the other, where the beasts went that they used to ride on; but the men whom they made use of in their journey stood in the house by the gate in a slumbering posture, sleeping against the wall (castle of Waldemar). In a huge large room of this house, they said, there stood a very long table, at which the witches did sit down; and that hard by this room was another chamber where there were very lovely and delicate beds. The first thing they must do at Blockula was, that they must deny all, and devote themselves body and soul to the Devil, and promise to serve him faithfully, and confirm all this with an oath (initiation). Hereupon they cut their fingers

(Odinism), and with their blood write their name in his book (Revelations). They added that he caused them to be baptized, too, by such priests as he had there (Antichrist's Sacraments).

And he, the Devil, bids them believe that the day of judgement will come speedily, and therefore sets them on work to build a great house of stone (Babel), promising that in that house he will preserve them from God's fury, and cause them to enjoy the greatest delights and pleasures (Moslem). But while they work exceeding hard at it, there falls a great part of the wall down again.

They said, they had seen sometimes a very great Devil like a Dragon, with fire round about him, and bound with an iron chain (Apocalyptic), and the Devil that converses with them tells them that if they confess anything he will let that great Devil loose upon them, whereby all Sweedeland shall come into great danger.

They added that the Devil had a church there, such another as in the town of Mohra. When the Commissioners were coming he told the Witches they should not fear them; for he would certainly kill them all. And they confessed that some of them had attempted to murder the Commissioners, but had not been able to effect it.

Some of the children talked much of a white Angel (Frigga as Christian tutelary), which used to forbid them what the Devil had bid them do, and told them that those doings should not last long. What had been done had been permitted because of the wickedness of the people.

Those of Elfdale confessed that the Devil used to play upon an harp before them (Tannhauser), and afterwards to go with them that he liked best into a chamber, when he committed venerous acts with them (Asmodeus); and this indeed all confessed, that he had carnal knowledge of them, and that the Devil had sons and daughters by them, which he did marry together, and they . . . brought forth toads and serpents (Echidna).

After this they sat down to table, and those that the Devil esteemed most were placed nearest to him; but the children must stand at the door, where he himself gives them meat and drink (Sacrament). After meals they went to dancing, and in the meanwhile swore and cursed most dreadfully, and afterwards went to fighting one with another (Valhalla).

They also confessed that the Devil gives them a beast about the bigness and shape of a young cat (Hecate), which they call a carrier; and that he gives them a bird as big as a raven (Odin's messenger), but white; and these two creatures they can send anywhere, and wherever they come they take away all sorts of victuals they can get, butter, cheese, milk, bacon, and all sorts of seeds ,whatever they find, and carry it to the witch. What the bird brings they may keep for themselves, but what the carrier brings they must reserve for the Devil, and that is brought to Blockula, where he doth give them of it so much as he thinks fit. They added likewise that these carriers fill themselves to full sometimes, that they are forced to spue ('Odin's booty') by the way, which spuing is found in several gardens, where colworts grow, and not far from the houses of these witches. It is of a yellow colour like gold, and is called butter of witches.

The Lords Commissioners were indeed very earnest, and took great pains to persuade them to show some of their tricks, but to no purpose; for they did all unanimously confess that since they had confessed all, they found that all their witchcraft was gone, and that the Devil at this time appeared to them very terrible, with claws on his hands and feet, and with horns on his head, a long tail behind, and showed to them a pit burning, with a hand put out; but the Devil did thrust the person down again with an iron fork; and suggested to the witches that if they continued in their confession, he would deal with them in the same manner.

The ministers of both Elfdale and Mohra were the chief inciters of this investigation, and both testified that they had suffered many tortures in the night from the witches. One was taken by the throat and so violently used that 'for some weeks he was not able to speak or perform divine service.'

THE WITCH FINDERS

Sax Rohmer

＊

With the increase of the sorcery epidemic uprose a class of persons whose business was the seeking out and burning of witches and sorcerers. Sprenger, in Germany, has the dubious honour of being the most active of these. He has laid down a regular form of trial, together with a course of examination by which his colleagues in other countries might discover the brand of Lucifer.

This individual alone made himself responsible for some 500 victims annually! Within three months, 900 perished in Wurzburg, 600 in Bamberg, and 500 in Geneva. One judge of Lorraine boasted that he had personally condemned 900; and the Archbishop of Trèves, ascribing the cold spring of 1586 to witchcraft burned 118 women at one time.

'Pricking' was the favourite mode employed by the witch-finder to learn if the suspected person were one of Satan's own, and the discharge of fourteen alleged witches by the Parliament of Paris, in 1589, appears to be the only notable instance of mercy throughout the whole black record. On this occasion, four commissioners – Pierre Pigray, the King's surgeon, and Messrs Leroi, Renard, and Falaiseau, the King's physicians – were appointed to examine these witches in quest of the devil's mark. Pierre Pigray relates that the examination took place in the presence of two Court Counsellors. The witches were all stripped naked, and the physicians examined their bodies with great care, 'pricking' them in all the marks they could find to learn if these were insensible to pain – a certain proof of guilt.

The poor women, however, were very sensible of the prick-ing, screaming when the pins were driven into them. 'Many of them were quite indifferent about life, and one or two desired death as a relief from their sufferings.' They were released, however.

A French theological Professor, who wrote in 1720, notes the following symptoms as being infalliable signs of a person having been bewitched:

1. The vomiting of needles, nails, and pieces of glass.

2. Continual burning and lancinating pains, especially in the region of the heart, inability to retain food, and a sensation as if balls were rising and falling in the throat.

3. Suddenly falling ill of a grievous complaint, and wasting away without any apparent cause.

4. Medicines prescribed having the opposite effect from their known virtues and intensifying rather than modifying the disease.

To such an absurd extent were the proceedings against witches carried on the Continent, that it is related how, on one occasion, a sow and a litter of pigs were prosecuted. The whole family was found guilty and condemned to death; but the infant porkers were reprieved on account of their youth!

The following is transcribed from an old chap-book which had a wide circulation in the seventeenth century:

'To help a Person under an ill Tongue, and make the Witch appear, or the Effect cease.

'Cut off some of the Party's Hair, just at the Nape of the Neck, clip it small and burn it to Powder, put the Powder in Sal-Armoniack, write the Party's Name you suspect backwards, and put the Paper, dipt in *Aqua Vitæ*, into the other two, then set it over a gentle Fire; let the Party afflicted sit by it, and diligently watch it that it run not over to catch flame, speaking no Word, whatsoever Noise is heard, but take Notice of what Voice or Roaring is heard in the Chimney, or any part of the Room, and then write how often you hear it, and fix before each writing this Character, ☽ – and if the Party who afflicts you appear not Visible, though you may know the Voice, repeat it again, and if she appear in no visible shape, it may make her charm impotent, and give relief to the Afflicted Party.'

Famous among witch-finders was James VI of Scotland; and, if his work on demonology has not rendered him immortal, by reason of his dealings with those suspected of witchcraft at least he is for ever execrable. The torturing of the young and handsome Gellie Duncan, and the infamous torments to which her reputed accomplice, Cunningham (Dr. Fian), was submitted, are but some of the items to the debit of James VI of Scotland.

Dr Fian was far removed from a saintly character but when his examination by James was concluded (restoratives having been administered again and again in order to render the victim conscious of renewed torture) he was less a man than a bleeding mass, for even the bones of his legs had been crushed to pulp in the boot; his nails had been withdrawn by pincers and needles thrust into his eyes to the sockets.

Euphemia Macalzean (another alleged accomplice of poor Gellie Duncan) was doomed 'to be burned in ashes, *quick* [alive] to the death'. This inhuman sentence was carried out on June 25, 1591.

In 1597 James published in Edinburgh his treatise on demonology. In the introduction he says:

'The fearful abounding at this time and in this country of these detestable slaves of the devil, the witches or enchanters, hath moved me, beloved reader, to dispatch in post this following treatise of mine, not in any wise, as I protest, to serve for a show of mine own learning and ingene, but only (moved of conscience) to press thereby . . . that the instrument . . . merits most severely to be punished, against the damnable opinions of two, principally in our age; whereof the one called Scot, an Englishman, is not ashamed in public print to deny that there can be such things as witchcraft . . . '

Other parts of his work James thoughtfully cast in the form of dialogue, to render it, in his own words, 'more pleasant and facile'!

England and Scotland, then, soon competed with the Continental countries in the burning of witches, and Zachary Grey, the editor of *Hudibras*, says that he himself perused a list of three thousand victims executed during the session of the Long Parliament alone. 1634 is notorious for the trial of the 'Lancashire Witches', but it remained for Manningtree, Essex, about the year 1644, to present to the world a master witch-finder, in the vulgar person of Matthew Hopkins. Assuming the title of 'Witch-finder General', Hopkins toured the counties of Norfolk, Essex, Hants, and Sussex, in quest of witches. In one year he brought no fewer than sixty to the stake.

The method of detection upon which he pinned his faith was that of 'swimming' – so highly recommended by James VI of Scotland. The right thumb of the suspected person was tied to the toe of the left foot, and *vice versa*. She was then wrapped in a blanket and placed on her back in a pond. If she floated – which we are told was generally the case when placed carefully upon the water – she was guilty, and was burned forthwith; if she sank, she was innocent!

Hopkins travelled like a gentleman, attended by his two assistants, always putting up at the principal inn of the town –

at the cost of the authorities. He charged 20s. per visit, with expenses, and 20s. per head for each witch convicted.

He had carried on his outrageous trade for three years when the Rev. Mr Gaul, of Houghton, published a pamphlet directed against the cruel rogue. In it he describes another method employed by Hopkins to detect a witch. He relates that the Witch-finder General used to place the suspected woman in the middle of a room, cross-legged upon a stool. Hopkins then caused her to be watched by his assistants for four-and-twenty hours, during which time she was kept without food or drink.

The interesting theory was that one of her imps would come during that time to suck her blood. As the imp might come in the form of a fly, of a wasp, or of any other insect, and as doors and windows were thoughtfully left open, visitations by imps were common under the circumstances. It was the duty of the watchers to kill any insect which appeared; if a fly escaped, it was her imp – the woman was guilty, she was sentenced to the stake, and Matthew Hopkins collected his modest fee of 20s. from the local authorities.

Of Matthew Hopkins Butler says in *Hudibras*:

> *Hath not this present Parliament*
> *A lieger to the devil sent,*
> *Fully empowered to treat about*
> *Finding revolted witches out?*
> *And has he not within a year*
> *Hang'd threescore of them in one shire?*
> *Some only for not being drown'd,*
> *And some for sitting above ground*
> *Whole days and nights upon their breeches,*
> *And feeling pain, were hang'd for witches;*
> *And some for putting knavish tricks*
> *Upon green geese or turkey chicks;*
> *Or pigs that suddenly deceased*
> *Of griefs unnatural, as he guessed;*
> *Who proved himself at length a witch,*
> *And made a rod for his own breech.*

One rejoices to learn that Matthew Hopkins was 'swum', according to his own recipe, in a Suffolk village-pond, and either drowned or was subsequently executed.

In Scotland, at this period, witch-finders flourished under the generic title of 'common prickers', receiving, like the talented Hopkins, a fee for each conviction. John Kincaid, the common pricker of Dalkeith, in 1646, was caused by the magistrates to exercise his craft upon the person of one Janet Peaston.

'He found two marks of the devil's making,' says Pitcairn, in *Records of Justiciary*, 'for she could not feel the pin when it was put into either of the said marks . . . they were pins of three inches in length.'!

Hundreds of innocent persons had suffered at the hands of the common prickers ere, in 1678, the Privy Council of Scotland sat to consider the appeal of an honest woman who had been indecently exposed by one of them, and expressed the opinon that 'common prickers were *common cheats*'.

THE WITCH BAITER

Robert Anthony

*

Mynheer van Ragevoort did not like the dark. There were things he could not see in the dark, but which he knew were there. But there were also things that he knew did not exist, which the darkness nevertheless conjured before his eyes. Faces. Spectral figures that floated and threatened and mocked. Many faces, many figures. And those of women chiefly, and girls. Of course, they had been witches, and he had condemned them to the torture, to the stake, to the rope. But why should they trouble him, dance about him, beckon him? He had not executed them; he had merely been their judge, the administrator of the Law. The Law forced him, and he was helpless. Still they bothered. Sometimes they seemed so real. . . .

Emphatically, Mynheer van Ragevoort, the Justice of Hegemonde, did not like the dark. Worse, noises often came from the night, noises that were mysterious and unaccountable. Sounds like the voices of people, especially sounds of women in pain, shrieking in torture, gasping brokenly.

There, the Justice started. He seemed to recognise a voice – yes, he heard it distinctly. It sounded like – ah, now he remembered – the voice of Melisande zer Honde, a slight girl, pale and pretty, a child of scarcely twelve. How she had screamed when the rack drew out her joints and stretched her muscles and ripped the ligaments. Yet she had confessed. He had been amazed that so young a child should be a witch. But witnesses had stated so, and under the torture she had admitted it. So he was forced to sentence her – to burning at the stake. How she had pleaded for life. How she had shrieked when the flames enveloped her. And then that appalling stillness, broken only by the crackling of faggots and the rush of flames.

And there was the sweet, innocent face of Gertrudis Bourdelaide. No, he doubted her accusers. He had known the girl since her birth; in fact he had lifted the child over the baptismal font as her godfather. Terrible she had been accused – and had confessed. They had to carry her away from the torture. He remembered how her crushed legs had quivered in agony, the white bloodless features, the maimed hands. She had endured much, but she had confessed. The rope and quartering. But those moans, long-drawn, haunting, unending. Never a shriek, never a cry, only moans. Would he ever forget?

The Justice shook himself. He flung his cloak around his head and moved down the road, carrying in his hand a small lantern, from which a candle shone weakly. 'Not much good in this thick gloom,' he muttered. There was a fog in the air, which scarcely stirred with his movements. Yet the stillness, the lack of motion made him feel unsafe, restless. What was behind the gloom?

Hurriedly he trod the road toward his castle, his home. This stood somewhat apart from the city, as became the overlord and Justice. Not for him to live among gossips and small tradesmen. Besides, it was the home of his fathers.

A faint rustling sound made him pause. He peered around

intently, but perceived nothing. Even his candle seemed unable to pierce the fog beyond his arm's reach. Silence around him. Well, he must move on, toward home, towards rest – perhaps. At least he would see his daughter. . . .

Something huge and light fluttered from the fog and fell over his head, covering him with soft folds. In fright he dropped his lantern and gurgled a shriek. He fought back the folds, but they enveloped him tighter and tighter, drawing around him till his arms were helpless.

And then hands seized him, on the right and the left, and a voice whispered: 'Come! But say naught.'

'What – what – ' he began. But an insistent prod of some pointed weapon made him move forward.

Forward. But where? Where were they taking him? And for what purpose? The cloth covering his eyes made little difference; he had been unable to see anything without it. They left the road, moved across ditches, over the veldt. Stops when he was lifted over some obstacle – a hedge or boundary mark, he thought. More veldt. And around him the faint thuds of numerous feet, slithering noises of mantle brushing against each other, muffled clinks of metal. God. What was in store for him?

The Justice stumbled through a ditch. Then hard and rounded bumps under his feet – ah, he was back in Hegemonde, in the city among people. If he called –

A sharp point pressed his side and a warning hiss apprised him of what would happen. So he was silent.

Some steps up which he stumbled, then a chamber. He felt himself led to a seat. How familiar that seat felt. With his feet he cautiously felt about himself. Yes, there were the legs of the table, and there his own footstool. It was his own: he was in the Court of Justice, his own court.

'Your own court. Your own dais,' came in deadened tones beside him. 'We are here to try the witch of witches, to try her under the Law. But she must not know us lest sorrow come to all of us. So speak not above a whisper.'

Routine. But why in the night? And who was the woman they called the witch of witches?

'Begin,' the dull command was given.

Routine. Well, he would go through with it. 'In the name of the Lord on High,' he intoned in a penetrating whisper, 'and in the name of His Majesty, the King of Spain and the Netherlands. There stands before us a – a – '

'A maiden,' prompted the voice.

' – a maiden, accused of having sold her immortal soul to the foul fiend in unholy conspiracy and of having exercised her black power in wanton sorcery and witchcraft to the detriment of man, woman and child, upon their property, their goods and possessions and upon their produce.' A pause, then: 'Woman, do you confess?'

Silence.

'Who witnesseth against her?' he continued.

'We all do witness against her,' whispered someone in front of him.

'Aye. Aye. It is true,' whispered many voices.

'We vow she hath bewitched us or those of our families and contributed to our loss, even the death of our loved ones,' said the accuser.

'Aye, she hath. We so vow it,' chorused the others.

'Doth the witch confess?' asked Mynheer the Justice.

Silence.

'Then to the rack with her – till she confesses.'

A scream of terror, quickly muffled, a sardonic cackle whose uvular tone seemed familiar, then the shuffle of many feet.

The Justice remained seated. No need for him to enter the torture chamber. Besides, he would not be able to see. In fact, he did not care to see. He had seen too many, too many. And they always confessed.

Through the open door he heard the spinning of rolls, the weak clatter of winding drums. A hush replete with indefinite sounds – they were fastening loops around the ankles and wrists of the witch. Then the squeak, a moan, a stifled shriek. A wait, then the splash of water. Another squeak of the drums. . . .

In accustomed routine the Justice leaned to one side of the great chair. Another twist of the rack, then would come the familiar sounds, and then – confession. He listened inattentively. For there was a bigger, a personal question. What were they intending to do to him? And why this secret trial? If they would only talk in loud voices, and not in those awful whispers. It was unreal – unreal.

Again the splash of water, then another squeak, followed by faint clicks and tears, joints giving way and flesh ripping. A ghastly shriek. 'God. I confess,' in a pain-shocked voice. 'A-a-h-h,' and silence.

Yes, that was the usual result, sometimes a little slower in coming, but not often. There. That quiet crackle. He knew it. No wonder – the skilled hands of the executioner were in charge.

The shuffle of feet once more and then a voice:

'Your Worthiness, she hath confessed her guilt. Your sentence?'

Mynheer van Ragevoort roused himself. Sentence. Very well. 'To be hanged by the neck until death do claim her. At once.' This would be sufficient, and few preparations necessary A rope and –

He must be short, he wanted to be away. Let them hurry and free him.

For a long time he sat there and waited – waited silently, for around him all noise had ceased. There had been a little shuffling of men entering the prison enclosure – to see the witch hung, of course – but nothing more. So he sat and pondered. He felt stifled. The cloth over his head impeded his breath, and drowsiness overcame him.

The tramp of feet aroused him. A moment later the fetters were removed from his arms and the cloth lifted from his head and shoulders.

He blinked in the sudden light of torches. Before him he saw a number of hooded figures, all with voluminous cloaks, faces hidden behind black veils. Were these the same men? he wondered.

'So it is here we find you, Sir Justice,' said the leader.

Mynheer did not recognise the voice.

'We looked for you in the castle. You were not there.'

Hm. So they looked for him. What did it mean? Why should they look for him when they had him already? And why no longer the whispers? At least he was thankful for that.

'Arise, sir, and take your place. You are to be tried,' said the leader.

Nine men in all, noted Mynheer. Two of them pushed him from the chair and led him down to a bench before the dais.

The tall leader at once occupied the chair of justice.

'Sir Justice, note what I say. You have been tried to execute sentence. We went to your home and waited for you. You did not come. Later we searched and found you absent. So at length we thought to look here. And here you are,' with sudden humour.

Mynheer van Ragevoort said nothing, only gazed bewildered at the speaker.

'Sir Justice, we are the Vehmgericht. In secret we met and considered you and the justice meted out by you. Sir, you have been an unjust judge. You have been a plague to this land. Like a wild beast you have persecuted the innocent and condemned them to death. Nothing has held you back – not friendship, not pity, not justice, not even the ties of blood. You lusted only to kill.'

He paused and seemed to wait for an objection.

Mynheer found the words. 'They were witches all. They confessed. The Law gave me –'

'The Law,' scorned the leader in stinging tones. 'Your wild superstition was the Law. Not the written Law. With you an accusation was the equal of proof. You never gave fair trial.'

'They confessed,' the Justice muttered.

The leader stood up and pointed an accusing finger at him. 'They confessed – under insane torture. They confessed – to escape further torture. They confessed – what you wished them to confess. Confession, indeed. So would you confess. Can an innocent child of ten – for such was Gertrudis Bourdelaide – know anything of wickedness, of sorcery, of witchcraft? Yet you forced her by the vilest tortures to say she was guilty. Did Melisande zer Honde know of witchcraft? She confessed to it – after you tore her on the rack. Did Roberta Deswaaters ever perpetrate any wickedness – she, a patient little saint, who spent most of her young life in pain? Yet you forced her to admit unholy practices – by means of the rack, the stocks. Did Margarete Van Voelker, or Pieta der Groote – oh, why name them all, the dozens of decent folk you put to death. For years you have sown terror in the land, you have revolted minds with your unheard-of cruelties. You were the scourge of the people until they wearied of it.

'Men came together and in secret protest asked the Vehmgericht for justice. When the Law is in unjust hands, man may, and must, take the Law from those hands and punish them. That is what the Vehmgericht has decided. Sir Justice, stand and hear your sentence.'

Mynheer van Ragevoort arose stiffly. It was all like a dream and still terribly real. For some reason he could not muster his thoughts to utter protest. Pictures of trials, of tortured women, of executions, raced through his mind. It was true, terribly true, what the leader had said. But he had not meant to be unjust. He, too, had suffered because of his duty. He had wanted to rid the land of the plague of witches, he had wished to make his land free of sorcery and witchery for all time to come. Many times he had wavered when friends, and even relatives, proved guilty; but resolutely, without fear or favour he had administered the Law.

The leader was speaking. 'You were sentenced to torture and death,' he said in sombre tones. 'Such was the sentence decided on.'

A pause – Mynheer twisted his hands, his face suddenly pale and beaded with cold drops.

Again the leader spoke, solemnly, impressively, and the eyes that gleamed blackly through the veil held something of pity. 'Torture and death. Such was the sentence. But this sentence will not be carried out – not completely. You shall not die through our hands. For there is worse than death that has struck you. Perhaps it is the Hand of God. We assembled tonight to carry out the sentence on you. But we found that others had been at work. We found that they had seized you – grief-stricken fathers they were, men fully as crazed with fear of witches as you – they had captured the witch of witches, as they thought – had tried her before your court, tortured her and hung her. Their vengeance is gruesome.'

What did it all mean? Mynheer van Ragevoort seemed paralysed. His eyes were wide, his mouth open, all his features expressed complete lack of understanding.

'You know not,' continued the leader, 'who the witch of witches was? Nor will I tell you. They blinded you, Sir Justice, and blind was your judgment. But a taste of the torture shall be yours, and then you will be freed. Perhaps – perhaps you will be more forbearing hereafter. To work, men.'

Strong hands seized Mynheer van Ragevoort and quickly-stripped him of his clothes. In a trice, so it seemed, they bore him to the torture chamber and looped the ropes around his wrists and ankles.

A spin of the drums, the ropes tautened and squeaked, pain unbearable shot through his limbs and scorched his joints.

'Another turn,' commanded the leader.

Agonised sweat rolled over the Justice's body, his mouth sagged and a croak came from his throat. 'I – I – confess,' he moaned.

'Confess,' exclaimed the leader in chill tones. 'Confess – what?'

The taut body could not even writhe – could only quiver. 'I – I – know not,' Mynheer gasped.

'Nor we.' The leader made a gesture, the drums swung back a half-turn and tightened with a jerk.

Suffering indescribable tore into him – the Justice fainted. Water, splashed over his head, awoke him. God. How he knew that crazy agony. He had sometimes wondered why the accused gave in so readily after a few whirls of the drums. He had been inclined to despise them as weaklings. Guilt alone could not endure, innocence certainly must. But now he knew. Oh, to escape this torment. Anything, anything – even death. But to escape.

A searing pain at his sides, yet he knew not whether it was hot or cold metal that touched him. And then the ropes became slack. What they did with him he scarcely knew – his whole body ached with tearing pains. And his head. It pounded and pounded and pounded.

A raw pain on his forefinger seemed to swell and swell until his arm – no, his body – grew large with the torment. What were they doing? He saw it – a pincer was plucking at a fingernail – slowly pulling it from its foundation. God. What could he do to get away from such torture? Waves of pain welled forth from the finger, greater than his body could endure.

Something else. They had bound his wrists behind him; his ankles also were bound and heavy weights attached. Why this? Why didn't they simply kill him and be done with it.

A hook slipped under his fettered wrists, there was a pull, and suddenly he soared, his weighted body suspended by the wrists. And then he dropped. Again they drew him aloft and dropped him. Shoulders twisted and cracked and ached, his body seemed an immense pain. He fainted.

A rocking motion aroused him. He was dressed and covered with a cloth; they were carrying him. He felt strangely numb, conscious of ever-present but subdued pain. And so weary, so weak, so exhausted.

At last the motion changed. They had entered some dwelling, and now they laid him down. Steps moved away, and then someone spoke – the leader.

'The sentence has been executed, Sir Justice. May it teach you to be more merciful hereafter. We leave you now – with your victim.'

Half-conscious, he wondered. 'My victim?' he asked, his voice muffled by the enveloping cloth.

'Look and see,' in a chilling whisper. There were quick steps, the slam of a door, and then silence.

Mynheer van Ragevoort scrambled painfully to his feet, weakened hands tore at the enshrouding folds. There. He saw light – the cloth fell away. But he knew that room – those paintings – that table. So they had carried him to his house, his castle.

He was thankful for even that. But why this strange, oppressive silence in the house? Where were the servants? And his –

His roving eyes caught sight of something. Over there, on the great divan, lay something very limp and still, covered with a white drape. That – that – his victim, the leader had said. But in this house – was it – everything was so silent – was it his – ? No, no, it must not be.

He crept weakly to the divan and tore the sheet from the still figure. 'God. Anne-Marie. My daughter.'

He stared at her, unbelieving, uncomprehending. His victim? Oh, no. Not that, not that. But it was his daughter that lay there, lifeless, features frozen in an eternal mask.

Slowly he inspected her. Quivering fingers felt the soft flesh, not yet rigored in death. He saw raw welts around her wrists and bare ankles. Around her neck an irregular stripe – they had hanged her.

His victim. It was she – Anne-Marie, his daughter – that had been tried as the witch of witches that night. They had tortured her and – and he – he had ordered the torture. 'And she confessed,' he groaned, 'I – I – ordered her execution – as a witch! God!'

The room reeled and he crashed to the floor.

Montague Summers

Augustus Montague Summers was born in Bristol, England in 1880. He was raised as an evangelical Anglican in a wealthy family, and studied at Clifton College before reading theology at Trinity College, Oxford with the intention of becoming a Church of England priest. In 1905, he graduated with fourth-class honours, and went on to continue his religious training at the Lichfield Theological College. Summers entered his apprenticeship as a curate in the diocese of Bitton near Bristol, but rumours of an interest in Satanism and accusations of sexual misconduct with young boys led to him being cut off; a scandal which dogged him his whole life. Summers joined the growing ranks of English men of letters interested in medievalism and the occult. In 1909, he converted to Catholicism and shortly thereafter he began passing himself off as a Catholic priest, the legitimacy of which was disputed. Around this time, Summers adopted a curious attire which included a sweeping black cape and a silver-topped cane.

Summers eventually managed to make a living as a full-time writer. He was interested in the theatre of the seventeenth century, particularly that of the English Restoration, and was one of the founder members of The Phoenix, a society that performed neglected works of that era. In 1916, he was elected a fellow of the Royal Society of Literature. Summers also produced some important studies of Gothic fiction. However, his interest in the occult never waned, and in 1928, around the time he was acquainted with Aleister Crowley, he published the first English translation of Heinrich Kramer and James Sprenger's *Malleus Maleficarum* (*'The Hammer of Witches'*), a

15th century Latin text on the hunting of witches. Summers then turned to vampires, producing *The Vampire: His Kith and Kin* (1928) and *The Vampire in Europe* (1929), and then to werewolves with *The Werewolf* (1933). Summers' work on the occult is known for his unusual, archaic writing style, his intimate style of narration, and his purported belief in the reality of the subjects he treats.

In his day, Summers was a renowned eccentric; *The Times* called him "in every way a 'character'" and "a throwback to the Middle Ages." He died at his home in Richmond, Surrey.

Francois Baculard D'Arnaud

Francois-Marie Thomas of Baculard Arnaud was born in Paris, France in 1718.His family hailed from nobility, and Arnaud was afforded an excellent education.He began writing poetry at the age of nine, and had already composed three tragedies by the time he turned seventeen.In his twenties he was appointed correspondent of King Frederick II of Prussia, and in 1751 became advisor to the French legation at Dresden.However, he maintained a love for Paris, and returned there in the late 1750s to devote himself to writing.Arnaud composed many plays, novels, short stories and poems – many of which are now forgotten.His best-known work is probably the black comedy *The Count of Comminges* (1790), and

his series of novellas *Les Épreuves du sentiment* inspired Vincenzo Bellini's opera *Adelson e Salvini*. Arnaud died in 1805, aged 87.

JOSEPH SHERIDAN LE FANU

Joseph Thomas Sheridan Le Fanu was born in
Dublin in 1814. His was a literary family of
Huguenot origins; both his grandmother Alicia
Sheridan Le Fanu and his great-uncle Richard
Brinsley Sheridan were playwrights, and his niece
Rhoda Broughton would go on to become a
successful novelist. Le Fanu's family lived in a
variety of locations around rural Ireland during his
youth – the folk superstitions of which are said to
have left a deep impression on him – and were
financially hard-hit by the agitations of the Tithe
Wars. In 1833, not long after the death of his father,
Le Fanu entered Trinity College, Dublin to study
law. While there, he was elected Auditor of the

College Historical Society, and between 1838 and 1840 published his first series of short stories, which were later collected as *The Purcell Papers*.

Le Fanu was called to the bar in 1839, but he never practiced and soon abandoned law for journalism. During the 1840s, he married, and spent time mounting a protest against the indifference of the government to the Irish Famine. He also produced his first two novels - *The C'ock and Anchor* (1845) and *The Fortunes of Colonel Torlogh O'Brien* (1847); both works of historical fiction – and in 1851 he and his wife Susanna moved to their house on Merrion Square, Dublin, where le Fanu was to remain until his death. In 1858, Le Fanu's wife Susanna died in unclear circumstances, and he became a recluse, setting to work in his most productive and successful years as a writer. Between 1864 and 1872, he produced ten novels, all in the 'sensation fiction' genre popular at the time.

At his peak, le Fanu was the leading ghost-story writer of the nineteenth century, and he is now seen as central to the development of the genre in the Victorian era. His work is credited with turning the Gothic's focus from the external sources of horror to the inward effects of terror, thus helping to create the psychological basis for supernaturalist literature that continues to this day. Arguably le Fanu's most enduring works are *Uncle Silas,* published in 1864, and the vampire novella *Carmilla* (1872), which influenced Bram Stoker in the writing of *Dracula* and has inspired several films. Le Fanu died in his native Dublin in 1873, at the age of 58.

SAX ROHMER

Sax Rohmer was born in Ladywood, Birmingham, England in 1883. Hailing from a working class family, Rohmer briefly pursued careers in civil service and the theatre before turning to writing. In 1903, his first published work, 'The Mysterious Mummy', appeared in *Pearson's Weekly*. Rohmer continued to write weird fiction, and his major breakthrough came in 1912, when the first Fu-Manchu novel, *The Mystery of Dr. Fu-Manchu*, was serialized over a period of eight months. Rohmer's story of Fu-Manchu – an evil genius described as "the yellow peil incarnate in one man" – played off the imagined threat of Asian immigrants which was common in that day, and was an instant bestseller. Fu-Manchu went on to star in thirteen more novels, and – combined with his more conventional detective fiction – made Rohmer one of the most successful and well-paid authors of his day. Rohmer was a prolific writer right up to his death, which came as a result of an outbreak of Asian Flu.